AN UNHOLY ALLIANCE

A Novel
by:

ELLA GUIDRY-HARRISON

AUNT HAGAR'S CHAPS PUBLISHING COMPANY INC.,
P.O. Box 19796, Baltimore, Maryland 21225

5-23-98'

To: Denise – thanks for your support!
There's a crown waiting for
you my precious!
Peace & blessings,
ella guidry-harrison

AHC

Aunt Hagar's Chaps Publishing Company Inc.,.
P.O. Box 19796
Baltimore, Maryland 21225

Library of Congress Cataloging-in-publication Data
Guidry- Harrison, Ella

An Unholy Alliance

I. TITLE

Library of congress catalog number: 96-86319
ISBN No. 0-9652651-1-0

REVISED EDITION

Printed in the United States of America
Publisher's Note:

Books are also available from publisher. To order books: Write or call:
Aunt Hagar's Chaps Publishing Co., Inc., P.O. Box 19796
Baltimore, Maryland 21225
Telephone: 1-800-337-6067
Voice: 410-590-3181: Fax number: 410-590-6881

Acknowledgments and thanks are due to my husband and son–my best friends–the two men in my life who never once wavered in their faith in my abilities and talents as a writer. Without their love, help, and support, *An Unholy Alliance* would not have been possible. They both have my love and gratitude. Gratitude to my mother, Leola Guidry-McFadden–a special, hardworking lady that would not accept less from her children. A heart-felt thanks to the readers who donated their precious time to read my manuscript–you know who you are. My loving thanks to all of the "voices" that gave me their love and support–you also know who you are. A special thanks to my two canine companions: "Maggie" and "Ebony" who spent many hours, sometimes into dawn, lying at my feet. And finally, "special thanks" to a fellow Louisianian, a famous trumpeter, a musical genius, whose music kept me "sane and focused."

"Beyond the Smiling."
Gospel song–author unknown

PREFACE

In my professional capacity as a social worker/family counselor, many sexually dysfunctional husbands in crisis, poured out their "tormented" souls to me. I was amazed to discover during further research that, millions of American men are suffering from impotence. I was also amazed to find that eighty to eighty five percent of "impotence" cases are not psychological in origin but physical–stemming from either the result of an accident or illnesses. Contrary to the stereotypical belief about African-American men's sexuality, there are millions of African-American men suffering from the debilitating condition labeled "impotence." The fictionalized character, Tousant, merely represents one of them. Reader, take special note: Tousant, the co-protagonist, is left undescribed. For Tousant is a universal character that symbolizes the millions of husbands, live-in mates, brothers, uncles, and cousins who suffer daily and are dying emotionally, by hellish degrees, from this debilitating condition.

Still, *An Unholy Alliance* is a positive love story between an African-American man and woman that rarely graces the pages of any book. It is a book about the daily interactions and the decision-making process that goes on in the context of church, family (however the structure of that family may be) and the community.

I believe that I have remained true to my resolve to write, not a sentimental, but a truthful depiction of the love and the deep bonds of the people of my childhood who embraced, protected, and kept me from "shattering" into a thousand pieces, people that had so much strength and determination that the many years of our oppression did not breed a sense of defeat in my mind. I was shown that above the "negative" voices, there were "positives" voices. But, deeper still, there was a "lovely spirit" that directed the movement of our lives, a "lovely spirit" that I, hopefully, have preserved and that remains unaltered in my life. I believe that I have remained true to my fidelity to these people who helped lay the foundation to my interpretation of life–an interpretation that cannot be defined or even understood but by a few.

Ella Guidry-Harrison

Wherever there are women having to learn to live without joy and peace, wherever there is a sense of hopelessness triumphing over a sense of hope, wherever there are women who are not allowed to grow, to change, to control their own destiny, wherever there are women who are forced to the other side of the wilderness, there are the makings of An Unholy Alliance.

This book is dedicated in loving memory of my late father—a writer and a great lover of books.

AN UNHOLY ALLIANCE

(NOVEL)

LOUISIANA

Rejoice with them that do rejoice,
and weep with those who weep.
Romans 12: 15

Chapter
One

1966

There was stillness. Something terrible had happened. Bree Jumppierre sat in a small waiting room at Saint Mary's Hospital in New Orleans. She had waited ten minutes or ten hours; she did not know how long she had waited. Her face was troubled. She knew that something awful and painful lay waiting. Her body trembled as she closed her eyes.

A doctor entered the small waiting room and spoke briskly to her. His face was blank, expressionless. "Your husband will live, Mrs. Jumppierre, but the accident has rendered him *impotent.*"

Bree looked unbelievingly at the doctor for a long time before turning her face away. Some seconds passed before she turned to face the doctor again. Even after she looked at the doctor's face a second time, she still was unable to believe what he had just said to her. But she was relieved to know that her husband, Tousant, was alive. She sat on the edge of her seat with tears streaming down her face, but made no move to wipe her tears away.

"Mrs. Jumppierre, we're taking good care of your husband," the doctor continued, curtly. "Your husband is a very valuable man."

On impulse, Bree asked, "When can I see my husband?"

"Mr. Jumppierre doesn't want to see anyone," the doctor stated flatly.

"Of course, Tousant wants to see me. I'm his wife!"

"He especially does not want to see you, Mrs. Jumppierre. I'm not being cruel. Neither is your husband. He wants to spare you. Mr. Jumppierre wants you to divorce him." The doctor blinked at her with dull, unconcerned eyes.

"Divorce him! Where is Tousant? Let me see him, please!"

She stared at the doctor, lips trembling.

"I'm sorry," the doctor said more firmly and made a motion to leave the room. He presented no further details.

"*Pas un sans de sentiment*," Bree whispered. "I will never divorce my husband. Tell him that I love him. I'll be waiting for him to come home to us—no matter how long it takes," she added.

The doctor exited the door without giving her a response. *The doctor should not have left her like that*, she thought. *He should not have handed her so much pain and walked away. He had spoken as though Tousant's injuries belonged only to himself. But Tousant's injuries were hers, too.*

Bree sat alone. Soft, background music flowed into the waiting room through the hospital's intercom. She recalled the telephone call that morning informing her of her husband's accident. It was strange how the morning began. There was nothing more than a surveying of mundane household duties. There were no indications, no customary anxious feelings, no uneasiness, no warning that something terrible had happened to Tousant. *Wasn't a wife suppose to be able to sense these things?* she thought. *Why hadn't she?*

Tousant worked as a physicist at the Manned Space Flight Center in Houston. He usually came home every weekend, but it had now been over two months since she'd last seen him. His work required too much of him and put too much of a strain on the family. He had never revealed to her the exact nature of his work. His work had always been shrouded by a veil of *secrecy*. So she had been content with what little he told her. A strong feeling came over her that she would never know exactly what had happened to Tousant. How could she be sure that the doctor was telling her the truth? How did she know for sure that Tousant was not dead? Had he been given some powerful drug that caused paralysis, and he couldn't speak or move? What if, right now, he lay defenseless needing her to rescue him? What if Tousant had inadvertently stumbled across some information that he wasn't suppose to know or see? *Do things like that actually happen in real life?* she thought. She sighed and shook her head. *Too many books. Too vivid an imagination.*

Beset by a fresh wave of terror, Bree fought an impulse to do a room-by-room search to find her husband. She sat undecided. Minutes passed. She rose on weak legs and walked slowly towards the outside door. She slipped quietly outside. As she walked across the hospital parking lot, she paused, and looked up at a red, Louisiana sunset. Though it was autumn, the days were still warm, and the air had a fragrant, warm softness. She walked past trees with yellow-gold leaves hanging precariously from their branches. A low moan came from some place deep inside her, and she felt her knees giving way. A moment later, she was on her knees embracing a tree, and she heard screams coming from some unfamiliar place.

A week passed. Bree was back home in St. Jamesville. She saw her family's comings and goings, but she was engulfed in a fog; oblivious to things happening around her. Tousant's sudden accident took a long time to accept. It was odd that she had never once thought of her family when she received the telephone call informing her of Tousant's accident. Not once did she think to ask her family for their assistance. Her actions were a puzzlement to her. It did not fit her past behavior. She found it odd, too, that her family never asked her the exact extent of Tousant's injury. The fact that Tousant was alive seemed to be enough for them. She did not deliberately mislead her family, but she had no intention of ever discussing Tousant's accident with anyone. She had a right to keep some things to herself, some things must be endured alone. How could she explain the end results of Tousant's accident when she did not fully understand the end results, herself. *Impotence* was something she did not know about. More importantly, she did not know all of the details of Tousant's accident, and she was still trying to make some sense out of what little she was told. A lot of unanswered questions still remained.

Lost in her own feelings, Bree struggled hard to make an

adjustment to things as they were. Daily meanderings through her mind showed only splinters—small bits and pieces–of her past life. At times, she tried to deny that the accident had happened, but the accident had happened. Otherwise, there was no plausible reason to explain not hearing from Tousant. Since he did not want to see her, she was left with an image of a mutilated body. She tried to rid her mind of such a terrible image, but the image clung with great tenacity. "*Mon Dieu*," she said, in a small, dry voice. Would Tousant ever come home? She wondered how long she would have to wait for him. This had to be a *test,* she told herself. God was *testing* her strength, her character.

Some nights, a fierce longing seized her as she lay there in the dark. Vivid "sexual images" flashed through her mind. Images that were so real she could almost feel Tousant's lips on her breasts. But it never took long before reality took over, and her face was bathed with tears. Sometimes she cupped her face with both hands and cried aloud. She felt ashamed at being so weak and confused. What was she supposed to do? She had always been as good as she knew how to be, and when *fate* twisted its cruel knife inside her, she felt it more than someone would have who did not value goodness.

As the weeks passed, Bree still had not heard from Tousant. From the reports she had managed to get from the hospital, Tousant was still hospitalized, but he remained undaunted in his decision not to see her. She wanted to go back to the hospital but she knew she could not.

Each day, she planned ways to get to see Tousant, but by the time she finished tugging at her plans there was nothing left of them. All she could see was an endless procession of grief-stricken days. So she clung to their son, Paupon, and waited.

It was a cold, sunless day, and the bitter morning wind howled. Bree stood next to the gas heater gazing out the living-room window reflecting on Tousant's accident. The gas heater burned her leg but not enough to cause her to move. Her life now was being driven by sorrow, grief, and pain. She needed a place where she could scream, reflect and survive, a place to either completely undo her or offer her complete salvation; but the place eluded her. As she wiped away tears, her eyes wandered to the oak tree that stood alone by the window. The tree stood bare, leafless. Sparrows had fluffed up their feathers against the cold. They were perched on the branches of the oak tree looking friendless.

Life had struck a heartless blow, and left Bree reeling with grief. Her suffering stayed constant, never leaving her. She had thought that suffering was suppose to make time drag slowly, but the weeks rolled swiftly by in a blur. And with the swift passing of time, something strange had happened to her, something had been stripped away, something that had great value to her. And the loss of this *something* had created a division; a gulf, that took her farther and farther away from the rest of humanity.

The day Tousant finally arrived back home in St. Jamesville, black crows sat in a long line on the power lines at the edge of his property, and dark storm clouds kept reforming themselves into ominous, odd-looking shapes. He glanced over at the crows and looked up at the dark, racing clouds. For no known reason, a chill crept up his back as he rang the doorbell of his own house. "I'll get it," Paupon yelled, running down the hallway. Bree did not respond to her son's announcement. She was laying on her bed with the monthly bills scattered about her. Tousant had always attended to the family's finances, so as she wrote out checks, her head ached. She stared at the pile of bills with dull eyes.

"*Père*," Paupon whispered, "*Père!*"

"*Fils*," Tousant said, standing in the doorway. He dropped his suitcase, and opened his arms to his son. Paupon flung himself into his father's arms with such force that Tousant lost his footing, and they both toppled to the floor crying. They held onto each other as their tears flowed.

"Oh, *Père*, I missed you so much," Paupon said, through a sudden burst of fresh tears.

"Everything's going to be all right now, *fils*. I promise you," Tousant whispered, as his own tears continued to flow.

"How come you stayed away, *Père*? Why wouldn't you let us see you? Was it because you loved us like *Mère la dame* said?"

"*Oui, fils.*" Tousant saw the puzzled look on Paupon's face. "You don't understand, do you?"

"*Non*, not quite. But I knew you would come home, *Père*. Because I prayed every night. And... because... *Dieu* said...Well, maybe not *Dieu*, but an *angel* said you would come home. Plus, *Mère la dame* said so."

My fils hasn't lost faith in me, Tousant thought. *And according to Paupon, Bree had not lost faith in him either.*

"I'm a lucky man," Tousant said softly, looking down at his son. Paupon's face was a beacon of happiness.

When Tousant reached the door of their bedroom, he stopped and simply stared. Paupon made an attempt to speak but stopped himself. Somehow he knew that he should walk away. He had never experienced anything like that before, and it left him confused and light-headed. He wanted to be alone. He looked up at his father, slipped his hand from his hand, and walked to his room closing the door behind him.

"I rang the doorbell. A little warning. I didn't want to just walk in and startle you," Tousant said. His voice broke, and his face was drawn and anxious. Bree, surprised by Tousant's voice, looked up. "Forgive me. That's my job," he said, in a shaky whisper. Bree stared; her heart quickened. She took in deep breaths as she rose slowly from the bed. Too overcome to speak, she let her eyes speak what she felt. For a full minute, they looked at each other without moving. Bree's feelings were so intense that tears sprang to her eyes. Tousant drew her into his arms. "Oh, Bree, Bree." His voice shook with deep felt emotions. As Bree held him, she stroked his back. She could feel his body go rigid under her hands. She realized then that Tousant was not the same man, but neither was she the same woman. Suffering and celibacy had changed her, too. Tousant released her and walked around to his side of the bed. Bree's eyes followed his movements. He lay down, and reached out his hand to her. He gave her a sad look that touched her. She crawled into his arms, and lay for a long while with her head on his chest. They lay there quiet like that. Finally, Tousant spoke. "Bree, we *will* talk, but not tonight." She lifted her head and looked deep into his eyes and shuddered. His eyes were *dead!* She looked into those "dead eyes" with horror. His once warm, lively, brown eyes had been replaced by eyes that had receded into dark shadows, and had formed their own shallow grave. This caused her to mourn for his eyes, not for the man, himself. She wondered whether she was equipped to rise to the challenge of living with a *dead* man.

Bree made a motion to reach inside the top drawer of her night stand. "Wait, lady, let me." Tousant got up, walked around the bed to her night stand, and opened her drawer. He picked up her little *music box*, and smiled as he handed it to her. She sensed that the smile Tousant had on his face then, would be the last genuine smile she would ever see on his face again. There were many times when she would have given anything for a moment like that. But now pain overshadowed everything. Tousant's homecoming wasn't exactly what she had dreamt it would be.

Disturbing thoughts of Tousant plagued Bree. She lay fingering her little *music box* in the darkness. The *music box* had been given to her by her paternal grandmother. Inlaid, gold wings covered the outside of the little, mahogany *music box*. She had slept with her *music box* underneath her pillow every night since she was a child. When she was a teenager, her mother took her little *music box* away from her, because her mother thought that she was too old to cling to a child's *music box*. But she became so depressed that her mother gave the little *music box* back to her, and never mentioned her *music box* again. How could she ever explain to her mother that *something* fierce and terrible lay inside her, something that she could not tame, something that only her little music box seemed to tame.

CHAPTER
TWO

Bree's life had changed forever. A new period had begun. Tousant had been home convalescing for a month. His physical strength had returned, and for a while, Bree had held a childish hope that a miracle would happen, that she would wake up one morning and find that Tousant was a whole man again. Then one day, she looked deep into Tousant's eyes again and had lost all hope. His eyes showed signs of "giving up." This made her go cold. At first, she thought she had imagined the signs, but as the weeks passed signs of Tousant "giving up" became more obvious. Before his accident, Tousant sat erect. Now, he slouched in his chair. Instead of lifting his feet as he walked, his feet scraped across the floor. Scraping, scraping, scraping... Scraping out painful, little squeaks as he shuffled along. He bathed daily. But he would not shave. He avoided mirrors.

The days that followed were hard and unusual. Bree wandered cautiously around the house. Silence was the only balm Tousant seemed to need. He avoided the enigmatic changes in their relationship the same way he avoided mirrors. She had got into the habit of not looking directly into his eyes. She could not bear to look him directly in the eyes without falling apart. If only she knew what he was thinking, or what it was she was supposed to be doing. She wanted to ask him about any follow-up medical care, but something warned against it.

Another month had gone past, and Tousant's accident still had not been discussed. He still showed no interest in anything. He lived in a kind of self-enclosure. His suffering claimed him completely. He never spoke. He never raised his head. Out of hollow, *dead* eyes, he sat in moody silence and stared out at nothing for hours. Sometimes Bree stood and watched him, her heart barely beating. His silent suffering was an awful thing for her to watch. Sometimes she caught him gazing at her, and when she looked back at him, he would not lower his gaze. He just kept on gazing as if he did not see her. She couldn't stand his *dead-eyed* gazes. She wanted to scream, and tell him not to gaze at her like that! But in those moments, his sorrow stopped her from thinking of a single reason why he shouldn't *gaze* like that.

Sometimes Tousant sat with his chair angled at the radio listening to Black commentators drone endlessly on about the perils of Black life in America: *racism, lynchings, beatings, high unemployment rate among Blacks, and the unequal distribution of "educational material" for Black children in segregated schools.* It seemed to Bree that he needed daily reminders of other existing pain in the world. He seemed to be always unraveling pain that was not his own; heaping more pain and grief upon himself.

Each night, Bree felt hot tears on her pillow. She wept because she was powerless to help Tousant find his way back. She could only stand by, and watch him in his silent suffering. How could she keep putting on a brave face, pretending that everything was all right, when everything was not all right!

Spring was in full bloom. The days were mild and sunny. In St. Jamesville all thoughts of winter had evaporated: Electric fans had been pulled out and cleaned, venetian blinds and windows had been washed in preparation for a long, hot summer, and a warm breeze billowed the thin, lace curtains and carried the scent of magnolia throughout the house. Paupon was heavily involved in school and after-school activities while Bree was once again deeply involved in the "Civil Rights Movement." Although Tousant was back at work, a sort of disquiet permeated the house. Their lives had a false normalcy, and a space hung between them waiting to be filled. Everything seemed to be hanging onto some untouchable, fragile thread.

Bree sat at the desk in her bedroom typing the monthly report for her organization. Her mind was disordered. Weariness was her constant companion. She was running on raw nerves. Her *situation* was a mental labyrinth, and it wore her out. Her face had become haggard with sorrow. When she looked into the mirror, her appearance shocked her. A hollowed-eyed image of a stranger looked back at her.

She had spent another sleepless night pacing the veranda until the exhausting night gave way to the morning sun. She had begun to feel uncomfortable in bed with Tousant. Sleeping in the same bed with him without him touching her was a hard thing. Night after night, she lay absolutely motionless, in one spot, to keep her body from touching his. Her muscles were tense; they screamed for release. Lying quietly beside him had become a burden. Guiltily, she sometimes wished for Tousant's death.

Bree had gone unto an emotional tailspin. Each day her *situation* consumed her more and more, and she thought less and less of other things. She wondered how long she could hold out. She felt the results of Tousant's accident had been avoided long enough, and she wanted desperately to pour out her torment to him; but she still found it difficult to approach him. Nothing in her life had prepared her for living with a *dead* man.

Bree's neck grew stiff from prolonged typing. She stopped periodically, and rubbed her neck. She tossed her pencil on her desk and walked out on the veranda. A few patchy clouds occasionally blotted out the sun. She watched the clouds as they slipped silently by. Though it was sunny, she felt chilled. She put on the blue sweater that she had draped over her shoulders. Her eyes wandered and rested on the oak tree that stood alone by the front gallery. Wild vines were coiled tightly around the tree's trunk, and the tree looked as if it, too, had some inner agony. She had a strong urge to be outside in the fresh air. She walked back into the bedroom, and gathered up her unfinished work.

She set the typewriter on the long table underneath the oak tree. She lifted a corner of the typewriter, and slid her papers underneath to prevent the wind from scattering them and went back inside the house to get a cleaning cloth. When she opened the drawer, her eyes fell on the paperweight Paupon had made for her. It was only a large, polished stone, but she cherished the stone because of the love and time Paupon had invested in it. He had polished the stone so well that the stone was slick to the touch. She walked outside with a cleaning cloth in one hand and Paupon's paper weight in the other.

The afternoon seemed empty. Bree sat lethargically in the warm sunshine with her hands folded under her chin. Her eyes scanned the landscape that sloped gently back from her house—land that belonged to her and Tousant. A lone robin sat chirping on a branch above her head. She tried to ignore the chirping but could not. She gave a quick glance up, but her eyes started to roam aimlessly again until they stopped and rested on her house. The house looked beautiful in the afternoon sunshine.

After the deaths of her grandparents, her father had given the house to her. After their wedding, she and Tousant had moved into her grandparents' house. Other than adding some modern amenities, they had kept the house in its original state. Eighty-three years ago, her paternal grandfather had designed and built the house with his own hands. It was a large, white house with: four large bedrooms, a living-room, a formal dining room, a sitting room, family room, and a large country kitchen. A circular gallery ran across the front of the house, and half way along one side until it connected to a sun room. The upstairs veranda ran along the opposite side of the house and stopped at their bedroom. From her bedroom, heavy French doors opened out onto the veranda. Though winters in Louisiana were short, her grandmother had insisted that a fireplace be built in the living-room.

The furniture her grandmother left her was made for comfort. The pieces were a hodge-podge of *Early American* and *French Provincial*. Generations of family photographs lined the hallways and other places throughout the house.

The house was too large for their small family. Until eight years ago, she had hopes of having more children, but Tousant had announced that there would be no more children. His announcement had hurt her. She still had not got over it. At the time, she wondered how men became so privileged? How could men make a decision on something, and make it a reality, a truth? And men never bothered themselves with the repercussions that may arise from decisions they made, either. Had God given men "special privileges?" Or had men simply taken these "special privileges" like they took everything else?

She stared at the stately, old house and remembered times—usually in late spring—when her grandmother gave tea parties on the front lawn. Her father made her go to her grandmother's tea parties so that she could learn how to be a lady. At the tea parties, she and other young girls sat, observed, and mimicked *les gens raffine's*: university scholars, people who sat on the boards of Black universities, attorneys, Black businessmen, and other prominent Black people of New Orleans. These were the people that instilled *les bonnes manieres*. There were days when her grandmother would stop what she was doing to instill "good breeding." She would look at her with serious eyes and a soft voice and say: "Bree, nice young ladies never let young men hold their hands, not if that young lady wants to be respected and become a 'debutante'. Bree, it's considered poor manners to look grown-ups full in the face. Bree, never pass by anyone without speaking and giving proper respect. Bree, being 'well-bred' means saying 'yes ma'am and no ma'am,' and 'yes sir and no sir.' Bree, never chew gum in public. Bree, don't ever be silly enough to associate with a girl that's in a 'family way." You are counted by the company you keep. Bree, this is most important; let your husband teach you your wifely duties." Her grandmother would always lower her voice when she said that.

Bree sighed with annoyance. "Bree, you should never... Bree, don't be a silly girl... Bree! Bree! Never! Never!" She was not comfortable talking to herself, but she felt unwell. She glanced at her bedroom, and her flesh crawled. Unconsciously, she started scratching herself, and pulling at her hair. She hadn't done that since she was a child. She turned her back to the house, but her mind was drawn back to the house. She got up, walked over to the front gallery, and sat down on the swing. The original swing had been duplicated and placed in the exact position as the old one. Along with her own gallery chairs, her grandmother's *berceuse à bras* still sat menacingly in its same position, too. Her grandmother's ghost still crowded the house. In her mind's eye, she could still see Grandmother rocking and patting her feet. Her grandmother always rocked at night, and there always seemed to be a moonbeam lighting up her face. She appreciated her ancestors, but sometimes...she wanted.... Knowing the uselessness of her thought, she let the thought go. "What path could I choose that would lead me to peace?" She spoke softly to herself. Restless, she got up and leaned against one of the white pillars on the gallery. She looked off, and in the distance saw her neighbor, Deacon Hebert, and his family cutting sugar cane. They were caught up in loud laughter. Though their laughter was not unusual, it sounded strange to her ears. She looked at them with listless, envious eyes. Deacon Hebert's grandchildren were on the headland of the cane field singing a traditional, childhood *ditty*. She had sung the same *ditty* as a child. She listened to the children for a moment, but her mind returned to herself. "I cannot live like this. I won't!" she said sharply. The task of rebuilding her life filled her with indignation!

As she looked about, her eyes traveled and stopped on the Poulet's old house directly across the road. The house looked sad and twisted and rheumatic in appearance. The Poulets' son never came back to Louisiana after their funeral. He left the house decaying from the lack of use. The whole place was overgrown by weeds, and saplings had grown around the pillars of the gallery in fantastically, twisted shapes. Low-hanging branches of surrounding trees lay over the roof and the sides of the house, blocking out the rays of the sun, hastening the house's decay. In places where the tacks came loose, the wind fanned out old, dried mink skins from the side of the storage shed. Bree studied the deteriorating house with a sort of casual absentmindedness. The red, brick tarpaper that covered the outside of the house made her think of blood. The house ignited something deep inside of her. She gave a slight shudder. Something was going to happen to her; some ill-defined calamity—she could feel it!

The whining sound of heavy machinery invaded Bree's thoughts. A construction crew was building a bridge across the canal that ran alongside the levee. The work had been delayed because of some legal technicality. She stepped off the front gallery and walked briskly toward the levee. She held one hand over her eyes to shield them from the sun. One machine was gouging the earth, making huge piles of dirt. Another machine was piling up black logs saturated with creosote. She stood and watched the men for a few minutes before turning back in the direction of her house. She walked with her head down, and her hands stuffed inside the pockets of her blue jeans. When she looked up, she saw a car coming down the lane to her house. The car created whirls of dust preventing its recognition. When the car entered her private driveway, she became curious but not alarmed. Strangers frequently mistook their driveway for a road, because the driveway circled in front of the house and led back out again to the main highway. As the car grew nearer, she saw that it was Tousant. She was alarmed by him coming home before the weekend. She called out his name as she ran to meet him.

Tousant stood outside his car and waited for her. When she reached him, she fell breathless into his arms. Her chest heaved, and her heart beat rapidly. "Why were you running, Bree? Look at you. You are out of breath," Tousant said.

"Oh, Tousant, I... thought... that... something...," She took gasps of breath between words. "I...thought...." She searched Tousant's face with inquiring eyes.

"*Je regrette, chèri*," Tousant said, with a worried look on his face.

"It's *d' accord*. As long as you are all right," she panted. He reached down and kissed her on her forehead.

"Let me carry you to the house. I believe the old man still has it in him." He picked her up.

"Tousant, don't! You'll wrench your back."

"Shut up," he growled, playfully, into her neck. "I'm still strong enough to carry your measly bones."

Though he teased her, Tousant was worried about Bree. She seemed to be falling apart, and he felt he had not done his duty by her. The thought hurt him. That past weekend, he had awakened and found her sitting barefoot in her gown on the veranda. Falling dew hung in the air, and the floor of the veranda was wet. She looked frail sitting there as the light of the moon fell upon her. He felt his throat swell. He had gone back to bed without disturbing her, but he had lay awake thinking most of the night. At the break of dawn, he saw her get back into bed holding her little *music box* to her breasts. Now, he had come home so they could talk about his accident. His mind was fully made up. He would not become a burden to Bree.

Tousant put her down gently on the gallery steps. They walked into the house with their arms around each other. When they entered the house, Bree walked towards the kitchen.

"Tisane de sassafras?"

"Non, chèrie. Je croit que non. I came home to take you for a drive—maybe even a walk in the woods," he added, "We have the whole evening ahead of us. Paupon can go to one of the neighbor's after school."

Bree stood in the doorway of the kitchen. "He'll have to. Unless he's reminded, Paupon never carries his house key."

"I'm not ruining any of your plans for today, am I?" Tousant asked.

"Oh, no. Nothing that won't keep. I wasn't getting very much done, anyway."

"I know." A strange look came to Tousant's face. "Where were you coming from?"

"From the levee. The construction crew started back to work on the bridge. I hope the bridge is finished before winter sets in."

"Are you ready to go?" Tousant asked, reaching for her hand.

"As soon as we get the typewriter and papers in," she smiled, but the smile did not reach her face. She was nervous.

They rode in silence. Tousant drove out of the city limits of St. Jamesville into the countryside. Bree refrained from looking at him. There were still times when she could not. Tousant seemed not to mind, but she knew that he did mind. She sat watching miles of tall, straight pine trees until her eyes grew tired and shifted to the shoulder of the road. She watched the powdery dust swirl as the wheels of the car passed over the road. Though it was a dry, hot day, the ditches along the shoulders of the road were filled with water. She could not suppress the thought that the earth had acquired its water from the tears that had dripped from the eyes of suffering women. Her mind was filled with the image of a woman, sitting, head bent, weeping. "I wish you could look inside my heart," Bree said.

"Why? What would I see?"

"Love enough to set the world on fire."

"That much, huh?" Tousant teased.

"Oh, Tousant, you know what I mean. I mean for you, Paupon, and my family."

"That scares me. I don't know whether I'm worthy of that much love."

"It's strange you should say that. Because I feel the same way. Am I worthy?"

"Of course, you are."

Bree, not knowing what to say, shifted her eyes back down to the shoulder of the road. Silence. "Stop the car, Tousant. Let's park and walk."

They walked through the woods smelling the pungent fragrance of pine trees. The only sound they heard was a 'bob white' off in a distance. They walked until they came upon a clearing. "You think we're trespassing?" Bree asked, with growing apprehension.

"Probably, so. But I don't think there's any danger. I doubt if the owner will mind. Let's sit here for a while."

"Would you look at that?" Bree said, pointing at a pecan tree.

Tousant stood up and brushed the dead grass from his pants. "Where?" he asked, looking in the direction of her pointing finger.

"How did that pecan tree get there amongst all the pines trees?"

"Grew," Tousant said, laughing.

"Very funny, Tousant." Bree started walking toward the pecan tree. Tousant walked after her. When she reached the pecan tree, she walked around the tree examining it. "I bet the pecan tree was here long before the pine trees."

"Probably," Tousant said, looking up at the branches.

"Maybe that's why this clearing is here. To let the pecan tree have its own pasture," Bree said.

Tousant sat down on a protruding root of the pecan tree, and leaned his back up against the tree. The picture of him sitting there underneath the pecan tree made her stir with pride. Tousant was still a remarkable man and very handsome. Before his accident, his brown eyes danced and reflected life. He needed and deserved a wife who could handle life's problems a lot more admirably than herself. "You want me to make the Pecan tree recite a *poem* for us?" Bree asked gaily.

"Sure," Tousant answered, closing his eyes. "I would love to hear it, my dear," he teased. "The birds and I will be its audience. The blue skies up above and the earth beneath us will be its stage," he said, pointing a finger to the sky. He brought his hand down and patted the ground. His eyes remained closed.

Bree got behind the pecan tree, and hid herself. "Ready?"

"Ready and waiting," he said lazily. "The Pecan tree may begin:

> *"I stand laughing, no mocking, the couple at my feet.*
> *I see their looks of endearment.*
> *They do not come to hear me speak.*
> *Still, I scream out my wisdom to the couple,*
> *but my wisdom goes unheard.*
> *The couple only come to talk.*
> *They never ask anything of me.*
> *They tune their ears to hear their own false dreams.*
> *Lies and truths rides on the wind.*
> *I only hold truths, but the couple take exception*
> *to the brutal truth. So I wait and watch the deadly,*
> *slow pace of their leaving."*

By the time Bree finished reciting her *poem*, her voice had reached a high, fevered pitch. She stuck her head out from behind the pecan tree, but she got no response from Tousant. He was sitting with a faraway look in his eyes. Her silence made him look up. "Are you finished?" he asked.

"I finished a minute ago," she said, staring down at him.

"I know. I was waiting. I thought there may have been more."

"No, I'm finished. You didn't know that a pecan tree could recite poetry, did you?"

Tousant closed his eyes again, and reached out his hand to her. She took his hand and sat down beside him. He had a weak smile on his face. "Was the Pecan tree just spouting words, or did the *poem* have some significance?" he asked, kissing the palm of her hand.

"I guess I was being silly," she said, ignoring his question. She felt an odd sensation surge through her body.

"You guess," he said, facing her. Bree bit down on her bottom lip and fought down the urge to run away.

"Bree, you're having problems coping with celibacy, aren't you?" Tousant asked, straightforwardly.

Without wanting to, Bree heard herself whisper, "Yes, I guess I am."

For a long time, she had prayed for them to discuss the accident. And now that it was finally happening, she suddenly felt tired. "It has been a long time, Tousant," she murmured. Her stomach felt heavy, nauseous. Her admission finally brought things out in the open. She hated her admission. Because it meant that she would be forced into a solution, a solution she did not have. "Tousant, we have always been honest with each other. It's not as bad as..."

"*Non!*" Though Tousant did not raise his voice, the anger in his tone stunned her, cutting off her words. "I have to know, Bree. It's been terrible watching you trying to cope. You may have remarkable strength, but you have reached your breaking point." He paused, gathering his thoughts. He passed a hand over his head. "Don't you see? That's been the problem all along. You're protecting me, and I'm protecting you. And we keep moving in the same old tracks. This time, lady, we'll tell it like it is. Say, *impotent!*" he yelled. "Say it! Stop calling it *our situation!*"

"*Non, non!*" Bree cupped her hands over her ears.

"Say it! Damn you!" Tousant tried to force her hands away from her ears, but Bree's body shook so violently, he stopped. A low moan escaped his lips as he cradled her in his arms. He gently stroked her face. "Just tell me the truth," he said softly.

"Okay," she replied dryly. Her words came haltingly. "Tousant couldn't you...use other methods...to satisfy?..." She paused, unsure of how her next words would affect him. "I mean... I know it would cause you to do things you wouldn't ordinarily do," she continued nervously, "but what about *oral* sex? Won't it be okay? I mean, as long as we both enjoy it." She felt Tousant's hot breath against her neck. She turned in his arms and faced him. Their eyes met. There was "something" in Tousant's eyes. She wished that she had not said what she said. But it was too late. Her words had been spoken.

Tousant stood up, ran his hand over his head again, and sat back down. "I didn't mean to say... I've got to be demented to even suggest such a thing. *Je regrette.* It's just that I think about the past a lot. Sometimes *je 'devenir folle,* Tousant! I cannot seem to make any sense out of *our situation.*" Life in general was just too much for her. All she wanted was one moment of peace.

"Shhh, come here. Stop it. Don't say that. You're not going crazy," he said, soothingly, holding her. "We have a serious problem. And we both know the solution is going to seriously alter our lives. Hopefully, the solution will be something we both can be at peace with." With his back to her, he walked a few paces away. Suddenly, he held his arms up high, and a shrill cry escaped from his lips. "Oh, damn this life anyway!" he swore loudly. He looked up into the sky, and shook his fist, a soul in torment. "Life's a bitch!" he said sobbing. His eyes burned with anger. But if he were asked, at whom or at what, his anger was directed, he could not have said. He was swearing at everything: at the poetic Pecan tree, at the melodious singing of the birds, at the perfectly blue sky, at his own life stretched out hellishly and endlessly before him. "*La dame*, you don't understand!" His voice cracked. "I have no *sexual* desires at all. It's gone—lost to me forever!" He fell to his knees and cried without shame.

Gripped by the reality of Tousant's words, Bree couldn't ask for a full explanation of his injuries. Instead, her floating mind tried to convince itself that Tousant's ugly words weren't being spoken. She could not breathe. Frozen in her spot, she watched him, unable to move, transfixed by fear. Before her was the human wreckage that had replaced her husband. Finally, she sobbed, ran over to him, and gathered him in her arms. She cried for him, for them both, and for the love that bound them together. *Why did this have to?... H*er thoughts vanished.

After a short while, Bree felt Tousant's muscles starting to relax. She gently removed her arms from around him, and hugged and rocked herself. Their lives had become a confusing nightmare.

"Bree, I'll do anything for you. You know that, don't you? But there is nothing *medically* can be done for me." He gave her a straight, somber look. "This is the end. There's no way out!"

Bree sat staring, wide-eyed. Tousant looked used-up. His face had collapsed, reminding her of a cracked mirror. There was so much pain around them, she could almost grab it by the handfuls. Tears lingered on Tousant's cheeks. She wondered whether their love was strong enough to survive a lifelong endurance of no "sexual" fulfillment? To her, a "lifelong endurance" sounded more like a prison sentence. She enjoyed sex. And now, regretted that she did. Other than for reproduction, what was the *real* purpose of sex? The questions kept coming. How much of love was sex? Could she find a *new* expression? Why wasn't she ever told that love could be an *ugly* thing too? Like a projector, the questions reeled themselves around inside her head, then paused, as if waiting for her inspection. But she knew that the answers to her questions would not be easily obtained. Because their *situation* had no substance. It was illusionary, like trying to reach the lake on the road on a very hot day. A person walked and walked, but never got to it. Death flashed fleetingly through her mind, but then the thought scattered, fleeing in panic. There was always a delicate balance between the old and new. It wasn't an easy task to be forced into examining her life in *new* ways and to speculate on the outcome–especially if the examination was based on something unimaginable. Any real change implied the break-up of life as she had always known it, and the loss of all that gave her an identity. It also marked the end of her *safety*. She would be catapulted into an area that was uncharted and unexplored. At that moment, she was unable to see, or dared to imagine, what the future would bring. Her whole world had been pulled out of focus. She wanted to cling to what she knew, or that which she thought she knew.

"I don't expect you to stay. I knew from the beginning that it was too much to ask of you." Tousant's voice pierced her thoughts. His voice was heavy with despair. He looked completely defeated.

Bree lifted her face to his and saw a tear fall. "Stop talking foolish, Tousant. For better or worse, remember?" Their eyes caught and held.

"No one—not even God—could justifiably hold you to those vows," Tousant said, his voice quivered in frustration.

Bree's eyes misted. "I know, I'm holding myself to those vows. Let's go home."

A smile lit Tousant's face. "Are you sure?" he whispered. He lifted her chin, and forced her to look directly at him. As she looked deep into Tousant's eyes, peaceful memories played briefly in her mind.

"Sure, of what?" she asked.

"Sure that you don't want your freedom? I pray not. Keeping our family together is more important than any needs we may have as individuals."

"I know that, Tousant. I won't divorce you. I never will. Love is an invisible adhesive. Divorcing you won't free me. As for my sureness on handling *our situation*, I'm not sure." Unlike, Tousant, who knew who he was, and always knew exactly what he was doing, she was less sure of who she was, and she didn't always know what she was doing. Their talk had left her a little less confused but that was all.

"Time will work things out," he said, as if he were reading her thoughts.

"Perhaps, it will. I have to believe that 'time' is all it will take, because I stay so tired all the time, Tousant. I use up so much energy trying to cope with celibacy."

"I know. Just give me some time to find a solution for us. Trust

22

me. Just be patient. Now, let's go home. I'll fix supper. My treat."

Since Tousant's accident, Bree had learned to understand every look, every expression, every kind of body language he used. But this time, she had misread him. She thought Tousant had planned on telling her that he had decided to leave her. Instead, something *inexpressible* had happened that left her without any means to focus on any one thing. "One more thing, Bree," Tousant said, his eyes dancing, "I want to make you an appointment with Doctor Laveau. You need something to quiet your nerves. I'll make the appointment myself," he said, patting her on the back.

"Yes, sir," she said, giving a strained laugh.

The evening was getting foggy. Bree walked to the car with a deep sense of foreboding. It was done. *Dear God, help me!* she thought, as she placed an unsteady hand on the latch of the car door.

Early the next morning, Bree pulled into her parents' driveway. She got out of her car and looked up at a cloudless, blue sky. As she stood, her eyes fell on the empty swing on the front gallery. Childhood memories flooded her mind, and she wished with all her heart that she were a child again. Her eyes wandered onto the large persimmon tree that stood next to the driveway. The tree brought a brief smile to her face. She thought about her long hours of play and peace in her doll house underneath the tree. The sweetness of ripe fruit drifted into her play house, causing her mouth to water. She could almost hear herself singing the childhood ditty that her grandfather had taught her to take her mind off the unripen fruit:

> *"Possum up dat 'simmon tree*
> *raccoon on the ground, the raccoon*

say you dirty hound, you better shoot dem
'simmons down. Oooh, come on Bree with your
suwie si. Oooh, come on Bree with your suwie si."

As she looked at her parents' house, an expression of longing shadowed her face for a few moments. She let out a great sigh. Something propelled her to the back of the house. She could hear her mother's housekeeper half-humming, half-singing a hymn as she cleaned. She smelled a whiff of *pralines* being cooked as she passed by the kitchen window.

When she walked around the corner of the house, her father was sitting on the back steps. Surprised by her father's presence, she stood and watched him. It was hard for her to tell what her father stared at, or what he was thinking, but his look always held her.

Each morning, dressed in his suit with his cowboy hat on, he sat and stared out at nothing while "country and western" music played softly on the portable radio beside him. He always rolled up the legs of his pants, and patted his bare feet to the music. His socks and boots sat neatly at his side. No one dared disturb him. Growing up, her father sometimes made her and her two brothers listen to "country and western" music. He said that "country and western" songs were about the "natural sources" of life. He claimed that "popular" music did not exalt enough. And he believed that *exaltation* was the key to life. "Aim high," he'd say. "A lazy mind may have a place, but not in my house. Set your mind high. Even if you miss the moon, at least you'll be among the stars." He would stiffen his back; stick his chest out with pride, and point his finger at each of his children for affirmation. Her mother would listen, and carry out his 'aim high' instructions to the letter.

Bree knew that if she walked past her father, he would not acknowledge her. During his morning ritual, he never acknowledged anyone. He merely lifted his socks and boots to let the person walk past him. After his morning ritual, he went inside the house; made his last minute preparations, and left for his office.

His dog, *Madame* Muscadine III, sat next to him. She was

temperamental but devoted to her father. *Madame* Muscadine III was a small dog, not much larger than a Chihuahua. The dog's appearance was unusual. She had short, wooly, gray hair with long beagle-like ears and a corkscrew tail. *Madame* Muscadine III was a *cur*. But if her pedigree were ever questioned, her father became highly upset. When one *Madame* Muscadine died another *Madame* Muscadine took her place.

As her father patted his feet, *Madame* Muscadine III wagged her "corkscrew" tail, and looked into nothingness like her owner. But Bree knew that the dog was watching her. The dog only kept quiet because she knew that her growling would displease her father.

She looked at the dog, then let her eyes travel down again to her father's brown, bare, patting feet. She turned abruptly, and walked back to her car. As she backed her car out of her parents' driveway, she saw her mother standing in the front doorway urgently motioning her hand to her. She drove off without looking back.

CHAPTER
THREE

*T*he past two months had been the most absorbing, challenging, and unpredictable months of Tousant's life. Bree had sudden streaks of recklessness that appeared out of nowhere. Her voice sometimes changed from being gentle and demure to loud and brash. She had bought a motorcycle. This deeply disturbed him. Bree had given weak excuses for canceling all of the doctor's appointments he had made for her. He had finally got her to agree to keep the last appointment he had made with Doctor Laveau.

It was a foggy Saturday morning. Bree sat in the waiting room nervously waiting to see Doctor Laveau. She had no idea of what she would tell the doctor. She knew that she could not ask for medicine to calm her nerves without giving an explanation. *Damn! I'm fine. What on earth am I doing here?* she thought. But she had promised Tousant that she would keep the appointment. She sat thumbing through the pages of a magazine for a minute. Then she got up to leave. As soon as she reached the front door, the nurse walked into the waiting room.

"Mrs. Jumppierre, you're next," she said, eyeing her suspiciously. Bree wanted to ask the nurse what business was it of hers if she were about to leave, but she followed the nurse quietly.

The nurse stuck a thermometer in her mouth, and started pushing up the sleeve of her dress to take her blood pressure. "Wait a minute," Bree said, taking the thermometer out of her mouth. "I'm not ill! I came to talk to the doctor about getting something for my nerves."

"It's routine, Mrs. Jumppierre," the nurse said, with a professional air. The nurse finished and walked briskly out of the room. A short time later, the nurse returned. "Mrs. Jumppierre, follow me," she said curtly. Bree followed her into the doctor's office. "Wait in here, please. The doctor will be with you shortly."

She watched the nurse walk swiftly out of the room. She disliked nurses. She hated their robotic manner. She had the same dislike for doctors. She thought of the doctor who had cared for Tousant after his accident and concluded that all doctors were the same—cold.

Doctor Laveau nodded his head mechanically as he walked into his office. He did not speak.

"Hello, Doctor Laveau." Because of Doctor Laveau's lack of warmth and good manners, Bree's voice was as cold as ice.

"What can I do for you, Mrs. Jumppierre?"

"I've been a little nervous, lately. I need you to prescribe something for my nerves."

"Why?"

"Why, what?" Bree asked, with flippancy.

"Why, are you so nervous?"

"Well... I..." she stammered.

Doctor Laveau gave her a long look, as if he were defying her to lie to him. "Bree, we have known each other for many years, but we have never got along. I personally like you, and I also have a great deal of respect for you and your husband. So I should not have to tell you that whatever you say to me will be held in strictest confidence."

She gave Doctor Laveau a hard look. She kept him as the family physician only because she felt one doctor was just as good as another. Medically, Doctor Laveau had done things to her satisfaction. There was nothing for her to do but explain. After she finished her explanation, Doctor Laveau sat tapping his eye glasses in his hand in deep thought. "Nerve pills will help some, but nerve pills are not a panacea. In a month, you'll be right back here in my office."

"That won't happen. Because I won't let it!"

"My dear, I admire your determination. But I'm afraid you don't understand the gravity of your problem. Both physically and mentally, sex has a very important function. From a medical standpoint, sex is not had for sheer pleasure alone. Among other things, sex is a natural way of reducing stress. Have you ever noticed a cat's behavior when she's in heat and locked up?" Dr. Laveau's voice was on the borderline of mockery. "Their nerves run wild like yours are doing now, Bree."

Bree detached herself from the doctor's words. She sat impatiently waiting for him to finish. It seemed that every day there was something else to burden down her already over-taxed mind. "You're over-stating my *situation,* Doctor Laveau. Anyway, I'm not a cat! I'm an intelligent human being very much capable of using reason," she retorted, getting up to leave. She wanted to shove Doctor Laveau's words back down his throat.

"Sit down, Bree, please. No harm was intended. I didn't mean to offend you. I was merely giving an example. No doubt about it, your nerves are shot." He reached for his prescription pad. "I'll prescribe something for your nerves—for this time only," he added. "You're going to have to come up with a way to handle your problem. I've never had a patient with your problem before. I don't feel that I'm qualified to help you. But I can give you the name of a good doctor who can help."

"I won't be needing another doctor, thank you."

"Your tenacity surprises me," Doctor Laveau said, in amazement, as he handed her the prescription.

Bree could have sworn she saw a smirk on the doctor's face. She got up to leave again, seemingly, untouched by the doctor's words. "You're a stubborn woman. Since you won't seek help elsewhere, if you need to talk, call me."

She gave no reply. She started out the door. "Mrs. Jumppierre, just a minute." *What is wrong with Doctor Laveau, anyway,* she thought. *It was Bree this minute and Mrs. Jumppierre the next. He seemed to change her name as his emotions shifted.* "Sit down, please," he said. His voice was so low that she barely heard him. She sat down and gazed deep into his eyes. As if vying for thinking time, the doctor took off his glasses; wiped the lenses with his handkerchief, put them on again and looked at her. "A friend of mine got hurt in a boating accident. And, like your husband, the accident rendered him *impotent."* From time-to-time, he has his best friend visit his wife. In

28

his absence, of course," he added. "Do you understand what I'm saying?" He put his glasses back on, and peered over the top at her.

She gave Doctor Laveau another hard stare. His words inflamed her. Finally she spoke, "Yes, I do understand what you're saying, Doctor Laveau. But I'm afraid that I couldn't handle a 'purely physical' relationship."

"Okay," he sighed, "call me if you need me. Have you tried masturbation? It won't harm you. I hope you don't think I'm painting a bad picture. That's not my intention. But I do want to paint a very *real* picture," he said, shuffling the papers on his desk. "How will you cope?"

Bree did not answer him. She rose from her chair and rushed out the door.

Bree sat in her car outside of Doctor Laveau's office. She closed her eyes in relief. Her *situation* seemed to set off something latent in the doctor. She thought that Doctor Laveau's behavior was sick and unforgivable. "Cats!" she cried, and lay her aching head on the steering wheel. "I will never come to Doctor Laveau again," she stated blandly. "There must be some *ugly universal law* that says without sex there is no loveliness, no grace, and no elegance between a man and woman. I'll never adjust to this! I cannot go back to my *Penelope mode* of waiting, waiting, waiting." she told herself.

As she sat there in the stillness of her car, something peculiar started happening to her that made her smile and lifted her spirits. An awakening. An unraveling. A *freeing* idea had started to take hold. When she looked up again, the fog had cleared, and the sunshine had started to peek through. The idea had such a profound affect on her that she didn't remember driving home. But ten minutes later, she was turning into her driveway.

As she approached her house, the front door opened, and Paupon ran out the front door to greet her. "Guess what," he said, hugging her waist, "we've got a surprise for you."

"A surprise. Then we should go right in. You sure you're not telling something that's supposed to be kept a secret, Paupon?"

"Nope. Besides, I just told you it was a surprise. I didn't tell you what the surprise was." When he looked up at his mother, his forehead was creased in a frown of seriousness.

"Well, I suppose if you want to get that technical. I guess you didn't," she said smiling.

When they walked into the living room, Bree did not see Tousant. She did not want to spoil their surprise. So she called out from the living room. *"M'sieu* Jumppierre, I'm home. Hello! Is anyone home?"

Tousant walked out of the kitchen with a dish towel thrown over his shoulder. "How did it go?" he asked. He had a concerned look on his face.

"All right. The prescription is in my purse."

"Bon. I'll go get it filled after dinner. The food will be ready in five minutes."

"Good. That'll give me a minute to change into something more comfortable." She walked into her bedroom loosening her clothes as she walked. She sat down on her side of the bed, and slipped off her shoes. Travel brochures were spread out on the bed. Lying next to the brochures, was a small, brown, velvet box. She picked up the brochure lying on top. On the cover was a picture of an attractive, brown-skinned woman, in a red bikini, lying on the beach waving her hand, smiling. The caption read: *"Fun in the sun in the Bahamas."* She picked up the velvet box with growing apprehension. When she opened the box, the sight of a diamond ring jolted her. She traced her finger over the most exquisite, diamond ring she had ever seen.

Tousant stood quietly in the doorway watching her. "I would give anything to keep that look in your eyes. I truly would," he said, his voice husky with emotion."

"I helped to choose it," Paupon said, happily.

"You did. *Merci beaucoup,"* Bree said, squeezing him to her.

"Well, some people can marvel at diamond rings, but us guys have pressing business in the kitchen. Right, *fils?"*

"Right!"

"Fils, run along to the kitchen. I'll be there in a minute."

"D'accord."

"What did the doctor have to say?" Tousant asked.

"Oh, nothing much. He wrote the prescription, and told me if I needed him to call."

"I want you healthy," Tousant said.

"I know. We'll talk about it later, okay."

"We'll discuss it now, Bree," he said, closing the bedroom door.

"Tousant, I'm not up to a long, drawn out discussion."

"All right," he said disappointed. "Dinner will be ready soon."

After Tousant left the room, Bree put the brown, velvet box, with the diamond ring inside, in her dresser drawer. Tousant had mistaken her bold, angry stare as shocked pleasure. He had no right to buy such cold substitution to appease a need in her. A need that ran so deep, she felt like dying. He had insulted her humanity! Who did he think she was? Some brainless doll to be adorned by precious ornaments! She reached into the drawer of the bedside table, took out her *music box*, and placed it on her stomach. Absorbed by the music, she wondered when in Tousant's eyes would she ever become a person, a human being. The thought gave her an uneasy feeling.

That night, after they had gone to bed, Tousant talked to her for hours about her taking a trip. "You know, I've been thinking," Tousant said, his voice carrying in the darkness.

"*Bon*," Bree teased.

"*Bon, que?*"“

"Good, that you've been thinking."

"Very funny," he smiled. "How did you enjoy supper?"

"I enjoyed dinner and supper. You're spoiling me."

"I want to help you. So, you think you'd prefer going to San Francisco to visit your *cousine*?"

"*Oui*, I've never been one for traveling aboard. Hey, I'm at peace," she lied. She lay her head on his chest.

"I want you to have a 'real' nice time on this trip," Tousant said.

"I will have a nice time. Now go to sleep, Tousant."

"You promise."

"Promise." *I will go on this trip to please you,* she thought. *But I cannot do what your voice implies that I do.*

"Bree, I want you to give up the motorcycle. Please! I worry. I think it's dangerous." Bree lay quiet. She heard the fear in Tousant's voice.

"I see no danger. Everything is tame to me now, Tousant. But if you want me to give up my motorcycle, I'll give it up."

CHAPTER
FOUR

B ree did not go to San Francisco. Tousant was not pleased. They had gone to bed early. Tousant, preoccupied with their problem, couldn't sleep. He had seen better days. His whole life had always been in order. He lay, hands folded behind his head, in deep thought. Occasionally, he turned his head to look at Bree. She slept curled in a fetal position with one hand underneath her pillow holding onto her little *music box.* Because of his fear of arousing her sexually, he resisted the urge to kiss her. As he pulled the cover up over her shoulders, it dawned on him in that stillness that Bree was the most beautiful woman he had ever seen. And he loved being married to her. Though he still felt that her motorcycle was dangerous, he now regretted asking her to give it up. The inner fire had left her. Not all at once—it was a sort of slow seepage.

Tousant shifted his attention away from Bree, and resumed his thoughts. He had got a substantial increase in salary, and he wanted to start construction on a game room for Paupon. He thought a boy should have some place special to entertain his friends. He had always encouraged Paupon to have his own identity, to be an individual. When Paupon was born, he had overcame his ego, by refusing to have his son named after him. He must be his own person, he had told Bree. Bree had protested, but her protests lacked importance to him. What was important was his son having his *own* name.

They had been married two years before he decided that they would have a child. It was he who had insisted that Bree give up her career and stay home to raise their son. He never asked her if she minded. It had never occurred to him to ask the question. He just assumed she should. Looking back, he remembered a change in her then, but he had attributed her change to the challenge of motherhood. But... now.... He shut his eyes and tried to force sleep, but his eyes immediately opened again. He sighed, and let his mind wander on.

For the past two weeks, Bree had been having nightly dreams. Her dreams deeply troubled him. Bree had broken under the weight of his *impotence*. Lately, when his back was turned, he could feel her eyes upon him. He knew with absolute certainty that his observations were correct, and not a figment of his imagination. He turned over on his side and looked down into Bree's face. He turned back over on his back. "Your attachment to the *music box* has grown. I cannot stand it anymore," he whispered. He spoke into the fold of his arm. "It's in your face. I dread looking at your face, Bree."

Though his pain was still too raw to touch, he was forced to do something; he had no choice. He could see his marriage crumbling. He had seen other troubled marriages grow soundless and cold, and he did not want that to happen to him, but he was horrified at the thought of putting his plans into action. In the past, he had always known what to do in any situation. If something didn't work, he worked at it until it did work, but the trauma from his accident left him afraid to try anything. The mere thought of *failure* broke up the smooth flow of his thoughts, and his thoughts started coming to him choppy, in small increments. His solution to the problem of his *impotence* was simple but dangerous. He would be putting his entire life on the line. It would be more than he could bear if his plans failed, and he lost his family. He was a living witness that life could suddenly go out of control, but he still couldn't understand how; especially for such a controlled person as himself. Something had been set in motion. But what! He groaned between clenched teeth and exhaled deeply.

Tousant lay a few minutes in silence before letting his thoughts flow again. He could not understand why God didn't give proper warning of impending doom. Why does He just let trouble loom up in front of a person?... frighteningly larger than any mere human being could hope to handle. It were as if God did not have a sense of fair play. God just let things come to a person and say: "There. You go away and figure it out" without leaving a person with a single clue as to how it was to be done. Was it just plain carelessness on God's part? Or was this God's punishment for his past infidelities? Had God grown angry with him and measured out the amount of sex he could have in his lifetime? Had God looked down on him in his infidelities and said, *"Enough!"*

But Tousant knew in his heart that the sudden, unexpected turn from peace to hell in his life was not God-made. *No,* he told himself, *it was all due to that bitch, Fate! What was the bitch, anyway? A sick, vicious, invisible entity with iron-clad, man-eating jaws. Where did the bitch, Fate, come from? Materialized from hell, no doubt.* He grunted.

Tousant's injuries had already stitched itself into the fabric of his life, and had erased from his memory all past sexual pleasures. His injuries made itself the primary focus of everything he thought of or did. He knew that there must be something medically he still should be doing about his injuries. But he had sought the help of experts, and they had failed him; he had failed himself. He had been failing while he thought he was succeeding. After a while, the prescribed *hormone* injections made him feel like a freak. In the dark, a painful look came to his face. Something had broken deep inside him, and he felt himself shaking with anger and resentment and useless grief. *So, now it's all over,* he thought. *Finished. The curtains had fell early in his life.*

Bree woke up, and she cried out. Her cries startled Tousant and broke up his thoughts. *"La dame, la dame,* it's a dream. You're having a dream," he said, turning on the light. Bree sat up looking crazily about the room, whimpering. "Lady, I am here. You're not alone," he said, folding her into his arms.

"Oh, Tousant, it was..."

"Shhh," he said, "don't think about it. It's all right. It's all right," he repeated, brushing back her hair, kissing her forehead. "Your gown is soaked." He made a motion to get up for a fresh one.

"No, Tousant! Please, hold me," she said. She clung to Tousant like a frightened child. They lay in silence.

"You want to tell me about this dream? You know you can," he said, stroking her arm.

"Tousant, I tell you, I'm going *mad!* Celibacy is doing strange things to my head," she said, tears had gathered in her eyes.

"No, no, lady. It's just a little nerves. You're probably tired. It's been an exhausting day for me, too. You've been pushing yourself too much lately. You've been dealing with Paupon's after-school activities and your organization on top of everything else."

"Yes, that must be what it is," she said. She wanted to believe Tousant. She wanted to believe that she was tired. But she knew it was still her nerves, because she had thrown away the nerve pills that Doctor Laveau had prescribed for her. The pills made her sluggish and sleepy.

"Come on, lie back down. You need your rest." She slid down underneath the covers. "You want to be rested up for the Woodward's party tomorrow night, don't you?" he asked, turning off the light.

"Tousant," she said, sitting up in the dark, "I want to tell you about my dream. It happens every night. Now I'm at the point that I hate to go to sleep."

Tousant turned on the light and held her hand. Her green, silk gown stuck to her small breasts. She looked lost. His heart ached. His brain seemed to explode. *Why did life have to change?* he thought. *Why did it mock? Why did it smirk? Why didn't it ever show any mercy?*

"Go on, *la dame*, I'm listening."

"You can never see the same beautiful sunset twice," she said, staring ahead.

Tousant was puzzled by her statement. "I don't understand."

"I don't understand it, either. But the words are stuck in my mind. You can never see the same beautiful sunset twice," she repeated. "I heard it, or I read it somewhere," she said, staring into empty space. "In my dream, I was driving along this dirt road. *Chevrefeuilles* were growing everywhere. The smell was so sweet that I wanted to kiss the air. Suddenly, steam started spewing out from underneath the hood of my car. I sat there staring at it. It was as if some magical mist was purposely sent to engulf me. When I got out of my car, I started laughing uncontrollably. A few minutes later, a black car drove up, and a man yelled out at me, 'You shouldn't have shut off the engine!'

The man got out of his car and stood next to me, but he didn't have a face, Tousant," she said, a desperate tone in her voice. "What do you make of that? Then, like a sleepwalker, I turned and started walking toward a grassy knoll. When I reached the knoll, I sat down. I could see the man still leaning over looking underneath the hood of my car. A short while later, he started laughing too. He walked to the knoll and sat down beside me." The man asked, 'Where were you going?' I couldn't remember, Tousant. He sensed my confusion and said, 'Oh, don't fret. Maybe you're already where you were going.'

"Yes," I said, "I think maybe I am."

'See,' the man said, smiling. And he caught me by my hand. 'Which part of your clothing do you need to take off to feel absolutely free?' he asked.

"My shoes," I said.

'Good! Because that's exactly what I have to take off to feel absolutely free, too.'

We looked out into what appeared to be an endless, green, open space. We started running. My sides started to hurt, and I said, "Hey, slow down. My sides are hurting me." But the man said, 'Shhh, hear it?' I heard it too, Tousant. It was a leaf falling from a tree.

'*Vite! vite!*' the man said, 'We must find the leaf.' *How can we find the leaf,* I thought. *There must be millions of leaves underneath those trees.* But in some strange way, that I could not understand; we found the leaf. The leaf was lying on top of a pile of dead, brown leaves. But this 'special' leaf wasn't dead. It was green, alive! I picked up the leaf. But the minute I picked up the leaf, the leaf started withering, dying. My hands were killing the leaf, Tousant. I struggled to put the leaf down but I couldn't. The leaf was stuck to the palm of my hand. So I started crying. Amazingly, when my tears fell on the leaf, right there before my eyes, my tears started reviving the leaf, putting life back into it. The leaf unfurled and changed back to its original green color. 'Hand me the leaf,' the man said. When I handed him the leaf, he reached up and hung the leaf back on the tree. The leaf hung there as if it had never fallen off the tree. I looked at the man's face again. Still, all I saw were the piercing, brown eyes and no face. 'Come.' the man said, 'Let us make love.' I don't know how long we made love, but I was hungry when we finished. 'There's a meadow,' he whispered. 'We can bathe and catch fish to eat.' There we were playing naked in the water. *Le poisson* just seemed to pop up out of the water into our hands, as if we had commanded them, and they couldn't help obeying. The man started a fire. 'Hold *le poisson* over the fire,' he said. Then he started walking into the woods. I wanted to call him back, but a strange sense of peace came over me, and I turned my attention back to the fish. Then a funny thing happened, Tousant. A triptych image of *le poisson* stood on its tail and started shouting foul names at me: 'Cheat! Whore! Sinful! Dirty! Adulteress! Yes, you are a horrible, sinful whore!' the fish screamed. Then a voice came from nowhere and whispered, 'Don't let that bother you, Bree. Look at what's calling you *foul* names. A fish! A goddamn, cold ass fish!' the voice giggled. 'A fish that's got itself caught and about to be eaten.' Then suddenly, ice rocks started raining down... pinging and knocking... jumping and dancing crazily upon the hot ground before sinking out of sight...that's it. That was my dream."

"That's quite a dream, Bree," Tousant said, brushing back her hair.

She slid back down underneath the covers. "I'm bewildered." she stated, simply.

Tousant lay in the darkened room and thought about Bree's dream long after she went back to sleep. He felt as though the ground had suddenly moved out from beneath him. Why was Bree still denying the reality of things? Would it have helped her if he had volunteered an analysis of her dream? *Suppression.* It didn't take a genius to understand Bree's dream and what was happening to her.

That Saturday night, Bree and Tousant attended the Woodward's party. The loud music drove Bree into the kitchen. It was late, and she was ready to go home, but Tousant was into a deep conversation with his best fried, Lawrence. She wandered upstairs in search of Nina, the hostess. As soon as she reached the top of the stairs, she overheard Nina telling three women how perfect Bree thought her life was, and how she was running Tousant into financial ruin with her high living. Bree had often wondered what people gained by trying to count up other people's money. "Have you ever been inside that house?" Nina asked her audience of women. They were standing in Nina's bedroom and did not see her. "Everything you put your hands on is money. I've never cared too much for *Creoles*, anyway," she confessed. "They're just too aggressive and high-minded." Bree was crushed. The air left her body, and she stood gasping. She had considered Nina to be her closest friend. She had always known Nina to be a gossip, but she had always thought that her gossip was harmless. But jealousy was an ugly thing, and she didn't have the stamina to cope with one more ugly thing in her life. She crept quietly back downstairs.

When Bree and Tousant arrived back home from the party, Tousant asked, "Did you enjoy the party, Bree?"

She slipped off her shoes. "The party was, okay. I know you enjoyed yourself. Look at you. Your face is all lit up," Bree said.

"There's a reason for my face being lit up," Tousant said.

"There is. Is it a secret?"

"No secret."

"Well, do I have to drag it out of you?" Bree asked, letting her dress slide to the floor.

"I've asked Lawrence to come over Tuesday night."

"Where is your head, Tousant? You know you won't be home until the weekend."

"I know," he said, staring at her. "*La dame*, I told Lawrence about my accident and what's been happening since then."

"Oh, no, Tousant, you didn't!" she wailed, "Not after keeping it a secret for so long. You just..." Bree sat down on the floor and held her head. She grabbed a handful of hair and gripped it tightly. Filled with rage, she sat there on the floor rocking herself.

"*La dame*, listen. It's not the end of the world! It was bound to come out sooner or later, anyway," he said, in a pleading tone.

"Now, everybody will know. You don't know what you've done, Tousant!" She could not believe it!

"*La dame*, Lawrence is my best friend. He wouldn't broadcast anything that was revealed to him in confidence."

"He's your best *amie*," Bree spat. "Until tonight, I would have staked a whole lot on his wife being *une amie*, but she isn't!"

"*La dame*, you shouldn't say that. Of course, Nina and Lawrence are our best friends."

"Not anymore," she said bitterly.

"*Qu èst-ce qui erreur?* "

"I don't know about Lawrence. But by Nina's own admission, she doesn't like *Creoles!* I overheard her telling some women in her bedroom a lot of negative things about me. Her criticisms shocked me. But when she said she didn't like *Creoles* that really hurt me, Tousant! A few years back, when the Organization had that sit-in at F. W. Woolworth's, this *Creole* was their leader! I was the one sitting there getting spat on. When that policeman hit me, and cracked two of my ribs, he didn't ask about my lineage. All he did was proceed to beat my watered-down, African butt! I was the one who lay in the hospital for two weeks. Where was Nina when all that was going on?" Bree asked, jerking off her stockings. Like most honest people, Bree had judged others as though they were honest too.

"I know it hurts, lady. But there are insincere people in this world."

"Insincere, hell! Nina is vicious and dishonest. I don't think as highly of her as I once did. I didn't know she was capable of saying such nasty things."

"Don't preach to the choir. Lawrence does not have that problem," Tousant stated, boldly, his anger rising.

"Maybe, maybe not. But I still don't want to go to bed with him. Look, Tousant, I know what you're trying to do. I've watched you at parties evaluating men. It won't work that way for me. If I do sleep with another man, he would not be a married man. Nor would I sleep with any man that we are associated with."

"I don't care who he is. Let's just hurry up and find this man. I want you healthy and at peace. You're not upset with me, are you?"

Bree sat where she was. She had to think. If she said that she was upset, that would cut off her own plans. But if she said that she was not upset, then Tousant could take it as her permission for him to run amuck evaluating possible lovers for her. She sighed deeply. "I guess not. Please, in the future, clear your plans with me first, okay?"

"I know that I should have talked my plans over with you first, but I became over-zealous and anxious, and I bummed out this time, but my intentions were good. Next time, we'll have a guideline based on your own preferences. I promise, okay. *C'est entendu.* We both agree that you're ready to take a lover."

Now that Tousant knew what he was up against, his plans were made easier. He would continue to search for a solution to their problem—with or without Bree's consent. He knew from experience how women can cloud up pristine water with their emotionalism.

"That's just it, Tousant. I don't know whether I'm ready or not. Your plan sounds right, but...."

"Sure, you're ready. Your body says that you're ready."

"But... I... Such an idea is beyond every law and rule I know of, Tousant. There are no secrets in St. Jamesville. Once word gets out, you cannot seriously believe that this will go easily down the throats of the people of St. Jamesville? Small towns don't usually harbor a large number of rational, intelligent people. And if you think that your plan will be acceptable to any of these people, you have completely lost your mind!"

"Forgive me, lady. But I really don't want to hear that shit! Because I give less than a good goddamn about what the people of St. Jamesville think or say. It's our life! We have a right to manage it anyway we choose." Tousant saw the confusion in her eyes as they watched him. "If we have to throw tradition to the winds, so be it! A person cannot always flow with society. Flowing with society can sometimes put a person too far away from where they need or want to be. I'm sure our solution won't be the world's *first* or the world's *last.* Anyway, nothing in life is ever clear cut. All we have to do is search until we find the right man. The Bible says, '*Seek and ye shall find.*' It's preached from the pulpit every Sunday," he said teasingly.

41

"Tousant, don't tease about church and the Bible. We'll have to come to grips with that soon enough. I think there's something you should know, Tousant. It's very important that I love this man. I cannot handle a purely physical relationship. I see no value in it. It's just not my nature. This man can't just be a lover. I need more. Besides, I don't like the idea of getting dressed and dashing out of here to go lay up with another man, with you giving me your blessings as I walk out the door. I like being in my home at night with my family."

"What do you suggest, then? Say it. Just let it fly. You are talking to your husband, remember?"

"I won't lie, Tousant. I have given *our situation* a lot of thought. Though I had no idea you were thinking almost the same thoughts."

"*Presque*," Tousant said.

"*Presque*," Bree said.

"How are our thoughts different?" he asked.

"I was... well..," Bree stammered, "can this man become my *second* husband? Why couldn't he live with us and become part of our family? If the man's the right person, it'll work." Bree's words hung heavily between them. She nervously cleared her throat.

Tousant hesitated. Then he threw back the covers and said, "Let's get in bed and talk."

When they got into bed, Bree lay very still on her side of the bed, thinking. Her words seemed to come out of their own accord. She never intended saying them. Had she gone too far? Had her words stripped Tousant of his humanity?

"You're not going to go to sleep, are you?" Tousant asked. "You cannot just drop a bomb and not say another word!"

After a long silence, Bree let out a soft sigh and said, "No, I was just thinking."

"*Bon!* Because so am I."

"Tousant, I think that I've hurt you, deeply. I was trying to think of a way to erase what I just said, to make some kind of atonement. What we're on the verge of doing is wrong, all wrong!"

"You have not hurt me. I'm a scientist, remember. Let's just keep an open mind about your proposal, okay? And we are not wrong!

Wrong is a relative term, anyway. Sometimes wrong overlaps on right and right overlaps on wrong. Besides, being right on a thing doesn't amount to a hill of beans! It's the end result that matters. Our family must take precedence over everything. Nothing else matters, nothing! I cannot stress that enough. As I said before, nothing in life is ever clear cut!" He added emphasis to his last two words as if his patience had worn thin with her. "I think it's time to smash up and destroy old gods."

"There is a *word* for what you're doing, Tousant. It's called, 'rationalization,' Bree stated. "But I do agree that our family must stay intact," she added.

"Frankly speaking, I don't care if I am 'rationalizing.' We are a *unit*, and this thing is about survival of that *unit*. I have to trust that no matter what happens, you will keep it that way, Bree."

"Will you marry us out on the veranda, Tousant?"

"Yes, I will. If that's what you want. There can be no changing of hearts and minds once things are set and put in place. So think long and hard, Bree. Leave no room for doubt."

"I won't leave any room for doubt, Tousant."

"Bree, there will come a time when we will look back over tonight with laughter."

Though she kept silent, Bree still did not feel as comfortable as she would have liked. She could not foresee a time coming when she could look back at that night with laughter. "Then, *c èst entendu,"* Tousant stated again, as if the mere repetitiveness of his words sealed and legitimized their action. He gave her a quick kiss on the nose. He turned over and shut off the bedside light as if his kiss had finalized their plans. But Tousant's kiss, and his total acceptance of the idea of her taking another *husband* who would live under the same roof with them, had not cleared Bree's doubts. His acceptance had only added more doubts. She wanted to pursue the discussion further. She wanted to explain to Tousant that this was her own truth, that it had nothing to do with him. Sometimes she felt as if she and Tousant had interchangeable body parts. They could exchange body parts; and Tousant would still be himself; and she would still be herself. But when would she ever stand alone? She was not comfortable with

Tousant having a hand in choosing a *husband* for her. She would not allow it. She, and she alone, would be the master of her own destiny. She had an urgent need to take ownership of her truth, to lay claim to it. She wanted to explain to Tousant how she wanted to run away with her hard, sought-after truth. She wanted to run away before someone took her truth away and labeled it a lie. Or condemned her truth by using words like loyalty, self-respect, and sin: no one could define these words for her. She wanted to explain how she had to hurry, and give up the place that knew her. And exchange it for a place that did not know her. For the first time in her life, she felt strong and in control.

CHAPTER
FIVE

*T*he late September sun infused Bree with sadness. It was the end of summer. Though the early morning hours still found her longing, her body on fire for want of a man, her decision to take a *second* husband was almost forgotten, pushed back by her busy, daily routine. She had spent the early morning hours of summer out-of-doors tending her flower garden. She watched with sadness as a pale, yellow butterfly rested itself on the petals of a fading rose. Her flowers had given her peace.

Early the next morning, Bree had decided that before the rainy season of fall set in, she would drive to New Orleans to the headquarters of her organization and do some shopping.

Bree had spent a busy day in New Orleans. She drove home, unhurriedly. As she approached the *Causeway*, she saw a stalled car up ahead. She slowed her car down. It was a common practice for motorists going in that direction to help each other. As her car approached, she thought she recognized the car as belonging to Reverend Littlejohn. But the hood of the car was raised and she couldn't see the owner. She pulled off the highway in front of the stalled car. "Can I do anything to help?" she asked, poking her head out of her car window. But the loud noise of passing cars and trucks made it difficult for the man to hear her. He pointed to his ear. "I said, is there anything I can do to help you?" she yelled. She got out of the car and walked in the direction of the stalled car.

"*Oui, Madame.* I would appreciate a lift into Mandeville. My father's got a truck, and he can tow me in," the man said. He had a strong *Creole* accent, and his pronunciation of 'father' rolled off his tongue with a heavy emphasis on the 'a' instead of the 'f'.

"Sure, I'll be glad to," Bree said, in an accommodating tone. "I'm going to St. Jamesville. I have to pass right through Mandeville."

"You goin' to St. Jamesville! This is my lucky day." He smiled a friendly smile. "I don't have to trouble you to go out of your way."

"It's no trouble at all," Bree said reassuringly.

"I can't think what is wrong with that car. It just came away from the shop, Monday. Today is only Wednesday," he said, holding her car door. He paused, and stuck his head inside the window on the passenger side of her car. "I don't want to get your car seat dirty. I work on the docks, and I gits sweaty and dirty."

"Please, don't worry about the car seat. It's just a car," she said, trying to put him at ease.

"Yes, you right. It is just a car," he said. But he still gave her an apologetic smile.

When she drove off, the man turned his head towards the car window. For some minutes, he sat looking out over the water. "You don't talk very much, do you?" she asked. He had not said a word to her since he got into her car.

"I talk, but not too often."

Bree drove leisurely for a few more miles before attempting to make conversation again. "So, you work on the docks?" she asked.

"*Oui, Madame*. Fifteen-years, I'm there."

"You like it?"

"*Oui, Madame*."

"Is it because it's out in the fresh air and sunshine?"

"I guess."

"You don't mind us talking do you?"

"*Non, Madame*. I don't care."

"How long were you waiting there beside the highway?"

"*Quelle heure est-il?*"

"It's four o'clock."

"Most of a hour. Maybe more."

"Your family is probably worried about you by now. That *Causeway* can be dangerous."

"I know; I been goin' on the bridge for fifteen-years, yes. Same way, every day. I hate drivin' the *Causeway* every day, but the *Causeway* is closest route to New Orleans." After a pause, he said, "I live with my parents. I don't think *mon mère* is too worried. She knows that my car won't behave and won't run the way it suppose to."

"So you can talk," Bree said, in a teasing tone.

"Oh, *oui, Madame*, sometimes."

"What do you do other than work the docks? Any hobbies?"

"Hobbies," he asked, a puzzled look on his face.

"Yes. Things you do for fun, for peace, other than your job."

"Well, I blow my music on weekends."

"Oh, you're a musician. Where do you play?"

"All over the State of Louisiana."

"What's the name of your band?"

"The Kingpins."

"The Kingpins. I don't believe I've ever heard of your group. But I very rarely go to nightclubs," she added, not wanting him to think that his band had to be unpopular. "How many are in your group?"

"Six."

"Nice size group. What instrument do you play?"

"I blow *sax.*"

"I bet you're good at it too. You look like a saxophone player."

"How do a *sax* player look," he asked. He surprised her with his question. Because up until then, she had led the conversation.

"Like you," she said smiling.

"And, how do I look?" he asked, looking at her for the first time.

"I walked right into that one."

"Now, how you gon' bring yo'self out of it?" He smiled. When he smiled, something stirred inside of her.

"By giving up, gracefully."

Bree watched him from the corner of her eye. He wasn't a handsome man, but he had strong male qualities. He was rugged and muscular with strong looking hands. His statement about "dirtying" her car seat made her think that he was a clean man. But he appeared crude. As if life were afraid to touch him and force upon him any refinements. He had a small scar under his right eye—which added to her assessment of him. "My ladies' club hires a band for our annual *Mardi Gras* ball. We were discussing the *Mardi Gras ball* at our last meeting. We've decided to do something different this year—maybe even hire a new band. The band we've always used just plays the same old arrangements. Who should we contact if we decide to hire a new band?"

"Just call me, and I'll have my manager call you. Offhand, I can't remember our manager's phone number."

"Oh," Bree said, giving him a full-faced look. "But if I call you, you'll remember his number, right?"

"I got his number wrote down on a piece of paper somewhere in my dresser drawer. You can write my name and my phone number down when you drop me off at my house."

"Okay. But I'm warning you, my ladies' club will probably audition at least two other bands before they make a decision. Price will be a large factor when we make our choice."

"You can't top our price, *Madame*. And we can *blow* too," he said, a proud tone in his voice.

"It was unusual for you to have to wait so long at the bridge for help," she said, changing the subject.

"The traffic moves the other way till the day brings itself to five o'clock," he said.

"Oh, yes. That's true," she said.

"I been workin' many hours over from my normal workin' day. I punch my time in for four o'clock at the beginnin' of the day, and I punch my time out at four o'clock at the end of the day."

"That's twelve hours a day. How long have you worked that many hours?"

"Eleven years. But no weekends," he quickly added. "I got to '*blow my music*' on weekends."

"We haven't even introduced ourselves. My name is, Bree Jumppierre."

"My name is, Farras Jourdan."

He directed her to a house just one block off the main highway. The small, white house, with its French style architecture, was old but did not show its age. Green and white lawn chairs were arranged neatly on the front gallery. The house was surrounded by a freshly painted, white picket fence. Cape jasmines ran along both sides of the fence. The shrubs grew naturally without harsh trimmings. Someone had left the gate open, and she could see small, circular cement blocks leading up to the front steps. A variety of flowers appeared to have been planted randomly. There were no particular patterns to the growing flowers. They grew out of seemingly odd places. Some flowers poked out of the openings between the wooden steps. Fading red and yellow roses grew in profusion, poking out of hedges and shrubs, filling the air with heavy sweet fragrances.

As Bree was putting her pen and address book back into her purse, Farras said, "I hope I hear from you soon." He got out of her car. "My name, my number, you have, yes?" Once outside her car, Farras leaned over, and started wiping the car seat off with his hand.

"Oui, oui; I have your name and telephone number."

She sat and watched him as he cleaned imaginary dirt off her car seat. Her eyes rested briefly on the hard muscles of his arms. His muscles rippled, generating a warmth in her that slowly crept over her body. Satisfied, he closed her car door and came around and stood beside her car door and smiled. "Much obliged."

"Bree could not describe the look that passed between them. "You're quite welcome, *M'sieu* Farras Jourdan." She gave him a warm smile. *Much obliged.* She hadn't heard that phrase in years. She chuckled to herself. She wondered whether she would ever see *M'sieu* Farras Jourdan again—or even if she really wanted to. She drove off with the sweet smell of cape jasmines lingering in her car.

Tousant arrived home that Friday earlier than usual. While having supper that night, Bree asked him if he had heard of the Kingpins."

"Yes. It's a band that plays popular music. They're from over Mandeville way."

"I've never heard of them—and Mandeville is only twenty miles away. But I don't go to nightclubs, either. Since you go out to nightclubs sometimes, I thought you may have heard of them. I met one of the musicians in that group today."

"Oh."

"Yes, his car had stalled at the foot of the *Causeway*. I gave him a lift into Mandeville."

"*Bon.* That's a dangerous place to break down."

"I know. His name is, *M'sieu* Farras Jourdan. He said that he works on the docks in New Orleans and plays—or as he says—*'blows my music'* on weekends. He lives with his parents."

Tousant's eyes lit up, and his face brightened. He laid down his knife and fork and leaned over the table towards her.

"This, *M'sieu* Farras Jourdan. Is he single, divorced, widower, what?" She knew what Tousant was thinking, and it made her uncomfortable.

"I don't know. I didn't ask! All I know is, he said he lives with his parents," she said, annoyance laced her voice.

"You like him?"

"I don't know, Tousant. He seemed nice enough, I guess. He's kinda crude, though," Bree said, her voice was still laced with annoyance. She wished that Tousant would change the subject.

"Crudeness can be an asset in a man. Does that bother you?"

"No... I... don't know," she stammered. "Can we please change the subject? I'm really not up to this tonight," Bree said, in a tired voice. She threw her napkin down on the table, and made a motion to get up, but Tousant's overpowering eyes fastened themselves onto hers defying her to move.

"You know how to contact this, *M'sieu* Farras Jourdan?" Tousant asked, ignoring her discomfort.

Bree sat, one hand underneath her chin, listlessly poking at her food with her fork. She answered wearily, "Yes, he gave me his telephone number, Tousant." She let her fork fall on her plate, and leaned over closer to Tousant and said in a harsh whisper, "I only took his telephone number to call him for his band to come audition for my ladies' club's annual *Mardi Gras* ball. That was my only reason then— and it still is!" Her voice rose, and she gave Tousant a cold, hard look. She wanted to strangle him.

"It's good that you know how to contact this, *M'sieu* Farras Jourdan," Tousant said. He ignored her reasons for getting *M'sieu* Farras Jourdan's telephone number.

"I know what you're thinking. But I cannot, Tousant. Not with the first strange man I meet! Just because *M'sieu* Farras Jourdan meets some of my requirements does not mean that I want to go to bed with him. Please, I don't want to talk about this anymore. Talking about this upsets me. I didn't think it would be like this!" she said. Her voice shook. "Let's just forget this. It's getting too worrisome." She bit on her lower lip to conceal its trembling. "I don't want to get to know *M'sieu* Farras Jourdan better." Even if an interest in *M'sieu* Farras Jourdan was there, Tousant had killed it. Even on matters of the heart, he could not respect her as his equal.

"I'll ask around. Let's see what develops." Tousant said in deep thought.

"Tousant, you're not listening to me. What in the hell is the matter with you!" she yelled. Her eyes had lost their softness. "It sounds as if we've got some conspiracy going here to entrap any unsuspecting man that meets our requirements. Has it occurred to you that *M'sieu* Farras Jourdan just may already have a *special* woman in his life. He just may not be interested in me? Anyway, it sounds as if you're getting some sick thrill out of all this."

Ignoring her last remark, Tousant spoke: "He may not be interested! The woman you are! Please, Bree." He looked at her as if questioning her sanity. "Any man breathing would be interested in you. Unless he's of the same 'gender' persuasion," he added.

"Tousant! I'm glad Paupon is having supper with my parents," she yelled. "You're letting this become an obsession with you. Lord, my nerves are in a shocking state," she moaned, as silent tears traced a path down her face.

Ignoring her tears, Tousant quipped, "Oh, shut off the waterworks, Bree!" He gave her a look void of emotion. "It's not as if we'd be taking something away from this, *M'sieu* Farras Jourdan, and he won't be getting *something* in return." Tousant continued as if convincing himself again about the *rightness* of his decision. "This, *M'sieu* Farras Jourdan, will probably be getting a hell of a lot more out of his life than he would otherwise get—or even had anticipated," he added.

"*Peut-etre*,"'Bree said, and stared at him. Just in the short time span of their discussion, she had started looking at Tousant with a new recognition. He had a *male-type* of control, a kind of vicious thinking, that she doubted any *female* could ever have. It was just one more thing about Tousant that she had started to notice and had started to despise. She was unable to overcome the feeling that something *bad* was on the horizon. Without any hesitation, she got up from the table and left the room, leaving Tousant with his own thoughts.

CHAPTER
SIX

Ella Guidry-Harrison

*I*t was in Bree's junior year of high school that her father had a tennis court put in at his high school. He thought that if a tennis court were accessible to his students, he would generate an interest in the game, but the students showed little or no interest in tennis. Consequently, she and Paupon had a free reign to the tennis court on Saturday mornings.

Bree and Paupon had finished their tennis game. As they walked towards her car, she saw Farras Jourdan leaning against her car door. He had his hands in his pockets looking in her direction. His presence surprised her, and some nameless emotion stirred and washed over her. As she and Paupon drew nearer, he waved at them. "Who's that man, *Mère la dame?*" Paupon asked, curiously.

"*M'sieu* Farras Jourdan. I helped him one day when I was coming home from the city. His car had stalled at the bottom of the *Causeway.* He's a musician," she added.

"Oh," Paupon answered, nonchalantly. When they reached her car, Farras stood, smiling.

"*Bonjour, M'sieu* Jourdan." Bree said, with forced cheerfulness.

"*Bonjour.* Please, call me Farras." Bree nodded.

"Okay, Farras. Please call me Bree. This is my *fils*, Paupon. Paupon, this is *M'sieu* Jourdan." She waited for Farras to correct her again, but he reached down and shook Paupon's hand.

"Pleased to meet you, Paupon," Farras said, smiling down at Paupon with a friendly, relaxed smile. His teeth were even and extraordinarily white. He wore brown slacks and a beige short sleeve shirt. The smooth skin of his freshly shaven face smelled of after-shave. He looked different from the man Bree remembered, and his voice appeared deeper.

"Pleased to meet you too, *M'sieu,*" Paupon said smiling. His small hand was engulfed by the over-sized hand. "You're a musician, huh?" Paupon piped up, obviously impressed. He stood smiling up at Farras Jourdan with his hands hanging from his back pockets. Bree stood watching them both. She realized that Paupon liked Farras. But she was not surprised. Paupon liked everyone.

"*Oui.* I've been blowing music since I was most your size," Farras answered. His *Creole* accent seemed more pronounced. For some reason that she could not explain, Farras' accent irritated her. Though English and French were commonly mixed together in conversation, Farras' accent was so pronounced that even when he spoke English it was hard for her to understand him. She wished that he would either speak French or English.

"What instrument do you play, *M'sieu* Jourdan?" Paupon asked.

"Sax," Farras answered.

"Can he come to supper one night soon, *Mère la dame?*" Paupon asked, with a pleading look. "He can play for us?"

"Most glad to," Farras quickly interjected. "If *votre mère et père* don't mind." He looked slyly at her. Bree hated the position Paupon had put her in. She wasn't sure whether she ever wanted to see Farras Jourdan again. He held her attention too long for her comfort, and his presence made her feel ill at ease. Her feelings and her thoughts about Farras Jourdan were two different things, and the incongruence confused her, but she did not put any effort into trying to understand it.

"Okay," she said, feeling defeated.

Two boys dressed in tennis outfits came up to them, spoke, and walked around behind them to the gate that led to the tennis court. The two boys sang in the church choir with Paupon.

"See ya' soon, *M'sieu* Jourdan," Paupon said, running off in the direction of the two boys. He ran moving his fingers blowing an imaginary saxophone.

"We'll be leaving soon, Paupon," Bree called after him. Paupon threw up his hand and kept running. She turned and faced Farras.

Again, she was aware of something being transmitted between them. It wasn't visual, or related to anything being said, but it affected her. Without wanting to, she found herself staring at him.

"My 'phone didn't ring from you," he said. He lowered his voice and stared deep into her eyes. She heard the disappointment in his voice.

"Yes, I know. My ladies' club had no occasion to use a band. We won't be needing a band until February. You know as well as I do when *Mardi Gras* is, *M'sieu* Jourdan." Bree said impatiently.

"That's five months from now!"

"I know when *Mardi Gras* is, *M'sieu* Farras Jourdan! I don't know what to say to you. Is your band that hard up for work!" she asked sharply.

"No, the work is too much to handle now."

"Then why are you out trying to drum up more?" Farras didn't answer her. He stood with his arms folded without breaking his stare. "How did you find me here at the tennis court? How did you find me— period?" she asked. She had a slight waver in her voice.

"I stopped at the grocery sto' when I came into this town. I asked if they know you. I asked where you lived. They tell me. The man said you had already passed by this mornin'. He said you and yo' son play tennis here every Saturday mornin'. He give me the directions how to get here."

"Small town," Bree quipped, and called for her son.

"I can't put you from my mind. Do I have to wait to *blow* my music fo' your ladies' club to see you again? What 'bout supper? You promised yo' son."

"I'm afraid I'll have to postpone Paupon's supper invitation. Sorry. I'm just too pressed by other things right now. I'm sure you understand. I'll call you to set-up a convenient time for my ladies' club to meet with you."

"But... Paupon," he stammered, "won't he be disappointed?"

"Please, don't fret over it, *M'sieu* Jourdan. I'll explain to my son about his supper invitation," she said, getting into her car. It suddenly dawned on her that, once again, she had let the *male process* take over. Even though she wanted to keep the conversation on a casual basis, Farras had carried the conversation where he wanted it to go. She was more angry with herself than with him.

As Bree drove off, Paupon waved his hand at Farras Jourdan and kept repeating, "See ya' soon for supper, *M'sieu* Jourdan."

Toward the middle of February, a mad gaiety overtook Louisiana. It was *Mardi Gras*. The whole state trembled and shook and bulged to its breaking point with merrymakers. Every town and city in the State of Louisiana had shedded its normalcy and joined in the madness. The roads of St. Jamesville were full of melodious music.

Endless planning and preparations had gone on for months. Bree had reached the point of total exhaustion. During the afternoon on *Mardi Gras* day, while attending to last minute details, she had entertained thoughts of staying home. But knew she had to go. She had a duty.

In St. Jamesville, the *Mardi Gras* ball ended at three in the morning. Bree walked across the ballroom floor holding a small canvas bag under her arms. She walked in the direction of the bandstand. The band was busily packing away their instruments. Farras Jourdan hadn't noticed her until she was upon him. "How did you like the music?" he asked smiling.

"You guys are great!" Bree answered. "Didn't you see everybody going crazy *Second-lining* on the dance floor? You have a nice group." She had to shout above the noisy crowd. A sea of fancy, colorful parasols and upheld white handkerchiefs filed toward the front door. The crowd spoke loudly and gaily as if music still played in their heads. "Your band is much better than the other band."

"Please, do not flatter us too much. Or next time, we charge you more," he teased.

"Speaking of money, I came to pay you," she said, hoping to break his stare. His stare unnerved her.

"Okay, let's sit down and tend to business," he said, motioning to a table in the back that ran parallel to the bandstand. He sat down across from her. "So we're better than the other band, huh?"

"Are you fishing for another compliment?" she smiled. "I said that your band is better—and I meant it," she added, unzipping the money bag.

"Look at me when you talkin' to me," Farras said, suddenly.

"*Quoi!*"

"I said, dammit, look at me!" Farras emphasized each word through clenched teeth. The intensity of his words surprised her.

"Your accent is worse when you get angry."

"I'm comfortable with it. Besides, people like you need people like me 'round."

"People like me?" She looked puzzled.

"That's right. *Pour le grand monde*. Shocked, ain't you?"

"*Oui.*"

"You should be."

"*Pourquoi?* What did I ever do to you except give you a lift home when you needed it?"

"I tol' you to look at me." She looked him full in the face. She didn't know quite how to react to Farras Jourdan.

"I'm in love 'wid you, Bree. What do you think of that? I didn't know for sho' 'til I saw you at the tennis court that Saturday," he said, looking at her with warm eyes.

"I'm flattered. But..."

"But what!?" he asked, his voice rising. She sat trying to collect her thoughts.

"Tell me you care 'bout me too, Bree. That's all I wanta hear." His voice held the passion of his deep feelings. She stared at him, speechless. "What? No fancy words, *Miss High Class Lady?* This is the first time I seen you speechless. What's the matter, *Miss High Class Lady?* Is this the first time you ever had an 'uneducated' man say I love you to you? You that hopelessly out of touch 'wid *des gens du commun.*"

"That's not it. I do care. But I'm married. And..." A tear rolled down her cheek.

"Oh, *bèbè*," he whispered, "I'm relieved. I thought it couldn't be possible fo' you to care fo' me. Oh, *Dieu bèbè, je t'aime*. I don't want to rush you into anythin'. But just tell me again that you care."

"Yes, I care."

"Then, we'll take it easy and go from here. Bree, the band is playin' in Baton Rouge next weekend. Come listen to me play, please. Afterwards, we can talk."

"All right," she sighed.

He reached and pulled a card out of his wallet. "Write yo' 'phone number down on the back of this card. I'll call you Thursday," he said, and laid his hand on top of hers.

"Don't do that!" Bree said.

"Do what?"

"Your hand. Someone might see." Reluctantly, Farras moved his hand away. She handed him the money. "Don't call me, Farras. I'll call you. I better go."

"Listen, Bree. Don't worry. I know you married. I ain't the kind of guy to cause trouble. I'll be careful. Everythin's gonna work out fine. You'll see. I wish the hell I could kiss you," he said, hurriedly getting up from the table. "But you already made me wait for five months without seein' you. I guess I can wait a few more days." As Farras spoke, Bree had already started walking away.

As Bree walked away, she wondered why she always hesitated when it came to making major decisions. Why was she always so painstakingly slow to commit herself to any?.. But there comes a time when even.... She let the thought go and walked briskly toward the clean-up crew.

∞

When Tousant returned home on Friday evening, Bree did not mention what had taken place at the *Mardi Gras* ball, but thoughts of

Farras Jourdan had remained with her. Once again, she felt pushed by someone else's timetable. She had to have time to think, to sort things out for herself. Tousant's little investigation of Farras Jourdan had proven positive. All that Farras had told her about himself was true. But he had not mentioned that his young bride of two months had been killed by a logger's truck.

Bree called Farras Jourdan that Thursday night. They made plans for her to drive to Mandeville that Saturday evening, and leave her car parked at his parents' house. That Saturday evening, Bree lied to Tousant. She told him that she had to attend a church meeting to plan for a benefit drive. When she heard herself lying, it made her nauseous. But what else could she do? What if nothing came of her attraction to Farras Jourdan?

That Saturday night, Bree and Farras drove back from Baton Rouge in silence. She sat watching his profile, and his self-assured way of driving. He caught her watching him. He let go of her hand, and pulled her close to him. "You didn't enjoy yo'self tonight, did you, Bree?" he asked, his eyes still on the road.

"It was fine, but I'm not particularly fond of nightclubs."

"*Oui, je sais.* I remember you tellin' me that when we first met. I won't take you to a nightclub again, promise. There's other places we can go to be together."

Farras turned into his parents' driveway, and parked his car behind hers. He reached over, and held her to him. "Do you have to go now?" He whispered in her ear.

"Yes, I have to."

"I won't pressure you to stay. There's plenty of time. I'm a patient man when I see somethin' I need and love and want. And I do want you, *Madame* Bree. Will you see me again, soon?"

"Yes."

"I'll call you Monday from work."

"That will be fine, Farras."

She turned and made an attempt to open the car door. "Wait, I'll get the door," he said. "I might not be *educated*, but I am polite. I was taught manners."

Farras went around and opened his car door for her. But when she stepped out, he held her tight against him, preventing her from getting into her car. He made a motion to kiss her. "Don't, please! I'm not ready for that yet."

"No good night kiss. It was innocent enough. I tol' you I won't force you to do anythin' against yo' will. I do have my pride and this masculine ego to protect." He held her out from him. "You ain't said you love me yet, Bree. I know you said you cared 'bout me. But carin' is carin', and love is love. There is a difference, you know."

"I know. Please, don't rush me, Farras. I need time."

"At least, you agreed to see me again."

"Yes, I will see you again. I better get going," she whispered, breaking their embrace. She got into her car.

"You take yo' time 'wid yo' feelings. I'll wait," he said, holding her car door. "But, if and when, you tell me you love me, mean it! Please, know what it'll mean to me. 'Cause the minute you say 'I love you, Farras Jourdan.' I'm gonna try all I know how, and use every means necessary, to take you away from yo' husband. I'm insanely jealous of you, Bree. I don't know why? I ain't never been jealous of a woman befo'. But I ain't sharin' you 'wid yo' husband or anybody else."

"Is jealousy the reason you behaved the way you did tonight?" she asked.

"Behave! I... don't.... What you talkin' 'bout, Bree?"

"I'm talking about your jealousy. I'm glad that you brought it up. I was going to speak with you about it, anyway," she said.

"Well, what do you want me to say? That I ain't jealous, that seein' other mens dance 'wid you, touch you, don't affect me. Hell, no! I ain't makin' that kinda claim. 'Cause it damn sho' do bother me. I can't stand it when other mens touch you—no matter how innocent. And don't you ever let it happen again. I meant what I said durin' intermission. I don't want you dancin' or holdin' a conversation with other mens. It ain't that I don't trust you. I don't trust mens. And I damn sho' don't want no man havin' the satisfaction of holdin' Farras Jourdan's woman in his arms. Do you understand?"

"Let's drop this discussion for now, Farras." Bree said, holding up her hand. Her voice softened. "I don't want to argue with you," she said, keeping her voice soft. "But I see that your jealousy can cause some very serious problems. But I guess you have your own reasons for being jealous. Jealousy never really made any sense to me. But this isn't the time, nor the place, to deal with your jealousy. It's late. I really must be getting home. But we'll have to deal with your jealousy."

"My jealousy is no problem," he said. "It never will be if you keep my feelings in mind. Never mind how my jealousy got there. You just keep in mind that I have very strong feelings 'bout some things."

"All I ask is that you keep your jealousy under control, Farras. I'm taking your word that you won't ever let it be a problem. Because I've always had freedom of movement. I just hope you have no plans of trying to change that."

"I said, no problem. But I would appreciate it in yo' actions 'wid other mens you keep my feelings in mind."

"There's a million things I could say to you, Farras. But it's late."

"A million thangs, huh? My jealousy really bothers you that much, Bree?"

"Yes, it does," she said, sighing. "But if you handle the things as admirably as you did tonight, I guess..."

"You guess it might not be a problem, right?" he said, finishing her last words.

"Right!" she said.

"Like, I said, I might not be a gentleman, but my parents did teach me good manners, *Madame* Jumppierre." He gave a short laugh and bowed to her in the dark. They both laughed.

"I really must go, now," Bree said, "*Adieu.*"

"*Adieu.* I'll call you Monday," he said. He reached his head inside her car window, and let his lips brush lightly against her cheek. "I'll follow you home. The highway can be dangerous at night."

"That's sweet of you, Farras. But I'm sure I'll be all right."

Bree could see Farras' headlights in her rear view mirror. After they had driven a few miles, Farras started brightening and dimming his car lights. She pulled onto the shoulder of the highway. Farras got out of his car and walked to hers. She rolled down her window. "I know, I'm driving too fast."

"No, I forgot to tell you how beautiful you are."

"Oh, you," she said laughing.

As Farras followed her into St. Jamesville, the miles went unheeded, as her mind drifted into thoughts of the future and Farras' place in it. She did not want Farras to demand more from her than she was willing to give. Mainly, wanting her to destroy her family for him. Three blocks from her house, Farras honked his car horn and sped away.

When Bree walked into the darkened bedroom, Tousant reached over and turned on the bedside light. "Did I wake you?" Bree asked.

"No, I had to go to the bathroom. I just got back in bed. You look radiant," he said.

"Do I?" she said, wondering what was the basis for Tousant's remark.

"Yes, almost as radiant as you did when we... I mean... before... well... you know what I mean, Bree."

"Yes, I do know what you mean."

"Are you too tired to talk?" he asked.

"No. Just let me change into a gown, okay?"

"Did you ladies get anything accomplished tonight?" Tousant yelled into the bathroom. Bree shut off the water, reached for a towel, walked back and stood in the doorway. She stood there in the doorway and stared into Tousant's face for a few seconds. Finally, she walked slowly over to the edge of the bed and sat down.

"I lied to you, Tousant. I didn't go to a church meeting," she said softly.

"I know; you lie very badly."

"I didn't want to tell you anything until I was sure," she said, throwing her towel on the chair next to the bed. "I saw Farras

Jourdan at the *Mardi Gras* ball. We talked. He's nothing like I initially thought. But he's still a crude man, and our 'dissimilarities' are alarming. Yet... I care for this man. We met tonight and talked again. I wanted to get to know him better."

"Did you?"

"Some. I'd like the freedom to learn more about this man, Tousant."

"If the interest is there," he gave her a long look, "then you do need to know more."

"Yes," Bree said, "but there's one major problem. He wants to take me away from you." Tousant laughed a soundless laugh.

"That's a natural thing for him to want to do. He doesn't understand the *situation*. Once you explain *our situation* to him.... Just how deeply does your feeling go for this man, Bree?" Tousant asked, with a look of puzzlement on his face. "I know you said that you cared about him. But do you love him?"

"I don't really know. I haven't been able to let him kiss me yet."

"Why?"

"Because of my loyalty to you, you silly man. I think my Catholic beliefs have a lot to do with it, too."

"I thought you gave up your Catholic beliefs when we got married? We decided together we would be Baptist."

"No, Tousant. *You* decided that we would be Baptist. That's not quite the same thing. But that's not important right now." After a brief pause, Bree continued. "It's not so much my Catholic beliefs, anyway. It's religion, period. I've had a lifetime of 'spiritual teaching,' Tousant. I cannot just erase it."

"You didn't think that our decision to live an *unconventional lifestyle* would automatically erase all prior religious beliefs, did you? It'll take some time. What we both will be going through in the future won't be easy. He stroked her face gently with the back of his hand. As long as it's understood that this is something that we both want. There will be times when we both will have misgivings, but we have to hang in there if this 'arrangement' is what we want. Nothing has changed for me. I still want it. We have no choice. Unless a miracle happens." He gave her a look that denounced the improbability of that ever happening. "Again, once we start there's no turning back, Bree," Tousant stated flatly.

There he goes with that "we" again, she thought.

"I know that, Tousant. I wouldn't won't to turn back. At least, I don't think I will. I know it's not exactly cheating. Still..." she paused, "I feel as if it is. You've never cheated on me before."

"You want to bet! I have cheated on you without having a reason. Except that it was offered, and I wanted it." Bree lifted her head to search Tousant's face. She was silent for so long, he was beginning to think that she hadn't heard him. They both sat staring at each other. Tousant did not blink an eye. "Did you understand what I just said, Bree." he asked.

"You're lying to erase my guilt, Tousant. I know you love me, but you don't have to be a martyr! If I go through with this, you'll be sacrificing enough."

"Oh, come on, Bree. Get your head out of the clouds. You're living in a dream world!" Tousant said, fiercely. Bree continued to stare at him; her head suddenly started pounding at the temples. "Of course I've cheated! Lots of times! I'm away from home, sometimes for months at a time. God, what do you think I did to fill all those lonely nights? I'd still be cheating now if the accident hadn't caused me to be, *sexually dysfunctional.* Who do you think I was with the night before my accident?"

"Stop it! I don't want to hear anymore!" she screamed.

"Well, you gonna hear!" he yelled. "Your failure to look reality in the face can diminish you as a person. You've got to stop for your own sake, dammit! I'm a man. I was lonely," he yelled in her face. "I'm not as perfect as you seem to think. Any other wife would have at least, wondered. But not you, not good old, protected Bree! All your life you've been protected. First, by your father and two brothers. Then after we got married, I joined the 'Protect Fragile Bree Club.' I'm not sacrificing anything! Look at me," he yelled, getting out of bed. "Move your hands away from your face and take a real good look. He pulled her hands away from her face. "What do you see? Let me tell you what you should see. You should see a man who has a perfect home life, but has a job that made it convenient for him to *fuck* all the women he wanted—without the slightest chance of getting caught. I have slept with enough women, before and after our marriage, to last most men two lifetimes. Guilt-free!" He pointed at his chest. Bree sat frozen with incomprehension and hurt. "I have had an accident that has rendered me *impotent!*" Tousant emphasized the word, *impotent.* "Oh, but wait. I'm still being a selfish bastard. I have put you through pure hell—even to the point of you losing your mental health. I'm as certain as I can be that you couldn't have done the same to me. Oh, for God sakes, Bree! I only agreed for you to take a *second* husband for my own self-interest, to protect what I have. I can still keep my family, and I can still live my life as I always have. Now, tell me. What am I sacrificing? Nothing! I'm letting a man have your 'physical' love. Big deal! If I thought you could be healthy without sex, I wouldn't even agree to do that! But I do love you. Christ, how I love you!" he said. He sat back down on the bed physically drained. "You still don't get it!" he whispered. "I can tell that you still don't get it. I believe you're still praying for a miracle, still praying for God to give you your husband back! Well, my little 'magpie' that's not about to happen. Accept it, Bree! You have not seen my body since the accident: the mutilation, the scars, and the lack of testicles. I refuse to take anymore *hormones* to turn me into a freak! Welcome to the real world, Bree!"

Bree sat in stunned silence. Not a muscle moved. Not even a blink of an eye. New emotions overtook her. She sat struggling with these new feelings. "I... don't know... *how* or *what...* I feel, Tousant." she stammered. "Anger... hurt... I just don't know what I'm feeling anymore," she stated blandly. But she refused to cry. She still loved Tousant, but her relationship with him had changed, permanently, into something else. She couldn't fully understand *how,* yet. But it had changed.

After a painful pause, Bree spoke. "I have been over-protected. And, of course, it's my fault. Because I allowed it to happen. I could have put a stop to it, but it pleased me. I'm as much to blame as my father and my two brothers. I have control over what happened or happens in my life. I'm an intelligent woman. I could have stopped it. But my life was so simple, so peaceful, and so easy. I'm ashamed to say that I enjoyed it. But that's all changed now. You can start by addressing me by my Christian name. My name is, *Bree Boutte-Jumppierre!* A name is important; it identifies me as a person. All the women of the world are called 'lady' at some time in their lives. You even have our son calling me 'Mother lady.' Don't ever call me 'lady' again, Tousant! I'm a human being. I'm a woman. I'm a mother. I'm a wife. In that order!" Tousant looked at her spellbound. "Other than that, I have nothing else to say to you! And I have been tormented to the point of insanity. I've finally realized that I am an angry person. I realize now, that I have been angry for a long, long time."

A fierce determination had sieged her. From that moment on, Bree made a silent vow to live her own life without compromise to anyone. Her mood shifted. She looked over her shoulder at Tousant. And for a full minute, she gave him a steady, cold stare. "So here we are," she said, her eyes filled with cold malice. It was a look Tousant had never seen in her eyes before. A chill passed over him as he turned his head away from the burning contempt in her eyes. "I want to see your body, Tousant."

"No, never!" he shouted. "And don't you ever ask again!" He leaped up off the bed and pointed an angry finger in her face. "Now you just back off from this, Bree."

"Okay, Tousant," she stated simply, in a hurtful tone. She stood up and faced him. "I won't ask you again. Oh, one last thing." She slapped him hard across his mouth. "You, my dear sir, are *impotent!* It was funny how the *word* came out so naturally. After months of using the euphemism *our situation,* there the *word* was. "You stupid bastard!" Her language shocked even her. But she also felt a liberating joy. "I'm sure if this were known on your job, they would frown on your *whoring* around." Tousant did not react to Bree's slap or to her words. He sat back down on the bed, stunned. "And another thing, I'm sick and tired of men telling me to *look* at them while they talk to me! What the hell is so important you men have to say that I have to *look* at you for you to say it? And here's another 'tidbit' of information for you to chew on: loving a man like you have not been easy!" She felt Tousant's eyes following her as she reached over, and picked up her *music box* from the bedside table and walk quietly out the bedroom.

When Tousant heard the faint, unmistakable melody of Bree's *music box*, he reached over and shut the bedside light off and burst into tears, but they quickly subsided. When his tears stopped, he wanted them back. They had offered him a brief reprieve from his pain. But he was unable to call them back. He wiped away the trickle of blood from his mouth that Bree's ring-handed slap had caused. He lay in the darkness laden with heavy, painful thoughts. *Fate walks on silent feet,* he thought. *Why did Fate have to always present something "unlooked" for? No matter what your plans are, Fate reaches out its mighty hand and tears them apart, shatters them! A man just has no means of protecting himself from Fate's terribleness. He had learned the hard way that Fate held peace less than a quarter of an inch away from hell. Why had he, by some sick whim of Fate, been singled out to live the rest of his life walking down some extraordinary path that took away his soul?*

Tousant's thoughts always turned to his family. Family was vital to his peace, his wholeness. There was no other life he wanted or needed except with Bree and his son. The image of the way Bree would be again invaded his thoughts. She would again be *sexually* wonderful. She would again, in the heat of passion, whisper wonderful words of love. She would again be all softly fleshed out. She would again become an exquisite offering. She... His thoughts stopped and died there. When his pain lessened, he would bury his pain in some obscure, subliminal place. His pain had to be sealed away and forgotten.

Tousant's feelings underwent a change, but he didn't have a clue as to what it was. At that exact moment, he wanted to scream. He didn't have a clue as to why he wanted to do that either. It was a crazy moment, and screaming just seemed to come closer to what he was feeling. There was just no accurate label he could put on his feelings–feelings that were so horrible and so cruel. Was it self-pity? If it was, he did not care.

Within seconds, the feeling to scream was gone. Silently, like its twin brother, *Fate*, the feeling just slipped away. He was glad that the feeling had fled. Because his feelings had got ahead of his thoughts, and he did not want that. He needed to think, rationally. Feelings could sometimes mislead. A person could *feel* untroubled by a thing; yet at the same time, be deeply troubled by it.

Was it possible, he wondered, for him to have and keep it all? He found something both pleasant and unpleasant about the thought. He turned his head in the direction of the faint melody coming from Bree's *music box*. He exhaled a lung full of air; turned his head away and said in a weak tone of helplessness, "Life's beyond me."

CCO

It was late night. The stars were shining brightly in a clear, limitless sky. Bree and Farras sat in his car looking out over Lake Ponchatrain. The evening breeze, blowing in from Lake Ponchatrain, was chilling. Bree sat toying with a small piece of Spanish moss. "Cold?" Farras asked, putting his arms around her shoulders. His voice trembled with desire.

"It is getting colder," Bree said, snuggling up closer to him.

"Let's go to my house where it's warm. We need to thaw out," Farras said.

Farras drove to his parents' house. He pulled his car underneath the carport. "Why did you come all the way underneath the carport, Farras? You have to follow me home."

"Not tonight, my pet," he said, opening the car door.

"*Mais qu'est-ce que vous* ?" she asked, her voice rising.

"You ain't goin' home tonight."

"Yes, I am. I have to."

"No, you don't. What did I tell you 'bout any means necessary? You tol' me you loved me three times tonight."

"*Alors!*"

"So, tonight I'm makin' you my woman. In every sense of the

68

word," he added, in a hoarse, passionate voice.

"But...."

"No, buts," he said, getting out of the car. "I have thangs all set. I have the *Portuguese* wine you love so much. The wine should be all nice and chilled by now. I got a soft, blue light bulb to add atmosphere, a brand new jazz album, and me! What mo' can a woman ask for?"

"Nothing, I don't suppose." Bree felt out of control. Farras was calling the shots, and she resented it. She hadn't asked for this. Life had given it to her. Though she wanted Farras, Tousant had been the only man she ever had sex with, and she wasn't sure whether she could handle sex with another man. Her feelings were confusing her.

"Well, let's get out of this cold car," Farras said. "There's one more thang that I ain't mention."

"What's that?"

"We have the house to ourselves. My parents went to visit my brother for the weekend. How's that for good timin'?"

"I don't suppose you had anything to do with their little visit?" she asked.

"Well, let's say, I pointed out how long it's been since their last visit. They went all the way to Houma," he continued, biting her ear.

"Don't be so full of yourself!" she snapped. Silence. "*Je t'aime*," she whispered.

"You sho' runnin' hot and cold tonight, Bree. You lucky I like temperamental women."

Farras' bedroom had its own private entrance from the main house. He unlocked the door and pushed it open. He gestured for her to come in. She paused outside the door. Some seconds later, she stepped, cautiously, inside the room. The room smelled of furniture polish. The scent reminded her of her own house. As she brushed past Farras, she felt her body tremor. "Don't be afraid, Bree. Trust me," he whispered, and gave her a quick kiss on her neck.

Farras walked over and turned on the bedside lamp. The room was clean. Farras' bed was on the opposite wall from the door. The bed was neatly made. The floral pattern of the bedspread made the bed appear massive. Sitting next to the bed, was a small, antique-looking night stand with a black, goose-necked lamp sitting on top. In the corner next to the bed, a turntable sat on top of a brown, modern cabinet with dividers for record albums. At the foot of the bed, sitting flat against the wall, was an old-fashioned, light and dark brown *chiffonier*. The floor was bare. The brown wood looked slick and shiny from years of being waxed. There were no pictures on the walls—except for a cast iron, African mask that hung heavily above the door. It was a common mask. Similar to pictures she had seen in her African art books. She stood and continued looking around the room.

Farras picked up the blue light bulb lying on the end table. He unscrewed the regular light bulb and put in the blue light bulb. The blue light cast a warm glow in the room, relaxing her. "Atmosphere," Farras said, turning to face her. "Like it?"

"Yes. It's much nicer, more relaxing."

"Good, because that's how I want you to feel, relaxed," he smiled. "I'll be right back." He walked into the kitchen and brought out a bucket with a bottle of wine nestled in ice. He looked around the room for a place to put the bucket.

"Why don't you push the lamp back some and sit the bucket on the night stand," she suggested.

"Smart lady," he said, tapping his head. He walked over to the cabinet and started looking through record albums.

"Not yet, Farras. Please, I need to tell you something."

"You ain't scared, is you?"

"No."

"Nervous?" he asked.

"A little."

"I love you. I won't hurt you. I won't never hurt you, Bree," he said, pulling her into his arms.

"*Non, j'ai a vous dire quelque chose.*"

"Let's lie across the bed. So we can relax. I have a feelin' this is gonna be a long one."

They lay across the bed. Bree's voice softened, and she became sad as she started to explain Tousant's accident to Farras. Farras listened, uneasily. She explained to him the only relationship that would be possible for them to have. Bree ended by saying, "So your plan of taking me away from my husband is out. We cannot even discuss that possibility."

Farras sat up. His face had turned to stone. He rested his chin on his hands and grew silent. Bree lay still. She was afraid that Farras would reject what she offered. "I said that I have never met anybody like you before, Bree. How true that is. Well, I be damn," he said, shaking his head. "I have to think 'bout this one. This explains a great deal. I wondered why a woman of your 'caliber' would give me the time of day. You not the *mistress* type." He sat silent on the side of the bed in obvious deep thought. Bree wondered whether Farras' long silence was a rejection of her? Had the unforeseenable happened?

"*Foutu!* How could you and yo' husband come up 'wid a thiag like this?"

"Tousant, didn't. I did. People do what they have to according to their own circumstances."

"This is beyond what most people would do. I heard of husbands who can't cut it no more, gittin' they wives lovers. But agreein' to let they wife have a *second* husband, and livin' under the same roof, never! This beats the hell outa me," he said.

"Like, I said. It depends on the circumstances." Bree repeated. "Farras, do you love me enough to do it?" Bree asked.

"Yes, I love you enough." He looked at her for a long time. "And your husband will marry us, huh?"

"Yes."

"Well, I be damn. We all gonna be one big, happy family."

"Yes. That's what I'm hoping for, anyway." she said.

"And yo' son. What 'bout him?"

"Paupon is a secure, well-adjusted child. But... I... We'll see."

"I really like him," Farras said.

"Do you, really?"

"Oh, yes. I love children. I always wanted a son. But what you talkin' 'bout doin' is no simple matter," Farras stated.

Farras knew without any doubt that Bree would stay etched in his memory, forever. He loved her in a way that he had never loved any woman before. He gave Bree another long look, and wondered about his quick attachment to her. Still, he wasn't sure about accepting her proposal. But he had been in the streets enough years to know that what a man wanted out of life, and what he got, usually were two different things.

A few minutes later, Farras picked up the conversation. "We'll see. First thangs first."

"But is there a strong possibility that you will do it?" she asked.

Farras lay back on the bed pulling her on top of him. "You think it'll work?" he asked, nibbling at her neck.

"It'll take time for you to learn about Tousant and Paupon and for them to learn about you. But if we all are patient and work together, I think it will work out all right. We have the most important thing going for us, love."

"That's true fo' you and me, and between you and yo' *mari et fils*, but what 'bout me and them? This thang depends too much on everybody's cooperation."

"That's right. That's one important fact we have to keep in mind. Above all else, my son's happiness is the most important thing. I'm concerned about Tousant's happiness, too. Because if Tousant is unhappy, our son will be too."

Farras got up and sat on the side of the bed. "Human nature. There's bound to be problems."

"That's true in any family with only *one* husband," Bree said anxiously. "I want you to look at this realistically, Farras."

"I live in the real world, *bèbè!* I am lookin' at it realistically. Probably, more 'realistically' than you ever could!" Farras quipped.

"Thanks a mint!" Bree snapped.

"Well, it's true. The first time I saw you, I knew then that you lived in a 'dream' world. It showed. It stuck out all over you."

"I don't anymore. So you've never had children?" she asked, changing the subject to what mattered to her.

"Oh, maybe a few strays. But the women would never let me claim 'em." Farras said, with a hint of pain in his voice.

"Why?"

"Because they were married women, that's why! After a while, a man don't have too much of a choice," he said, getting up. He stood and began undressing. He took off his shirt and undershirt and stood naked from his waist up. She stared at his body. In magazines, she had seen pictures of men with magnificent bodies, but Farras had the most magnificent body she had ever seen. "Come," he said. She was glad that he called her. She got up and almost ran into his arms. She wanted to touch him. He held her face in his hands and kissed her long and passionately. She felt her body start to come alive. All her sexual frustrations started to melt away. She clung to him, moaning. He whispered hotly in her ear, "I'm gonna take you, and make you Farras Jourdan's woman. I want to love you so long and so hard that the moon will weep. Oh, God, *bèbè*" he said, squeezing her even tighter to him.

"Farras, wait," she whispered.

He continued to moan holding her tight against him. She stopped embracing him and tried to push him away. Farras became angry. "Damn! What is it now, Bree?" he asked, breathing heavily. He walked over and sat on the bed again.

"Please, don't be angry with me, Farras."

"Why shouldn't I be mad? All this damn talkin'. Talk! Talk! Talk! That's all you ever wanta do," he said, gesturing despairingly with his hands. "There's a time for talkin', but this just don't happen to be one of 'dem times! There's also time to do. That's all you *educated* peoples know how to do is, talk, talk, talk! Spittin' out a lotta fancy words. Words that don't mean shit or mount to a hill of beans! This life calls for action, *bèbè*, not ass sittin' and talkin'." He leaned over, and sat with his elbows resting on his knees.

"Don't be mad," she pleaded. "I agree with you. But this time...."

"This *time!*" he broke in. "Next *time!* I ain't never heard so many labels put on *Time* befo'. Go on, say what you feel you have to say. If we keep this up, it'll be Monday mornin'."

"I have to be honest," she said, making one final effort at explaining.

"Do!" Farras said, in an aspirated tone.

"What if you can't satisfy me? I... mean... that would change things. I can't deal with *two* men in my life not being able to satisfy me sexually. The thought of it frightens me, Farras. What am I

supposed to do then? I cannot go jumping in and out of men's beds
trying to find the right man to satisfy me. Maybe it's written down
somewhere that I should live the rest of my life in celibacy. Maybe the
wisest thing to do is to keep things the way they are."

"Oh, God! Why didn't you tell me this in the beginnin'?"
Farras asked. Bree could give no answer to his question. She only
looked at him. Her eyes pleaded for understanding. "At least, then, I
would have had the mind to accept losin' you. Why did you wait?
You coulda tol' me all of this the very first night we talked. Maybe,
then, I coulda pulled away from you. But...now...I'm in love 'wid
you, Bree. All my life I dreamed 'bout a woman like you. Do you
have any idea of how long I been out there in the streets? I been in the
streets most of my life: runnin' after other mens wives, hangin' in bars,
partyin'. Now I found what I been lookin' for, what I been prayin'
for. I'm tired of the streets, Bree. I wanta family. I don't understand
what you mean when you say: 'what if I can't satisfy you.' He gave
her a frustrated look. "Bree, you can drive a man crazy! Damn it!
Finally, I can feel the life I always wanted dancin' in the palm of my
hand. I don't know what to do."

"I know I was wrong for waiting so long to tell you this,
Farras."

"I can't give you up, Bree. I just can't. I ain't a super stud.
I'm a man. All I can do is give you, me. If you ain't satisfied, and you
still wanta walk out of my life after I give you all any man can give,
then...." He threw up his hands.

"Then, what?" she asked.

"I'm gonna beat yo' ass!" Farras said, forcing the words past
his lips with great intensity. "Don't you come here tellin' me if I can't
fuck, I better leave you the *fuck* alone! Now, I'm gonna get into that
bed," he said, pointing at the bed. "And you damn well better come to
me." Farras' voice went rough with passion.

"I've never had anybody talk to me that way before, Farras,"
Bree said. "I'm not sure whether I like it."

"You ain't, huh? I don't like talkin' to you that way, either.
But I'm tired of all of this damn talkin'! Maybe somebody doin' some
'street' talkin' to you is what you been needin' all these years," he

said, pulling her into his arms. "I'm gonna get in bed, and I want you to stand right where you are and take your clothes off." She sat on the bed beside him, quickly examining the full length of his body. He reached over and kissed her. She got up, and took her blouse off, not because Farras told her to, but because she wanted to. She hesitated before pulling her pants off. She stood naked before him. He gasped and took in a deep breath. "Oh, my God," he whispered, breathlessly. His voice became hoarse with passion. He moved farther back in the bed. He wanted her body, urgently and desperately. "Come to me," he said, reaching for her. "How long has it been for you?" he asked. But Bree was no longer listening.

"Look, *bèbè*. I want you to relax. Nobody is watchin'. Ain't nobody here but us. I ain't not gon' hurt you, but I ain't gon' treat you like a 'China doll' either. I'm gon' to make love to you like the woman you are." As he caressed her breasts, she lay begging him to take her. "Oh, Bree, it's *doux doux, bèbè, doux doux,*" he whispered. He kissed her pushing his tongue deep into her mouth.

"My body hears, my darling," she moaned. Each touch, each kiss, set off tiny detonators exploding inside her body, sending her into rapturous joy. Tousant had never come close to making her feel what she was feeling then. She was whirling in ecstasy; flying, being carried out as strong winds carried a weightless feather. She and Farras had broken through to the other side of ecstasy, where very few couplings go, and they lingered and lingered and....

Afterwards, Farras did not move. He lay atop her kissing and talking to her. She began to feel him swell inside her again. Farras made love to her again, with a fire and a passion, she had only read about in books.

Bree had surprised Farras with her burning passion. She had caught fire right there in his arms. He hadn't expected such fierce passion, such encompassment, such total abandonment from her! It excited him to know that beneath all that sophistication was a passion that could grip his soul, that could leave him senseless in love with her. He knew that he was quickly becoming obsessed with her. And he knew, too, that there was no turning back. He would share his life with Bree and a *hundred* husbands if that was what she wanted. At that moment, as he held her underneath him, he was afraid that the whole thing was just a wonderful dream, and he would wake up to his old life of chasing worthless women and feeling empty all the time. He couldn't stop looking at her or touching her. Somebody or something had placed Bree there for him. She was a "gift" for his empty soul, a "gift" from the gods. And he had no intention of throwing his "gift" away. It had all become very clear. This was the *part* of her he would have for himself, alone. Oh, how his heart rejoiced.

In a low, husky voice that expressed his needs, Farras spoke. "I'll be honored to be yo' husband, *Madame* Bree." He had made the right decision. He was sure of it. *Qui ne risque rien, n'a rien,* he thought, wildly. Outside the crickets made loud, melodious sounds in the crisp, autumn night.

The sun showed itself through the tiny space between the curtains, The light falling on the bed, beaming onto Bree's face. "Wake up, sleepy head," Farras said, shaking her foot. "Let's eat some breakfast." Bree turned tiredly over onto her back. She squinted her eyes trying to block out the sunlight. For a moment, she forgot where she was. "What time is it?" she asked.

"Seven o'clock," he said, slipping into his pants.

"I've only been asleep for two hours!" she moaned, covering herself with the sheet. "I ache," she announced, turning back over on her stomach. "What did you do to me? Sex with you certainly wasn't a disappointment." She winked at him and smiled serenely.

"As the song goes, I guess the pain makes the pleasure nice. Sweet and wild. That's the way it gots to be, *ma chèrie.*" He winked back at her.

"You sadist. Go away," she groaned playfully, pulling the sheet up to her chin. She lay on Farras pillow and smiled warmly up at him. Farras stared down at her, overwhelmed by her beauty and his unexpected fortune.

After breakfast, Bree was anxious to get home to her family. "Thanks for the breakfast, *mon amour!* It was sweet of you to fix breakfast in bed for me," she said, searching through her purse for her car keys.

"You sho' you don't want me to follow you home?" he asked.

"No, for heaven sake, Farras. It's broad daylight. I'll be all right. Don't fret," she said, putting her arms around his waist.

"My, my, my. How the gods done smiled down on this lowly man. So this is what *joy* is," he said. *"Joy! Joy! Sweet joy!"* He almost wept. He thought he would burst from so much happiness. He wanted to shout, to scream out his joy. He wanted the world to know about his great fortune.

They stepped outside his bedroom into the bright, morning sunshine. "This is a shinin', new world. I didn't know God could make a whole new world overnight. I thought it took Him six days." Farras gave a deep-throated laugh. She gave his hand a gentle squeeze. When he looked at her, he was surprised to feel his eyes had moistened. "Be careful on the highway, Bree. I'll call you tomorrow. Maybe, I should call you later today to see if you got home all right."

"That'll be fine. Will you kiss me, please. So I can go home?"

"Kiss you. In broad daylight! Oh, dear, dear me. What will the neighbors think?" he teased.

"Who cares? We're practically married."

"Vrai, vrai," he said kissing her. *"Au revoir, doux doux,* Bree. Don't ever give me a reason to doubt yo' love, Bree. Because I might...We'll talk 'bout it later," he said, closing her car door. Farras trusted Bree completely, but his mind ran wild with scenes of other men trying to touch her. In time, he hoped that would change. Perhaps it would after his mind had convinced itself that Bree was truly a part of his life.

"Yes. But we'll have to talk some more. I want you to understand that I made love to you because I wanted to, not from anything you may have said or done, Farras."

"What are you talkin' 'bout, woman!" he asked, taken back by her statement.

"I'm talking about giving my body to you, Farras. I gave my body to you because I wanted to. In other words, I don't feel duty bound to give my body to you. Just as you shouldn't feel duty bound to give your body to me. I want control over my own body. That's a basic human right," she said, gripping the steering wheel. *"Est comme ca."*

77

"I don't know what the hell you talkin' 'bout, Bree. But I can't deal 'wid that women's lib' stuff. A Black man's got enough shit on his plate already without havin' to fight with his own woman. That would be too much!"

"We'll talk later." Bree said, starting up her car.

"Somethin' tells me I got a lot to learn," Farras said smiling.

"Yes, you do," she said.

"God, that woman's full of fire!" he teased.

"We both are." Bree said, and winked at him. "Bye, precious. I'll be waiting for your call."

As Bree drove home, she thought about her night with Farras. She knew that most men did not look for strong, goal-oriented women, no matter how beautiful. She wanted Farras, but not at the expense of her being submissive to him. She could never be submissive to a man again.

Bizarre as it was, chancy as it was; and yes, even as painful as it was, she needed and wanted Farras Jourdan. And she was certain that she could achieve what she wanted in her relationship with *two* husbands. She knew, too, that she needed to learn quickly if she were to become the woman she wanted to be, and get what she wanted from her relationship with *both* men. She sighed contentedly as she increased her speed.

CHAPTER
SEVEN

*T*he next Saturday evening Bree, Tousant, and Paupon sat at the dining room table discussing her relationship with Farras. As soon as they ended their discussion, Paupon got up from the dining room table and walked into the kitchen. It appeared that he understood, but Bree sensed that something was amiss. Tousant had sounded too mechanical, too void of feelings in his explanation about her relationship with Farras.

Bree got up from the dining room table. She walked down the hallway to the closet, and took out a jacket for herself and Paupon. If Paupon was not at peace, everything else was meaningless. If there were any danger of Paupon being confused, or touched in a negative way, she had hopes of correcting it. When she stepped into the kitchen, she found Paupon still at the kitchen table with his hands underneath his chin, his forehead creased in a frown. She handed him his jacket. "Come with me to the levee, son." Paupon gave her a weak smile and followed her.

They walked through the tall weeds that had been last summer's garden. As they walked, Bree pondered over the rightness of her decision. How could she make Paupon understand precisely when she had trouble understanding her *situation* herself.

They reached the top of the levee and sat down. Paupon pulled up a dried weed and sat running it across the top of his shoes in silence. She sat down beside him, and cupped her son's face in her hands. His eyes were bright. "*Mo p'tit' zange.* You appear to be on the verge of crying." She smiled at him, sadly.

"I don't want to cry. It's my eyes. They want to cry," Paupon whispered softly. She pressed her lips gently to Paupon's forehead and tried again to explain to him. And she would keep explaining until she was certain that Paupon understood enough to accept their *unconventional lifestyle.*

"You're ten-years old now, Paupon. No more *Mère la dame's* little boy," she said. Her eyes moistened. She swallowed and continued, "I get so afraid sometimes, Paupon. I'm terrified that my actions will hurt the very people that I love and hold so dear. The trouble is, sometimes it's hard to tell how, or even if, you're hurting them. But this time I'm as sure as I can be that what I'm about to do is right for me and your father. But I'm not sure whether it's right for you and Farras. I have no guidelines. There are no books for me to read to teach me how to go about doing what I'm about to do. I'm hoping that my love for the three of you will help guide me through all of this." Paupon put his arm around her shoulder. "*Fils*," she continued, looking at him, "I'm just so afraid." Tears streamed down her face. Paupon reached into his jacket pocket, took out his brown, knitted cap, and wiped her tears away.

"Don't be afraid, *Mère la dame.* I don't want you to be afraid. I'm here. I'll always be here for you," he said, stroking her face. Bree heard her own words being spoken back to her. They looked deep into each other's eyes. Paupon's brown eyes reflected his love for her. She felt sure that his love for her would help him to accept anything he thought would make her happy.

"*Mère la dame*, are you really sure that you want *M'seiu* Jourdan to be your *husband*, too."

"*Oui, fils.* I do."

"Yes, but how do you know for sure?"

"I don't really know for sure. How can I? But I'm as sure as I can be. There are no certainties in life, *fils.*" Paupon seemed to ponder her answer for a few minutes.

"Then you have to do what you really think is right," he said. "That's what you always tell me."

"St. Jamesville is a very small town Paupon. It won't take long before news about me and Farras gets around. *Fils*, I want you to know that most people will condemn us." It annoyed Bree that everyone in St. Jamesville always knew everything about her.

"It is none of their business," Paupon said, his eyes blazed fire.

"Maybe, it isn't, but we are dealing with human beings here, Paupon. They will make it their business. I must forewarn you; people tend not to like things they don't understand.

"*Pourquoi?*"

"It's just human nature, I guess."

"But we won't be hurting them. I'll hate them if they try to hurt us."

Bree looked at her son, whose voice had not yet deepened, and said, "No, you won't. You're not being raised to hate anyone. Hate is a vulgar thing, Paupon. At school, the children may tease you, and react in a way to make you think that what I'm doing is a bad thing. How would you defend yourself?"

"Don't worry, I can defend myself."

"I'm sure you can. But I wish that you didn't have to. It'll all blow over in a short while. You remember the old bridge, how unsafe it was?" she asked.

"Yes, I used to be scared to cross it with my bicycle. That bridge felt as if it was gonna crumble any second."

"Now, we have a new bridge. A stronger, sturdier bridge that will probably last my lifetime. Life is like that sometimes. Sometimes the old things stop working, and we have to build something new."

"Like replacing old, worn out shoes, or a jacket that you have outgrown," Paupon piped up, pleased with himself.

"Yes, but there are some things that endure. Some things get better with time."

"Like cheese or wine," he said, pleased with himself again.

"How did you get so smart, *fils?*" she teased.

"I read too, you know," he said, smiling proudly. "Besides, Uncle Batiste tells me things." Paupon's brow wrinkled as if he were concentrating hard on something. "But, *Mère la dame. We're* talking about things, not people," he said.

"You're right, and there is a big difference. I only mentioned these things to show you that some things change and don't always stay the same. The same goes for people."

"Yes, I know."

"As long as you keep that in mind, we'll be all right. Right?"

"Right!" he said.

"Will you do me a favor?" Bree asked.

"Yep."

"Will you hold me in your arms for a little while? Suddenly, I feel like a little girl." Paupon put his small arms around her neck, and patted her on the back as if she were his child. "I love you Paupon. And I'll always nourish your soul."

"It's nothing wrong with you feeling like a little girl. If I can feel like a man sometimes, you can feel like a little girl sometimes. That's what's wrong with grown-ups. They think that they have to be grownups all the time, but they don't. *Oncle* Batiste said that grownups stop believing in fairy tales, and that's foolish. Look at *Old Minnie* over there," Paupon said, pointing.

"Old Minnie."

"The old oak tree. That's what I call her, *Old Minnie.*" They stood up, and Bree looked intently at the oak tree with Spanish moss hanging from its branches. "How old do you think she is, *Mère?*" Paupon asked.

"I don't know, but she's been around a while. How do you know whether, *Old Minnie,* is a she?" Paupon looked up at his mother and laughed as if her statement were a joke.

"Let's just say that I know, okay." he said, and winked his eye at her. "Anyway, *Old Minnie* might be old on the outside, but she's young on the inside, because in the springtime, she sprouts buds."

"Out of the mouth of babes," Bree said, smiling at Paupon with pride. "Hey, didn't I hear you call me, *Mère*? Now it's my turn for questions. Why?"

"I don't know. You just seem more like a plain *Mère* now. From now on, that's what I'll call you."

"Thank you, Heavenly Father," Bree said, as she stared into the setting sun. "It's getting colder. Let's go home. Hey, you know what, Paupon? You sure are a nice person. One day you're going to make one hell of a noise in this world. I believe that you have been here before. You must have!"

"You never know. This world looks awfully familiar to me," Paupon stated, sounding mysterious. *"Mère,* will you still play your little *music box?"* he asked.

"Yes, why?"

"I just wanted to know." She gave him a questioning look.

"Let's go back to the house, *Mère,"* Paupon said quickly.

Although Paupon seemed to completely accept her relationship with Farras, Bree did not see the reappearance of a smile on his face. And smiling had always come easy to Paupon. She walked at a slow pace. Paupon walked briskly ahead of her. Bree felt an uneasiness about her conversation with Paupon. His words were too mature for a ten year old. He spoke as if he were merely mimicking the conversation of an adult. She let out a lung full of air. She had been holding her breath without realizing it. "Perhaps I'm mistaken." Bree spoke softly to herself as she walked. "Perhaps all *enfant uniques* sounded like adults.

A week later, a sleeting winter's rain added a bleakness to St. Jamesville. The wind blew ominously and filled Bree with apprehension. It had been raining heavily throughout the week, and the sleeting rain showed no signs of diminishing. Each morning, Bree woke to find it still raining. A week before, glistening, paper-thin ice covered the ground. Southern Louisiana could get miserably cold, and it could, sometimes, snow.

In the living-room, Tousant had made a fire in the fireplace. In deep thought, Bree sat on the floor on a large pillow staring intensely into the flames. She was unmindful of Tousant and Paupon sitting opposite her playing chess. She had discovered that to live her life based on her own terms brought about its own confusion. But she would just have to wade through her confusion. Never again would she accept anything based on someone else's "terms" or someone else's "truths." Any mistakes she made now would be solely her own.

The house was quiet. She glanced at the clock sitting on the mantle above the fireplace. It was seven-thirty. Farras was expected soon. Bree was suddenly made nervous by her nagging doubts. What if Tousant didn't like Farras and rejected him as her choice for husband? What if Paupon, upon a closer examination of Farras, totally rejected him? What would she do then? What...would?... Talk was one thing and reality was yet another. It was simply a decision, she told herself. She got up, parted the folds of the drapes, and stood at the window peering into the darkness. "Maybe I should call and have Farras come another night. The weather's so bad," she said, turning from the window. She received no reply. The room remained silence. Her words had failed to break Tousant and Paupon's concentration on their chess game. She averted her eyes back to the burning logs in the fireplace.

Finally Tousant spoke, "Too late, now." He kept his eyes on the chess board. "He's probably left home by now. Don't worry so much, Bree." Engrossed in his chess game, Tousant still did not take his eyes away from the chess board.

She had thought about Farras' visit throughout the day. "I guess, I shouldn't worry... but...." Her eyes turned from the fire, and rested on Tousant's face. Then she turned her attention back to the burning logs. Her heart raced at the thought of Farras' touch again.

When the doorbell rang, Paupon got up to answer it. Farras stood in the doorway holding a long, white box. Farras spoke as he walked into the living-room. Bree could see that Farras was nervous. She wanted to kiss him, hold him, feel his body next to her own, but she held herself back. Paupon took Farras' raincoat, and Tousant offered him a seat beside him on the divan. Bree could feel the tension in the room, but she couldn't move from where she was seated. She was rooted to the spot, held there by some invisible force. Tousant offered Farras a drink. "Scotch would be fine, if you have it. Thank you," Farras added. His eyes followed Tousant.

"I'm a Brandy man, myself," Tousant said casually, as he fixed their drinks.

While Tousant fixed their drinks, Bree gave Farras a brief, reassuring glance. Her eyes told him that she loved him. When Tousant handed Farras his drink, he seemed more relaxed.

"Oh, I brought you some roses, Bree," Farras said, picking up the box that lay next to him on the divan. "I know you love roses."

"Thank you. I better put them in water," Bree said, getting up. Paupon got up too and sat down next to Farras on the divan.

"Did you bring your saxophone with you, *M'seiu* Jourdan?" Paupon asked anxiously.

"No. But when I come to stay, it'll be the first thing I'll bring through the door," Farras said, squeezing Paupon's shoulder with affection.

"Mère," Paupon said, as Bree walked back into the room, "if you and *Père* don't mind, I'd like to call *M'sieu* Jourdan, 'Papa J.' " Bree held her breath, and glanced quickly over at Tousant to see his reaction, but she saw none. He held his eyes on the drink in his hand. He did not look up or raise any objections. Still, she thought that Paupon's decision to call Farras, *Papa J,* may have been made too hastily. But it did indicate to her that Paupon had given her and Farras' relationship more thought after their discussion on the levee. She glanced over at Farras sitting with his arm draped over Paupon's shoulder. Like her, he appeared to be holding his breath. Tousant looked at Paupon and nodded an emotionless approval.

"May I be excused? I have a ton of homework to do," Paupon said, getting up from the divan. "I better say good night, too. Because when I'm finished with my homework, I'll be tired and sleepy. When do you think you'll be moving in, *Papa J?"* Paupon asked. The words, *Papa J,* sounded alien to Bree's ears, but she knew in time she would get used to it.

"I don't know exactly when I'll be movin' in, Paupon. But it'll be soon," Farras said.

"When you move in, I'll help you unpack, okay." Paupon said. Bree knew that that was Paupon's way of welcoming Farras into the family.

"Okay." Farras said, as relief washed over his face.

"He's trying to let you know that it's all right, that he'll meet you halfway," Tousant said. "He's expecting you to do the same, Farras. He's not a perfect boy. He has his days. If you feel that Paupon should be reprimanded for some inappropriate behavior, consult me first. That's all that I ask. After all, Paupon is *my* son. I won't ask for fondness from you," Tousant continued. "But I expect you to respect me. Just as I will respect you. It is of the utmost importance that we get along and keep peace in this family."

"I want all of the same thangs, Tousant. I'll bend over backwards to do my part," Farras said.

"Then *c'est entendu*," Tousant said, walking over to shake Farras' hand. "You'll stay in the guest room for now. In a week or so, we'll start construction on living quarters for you above the garage. I think you'll be pleased at the arrangements. I'll get some paper and pencil to show you what I have planned." As Tousant walked out of the room, he added, "You may have some suggestions of your own."

When Tousant re-entered the room, he sat down closer to Farras, and spread out his drawings on the coffee table. Bree thought she caught a quick, painful expression cross Tousant's face as he began to discuss the drawing. "I decided to build your room with its own private bath above the garage. One corner of the room could be used as a small sitting area. For privacy, your room will be entered by stairs from inside the kitchen. This will separate your room from the main house." As Tousant pointed out that part of the construction, Farras' attentive eyes followed his finger.

Tousant discussed financial arrangements, and Farras' financial contribution to the household. When the discussion ended, Farras sat staring in deep thought. "Farras, you seem dissatisfied. Is there something that I have missed, something you would like to have corrected? If so, speak up, man. We have to keep a line of communication open if this arrangement is going to work," Tousant said.

"Oh, I'm satisfied. The plans for my livin' quarters is fine. It shows you put a lot of thought to it, Tousant. It's just that you don't appear to be a jealous man. I hate for us to start out 'wid problems, but I have to say what I feel."

"By all means," Tousant said.

"You see, I ain't never had or knew nobody like Bree. Everythin', all of this," Farras waved his hands around in the room, "is a dream come true fo' me. I'm so scared I'm gon' lose Bree that it got me crazy jealous of her," Farras concluded. His words had softened his harsh features.

"That's a problem that you and Bree alone must deal with. I cannot make it my concern. If, from time-to-time, you need to talk about it, I'm here. But I don't know how I can help. Bree and I have never had a jealousy problem."

"That's 'cause you both always had yo' dreams come true. You always had what you both wanted out of life."

"Not always. But we have always been sure of each other's love," Tousant said.

"That's my point. I ain't sho'. Maybe, in time, I will be," Farras said.

"I certainly hope so. I have seen the results of jealousy. It destroys love. You end up losing the very thing you're fighting to keep."

"Then I'll have to work on my jealousy, won't I?" Farras said. Tousant gave him a disinterested look.

"Well, it's been a long day. I think I'll turn in," Tousant said, getting up from the divan. He stretched and yawned. "I'll tell you two good night." His instincts told him he could trust Farras Jourdan. But the word, *impotent*, flew into his mind. No matter how he looked at it, or thought of it, or wished it away; his injuries did not change to no injuries. Now, some kind of hideousness, laced with goodness, was about to take place. *Copy book standards* didn't exist anymore. But he told himself that it was all right, that it didn't matter! But a 'sick-to-the-soul' pain ran just beneath his thin, tender, and raw surface. A 'sick-to-the-soul' pain that caused him serious suffering. A 'sick-to-the-soul' pain that had erased itself outwardly, but had burrowed inwardly, and had found itself a soft, vulnerable home. He had to keep reminding himself that, it was he who had made the final decision for their *unconventional lifestyle*. If he had insisted, Bree would have lived her whole life through on nerve pills and masturbation. He gave Bree a defeated look and turned to Farras. "I know there must be some things you two will want to discuss. I'll see you, soon. Welcome to the family. Farras. I put a lot of thought into everything that I say or do," Tousant said. "Bree is a wise woman. I counted on and trusted her to make the right choice. Now that we have met, I believe that she has." He walked over to Bree. She was still sitting on the pillow before the fireplace. He pulled her up to her feet, and held her tightly to him. He stared deep into her eyes before kissing her forehead. He squeezed his eyes shut reluctant to break his embrace.

Farras rose from the divan. Tousant pushed Bree gently towards him. "God, keep us strong," Tousant said, as he walked out of the room.

As soon as Tousant left the room, Bree ran into Farras' arms. I've been waiting to do this."

"Why, didn't you?" Farras asked.

"I didn't want Tousant or Paupon to..."

"Now, listen," Farras said, as he held her out from him, "look at me. I'm gonna be yo' *husband* soon. *Second* husband, I grant you. But, nonetheless, I am yo' *husband* too. Which means I have all the rights and privileges as Tousant. We have to start this thang off right. What happened to yo' open, honest attitude?" Farras asked. "If we want to show affection towards each other, no matter where, when, or who's here, we will. We ain't got nothin' to hide. We ain't got nothin' to be shame of. In the beginnin', it may be a little awkward fo' us, but that'll pass."

"I'm glad you called me on it," she said.

"Let's keep callin' thangs the way they are," Farras said.

"Okay," she said, putting her arms around him. He held her face up to his and kissed her. "When will you move in?"

"I'd like to move in tomorrow night. But I thought I'd give Tousant the rest of the week alone 'wid you and Paupon. He may be an unusual man; still, he's a man. I hope to God I don't ever forgit that."

"That's really very thoughtful, Farras."

"It's just the right thang to do. The man's willin' to share his family 'wid me. Fo' that, I'll always be grateful to him. I shudder at the thought of his courage and his love fo' you. I know I couldn't do what he's doin'."

"I love him too, Farras."

"Since I met him, I can see why."

"Your jealousy doesn't include Tousant, does it?"

"*Non.* Oddly enough, it don't. The man overwhelms me. I'm just so grateful to have the woman I love. If you had been married 'widout these 'special circumstances,' I couldn't have had you. You not the cheatin' type."

"How do you know?" she teased.

"You better not be!" he said, a serious tone in his voice.

"If you know that, then why are you so jealous?"

"Being cautious. Watchin' out fo' my own interest. You just 'bout perfect, Bree. But you still just a human being. Tousant's education makes him too logical. I bet he thinks if you did git somebody else, logically, he can't do nothin' to stop it. But I don't feel that way. I believe I can stop it, prevent it, whatever." He chuckled.

"I can handle it."

"Oh, yes, lady. I know you can. You quite a woman."

"What about your jealousy and Paupon? He's still just a child, no matter how grown up he appears to be or likes to think he is. Paupon still needs a lot of love and attention. I must have the freedom to give him what he needs for as long as he needs or wants it. Don't ever make me feel like you resent it. I couldn't stand that. Paupon has to come first. Before you, Tousant, or myself. I love my son. I cannot hope to have a life unless he's happy. You are one of his parents now, Farras. And you have a responsibility to him, too. The three of us have to be committed to love him, and to see that he grows up to be a healthy, loving, and a well adjusted person. So far, thank God, he's maturing nicely."

"I know you gon' think this is impossible, but I care fo' Paupon already. I know my carin' fo' him can only grow stronger. It started that Saturday at the tennis court. He ain't a hard person to care 'bout. You and Tousant is to be commended. I think he's fond of me, too. I won't kid myself into thinkin' that he respects me. I know I have to earn that. I know, at times, it's gon' be hard. But I'm willin' to try. I think that Paupon showed the three of us tonight he's willin' to try, too. I have to make sho' Paupon knows that I ain't ever gon' try to take his father's place. Friendship is all I want. I got to make sho' Tousant knows this, too. If somethin' happens to Tousant, then I'd try like hell to be Paupon's father. I always wanted a son so bad At times, I may go a little too far. That's where you can come in, Bree. Point it out to me. I'm gonna work on a 'special' relationship for me and Paupon."

"It makes me feel good to hear you say that, Farras. Just don't ever hurt him."

"I'll make you a promise. Befo' I deliberately hurt any of you, I'll walk away from this house. I promise you, too, that the only thang that I'll ever be guilty of is spoilin' Paupon."

"*Merci*," she said, her voice choking up with emotion. "Farras, it's going to work out, isn't it?"

"Yes, it's gon' work out. It's got to work out. We four of the greatest people on this earth. We'll make it work," he said, a determined look on his face.

"Farras, did you tell your family about us?"

"*Oui*."

"What was they reaction?" she asked, sitting down on the divan.

"They think we *folle*. *Mère* started rantin' and ravin'. She said Tousant must be *voodood*. She believes the spell gon' be broke one day, and he gon' kill us both. I didn't tell them 'bout Tousant's accident."

"Why not? Bree asked, "It would have made things easier for them to understand."

"In the first place, it ain't they business. And in the second place, I didn't feel I had the right. They should trust and respect my decisions as a man. They had to admit to theyselves that I'm mo' at peace now than they ever seen me. *Père* kept walkin' around shakin' his head, talkin' 'bout how dangerous this *situation* is. '*Fils*, ain't no woman in the world worth gittin' yo' self kilt over. Ain't no love on this earth that strong.' Mines is, I tol' him. *Me're* got her *livre de priere*, and held it up with tears streamin' down her face. 'Don't do this! Lord, *fils*, don't do this! Ya'll headin' down the pathway to *hell* and destruction!' she hollered. 'Destruction! Jesus! Destruction!' She held up her *livre de priere* and shielded her face from me. I tried to hol' and comfort her, but she pushed me away. She said she didn't want me to touch her. She kept holdin' up her *livre de priere* like she was usin' it to shield my sins from her. She said it's a sick and sinful way to live. Then she started *toutes les larmes de son corps.*"

"So it has started already," Bree said, staring at nothing.

"It's nothin' we didn't expect," Farras said, sitting down beside her. "They'll git over it, Bree. After they meet you and see what a decent, wonderful person you are, they'll fall in love 'wid you too."

"And, if they don't?"

"Then it'll be my parents' loss. What 'bout yo' family? How did they take it?"

"I haven't told them yet."

"What!" Farras said, in astonishment. "You mean to tell me, as important as this is, you ain't tol' 'em yet? Do you realize this is gon' 'fect they lives, too?"

"I know. I wanted everything worked out between us first. I'll tell them soon. This week. Before you move in."

"*Demain,*" he said.

"I don't think that it'll be a big problem with them."

"Oh, you don't, huh! Sometimes peoples act the exact opposite from the way that you would think."

"That's true. But in my case, I don't think so. All my family wants is my peace."

"*Chèri,* you ain't being realistic. You still hangin' onto some of yo' "dream world" ideas. This ain't like you decidin' on what college you gon' go to. You talkin' 'bout havin' *two* husbands, and livin' 'wid both *husbands* under the same roof! Believe me, this is gonna blow they minds. They prim and proper daughter will be the talk of the town, maybe the whole State of Louisiana. Parents are funny. They feel if they children is being condemned, somehow, they being condemned. Please, *bèbè,* expect the worst."

"They love me," she said passively.

"My parents loves me, too. But look how they reacted."

"My father is a businessman and an educator. He's used to dealing with all types of people and situations. I'm depending on him to make *mon mère et mon deux freres understand.*"

"Maybe, so. I hope you right. We'll see. At any rate, we have our own lives to live," Farras said.

"We cannot isolate ourselves from the world, Farras. I need my family. I cannot live without them. I need my friends, too. We cannot live in this world without other people."

"Well," Farras said, standing up, "I have to go to work tomorrow. It's late."

"Please, be careful on the highway, Farras."

"I will. Oh, one more thing. What 'bout sleepin' arrangements? We didn't discuss that," he said.

"Tousant and I decided that I would share your bed. I'll know the nights that Tousant will need me to share his bed. As long as you understand that, and not feel neglected."

"I tol' you I understood, and I do. After all, he is yo' husband, too. At times, he gon' need you in his bed. I 'cept it as a fact. There are times when I wanta be by myself, too. I need to hear my music. Believe it or not, sometimes I do think."

"Each of us has to have our own space," Bree stated.

"I'm glad I brought this up. What 'bout my music? I still like to *blow* my music on weekends. We rehearse every Wednesday night at the school auditorium in Mandeville. You already know how the band travels to different little towns on weekends."

"No problem. Your music is a form of self-expression. Actually, I'm glad that you'll be still keeping your musical interest, because Tousant is only home on weekends, and he'll need some uninterrupted time to spend with me and Paupon."

"Self-expression. Is that what my music offers me?" he teased.

"That's what it is."

"Well, you learn somethin' every day," he chuckled. "I better go, now."

"Please, be careful," Bree said, with concern in her voice.

"One other thing, Bree. Do yo' family know how the accident affected, Tousant?"

"They didn't ask, and I didn't say."

92

"Will our thang affect Tousant's job?"

"I don't think so. They know how the accident affected Tousant. They probably know more about it than I ever will. I still don't know how it actually happened. Tousant never said, and I never asked. It's getting late. You better get going, Farras. Please, drive carefully," she cautioned."

"Right," he said, pulling her to him. He kissed her. "If it wasn't so late, I'd..."

"Shhh," Bree said, putting her hand over his mouth. "It is late. And we have the rest of our lives to make love."

"We do?"

"*Oui.*"

"In that case, *adieu,*" Farras said, kissing her again. Bree stood in the doorway and watched him drive off.

After Farras left, Bree sat down on the pillow in front of the fireplace. She sat quietly. The house had a hush to it. The glow from the dying fire gave the room an oppressive atmosphere that pressed in on her, and her confidence in her *unconventional lifestyle,* fled. New thoughts troubled her. She was gripped by thoughts of her family's rejection of her *unconventional lifestyle.* The question was, if her family rejected her *new* lifestyle, could she hold her own against them? God, help her. She still needed her family's permission and blessing. There was no need in haggling herself about it when she knew that she did. Somehow, her father had always made her feel helpless and inadequate. He was scary to talk to, but that didn't mean that her father couldn't sometimes be a comfort. He just did his comforting in an authoritative way. For her entire life, she had hidden her *real* feelings from her father. She had hidden her feelings so well, she doubted if her father ever suspected that she was a different person from the Bree he thought he knew.

CHAPTER
EIGHT

lmost before Bree knew it, Christmas was upon them. It was at Christmas time that she cherished the illusion that all was well. Christmas meant family and traditions. A time which could not be disturbed. She had been forced to examine herself in ways that were unthought of the Christmas before. But something good had been gained. That year, she had made some hard choices, scary choices. But she had found her way, or was finding her way, and she hoped that this Christmas really was the season for miracles.

Bree and Paupon worked together decorating the Christmas tree. She paused occasionally to admire their work. The Christmas lights blinked warm, bright colors. Bree's throat was suddenly swollen thick with tears. She turned away from the tree and stood, arms folded, looking wistfully out the living-room window. Though the sky held a gray overcast, and it threatened to rain, St. Jamesville gave off a sort of calm beauty.

She had broken her promise to Farras about telling her family about them. The holiday season had always been a "special" time for her family, and she couldn't stand the thought of destroying that specialness. She explained by telling Farras that it was too close to Christmas. She had given him a tender kiss and begged him to understand, but the warmth had left Farras' eyes when she asked him to wait until New Year's Eve to move in. Farras, unhappily, agreed. The truth was, she was not sure what her family's reaction would be. If her family rejected her, she was not sure if she was strong enough to cope.

Christmas passed as all Christmases do. There was plenty of peace, song, food, and presents. But Bree missed Farras. They planned on having their "special" wedding on New Year's Eve night. She thought it appropriate for them to marry on that day. A new year, a new life, a new beginning, she had told Farras.

Three days after Christmas, Bree ran around in a frenzy from store to store buying champagne and renting tuxedos. She had purchased her wedding dress the same week Farras agreed to be her husband. In the midst of all the activity, it occurred to her just how good she felt. Things were not perfect, but she was at peace.

By two o'clock New Year's Eve day, all wedding arrangements had been made. Bree had made arrangements for the wedding cake to be delivered. She felt that cake and champagne would be enough, because there would be no one else attending her and Farras' wedding but the four of them and her Uncle Batiste.

The day before her wedding, Bree called her mother and asked if they could come over after supper that night. Her mother hung up the telephone sounding puzzled. Her call to her two brothers was brief. She had hung up the telephone before her brothers could ask her any questions.

By seven o'clock, her family was sitting in her living-room with anxious looks on their faces. With a voice of pride and forced strength, almost without taking a breath, Bree explained her "new lifestyle" to her family. She left out the results of Tousant's accident. Her eyes scanned the room, momentarily pausing on each family member's face. Her father was a serious man. He was known for his honor, and his fierce protection of his family. In appearance, her older brother, Durant, was almost an exact replica of her father. But he had their mother's temperament. Durant was too serious, too quiet, and he had no sense of humor. His profession suited him. He had an excellent personality for being an attorney. It was always hard for her to fit Durant accurately in her mind. He was six years older than she, and like her father, had over-protected her. Durant was never friendly to any of her boyfriends. The severe questions he put to them drove most of her boyfriends away. But Tousant had stood his ground.

Her younger brother, Manuel, was outgoing, strong-willed, and had a mind of his own. He was the type that would die for a principle.

He had a personality more like their Uncle Batiste. He stood over six feet with curly hair and green eyes. She had always thought him odd-looking but handsome. He was the athlete in the family and had been very popular with the girls. His profession as a high school coach fitted him. Her mother stood slightly above five feet. She had smooth, satiny, light-brown skin with keen features. According to her father, her mother once had a figure that would melt ice. Her mother's good looks, though fading, always surprised her.

While Bree spoke, her father stood with his arms folded across his chest. She sensed that her father had closed himself off from her words. But she never took her eyes off his face. Tousant added comments from time to time. The rest of the family sat, seemingly, without sight or motion. There was a strained silence in the room. The quiet was fully charged with thoughts and emotions and words not yet spoken.

When she finished, her father looked at her. His facial expression was indescribable. When he spoke, his voice was low, and he appeared to be putting forth a great effort to speak. "What's happened to you two? How long has this stupidity been going on?" he asked, in a soft whisper. "Bree, why are you doing this? This is obscene! It's disgusting!" His words seemed to be causing him great pain. His face twitched. "There is a limit to human recklessness," he continued, maintaining his intense whisper. "You two have over-stepped your boundaries. You two are out of order!" There was an acidity in her father's voice she had never heard before.

"We had a problem," Tousant interrupted. "But we don't anymore. We have already taken care of it. This way is right for us. I know what we're doing goes against everything we were taught. And I know, too, that we're going against all of the 'mores' and 'folkways' of Western society. But we've spent many hours, days, months even, discussing this. We have taken everything under consideration, and we both have decided that this *unconventional lifestyle* is right for us. We know people are going to talk. But after a while, the talk will stop. We thought you loved us and would want to see us at peace," Tousant said, looking at Bree's father. "We're perfectly *sane*." Tousant emphasized the word, *sane*. "We were certainly counting on your support and blessings. We didn't think that asking for moral support and blessings from our family was asking too much. But whether our families gives us their support and blessings or not, we're going ahead with our plans. We're two responsible, intelligent adults, and we know what gives us peace."

M'sieu Boutte flew into a rage. "What about *la famille*? Do you think I'm going to let you undo what past generations of Bouttes have accomplished? Maybe you two are too selfish to care about our reputation and the gossip," *M'sieu* Boutte shouted. "But I have worked too hard to keep this family's name decent and respectable— as my father did before me and his father did before him," he added. His rage mounted. Bree looked at her father's face and saw blind terror. "This waywardness is unbelievable! Incredible! Why are you two trying to destroy what this family has managed to achieve?" he asked, shaking his head. With a hardened expression, he glanced over at his wife and two sons. Her mother gave her father a long, searching look.

"Correction. Your family practically built this town, Papa Boutte. I doubt a little tarnish on its reputation will hurt," Tousant said. "I think the discomfort your family will suffer will be minimal. It's a small price for your daughter's health and peace. I doubt you'll lose your position as a good, outstanding, *Negro* family in this town. Our objective is the same as yours—to keep our family together."

"You certainly have a strange way of keeping *la famille* together." He shook his finger at Tousant, his eyes projecting anger and horror. "I ought to get a doctor to declare you both mentally incompetent!" *M'sieu* Boutte yelled.

"You'll only make a fool of yourself and cause your daughter a great deal of embarrassment. Because you know, all of you," Tousant said, looking around the room, "that we both are perfectly *sane*. I'm trying to save my family, Papa Boutte. *A*nd you're only concerned about protecting the family's name."

As Tousant and her father argued back and forth, Bree stood biting her bottom lip. She realized that it was useless to try to talk further to her father. She was tired. And she wanted her family to leave.

"Bree, sugar, listen to your *père*. You're letting your, so-called,

97

love for this Farras Jourdan, and your own selfishness to have your cake and eat it too, overrule your senses. You're being absolutely unreasonable. You young people live in such a 'feel good society.' You want to do things that 'feel good' rather than 'being good!' Well, my *chèri*, being part of a family brings *responsibilities* to that family. You just think about that!" he spat.

Bree had always exercised great care with the words she spoke to her father. Attempting bravery, she spoke up. *"Père,* if we didn't feel any *responsibilities* towards our family, we would not be having this discussion right now! Please, do not tell me what I feel or think! You have not been blessed with the gift to mind read." Her words to her father shook the very foundation by which she had been raised: *Honor thy father and thy mother.* But her calmness surprised her. She had always been afraid to talk to her father. He had always appeared larger than life in her eyes. She took a deep breath, and looked her father full in the face. She saw a glimpse of "something" in his eyes, but she was puzzled as to what it was she saw. Her father ran his hand over his head.

"What about, Paupon? How do you think this will affect him in dealing with his friends? Your selfishness is going to turn your son's world upside down and stand it on its head. Bree, you are going to cause incalculable damage to your *fils.* You got to be crazy to expose his young mind to this sinful thing!"

Bree felt as though *Armageddon* had arrived, swiftly, and without mercy. "You make it sound like I'm naturally wicked and sinful, *Père."* She spoke her words in a half-whisper. She rubbed her temples. She knew, for the first time in her life, that she had to verbalize her feelings to her father, because her father had always misunderstood her. The misunderstanding came about, not because of anything she had ever said to him, but because of the things she had not said to him. She had always left most things unspoken. In her father's company, she was not so much a quiet person as she was silent. "You don't have to be concerned about Paupon. He's our son. We love him a lot more than anyone else ever could. If we thought that our *unconventional lifestyle* would affect Paupon negatively in any way, we wouldn't do it!" Bree said, with resentment in her voice.

"I'm proud to say that Paupon has a lot more understanding about love, and a person's right to peace, than all of you seem to have. Children's hearts are pure. Paupon was honest with us, and we were honest with him. We have chosen an *unconventional lifestyle*. That's all. That's it! Nothing complex! You won't even try to understand. You surprise me, father," she said coldly. "I had hopes of you at least trying to understand."

"I'm sorry to have to disappoint you, Bree. Don't you see?" But Bree did not see. "Love is not reason enough for your behavior. A *bird* can fall in love with a *fish*, but where would they live! I have never met a woman with *two* husbands with the *first* husband performing the wedding ceremony for the *second,* *a*nd with all of them living under the same roof like one big, peaceful family! It's unheard of! It's perverse and beyond spiritual pardon. I tell you, it's sinful! *Zut alors! Vous avez fort!* It's an *unholy alliance, D*aughter!" He looked deeply into her eyes and repeated, *"It is an unholy alliance!* That's all this can be! All it will ever be! And you're going to pay for this dreadful sin. Don't bother trying to justify yourself to me," he said, with wide eyes. "My words are like dust in the wind to you now. But you shall see, Missy! You shall see," he repeated. "Don't be a fool, Bree. Your behavior is outlandish!"

"By whose standards?" she asked.

"Dieu's!" he yelled. "And I don't care who marries you, it won't be legal!"

"Père, you're missing the point here. For us, it's just as legal as the paper that says that Tousant and I are married. Because the thing that binds us is love, not a piece of paper! The same will hold true for Farras and me. Just because something is legal doesn't necessarily make it 'moral,' *Père."*

"You're rationalizing," her father stated flatly.

"No, I'm not. It is a solid fact!" Bree never saw her father so angry. She could see that her decision had both frightened and saddened him. And he had a right to be frightened and sad. Their *unconventional lifestyle* would destroy the old, and it was the old that made her father the man that he was.

"Well, I can see we're not getting anywhere here. May God help us!" her father moaned. "This family would go *a la debandade* without me overseeing it. I won't put up with your impiety, Bree." Still dumb-founded by the dreadful taboo, her father looked at her as if he didn't know her from a stone on the ground. Bree turned her head, and met her father's steady gaze and thought: *a lot of fathers get angry and say mean things to their children they don't mean.*

Her mother was sitting in the corner of the divan, whimpering, making *un signe de croix* and mumbling something about, *unbecoming.* She looked at Bree as though she never existed until that moment.

Her mother looked sadder and heavier. Her younger brother, Manuel, took her hand in his, but she was inconsolable. He gave Bree a disturbing look. Her oldest brother, Durant, humped his shoulders and gave their mother a sad, defeated look.

As she looked at her mother, Bree's expression changed to helpless concern. Her mother's face showed a depth of feelings she wasn't aware that she could feel. It was an odd feeling seeing her that way. She gave her mother a gentle look.

The memories she had of her mother were that she always smelled of *rose water,* and she was predictable. And she used the word "unbecoming" to describe any inappropriate behavior. She thought that her little *music box* was *unbecoming.* If Bree slouched in her chair, that was *unbecoming.* If she acted in a way that her mother thought was unladylike, that was *unbecoming.* If she misbehaved, her mother pointed her finger and said, *"unbecoming."* Then her mother would grow silent and lock herself up in her bedroom. Those were the memories that she had of her mother, not of a woman capable of deep feelings.

Her mother had been sent to Xavier University to find a proper husband. But before her marriage, she had already graduated from Xavier University. Her career as a mathematics teacher was brief. When she met and married her father, like a dutiful wife, she left her life in New Orleans and followed her husband to St. Jamesville. The transition to St. Jamesville had been hard for her. She missed the city. Not unlike the women of her day, her mother was forced to push her own needs aside for her husband and children. All her dreams, all her education, wasted. She often wondered whether her mother loved her father and if she had peace. The answer to that question was soon answered when she saw her mother give her father a look akin to worship.

Though her mother's family owned a chain of funeral homes, and her grandfather sat on the board at Xavier University, Bree never cared for her mother's family. They were caught up in the "brown paper bag syndrome." Anyone darker than a "brown paper bag" was automatically rejected. When her grandfather died, he willed his funeral homes to her father.

The room grew quiet again. Bree's thoughts fell on her *music box* and stayed there. "Nobody will sympathize with you. Because what you're doing is against a woman's nature," her father said. Bree let her own thoughts go, and brought her attention back to her father.

"Did you say that my *unconventional lifestyle* was against a woman's nature, *Père?* Nature has no perception or intelligence, but I do! Most men have at least one other woman on the side. Why cannot women have more than one man? I'm not asking for sympathy, *Père.* All my life you told me that I can be, or do anything I wanted, didn't you? How many times have I heard you say, 'Aim high, Bree.' Her father stood in silence. "*Nest-ce pas?* Well, I'm aiming high, *Père.* I'm aiming for the moon, the stars, and the sun too! The whole damn "Milky Way Galaxy!" Bree said, her voice rising slightly."

"Don't you say that to me, Bree! Don't you dare say that to me!" Her father's voice trembled. "Again, I ask you. Why are you doing this?" he bellowed.

"I cannot tell you. You just have to trust me. Assume my reason has some validity."

"There is no 'valid' reason on this planet you can give to justify this kind of behavior!" Her father turned abruptly and walked towards the door.

"That's right. Leave, *Père!* But stop crucifying me! I have already gone through a terrible self-chastisement. If this were your two precious sons, this would not be a problem. The only advice you would give your sons would be for them to just keep their mouths shut about their affairs. You'd tell them to finish up what they were doing out there in the streets and go on home to their families. And you would go about your own business, *Père.*" Her father looked startled. He stood motionless, his eyes were averted downward. He lifted sad eyes, and gave her a long look before he walked towards the door again.

"You're the one who told me that families had to stay intact at any cost," she yelled after him. Her voice was as cold as ice. "I apologize for not being able to heal the sick, raise the dead, and walk on water!"

Her father ignored her words. "Bree, this is another way of you waving your *magic wand.* 'If I wave my *magic wand* everything will be right and reasonable and proper.' Do you remember saying this as a child? Well, I gave you that *magic wand.* And now, I'm taking back that *magic wand.* Grow up!" His voice shook.

"I'm trying very hard to do that, *Père!*"

"Anyway, this, Farras Jourdan, *c'est de la communaute.* He's most unattractive. Frankly speaking, he's an ugly man, and the wrong type of *Creole.* He's blacker than midnight!" Her father's description of Farras stunned her. Ugly and black were not what she saw when she looked at Farras. "Don't look so shocked, Bree. I saw you two from my office window on the tennis court. The janitor knows him, too. And now, I know more about this, Farras Jourdan, than you do." He gave Bree and Tousant a hard look. "Make no mistake about it, Bree. The blood is on your side of the bed. Like my father used to say, 'If you don't know what you're doing, you better ask somebody.' "Such is the *Breeness* of Bree," he said, and shook his head in disappointment. "In the end, such is the *Breeness* of Bree. Is there anything else I need to know that no one's bothering to tell me?" He looked at her. "This won't work! I'm telling you, *Fille.* It won't work! After getting no reply from Bree or Tousant, he said, "Well, I'll leave you in the hands of *Dieu.*" He stormed out swearing to himself.

As *M'sieu* Boutte stormed out of the front door, *Madame* Muscadine III gave Bree a cold look, and ran to catch up with her owner. Her mother and her brother, Durant, walked quickly out of the door behind her father. Bree looked at the open door that they had just walked through and said, "God, help me. Please, help me!"

"You're not wrong if it brings you peace. I cannot see it harming anyone." With watery eyes, she looked into her younger brother's face. "I wish that I had the guts you and Tousant have. I'll stand by all of you," he said warmly. "Maybe your experience can teach me something about my life." Bree thanked her brother, Manuel, with her eyes. She was both thankful and amazed at her younger brother. She had thought that if one of her brothers would ever go against their father, it be her oldest brother, Durant.

"All my life decisions have been made for me," Bree said. "Why do I have to continue to conform?" she cried.

Tousant and Manuel sat on the divan crying in their hands. Manuel looked up at her with tears streaming down his face and said, "You don't, Sis. Trust yourself. It'll all work out. Stick to your decision," Manuel said, through his tears.

"*Ainsi soit-il!*," she said softly.

By the time all of the family left, Bree was exhausted. It was odd. Her mother never lifted her head; not once did she come to her defense. She had counted on her mother. A numbing feeling of being let-down possessed her. Strangely, she was not angry with her mother. She even felt a remote pity for her. Actually, her mother's reaction was true to form, but she was still disappointed. She had thought that this time her mother would have.... She dropped the thought. She was finally beginning to understand why her mother never showed her father, or anyone else, the face that she showed her in their *private* times. In their *private* times, her mother showed her *true* self. Her fake benignity would erupt into malignant anger. But after those *private* times, her mother's image would change back to her *old* self, and she would think You hypocritical bitch! But her mother's mask did not conceal everything, because after their talks, her mother's eyes always sent out a warning message that said: know this but don't know this. Each time her mother did that, she wanted to slap her, to hurt her for handing her something that she clearly saw weighted down women. Sometimes for weeks at a time, she walked around in a stupor; trying to rid herself of the terrible feelings. Each time, she would tell herself that that was the very last time she would listen to her mother's *purgings*—the last! She would stop her mother's pathetic game of "let's bury ourselves."

All her life, her mother had preached to her about "going against the grain"—saying that there was no peace in it. But it had always seemed to her that "peace" was precisely in it! Because "going against the grain" was venturing into something new, something unknown, something untried. It maybe painful and terrible, but in the end, may prove itself to be good. But then, she was different than her mother. She didn't mind letting "something" painful and terrible take place inside of her. Her mother would never let "something" painful and terrible take place inside of her.

Without a word, Bree walked quietly out of the room, leaving Tousant to weep alone. A moment later, the bedroom was filled with music from her *music box*.

At seven o'clock the next morning, Bree heard a loud banging at the back door. She tried to ignore it. Last night's discussion with her family had left her drained. She hadn't slept well. She kept waking up. Her eyes felt gritty, and she had a slight headache. But the "Knocker" was persistent. She wondered why the "Knocker" didn't use the doorbell. When she opened the back door, her Uncle Batiste was standing at the door holding one, brilliant red rose and a white envelope in his hand, looking offended. His brown, wavey hair gleamed in the early morning sunlight. Like her father, her uncle was a big man, well over six feet tall. He was light brown-skinned with green eyes. His tranquil expression always reminded her of a *Buddha* in permanent meditation. His mind was wisely elevated above, or tranquilly settled below the cares and complexities of the world. He took his life into his own hands, and managed his life to his own liking. Her uncle was as different from her father as two brothers could be. After the war, her father couldn't get his brother to stay in one place. He was older than her father, but he had a free-spirited, recklessness about him. Where he kept himself on his visits to Louisiana was a mystery to everyone. His car was his only earthly possession. He had no home. Wherever he happened to be when darkness fell, was where he slept. Wherever he happened to be at meal time, was where he ate. He kept his few belongings at her father's house. It upset her uncle if her father offered him anything. There was nothing to do about him.

Uncle Batiste had a short temper that seemed not to mellow with age. He was a "third generation" chef. His grandfather and father had been a chef at the same restaurant in the *French Quarters* until his father opened his own restaurant. Her uncle had refused to work for her grandfather. He got a job as a chef on a ship. Now, working on ships was the only place he would work. He derived great pleasure from roaming the earth. Her uncle was one of the few people whose company she enjoyed. He shared most of her beliefs and was always a dutiful listener. He was the most *sane and sensible* person she knew. What he said or thought had always been important to her.

When she was a child, when her Uncle Batiste wasn't on one of his faraway journeys, he spent his time teaching her about life and about the places he had been. He never talked seriously to anyone else. He was awkward around other people. He believed that people wouldn't understand what he was talking about, anyway.

Bree were both surprised and elated at seeing her uncle. He was not a sociable man, and he rarely visited anyone. "Will you let me inside, or do I have to stand here until my behind turns to ice? I'll *fait tres froid ce matin*. You know I always enter houses from the rear. It's closer to the kitchen and coffee," he growled. She stepped back from the door, smiling, and let him walk past her.

"Why do you always grumble instead of talking?" she asked.

"I act grumpy with everyone. It's my way. You know that, niece." Her uncle had a kind heart, but he kept it hidden. "You gon' take this rose and envelope, or do I have to stand here holding them for the remainder of the day?" he asked, extending the rose and envelope to her. "Roses are your favorite flower, ain't it? It sho' damn snake better be. Since I had to drive all the way uptown to the florist to get it—and don't you open that envelope until after I'm gone," he added.

"Yes, sir. Roses are my favorite flower. The rose is beautiful, Uncle Batiste. *Merci beaucoup.*" She gave him a quick peck on the cheek. He seemed embarrassed. "I won't open the envelope until after you're gone," she said, holding up her hand as if she were swearing an oath, "*Avez-vous du cafè?*"

"*Oui, j'en ai.*"

"You drink too much coffee, Uncle Batiste."

"You let me be the judge of that. I been drinking coffee all day long since before you were born. I ain't had a sick day yet. So I'll proceed in telling you to mind your own bees wax."

While she fixed her uncle's coffee, from the corner of her eye, Bree could see him watching her. "I've got to say one thing for you, Bree. When you make a move to do something, it's a *lu lu!* He had stopped by her father's house for his usual morning coffee, and he had overheard them discussing Bree.

"Think so," she said.

"Know so. Even I wouldn't have thought up this one," he said, shaking his head in awe.

"What do you think about it?"

"*Chacun son gout.* I've always been a man for change. I can't stand to see life looking the same from day to day. A man would be a fool to think 'cause he's gone and got himself old that he's seen everything. Take me, I've been around the world. I've been in a couple wars, too. But I ain't never seen nothin' like this before! Folks don't understand that just because something is different, don't make it's wrong," he said, stirring his coffee. "I believe a person should live their own *epitaph.* I know that I've lived my own. The world sho' damn snake better believe it! 'Batiste never walked over *covered* ground.' That's what my *epitaph* will read. Want be no need to have lies said into my dead ass face. And yours, Bree. What would your *epitaph* say?"

"Mine's will say: 'Here lies Bree. She inadvertently went against the grain.' Fear reflected in her eyes. "There's going to be a lot of talk, *Oncle* Batiste," she said, running her rose across the back of her hand.

"*Bon.* This town needs something to shake up its brains—

especially the ignorant ones."

"Oncle Batiste, I cannot tell you what it means to have you come," she said, giving him an affectionate look. She put both feet up in her chair; draped her arms over her updrawn knees, and looked at her uncle with misty eyes.

"I've always had a weak spot in my heart for you. And don't you go blabbing that around, either," he said, pointing his finger at her. "Besides, I always have liked *algarade* from time to time. The pitiful souls in this town all act, look, and talk alike."

"Oncle Batiste, you have always had a type of shrewd mentality that I have always admired," Bree said smiling.

"Don't let *votre père* hear you say that. He thinks he's life's greatest *professeur.* That brother of mines thinks that he has the power to sit his behind on a thumb tack. He just looks so pleased with himself all the time. He reminds me of our father. Your grandpapa had a *conniption* because I had my own mind. I drew the line at his plans to send me away to college. You sho' damn snake better believe it. I tol' him ain't nobody on this earth was gon' smooth me out, and shine me up like a new penny. *Père,* had taught me all he knew about being a *chef,* anyway. Or anythin' else, to my way of thinkin'. So I got the hell on with my life! You sho' damn snake better believe it."

Bree looked at her uncle's face. He had gone to another time and place, back to some childhood grief. She could not look away. At that moment, it was clear to her why she loved him. How are they? *Mère et Père?"* Bree asked. Her uncle did not respond. "How are they? *Mère et Père?"* Bree repeated. Her uncle looked slowly at her, and the warmth returned to his eyes.

"I'm sorry, lil' darling. What were you saying?"

"How are they? *Mère et Père."*

"As always, your mother is performin' her 'wifely duties' by sticking to her husband's views. She always has been faint-hearted. She has taken to her bed, poor soul. Your father's walkin' around visibly shaken, talkin' his usual *betise.* Because he can't push his way off on you anymore. This is blowin' the fuses of his thoughts. He don't want you tamperin' with things. He made you a princess and now it's backfired."

"Last night, *mon mère* was *désolée, a*nd I thought *Père* was having *un coup d'apoplexie! B*ut my dam broke and all of my *real* feelings just came out."

"But you stood your ground. It gives me a personal thrill to see that you've finally got a mind of your own. You are brilliant! And you use that brilliance with your organization, but when it comes to family and your own personal life, you loses that brilliance, Bree. But you're finally learnin' how to out-talk a man—one of the easiest thing in the world to do."

"Life is crazy, isn't it, *Oncle* Batiste?"

"Yes, it is. But I've found an 'unbothered' place for myself," he said smiling, contentedly. "Bree, I wanta ask you something. If I'm puttin' myself where I ain't wanted, you stop me."

"*Oncle* Batiste, I don't mind you asking me anything, you know that."

"Well," he said, clearing his throat, "sometimes the simplest things are the hardest to say. You sure it ain't more to this thing than you tellin'?" Bree sat running her fingers over the petals of her rose. She didn't answer her uncle. She gave no indication that she had even heard him. Her uncle took her silence as a signal to end the discussion. The morning paper had been left unopened on the kitchen table. He unfolded the *Louisiana Weekly* and began reading the headlines. He sipped his coffee. After a few minutes, Bree turned her attention back to her uncle.

"It's all right, *Oncle* Batiste. I don't mind telling you." She told her uncle the 'whole story' including the results of Tousant's accident.

"Did you tell your father the whole story?"

"*Non.* I simply could not, sir. I have had too many years of hiding things from, *Père.*"

"I didn't think you had. If you had, he wouldn't be carryin' on so. I knew that it was more to this than what I overheard. Why don't you tell him? It would help save time and trouble."

"I wanted to. But at the last minute...."

"It still hurts to talk on?" he asked.

"Somewhat, but not so much that I couldn't have told them."

"Then, why didn't you, child!?"

"*Je ne sais pas.* I felt they should have trusted me. They should have respected my decision."

"That may very well be true. But there are many ways to tell the truth. They sho' damn snake should be tol' the 'whole' story now."

"No, *Oncle* Batiste. It's too late now, sir." Her voice was barely audible, and her eyes revealed the beating she had taken from her father.

"No, it is not! You stop saying that. It's stupid! What if you were sick, and you went to the doctor and said, 'Doctor, I'm sick!' And the doctor asked you to tell him *all* of your symptoms. If you refused to tell him everything. The doctor couldn't help you. Unless the doctor's a damn fool! The doctor needs to get at the cause of the pain. Well, it's the same way when you're dealin' with your family. You got to give them *all* the reasons for your actions, the cause. Most times, they pretty much can understand," he advised.

"Yes, sir. But *Père* thinks that I have gone mad. Apparently, loving a man like Farras proves my madness."

"That's 'cause he went on what you told him. You didn't give your papa *all* of the symptoms, *all* of the reasons for your actions. Very rarely can human problems be summed up on what's right or wrong. Nothin' is that simple. I can go right now and tell them—or is it best that you tell them?"

"*Cela est egal.* I talked out last night. You tell them, *sir.*"

"I'll be glad to. And will you please stop with that 'sir' business. That 'sir' business never did set right with me. You can give your uncle respect without such formalities. When is the wedding?"

"Tonight at eight o'clock, sir. Sorry, habit. We're keeping the wedding simple. *Sans tambours ni trompettes.*"

"Is it all right for me to come?"

"Of course it's all right, *Oncle* Batiste. *Ca va sans dire,*" Bree whispered. She gave her uncle a light smile and grew silent.

Her Uncle Batiste sat quietly watching her. He looked up at the kitchen clock. The sound that came from the clock was too loud and too fast. It was as if the electrical currents sped up to overcompensate for the quietness that engulfed the warm kitchen. He had only watched the clock long enough for the second hand to swing itself full circle, but it seemed he had been watching the clock longer. He stirred uneasily in his chair, and stroked his chin thoughtfully. He could tell by Bree's silence what he would see when he brought his eyes to hers again. It was a familiar look, a look he had seen many times through her growing years. It was a stern look with eyes gripped by sadness and confusion. Eyes that tried to appear young and brave but were old and fearful. Her hazel eyes had always left him feeling unlike himself and sinking into a depressive, weariness that lingered about him sometimes for days. He feared that the years had not changed that.

It was Bree's eyes that always struck a person first. They were such a pale brown that they bordered on some other color. Her fine-textured skin and long hair had the same pale, brown color as her eyes. *Honey,* he thought. *She was all golden honey.* This gave her an uniqueness that was commanding; in that, she defied any suitable description. A person's brain described her, but they still could never be sure if that was the description they wanted. Her image constantly changed in the course of a conversation. As Bree's looks changed, so did her behavior. She had been a fairy-like child and walked with small, delicate steps. Though Bree was now in her thirties, she looked youthful enough to be in her teens. *Women like Bree never aged,* he thought. *Their beauty merely dimmed and dimmed until death captured the last dimming.*

He could still feel her relentless, unmerciful gaze. He laid the newspaper aside and toyed with the pepper shaker on the table and waited for her to speak again. *"Oncle* Batiste." Her eyes were still on his face. He looked up trying to avoid any contact with them. He focused his eyes on her bow-shaped lips. He hoped to hold them there during the full course of their conversation. He had learned that Bree's eyes could never be trusted. "I have found my answer, *Oncle* Batiste." Bree stated, drawing him out of his thoughts.

"Answer," he said, maintaining his focus on her moving lips.

"Oui," she said. "I don't feel the old Bree inside me anymore."

His eyes held steadfast as he nodded his head to acknowledge his listening. His heart was aching. "Sometimes we can live out our entire lives knowing only the *self* someone tells us that we are. Then something drastic happens to us—a crisis—waking up the *real* self.

The person wakes up one morning, looks into the mirror, and sees someone *new*. Then the person has to stand there going through some 'mental metamorphosis,' wondering how to introduce the *old* self to the *new*.

She leaned across the table closer to him; her face was drawn and tired and weighted with despair. The desperation in her voice forced him to look into her eyes. His body went rigid. He wanted to pluck her eyes out of their sockets, and replace them with young, sparkling ones that showed nothing but love and innocence.

"Mental metamorphosis," huh?" he answered. He glanced at the clock again. Her eyes remained fixed on his face. He could feel them tugging at something deep inside of him. This forced him to look, against his will, into her eyes again. He looked, and then looked quickly out the kitchen window. His eyes hurt. They felt as though they had been torn, physically, from their sockets by Bree's pair of staring, odd-colored eyes.

He pushed his coffee cup aside, got up quietly from the table, and stood looking out the kitchen window at nothing. He looked down and ran a finger through imaginary dust on the window sill. "Mental metamorphosis," he repeated. "So that's what you're callin' it."

"*Oncle* Batiste, I...." He held up his hand stopping her words.

"You call it what you want, Bree. But I call it just being *strange*." He threw up his hands in some rare emotion that he felt but never understood when in Bree's presence. "That look. Those eyes. The way you are now. I've seen before. You were always a good child, Bree. But, *chèri*, you were *strange* too. I don't think your mother, bless her heart, will ever understand you. And your father..," he paused and sighed deeply, "your *père* is so wrapped up in your 'physical perfection' that he can't see much else—which only goes to show you how much your father knows about you," he interjected. "You were his *perle de perfection*. Nonetheless, I've always known you. People like us: you, me, your *petit amie* Harriette, are just different some kinda way. I don't even know why. I wished I did. I'd use it to keep myself still sometimes. *Daring!* That's the word I've been searchin' for all these years, d*aring*. That's part of our *strangeness* but not all. But you've finally come to realize what I've known all along. That we have the capacity to *love, love, love!* It doesn't matter who or what. Just love, damn it!"

"But you seem at *la paix* with yourself, *Oncle* Batiste. Even Harriette," Bree whispered in a raspy voice, "seemed at *la paix*."

"I don't know about, Harriette. I can only speak for myself. I am at peace. I've learned, just as you finally have, that we all have to define 'ourself' for ourselves," he said, holding his hands to his chest.

As her uncle spoke, he had a strong urge to hold Bree the way he did when she was a child. He had always felt responsible for her. He gave a compassionate sigh and looked over at her with sad eyes. "Defining one's *self*," Bree repeated. "A difficult task. I wish I could be a *self* not subjected to approval from family, friends, and the community."

"*Oui*, but there's no way around it. Still, it's better to be wrong about a *self* that you have defined than to be wrong about a *self* that someone else has defined. Sooner or later, we all have to face up to who we *really* are." He rubbed a stiff hand over his week old beard and heaved a great sigh. "Now, everybody knows that I'm a rambling man. I don't like walking over *covered* grounds." He stopped talking. After a brief pause, he said, "We've had this talk before, Bree. So, please, let's not ever talk on this subject from this day forward and forever more. It puts me in a fog for days. I don't know about you, but this kind of talkin' locks up my brain. It makes me talk one way this minute and another way the next. Nobody has ever been able to do this to me but you. But you are on the right road. Nobody has a right to judge you." Tears touched Bree's cheeks. She nodded her head. "No matter what happens," he said, pointing his finger at her, "you are on the right road. I believe you know that. You've finally learned to listen to the drums of the *Congo*. You don't feel guilty, do you?" he asked. "Because if you listen to people in this sorry-ass town, they'd have you feeling guilty about everythin': steppin' on ants, steppin' on green grass; 'cause it's alive too! They would try to stop you from lookin' up into a cloudless sky. They would claim that the sky's naked! And Lord knows what else."

"Guilty, about what?"

"Having *two* husbands, that's what!" he said impatiently.

"No, I have no feelings of guilt. *Oncle* Batiste, why is it that society feels that women are not supposed to be *sexual* beings? If a woman denies her own *sexuality*, would that automatically increase a man's *sexuality*? Aren't women and men both of the same species? But society makes *sex* normal and right for men and abnormal and wrong for women. *Oncle* Batiste, I'm sure that what we're doing is right for us. I'm sorry that the family had to be touched by my decision. But in this life, there are no innocent bystanders."

"How well I know that. The three of you saw your answer; therefore, ya'll made this decision. It's simple to me. People do what life calls for them to do. Different people have different requirements in their lives. Enlightened people knows this. I'm glad you're not carryin' around any guilt. But don't let this 'escape hatch' become your trap. Do you still remember the three questions I taught you to ask when somebody's tryin' to push their way on you?" Her face lit up. "I'll say them for you," Uncle Batiste said. "Number one-do I really think this? Number two-do I really feel this? Number three-do I really believe this, or am I spoutin' out words I've been brainwashed to say?" He ticked each question off with his fingers. "Please, tell me that you've at least reached the second level." His eyes held hers. "You must have! Otherwise, you would not be in your present dilemma.

Bree spoke quickly. "Your wisdom will finally not go to naught." His face relaxed, and a warm smile wrinkled the edges of his eyes. Abruptly, he pushed up the sleeve of his sweater, and gave a quick glance at his watch. He reached for his coat that he had thrown over the back of the chair next to him.

"I must be going." He gave her a slight bow, and walked hurriedly towards the back door without giving her a chance to leave her seat.

Her uncle's abrupt departure left her puzzled. Bree stared at his empty seat for a few seconds; shrugged her shoulders, and got up from the table. She walked over to the sink, refilled the kettle, and placed the kettle back on the stove to boil for a fresh pot of tea.

A short while later, Bree sat back down at the table sipping a steaming cup of tea. She picked up the white envelope from the table and tore it open. She sat reading with trembling hands. When she finished reading the note, she laid it on the kitchen table and stared at it. She held her head slightly to one side, as if she were listening to her uncle's words speak to her. After a few seconds, she picked up the note again and re-read it, silently moving her lips:

> *"Even if I could cry all of your tears for you, or*
> *could feel all of your pains for you, I would not.*
> *Forgive me lil' darling, but I want this town to kick*
> *your behind, righteously. I want them to really hurt you.*
> *You'll understand my words by and by. I do promise*
> *you this, as long as I live I will never forsake you.*
> *P.S. We both are folle, you know.*
> *P.P.S. Finally, you're seeking. It's a miracle! (smile)*
> *Oncle Batiste"*

She didn't completely understand her uncle's note. But she held his note to her breasts and thanked God for him, anyway. He had brought her some of his peace. She still had nagging doubts about having *two* husbands. Sometimes her doubts were even strong enough to keep her awake nights, sometimes she became afraid for, seemingly, no apparent reason. But she felt the exquisite joy of triumph! *"Merci, encore, Oncle* Batiste."

Farras moved in on New Year's Eve. Paupon helped him unload his car, and they got everything unpacked and put away. "Did you talk to your family again, Farras?" Bree asked.

"Yes, I tol' them that I was gettin' married tonight."

"*Et.*"

114

"*Et*, nothin's changed. Maybe, a little bit better. At least, *Mère* stopped prayin' for my sinful soul, a*nd Père* stopped preachin' 'bout *voodoo.* So, maybe there's hope."

"Maybe."

"Oh. My brother, Jimmy, and his wife is comin' to our weddin'."

"Oh."

"They don't see where our "new" lifestyle is so bad—just different."

"Different?"

"Yes, that's what Jimmy said. That it was different. I was tellin' him that for so long every woman I touched b'longed to someone else. Now, I have someone that b'longs to me, and I b'long to her. I have a family of my own now. This feels like home to me already." Bree looked at him and thought: *I do not belong to anyone!*

In the early January darkness, Paupon knocked on the bedroom door. "Hey, Papa J, we're ready. We're waiting for you."

"Be out in a minute." Over-anxious, Farras fumbled with the button at the neck of his shirt. *I must be gainin' weight,* he thought. His hands shook.

Paupon had asked his mother who was coming to her wedding. Bree had told him that, except for Uncle Batiste, no one. It was going to be a private ceremony. "I'm gonna give the bride away and be the best man, right!" Paupon said.

"Right!" Bree said. "With the stars and the moon shining God's blessing."

They all stood outside on the veranda. A beige, lace *tippet* hung beautifully from Bree's head and fell softly around her shoulders. The ends of the *tippet* hung down in front of her beige, lace wedding gown.

Tousant unfolded his paper to begin the ceremony. He had written his own "special" marriage vows for them. Uncle Batiste had elected himself to take the wedding pictures. He beamed. He felt that he was taking part in a sacred act.

When the doorbell rang, Uncle Batiste rushed to answer it; swearing under his breath. When he opened the door, his mouth dropped in surprise, and he stood holding the knob of the door.

"Batiste, are you planning on letting us come in?" his sister-in-law asked. *"Bonne Annee!"*

"A vous de meme. But... I... thought," Uncle Batiste stammered.

"That's your trouble, Batiste. You think too much." They walked in with food and presents. *Madame* Boutte, placed the food on the table chattering, excitedly. "I cooked some *gumbo z'herbes* Otherwise, we would not be assured to have food for the coming year. I made some *pain-patate.* Bree, Bree, *Bonne Annee!* "

"Will you stop yelling, Angelic," Uncle Batiste said. "The wedding's started already.?"

"Cannot I be at peace? Bree is my daughter. Where's the wedding taking place?

"Out on the veranda."

"It's so cold out there."

"It's what the bride and groom wants!" he quipped, looking at his sister-in-law with cold eyes.

"Oui, oui; je regrette."

When Bree looked up and saw them, she couldn't move. Following close behind her mother were her *marraine et parrain.* *"Bonne Année!"* They all shouted.

"A vous de meme. Oh, *Mère*, I'm so happy you came."

"I have always gone along with what your father wanted. But I'm the one whose breasts you've suckled. I draw the line when it comes down to me having to give up my children."

Her godparents said. "Don't forget you have us too, Bree. You belong to us, too. We love you to death, darling."

"Come on, Bree. We came to attend a wedding," her mother said. "Let us give you a big hug for good luck. Let your mother hold you to her breasts once again. These breasts are yours to lie on anytime you need to. Now, let's go get married." She gave Bree a wet-eyed

116

smile.

After the wedding, they laughed and talked and drank champagne. But Bree could feel the tension. The laughter was too loud. Still, she was thankful that her mother and her godparents were really trying. When they cut the wedding cake, Bree and Farras kissed a lingering kiss for Uncle Batiste to have time to take pictures. There was a *hush* in the room until Tousant yelled out, "Anyone for more champagne?"

"I want to drink to *Mère et Parrain et Marraine.*" Bree lifted her glass to their applause.

The doorbell rang. Uncle Batiste hurried to answer it. A few seconds later, Farras' brother, Jimmy, and his wife walked into the room. Farras' parents walked in behind them. His mother was small in stature, and she stood gazing up at Bree with cold eyes. In appearance, the father was an older version of Farras. He stood next to his wife and joined her in her gaze.

Bree walked over to them, smiling. "Welcome." She attempted to embrace Farras' mother, but she slapped her arms away.

"Get away from me!" she snapped. "Don't you dare touch me, you hussy! Don't you ever touch me. I came to see this weddin' to believe it. This is disgraceful!" She gave Bree a look of pure hatred as she and her husband turned towards the door.

"Now, wait a...." Tousant said furiously, coming to Bree's defense.

"It's okay, Tousant. It's all right," Bree reassured, stopping Tousant's words. "Really, it is," Tousant's eyes blazed with fury. *An unholy alliance.* Her father's words echoed in her mind. Bree's stomach felt queasy as she bowed her head slightly to Farras' parents. "I won't ever bother you, *Madame* Jourdan. I respect your feelings," Bree replied softly. Paupon ran and buried his face in his father's chest. Tousant took his son by the hand and left the room.

"Why did you have to come?" Farras yelled. His heart felt like it was, literally, breaking into pieces. Bree placed her fingers over his lips.

"Hush. Shhh. It's all right, Farras," Bree said soothingly. Farras stood glaring at his parents, his nostrils flaring.

"On our way over here, one lightenin' bolt shot down from

Heaven, son. Lit up the hol' sky! It's a sign from on high. That mean God's gon' really bump some rump! Think 'bout what you doin' please, son," his father pleaded. "Yo' looks ain't the best, and you ain't never been too smart. Now ask yo'self why would a woman of *Madame* Bree's caliber wanta take up 'wid you. There's somethin' more ta this foolery. You just ain't smart 'nough ta see it yet. No man, not even a dumb one like you Farras, would go 'long 'wid this foolery. But we don't fault you none, son. Any man on this earth would find it hard ta say 'no' ta that woman. No woman on God's good earth supposed ta be as good lookin' as she is, anyway. God don't make a woman that good lookin'—the devil do! She's smarter than anybody I know. Smarter than smart! I saw her on the television with that 'civil rights organization' she heads up. I'm tellin' you son that woman kin talk the 'silver' right out of a silver dollar. She's the devil, son. You sleepin' side by side 'wid the devil. Plain and simple. Every time peoples look at that woman, she keepa changin' her looks. Right there fo' yo' own eyes. How can any man keep up with a thousand womens? Ask yo'self another thang, Farras. How come the Bouttes is so different from all the other Negroes 'round here? Do you have any idea of how much land these peoples own? Even the White peoples 'round here don't own that much land. It's just evil the way the Bouttes keepa openin' up funeral homes all over the State of Louisiana. Everybody in this state knows 'bout these peoples. They family been ownin' a restaurant in the city every since the world begin. I heard if a person eats there just one time, they can hang it up! 'Cause they can't stop theyself from goin' back to the Bouttes' restaurant to eat again. Everybody knows that but you, son. Even Roy Madison and other famous peoples can't stop theyselves from goin' back to they restaurant. That's a shame too! 'Cause po' Roy Madison is blind as a bat." A look came to Farras' face, as if he were trying to hold back laughter, but the seriousness of his father's face held back his laughter. He hung his head. When he looked up again, his face held the seriousness that befitted his father's words. "If you don't believe me, Farras. Go ta they restaurant. They got a 'special' family room there. I'm tol', they's pictures of they family everywheres. Peoples say it's spooky as hell."

"Papa, I want you to stop this now." Farras voice shook with anger.

"Yes. Stop it right, now!" Tousant's angry words exploded as he re-entered the room. "Leave our home this instant!"

"Be quiet! I come here fo' a purpose, and I aims ta complete my purpose. I'm talkin' ta you too, *M'sieu* Jumppierre." Farras pulled out a chair from the dining table and sat down. He sat silently twisting his new wedding band around on his finger. "If you mention Africa, France, and Choctaw Indians, these peoples can go step on the 'exact' spot they ancestors *life cord* was cut," he continued. "Ain't no Negroes we know able ta do that! It's *voodoo* plain and simple. That *voodoo* got you where you can't hear or see nothin' no mo', son! These peoples got you messed up. You these peoples slave. They don't look upon you like you one of 'dem. Why you think they picked somebody out of they element? 'Caused they knowed you'd go long 'wid what they tol' you. These peoples gon' pick po' robin clean. I'm tellin' you, son. You can't fight the *Mojo* and that woman's good looks all by yo'self. She done put you in a *mojo world* where ain't nothin's real. You need ta be cured. Let us take you over the river ta *Algiers,* and have the *Voodoo* peoples who know 'bout these thangs, help you. Don't be a fool!" His father paused, looked at his son, and resumed talking. "You hear what I'm sayin', Farras?" Farras did not respond. "Me and *votre mère* done search this thang out. We done already found somebody that's got some strong *voodoo* powers. Stronger than the *voodoo* powers they usin' on you, Farras."

Farras' mother interjected, "They can 'free' you where these peoples can't touch you! But you got ta leave with us right now, son." Her eyes pleaded with her son, but Farras did not look up. He kept his eyes averted to the wedding ring on his finger. "That *voodoo* got you plumb crazy, son. Can't you see a man in his right mind wouldn't do this!" Farras did not answer his mother. His mother heaved a sigh and looked at Bree. "You ain't gon' have no good luck, and you sho' ain't gon' have no peace. We don't need a lot of money ta undo what you done done ta our son, *Madame* Bree. That's one good thang 'bout it. We gon' fix you, *Miss High and Mighty.* If you don't 'free' our son, you sho' ain't gon' see no peace on this earth.

You mark my words." Silence. Farras did not move.

"Like that song say, 'Give you a list of what's not ta be done, and you sho' gon' start doin' it today.' Right, Farras?" His father's voice was hard, and his facial expression matched his voice. His wife continued looking into Bree's eyes, as if she had caught sight of Bree's soul, and had discovered its wickedness. "Farras, I don't want you comin' 'round hurtin' yo' mama no mo', you hear me? This thang's killin' her."

"Papa, look..." Farras said. His father shook his head, and threw up his hands.

"One last time, Farras. Come on home with us, son."

Farras stood up from the table with a determined look in his eyes. He draped his arm around Bree's shoulder. *"M'sieu and Madame* Jourdan, I would not move one hand against anyone." As Bree spoke, her eyes pleaded for understanding.

They gave her a disbelieving look and walked out the room. Farras' brother, Jimmy, and his wife followed them. As they reached the front door, Farras' father stopped and said, "We don't know what we coulda done to make God punish us thisa way." He wept, and quickly covered his face; then lifted his head and gave Farras a sad look. Bree forced down hot, thick saliva that had accumulated inside her mouth. She ran to her piano and started playing an upbeat tune. "Come, everyone, dance," she said, with forced gaiety. They clapped hands and danced with false smiles on their faces, disrupting the quietness.

At eleven o'clock that night, Bree and Farras were alone in their bedroom. "Everything turned out better than I expected," Farras said undressing.

"You can still say that after what your parents said?"

"Yes, I can. They only performed like that because they love me. They think they protectin' me. Let's give them time, okay, Bree"

"Sure, let's give them as much time as they need. I almost fainted when I looked up and saw my mother and my godparents. They're trying hard to accept this, too. To accept something this alien is hard for them. Try to understand, it's hard for your parents too, Farras."

"Yes, I know. It's the only way I can explain my parents' behavior. You saw how they acted. I thought *Père* was on the brink of insanity, and *Mère* looked like she was 'bout to kill us."

"They'll come around."

"I don't know. Maybe."

Before they got into bed, Bree opened the drawer of the night stand to get her *music box*. She searched inside the drawer, but she could not find her little *music box*. Farras lay on the opposite side of the bed looking at her. Frantic, Bree got down on her knees and looked into the drawer. She panicked and jerked the drawer out of the night stand. She searched through the drawer again, but she still could not find her little *music box*. She started screaming and ran to search in Farras' drawers. After coming up empty-handed again, she searched the night stand on Farras side of the bed. "Have you seen it?" she shouted.

"Seen, what?"

"My *music box*," she panted, "have you seen it, Farras?"

"I put it away. You don't need yo' little *music box* no mo', Bree. You got me to satisfy you now."

"You don't understand," she shouted, "all my life I have had my little *music box*. Give it back!" Bree continued to shout. Tousant was sitting at the kitchen table. When he heard Bree's shouts, he bolted through Farras' bedroom door.

"What's going on in here?"

"It's my *music box*," Bree said, tears rolled down her face. "Farras hid my *music box*, Tousant." She ran into Tousant's arms. "Tousant, make him give it back to me!" Farras lay confused.

"What could be so important 'bout a child's *music box*?" Farras asked, trying to understand. He had hurt Bree without intending to.

"Give the *music box* back to her, Farras. Now!" Tousant ordered with fury.

"I'm sorry, man. God knows, I'm sorry. I didn't know. I don't understand," he said, getting up.

Farras walked over to the closet, and opened up his saxophone case. He took out the little *music box,* walked over to Bree, and deposited it in her hand.

"Don't ever take her *music box* away again, Farras. She had it when we met. I have never questioned her about it. There's some areas of a person's mind one should never tread. Her father told me once that Bree physically attacked her first grade teacher for taking that little *music box* away. The results of her teacher's actions only made her cling to the *music box* more. Do you want the same thing to happen to you, Farras? If I hadn't come in here when I did, she may have attacked you. Bree's not a violent person by nature. But her little *music box...* Surely, you cannot be jealous of a child's *music box!*" Farras stood looking confused.

"*Chèri,* forgive me. I wouldn't hurt you fo' nothin' in this world. You know that, don't you?"

Bree turned her face from Tousant's chest and looked at Farras. Farras went into the bathroom and came back with a wet towel. "I'll take care of her now, Tousant. She gon' be fine."

Tousant looked at Bree. "I'm fine now, Tousant," she nodded. Farras held her, and wiped her face with a cold towel.

Tousant turned to leave the room. "I won't ever hide Bree's *music box* again, Tousant. I still don't think she needs it," Farras retorted.

"Don't any of us know all of a person's needs, Farras. In time, the *music box* will not bother you." Tousant defended Bree as he walked out of the room.

∞

Bree and Farras had been married for two days when a tornado touched down in St. Jamesville. The tornado had moved swiftly sucking up all sounds inside it. If a person screamed, the tornado stole the sound. All the person standing next to each other saw was a stretched mouth, and eyes that bulged in fear. The tornado skipped and jumped houses as if playing a childish game of hopscotch. Some houses were completely destroyed, some had major damages, and some houses were completely spared; untouched by the debris of their neighbor's airborne houses. There were no deaths, but broken bones, scrapes, and bruises covered the bodies of many. One man had a broken leg. A small child had a broken foot. One woman had a large bruise on the side of her neck and a sprained back. She walked around with a severe stoop.

The townspeople milled around in a crowd. Those whose houses were destroyed, wept. Some people stood around in awe, while some walked around like zombies, their eyes glazed over in disbelief. Bree and Tousant offered to help them, but they gave Bree a look filled with venom, and turned their backs to her. One man, with a bandaged wrist, left the crowd and walked up to Bree with tears in his eyes. "You the blame for all of this, Bree!" He pointed an angry, accusatory finger at her. "God ain't gon' leave us alone. This just the beginnin' of our troubles. God is mad as hell at us because of you and yo' doings. But I see the devil protected your family's ill-gotten gains." He walked angrily away; found his place in the crowd, and resumed his crying.

Bree reached a trembling hand out to the crowd crying, *"Ce n'est pas ma faute.* I'm not to blame!" She fell to her knees, raised both hands up to the sky, and screamed. Tousant lifted and carried her screaming back to their car. Bree sat in the car next to Tousant, screaming, *"Non! Non! Non!* Why don't they hate you too, Tousant? *Ce n'est pas ma faute!* As Tousant drove home, the car was filled with Bree's painful screams.

After the tornado hit St. Jamesville, each morning Bree saw her nearest neighbor sprinkle "lime" from a large bucket around his house. Nothing in St. Jamesville went unnoticed. The following morning, all of St. Jamesville was sprinkling "lime" around their houses. The townspeople cleaned up the debris, rebuilt, and had their houses blessed. They said nothing. But they kept a vigilant eye on Bree.

CHAPTER
NINE

News of Bree's marriage had spread throughout St. Jamesville. Day after day, the local newspaper wrote flaming articles that branded Bree and her chosen lifestyle. Bold headlines read: *"SCARLET WOMAN RESIDES IN ST. JAMESVILLE."* Sub-headlines read: *"Is This a Prelude to the Family of the Future?"* The first article stunned Bree. A reporter got a picture of the four of them as they left church. There was also a picture of Paupon standing holding his bicycle. A female reporter constantly followed Bree everywhere she went wanting her side of the story. But Bree ignored her. Some reporters made an unsuccessful attempt at interviewing Tousant and Farras. Tousant ignored them. But Farras was more aggressive, he chased them off the property. Bree had learned one thing about reporters, they had a lot of nerve. She had placed a telephone call to the editor inquiring why he felt her life newsworthy.

"Mrs. Jumppierre, you come from a prominent family in St. Jamesville. And you ask why we wrote this story?" the editor had said, irritably. "That's news. Your *unconventional lifestyle* alone would be news. You're not talking censorship, are you, Mrs. Jumppierre? I have noticed that you don't mind your name being in the news when it has anything to do with that 'organization' of yours." Bree had been too angry to reply. She hung up the telephone shaking with rage.

The articles continued. St. Jamesville was full to the brim with people who had expected *saintly* things from Bree. Soon after the first newspaper articles appeared, she started receiving anonymous letters.

Most of the hate-mail came from wives accusing her of generating distrust between husbands and wives. Some wrote that she was a shining example of a good person gone bad; others pleaded with her to give up Farras; others wrote that they secretly admired her, but cited weak excuses why they could not risk supporting her publicly.

After the initial articles, the letters tapered off, though a steady flow continued. Tousant had all mail held at the post office for his pickup. The articles and letters deeply disturbed Bree, but she forced herself to keep up her daily routine. It was during this time that she got a brief note from Nina offering her support. She folded Nina's note, and placed it in a box with other mementos.

Day after day, the humid heat hung heavily over St. Jamesville. There was no rain, no breezes, and no stirrings. Yards and galleries were empty. Fans hummed tiredly. During the day, Bree stayed indoors; kept her venetian blinds closed, and tried to keep the sweltering heat at bay. Her family sipped cold lemonade and iced tea and waited for the blazing Louisiana sun to go down. She had stopped looking at the outside thermometer.

A little past noon, Paupon walked into the kitchen, opened the refrigerator, and poured himself a tall glass of cold lemonade. Bree was in the kitchen preparing the noontime meal. She looked up at Paupon and gave him a tired smile, "Dinner will be ready soon."

"Guess what Freddie just told me?" Suddenly curious, she looked at Paupon. "Freddie said his father walked out on them a few weeks ago, and his *mère* is ill in bed. I mean, really sick,"
Paupon said, with wide eyes.

"Has she gone to the doctor's yet?"

"I don't think so. I don't think the father left them with any money. Freddie said they have run out of food, too."

"*Quel dommage!* Is anyone helping them? What about their relatives?" Bree asked.

"Freddie said his mother won't ask anyone for help. Boy, he sure was hungry. I gave him the whole five dollars I had in my piggy bank."

"I'm glad you did that, Paupon."

"Freddie said he'll pay me back. He says he's looking for a job, any kind of job."

Even though Paupon and Freddie were best friends, Bree had never visited Freddie's mother, Delphine. She started gathering up food. She hoped Delphine's pride wouldn't stop her from accepting the food.

The heat had lost its importance. Bree shifted the red croka sack of food over her shoulder. "*Mère*, it's so hot the birds won't fly," Paupon said wearily, as they walked. Preoccupied with their errand, they cut across *Madame* Blanque's yard forgetting the mean, female, mongrel she owned. But the mean dog gave no barks of warning when they trespassed into her domain. The dog had dug herself a deep hole underneath a large chinaberry tree. Restless, she kept getting up turning herself in the stifling, noonday heat. She gave them a listless, eyelids-drooping look as they walked past her.

"Swallow your embarrassment, son. Walk underneath my parasol with me." When Bree said that, Paupon widened the space between them. Bree smiled.

"Why didn't we drive the car to Freddie's house?"

"Paupon, please. You don't drive a car like ours to someone's house that's hungry."

"I just didn't think. I guess, that's why I need you." He smiled at his mother with affection, and quickened his pace. As they walked past a weeping willow tree, Bree noticed dragonflies resting lazily on the leaves. The humid heat had caused them to tirelessly move their frail wings up and down, as if fanning their hot bodies.

"It's your turn to carry the sack now, Paupon." She handed Paupon the croka sack. He threw the sack over his small shoulder and walked ahead of his mother. He walked tall and straight with pride, as if he were trying to impress his mother with his manliness.

When they arrived at Delphine's house, Freddie opened the door. He looked surprised at seeing Paupon with his mother standing on their rain-rotted back steps. He asked them in and pointed past the kitchen door to his mother's bedroom. Bree and Paupon stepped into the kitchen. A young girl and boy were sitting at the kitchen table, silently staring down into two empty bowls.

When Bree entered Delphine's bedroom, she was staring into space with a lost look in her eyes. Her parched, cracked lips were silently moving. She held the familiar *traiteur's* string, with seven knots, in her hand. She slipped the knots through her fingers as she prayed. Delphine had apparently sent for the *traiteur*, the healer of St. Jamesville. *"Allo*, Delphine," Bree said.

Startled, Delphine lifted her eyes in surprise. *"Allo*, Bree," Delphine spoke in a frail voice. "It's sho' nice of you to come see me."

"Comment allez-vous?"

"Mal. I'm really weak, too, Bree."

"I brought food. I found out just minutes ago that you were ill."

"Merci beaucoup. We sho' can use the food. I ran everybody else away," she said. "'Cause they'll talk 'bout me behind my back like a dog. Meddlers. That's all they is, anyway." Bree nodded a silent agreement. "I thought I didn't need nobody. I've been sufferin' for over two weeks now, and I don't have money for food or a doctor. Lordy, mercy! That man left me high and dry, Bree. That Negro sho' can be evil when he wanta be. It's so hot. Lord, it's just so hot in here," Delphine moaned, as tears escaped from underneath her closed eyelids.

"It sure is awfully hot in here, Delphine. I'll bring two fans back. But you shouldn't have run people away."

"Ain't no secrets in this town. I was just shame for peoples to see the shape that man left me in."

"You're right, Delphine. In St. Jamesville there are no secrets. This is a town without strangers. But right now, we have more important things to do. First, let's get some nourishment into your body. Then I'll get you and your bedroom cleaned up." Relief flooded Delphine's face as she followed Bree's instructions.

Three hours later, Bree sank tiredly down on the edge of Delphine's bed. She gathered Delphine's hands in hers and smiled. "Is there anything more I can do for you, Delphine?" Bree looked around the unfamiliar room.

"No, you done so much already. I wanta thank you again, Bree," Delphine said. Her eyes misted over.

"Please, don't thank me, Delphine. I'm so glad that I can help you. You want me to call your relatives and tell them that you're ill?" Bree asked.

"I don't have no relatives here in St. Jamesville. All of my peoples live deep in the swamps in *Bayou Manchac*. They're worse off than me." Delphine did not have to tell Bree that she wasn't from St. Jamesville. Just by the dialect, every Louisianian can tell what part of the state the other came from.

"Won't you let me call the welfare office?" Bree asked.

"No, Bree. No welfare! I worked all my life. I don't want no charity," Delphine said.

"That's the reason you should call the welfare office, Delphine, because you have worked all your life. Then let me help you until you are well and back on your feet again? No strings. I give simply because I have it to give."

"I believe you, Bree, but I'm still gon' pay you back every penny." Delphine replied, in a prideful tone.

"The *Traiter's* medicine is not working. You need medical attention now, Delphine. Rest easy. I'll be back to take you to the doctor's."

"Lordy, mercy. I ain't never asked anybody for nothin'." Delphine covered her face with her hands and wept. Her body heaved with weak sobs.

Bree sat down on the edge of her bed again and stroked her face. "I cannot win unless you win, Delphine. It's an ancient, African law. Now, you don't want to be responsible for breaking that precious law, do you?" Delphine looked confused. But when she saw Bree smiling, she gave her a weak smile.

As Bree rose up from the side of the bed, she placed money delicately into Delphine's weak hand and looked the other way, as if it were an absent-minded gesture. "I'll take your soiled laundry home with me. Send Freddie over late this evening to pick up the laundry," Bree said. "I'll be back to dress you and take you to the doctor's."

"Bree, Freddie tol' me how these old, low-down peoples been talkin' 'bout you. How in the hell can you cause a tornado! I wish somebody would explain that to me," Delphine said, with weak, bitter fury. She had raised her weak body up supporting herself with her elbows. They're puttin' you through holy hell."

Delphine looked at the pain in Bree's eyes that she tried valorously to cover up, a pain that silences a woman's soul if left unchecked. Except for herself, Delphine had never seen pain like that in another woman's eyes. "It'll die down," Bree said quickly. Although Delphine had always been pleasant in passing, Bree did not want to discuss her life with her.

Bree's falsifyin' her real feelings, Delphine thought. She had a long history of doing that too. "Freddie," Delphine weakly called out, "show *Madame* Jumppierre where the dirty clothes is. I'm sorry you have to pass back through that dirty kitchen to get to the bathroom, but the bathroom is where I keeps my dirty clothes." Delphine gave Bree an apologetic, embarrassed look.

"Don't worry about your dirty kitchen, Delphine. I'll leave Paupon here to help Freddie clean up."

After collecting the dirty clothes, Bree ordered Freddie and Paupon to clean up the kitchen, then ordered the two silent children to follow her home. They rose from the table and obediently followed her.

Bree stepped back into Delphine's bedroom. "I'll be back to take you to the doctor's, Delphine. And it's not open for discussion— we're going."

"Yes mam, *Madame* Bree," Delphine gave her a weak smile. "Thank you so much," Delphine said again. Her eyes followed Bree as she pulled the sheet full of soiled clothes behind her.

"*De rien.*"

"Bree, most...peoples...of yo'...statue," Delphine stammered weakly, "wouldn't come... to the... back door."

"I think that my present 'lifestyle' would probably disqualify me from the 'most people' club right now, Delphine," Bree said firmly, stopping any further discussion. "Anyway, that's not...the reason... I...." She gave Delphine a womanly smile as she exited her bedroom door.

Bree stepped outside Delphine's back door with a troubled expression on her face. As she walked, she thought about St. Jamesville and its people. St. Jamesville could not be described by a word like "beauty." It was a clean town. There was not one speck of dirt where dirt did not belong. If during the day, there was litter on the streets, the next morning it would not be there. It were as if the town had an "invisible night maid," and while the townspeople slept, the "invisible night maid" rushed out and cleaned the town.

The houses in St. Jamesville always had a fresh, washed-down look. Clean clothes always hung on clotheslines embracing the sunshine. Every night, through open windows, children could be heard howling from being scrubbed with stiff-bristled brushes while *Octagon* soap burned their eyes and went up their noses.

Bree thought about how mindlessly Delphine's children followed her. A bitter taste came up in her mouth. Church members, school staff, and every adult in St. Jamesville spied on the children. They wanted their children to become clean and hard working like themselves. Negro children were getting bombed in churches, and they were still raising their children to be seen and not heard. She thought of the danger in that and wanted to scream. She forced the scream back down her throat, and held the corner of her lower lip between her teeth. She remembered the townspeople's reactions when she hired a college student to help her with the housekeeping. Each time the student interacted with the children, their parents accused the student of trying to destroy their way, and swelling their children's heads with things that would separate them from their families. They called the student, *p'tit diable*. Loud complaints were voiced to her father about her part in the conspiracy. Her father had strongly suggested that she let the student go. In their quest to keep their children clean and hard working, the parents forced them to work in the blazing sun alongside them in the cane fields. The children always appeared to be in silent prayer; calling on their God for some assistance, but their God must have agreed with their parents because

130

no assistance came.

The children were never allowed to have an idle moment. If idleness was suspected, parents became agitated and would say, "Do this while you resting," and give the children some silly task to do.

The townspeople wanted to work all day on Saturdays, but their children made a pest of themselves. They pleaded with sweaty, busy parents to take them uptown. The parents tried to ignore them, but the children stood around looking hurt and angry.

Uptown on Saturday evenings, St. Jamesville was overrun with children standing silently; their clean skins glistening in the sunlight licking dripping ice cream cones, while their parents stood around talking, mundanely, about nothing. Every so often, they looked around to reassure themselves that nothing had changed, that nothing had moved since the week before. Satisfied, they smiled contentedly and continued to talk about whatever it was they were talking. But they were not comfortable. The red, setting sun reminded them of their *lost* hours of work. Periodically, they gave a quick look in the direction of their children, and wondered why their children needed such pampering.

Jobs were limited in St. Jamesville. Most of the townspeople held jobs in New Orleans, but working to earn a living was not sufficient work for them. They still planted sugar cane and other vegetables. When they came home from their jobs, some without stopping at their houses, went directly into their fields. They worked in their fields until it was too dark to see. When their own work was finished, they went to neighbors and tried to take over jobs in their fields. Some of them even pressed their luck and worked on Sundays. Eventually, Father Andreau got news of it, and put terror into their souls. That stopped them temporarily, but as time passed, they found themselves back in their fields again on Sundays. When they were caught again, Father Andreau merely repeated himself. For some unknown reason, Father Andreau did not understand that work *was* the people's salvation.

The only pleasure the Negroes of St. Jamesville really wanted was their yearly trip to the "Crab and Crawfish Festival" in *La Combe*. Every year, they sat at long tables underneath oak trees with large platters of crawfish and crabs before them. Tubs of cold beer sat at both ends of the tables. *Zydeco* music, or the *Blues*, spilled hotly out of large speakers hung up on branches of trees. The crabs and crawfish were so hot with red peppers; their eyes teared, and their noses ran. Yet they smiled, smacked their lips, and sprinkled more *Louisiana Hot Sauce* on their food. It was as if all year long they kept their spirits and bodies cold, and for that one day a year in *La Combe*, they wanted their spirits and bodies to burn, to spit fire!

Caught up in her own angry thoughts, Bree walked at a fast pace. She had not seen Malik X sitting in the swing on her front gallery. When she reached the edge of the gallery, Malik X stepped down from the gallery and embraced her. Their arms were still around each other's waist when they stepped back up on the gallery and sat down in the porch swing. Delphine's two silent children struggled to pick up the sheet of soiled clothes. *"Non, bèbès.* You two go inside where it's cool. Look in the refrigerator and pour yourselves a cold glass of milk. Turn the television on. I'll be inside, shortly." Bree looked at Malik X. "You look like you could use a glass of cold milk, too."

"Yes, indeed, Sister Bree."

"I'd invite you in, but the neighbors..."

"No need to explain. The newspapers said it all. As a matter-of-fact, that's why I'm here, but I would appreciate some refreshments first."

Bree went inside the house. She was glad that Malik X had come. She was fond of him personally, but her admiration for his commitment to their people's struggle for "equal rights" went far beyond admiration, and bordered on hero worship. Though Malik X was not a Muslim, without an explanation to anyone, he had discarded his birth name.

Bree brought out a tall pitcher of cold milk and two glasses. Malik X stretched his legs out and gave her a long look. "So, what's this we're reading about you in the newspapers? The papers said something about you destroying the whole *damn* family structure of the *Western* world! Hell, I didn't know you were that powerful, Bree. What in the hell happened to all that 'Black power' when we were getting shot at up in Mississippi?" He tried to stifle the laughter in his throat, but he failed, and fell into a fit of hard laughter. Bree looked at him and laughed too. When their laughter subsided, Malik X put a serious look on his face. "Last week, *Headquarters* received your letter of resignation. Look, Bree. I don't want you to hand me the reins to the Organization. You know me. I don't always keep a cool head when I'm supposed to. That's why you're our president, remember? Why don't you just take a little time off until your life settles down. We'll keep the 'home fires' burning."

"Malik, I don't think the chapter here in St. Jamesville will go along with your proposal."

"The Organization is state-wide. Each chapter, based on membership, only have so many votes. You know that, Bree. *Headquarters* sent out letters to all chapters informing them of your letter of resignation. All each chapter had to do was come in to the city and cast their votes. The St. Jamesville chapter didn't respond. The motion was carried. You are still our president. We aren't accepting your letter of resignation, and we aren't going to take no static behind it, either. We're all in this 'equal rights fight' together."

"Malik, I won't stand for a division in the Organization. I'll walk away before I allow that to happen. Malik, for true, is that the way most of the members voted?"

"For true, Bree. You got the brain power, and your *war* wounds are not taken lightly."

"We're a strong organization, Malik. We have made great strides. Our work must continue." She gave Malik X an apprehensive look and let out a deep sigh. "All right. I'll stay. I'll write a letter of thanks to *Headquarters* for having so much faith in my abilities."

"Now, that's the sister I know." Malik X squeezed her hand.

"I'll stay as long as I'm making a contribution, but if I see that I'm hurting the Organization in any way, I'll leave, okay?"

"That's fair. Bree, listen. Now, if I'm putting myself in a place that I ought not to be, stop me."

"Don't fret, I will."

"You changed after Tousant's accident. I don't have to be a genius to know that something ... well... must have gone wrong on the 'intimate' front. Bree, we went to college together. Everybody knows that you have never been fast up behind a man. I mean...how do I put this in a *delicate* manner? It's all right with us. We want you to know that. We know how you and Tousant feel about family. You know what I mean?" She nodded her head and looked away. "The media is always getting people stirred up, Bree. They are always 'sensationalizing' everything." He stood up, and straightened out his *Dashiki.* "Well, I said what I came here to say. Do you need anything, sister? Anything at all." She shook her head, no. "Okay. All you got to do is ask. You know that, Bree. It would be easier on me if I could have come and stayed with you for a week. We really need to discuss some strategies. The telephone is not safe anymore. Will you at least commit yourself to one day a week? No field work. Merely, to discuss strategy," he added.

"I think I can manage that. If anything comes up that's urgent, call me and ask me to call you back."

"I'll go to a pay 'phone and call you back. I know damn well our office 'phone is *tapped*, Bree. I'm sorry to put you through this, but it's the safest way. These are crazy times. It's a shame we have to live like this! I'm sick and tired of the battle to survive! Violence doesn't make these times terrible; it's the constant battle to survive. We have a right to claim a life of our own like everybody else! The only thing that makes this Black man truly happy is knowing that White men fear me." He looked deep into Bree's eyes before asking, "Tell me, how's Tousant? He still thinks the agenda for the Organization is all wrong? Hell is breaking out all over, and Tousant thinks education is the panacea to everything."

"I thought we made a rule that we weren't going to talk about Tousant's ideology, Malik." Bree spoke softly. She had become slightly nauseated by Malik X's words on survival.

"You're right. My mistake," He held up his hands in surrender. "It won't happen again. How's, Paupon?"

"He's fine. He'll make an excellent leader for our people one day."

"Lord, yes. We know he's being groomed. As you know, a lot of funny-style stuff's going down. How can a place as pretty as Louisiana have so much *foul shit* going on?" Pain crossed Malik X's face as he spoke, and his eyes held his suffering. He had learned to despise his own country. "It's hell out here, Bree. Try to make it back soon." He looked at his watch. "Sister, I've got to run. These days, Black people only have time to think about doing things detrimental for our survival." Malik X took one step towards the steps, paused, and turned around facing her. As he stood silently gathering his thoughts to speak, Bree watched a white Egret fly low against the horizon. She gazed at the bird until Malik X's words broke her gaze. "The world don't see us trying to find 'new' ways to survive. They don't see that the whole 'pattern' to our lives is nonsensical. Even without a history of enslavement and oppression, it has taken the White man over two hundred years to get where he is today, but they won't even give a Black man two weeks to get his program together. I've studied the histories of oppressed peoples throughout the world, and considering our history of enslavement and oppression, we have progressed with remarkable speed."

He reached in his back pocket and took out his wallet. He fished through his wallet until he found what he was looking for. "I'm never caught without a copy of the *Fourteenth* and *Fifteenth Amendments* to the *United States Constitution*. You wanta know why?" Before Bree could ask him why, he said, "To remind me that we have to keep on rebelling and rebelling and rebelling, for as many generations as it takes!" As Malik X preached, a thousand memories flashed through Bree's mind. "You wanta know why?" Malik X plowed on. "Freedom will be ours because we will survive and out-last oppression. We will struggle until the end of this world comes. No matter how many *Christian* laws they concoct to destroy us, no matter how many vicious lies they spread about us, no matter how many destructive vices are placed in our communities, we have our *own* God; and we *will* prevail!" He gave Bree a long, agonizing look. "Lord have mercy, Bree. Who will protect and write about our sufferings in this place? Not just our own people's suffering, but Native Americans, Latinos, and Asians too."

Malik X hated the White man's power and his laws and the present times. He could understand, in the end, how some Black men finally came to give themselves "unconscionable" permission to do any and every bad thing they wanted; because any and every bad thing had been and was being done to them. He, himself, had had to struggle a ceaseless battle over so-called "criminality." He had escaped solely because of his father's strict, heavy-handed, Christian discipline. His parents had not taught him to hate, but he ended up hating them both because they had not—especially his father. But in his childhood, he had taught himself to hate. Always fearing for his life; he had learned to hate the people who caused his fear. His consuming hatred had led him to a pathway of war.

His father was not consumed by hate. He had never expressed any hatred for the *Ku Klux Klan* for their merciless slaughter of innocent Blacks. He had never expressed hatred for White politicians who made "bogus" laws to stop him from breathing. He had never expressed hatred for any American president. He loved America. And he simply adored Louisiana with its deep, variegated greens of beauty, with its foods, with its fishing and crabbing and shrimping, with its magic and music–and he guessed–with its "Jim Crow."

He had asked his father about the lynchings and the tortures of innocent Black people in the past. His father had told him to "Shut up his mouth 'bout yesterday." And his father walked around in tight-lipped silence for days. To his knowledge, his father had never challenged a *wrong*. He always said, "Let God be the judge and take care of it." But he was nothing like his father. He had never bought into *his* philosophy. And he had never paid any mind to his father's fears of him being lynched, either. Some things were worse than death. And, unlike his father, he knew that his black skin would not stop his "greatness." Because he needed no one, not even his own father or his God, to validate his humanity.

As a teenager, he kept running up against barriers. He'd clear one barrier, only to reach another. He kept clearing and clearing barriers, but there were always more to clear. It had kept him confused for a long time. He had done well in school only because he wanted to be trained how to think in a methodical and logical way. Now, as far as he was concerned, he had no limitations!

Malik X stepped off the gallery, picked up the sheet of soiled laundry, and laid it on the edge of the gallery. He stepped back up on the gallery. "May *our* God bless you real good, Sister Bree. *Adieu*"

He gave Bree a quick, tearful embrace and left.

Malik X had preached. He had "purged" a small piece of his sick soul, and took his leave. But a profound and ancient *presence* still hung in the air, a found and ancient *presence* that was left by all "warriors" fighting clouds; a profound and ancient *presence* that would prevail long after: Roy Campanella coming to St. Jamesville with the Brooklyn Dodgers, adding a "steel rod" in Negroes' spines, long after: meetings, beatings, murderings, strategies, fear, hate, and threats. She let out a heart-wrenching sob, for Malik X epitomized her people's suffering. She could feel the eyes of the two children upon her. They stood silently in the doorway, seemingly absorbing her pain, looking undecidedly as to whether they should cry too. When she looked again at their faces, there was some unexplained "something" resting on their small faces. She turned her head away from them and quickly wiped away the wetness. She sat quietly swinging, humming an old spiritual.

It had rained the night before, and the morning air was crisp and fresh. The bright morning sun created a tranquil canopy over St. Jamesville. *M'sieu* Boutte stood at Bree's front door ringing her doorbell. *Madame* Muscadine III stood loyally beside him. When Bree opened the door, her eyes widened in surprise. "Coffee," her father said, as he walked briskly past her towards her kitchen. He did not speak. Bree put a stern look on her face and followed him. He sat down at the kitchen table; folded his hands on the table before him and looked at her. Trained well by her owner, *Madame* Muscadine III went quietly underneath the table and lay at his feet.

Bree stood at the kitchen stove positioning the kettle over the fire. "Who has any patience these days?" It was a question more for himself than for her. She glanced over her shoulders at her father. He looked at her as if wondering what he should say next. The kettle started to whistle on the stove. She busied herself with preparing coffee for her father and tea for herself. A few minutes later, Bree placed a steaming cup of coffee on the table before her father and sat down across from him. "You have caused many houses in St. Jamesville to have lights burning way into the night, Bree." His voice dropped and sounded grave. A sadness came over his face. "I know you love this town, but you have added a 'negative.' A 'negative' we really don't want or need. I am genuinely respected in this town, Bree. Some very prominent people in this town have been grooming me for politics! The plan is for me to become St. Jamesville's first Black mayor. Times are changing, and we all must be ready. Everything must be put into place now, or what's being fought for will be meaningless. What am I saying? You already know this."

Bree nodded, and gave her father her full attention. As her father spoke, she was surprised at how mild-mannered he had become, almost humble. Politics. Her mind could not connect her father to anything but education and business. She looked at him, and a whole new transformation took place in her mind. He was another man. "We have decided that I should make another plea to you to give up this thing."

"Wait a minute, *Père*. We. We who?" Bree spoke harshly,

"That's not important."

"It is to me!"

"I cannot see why knowing who's backing me politically should make a difference to you. Let it suffice to say that I have met with some very important people." She opened her mouth to speak, but her father held up both hands and stopped her. "Let me finish, Bree. Then I'll listen to you. Bree, how can I be the mayor of a small town like St. Jamesville with my daughter living openly with *two* men? If I get elected mayor, it will be uplifting to our people. Bree, listen to me, sugar. Yesterday, I closed a deal on a little house in Mandeville. Here, take this key." The forced smile died on his face. He held the key out to her. But Bree did not reach for it. She sat calmly sipping her tea, giving her father an inquiring look. He laid the key down on the table. He gazed at her and took a large swallow of coffee. He spoke with his mouth to his cup. "The house is convenient. Go there to meet this, Farras Jourdan, whenever you need to. Say, once a week. Then, wash your hands of him until the next time. Take your rightful place in St. Jamesville, Bree." He spoke with urgency. "This is the best way, Bree. It'll work out better all around. No fuss! No mess! Anyhow, the way I see it, you don't have that many choices. It's our *whole* race of people or this, Farras Jourdan. How much are you willing to sacrifice for him? You're not being fair to the Organization, either. An organization you started, I might add. This Farras Jourdan, just don't fit into our program. I don't care how much you try to stuff knowledge into his head, he'll never make a good 'warrior' for our people. We all should be doing our part. We have got to help ourselves in this world. The whole family fears for your life, Bree. When you go back out there in the field, what's this, Farras Jourdan, going to do? Get in the bed and pull the covers up over his head. That *boy* don't know nothing about protecting, supporting, and trying to keep a family safe."

An involuntary shudder went through Bree. She let out a lung full of air and got up from the table. She walked over to the counter, and poured herself another cup of tea. She held the cup and saucer in her hand and leaned against the kitchen counter facing her father. She gave him a long stare. "Don't do this to me, please, *Père.*" Her voice sounded tired. Weary.

"Well, I am doing this to you! I came here for some straight, sensible answers." His voice shook with emotion. "Find some other way to fix this! You are a highly intelligent, creative young woman, Bree. I'm sure that if you looked carefully, you could find a more appropriate way of dealing with this ...*situation.* Your Uncle Batiste told us about you and Tousant's ...*situation.* It's unfortunate. But it's not the end of the world! It hardly justifies what you're doing. *Celibacy* cannot be that bad. Nuns and priests are *celibate* all of their lives. But since you cannot seem to cope, I'm offering you a viable alternative. Take it!"

"*Non*! I have fixed it. Why don't you ask me to just make another world, *Père.* It would be easier." *M'sieu* Boutte heard the pain in his daughter's voice, and he reached his hand out to her. Bree moved

139

away from him.

"Calm down, Bree. You're a good girl. Oh, for Christ sake, don't cry!" He hated to see her cry. It had always seemed to him that Bree's tears were more than her own tears. Her tears, somehow, signified something deeper. Though he never showed it, her tears always undid him.

"I'm not going to cry, *Père*. I just find your proposal, shocking. It's really shocking my senses." A determined look came to her face. She would cry later. But when her eyes dried, Farras would still be her husband. Nothing could change her feelings. She felt what she felt. "You don't need my life to be 'picture perfect' for you to win an election. For generations our family has stood on its own merits. You're already uplifting to our people," Bree said. Her father took a deep breath and looked at nothing. She cleared her throat and poured him another cup of coffee. *Madame* Muscadine III raised her head, listened, and lay her head back down at her father's feet.

He looked up at Bree. "Angry?" he asked calmly.

"No. Actually, I would have been disappointed if you hadn't tried something else." The beginning of a smile appeared on Bree's lips. As the seconds passed, her smile broadened into a wide grin. Finally, they were both laughing, but it was not happy laughter. Their laughter implied something deeper, something left unspoken. Her father shook his head and motioned for her to sit down. *Madame* Muscadine III gave Bree an indignant look, and plopped herself angrily back down again. She growled to herself. Bree ignored her.

M'sieu Boutte's posture changed, and he smiled a pleasant smile. He took out a handkerchief from inside his jacket pocket, and blew his nose. "Do you remember the time your mother had to call me at my office to come home? It was storming, and you were afraid. You have always been terrified of storms. Your mother tried to hug you to quiet your fears, but you started putting up a fuss. When I arrived home, you were still screaming. I said, 'What's this? What's this?' You ran into my arms, screaming. 'Make her stop. She hugs me too tight, and it makes my skin burn.' Her father chuckled. "You looked me straight in the eyes and said, 'She's afraid, too. That's why she hugs me so tight. She's trying to cover up her own fears of the storm.' When you said that, your mother almost fainted. I found your statement profoundly perceptive for a child so young. You couldn't have been more than six or seven years old. So many memories. I will never forget the time you saw this little, blue, velvet coat–or was it turquoise? I forget which. You tore the page out of a magazine, got on your bicycle without permission, and brought the page to my office. '*Père,* please, you must buy this coat for me. The coat has to be exactly like the picture.' That Saturday, your mother and I went to New Orleans, and we searched and searched for that little, blue velvet coat. Your mother was so exhausted that she wanted to buy some other coat, but I said no. This coat is for my little, precious pearl. So we went to a tailor's shop, and had him make that coat for you. Finally, the day came, and your little, blue, velvet coat was finished. When we brought the coat home, and put the coat on you, you twirled and twirled around the room. The family gathered around you and applauded. Oh, how your little face beamed. You smiled and curtsied like a lady. You remember that?" Bree smiled, warmly, and nodded her head. Her father reached across the table and gave her hand a gentle squeeze. "What can I say to you my little, precious pearl? How can I convince you to give this man up?"

Bree's face clouded over with the thought of her father's emotional betrayal. He had preyed upon her emotions for his own benefit. She slowly rose from the table and said, "Please leave, *Père.*" There was venom in her voice. "I pity you. You are a man with no imagination and no vision. Actually, you're a well-oiled machine."

He shrugged his shoulders, stood up from the table, and faced her. "The truth is, Bree. You have always done things in the extreme. You were always shaming and humiliating this family. That summer I sent you to New York to visit Professor Wilson and his family, look what a mess..."

"Stop it!" his words stunned her. "Why are you bringing this up after all these years?"

"To stop you from ruining your life and our family's good name. I want to remind you of the dreadful mistake you almost made in New York city. If it hadn't been for me, and that boy's family's intervention, you two young fools would have ruined your lives!"

"Stop it! You're being cruel, and it's uncalled for. The past cannot change what's happening now."

"I will not stop it! Because this thing you're doing now falls under the same category. After your freshman year in college, I sent you to New York City to expose you to some culture. You were told this. You were not supposed to go up there and meet some boy out of your own race! Thank God, the boy was Jewish. His family's values are rooted in kinship, tradition, and religion like our own. His family agreed with me. And they were more than willing to do their part toward the dissolution of the relationship. You two had to be stopped from running off to California, remember? You had a brilliant future with your own people, and that boy had a brilliant future with his own people. His parents were weakening, swaying to you two's madness. But they were more than grateful to me for pointing things out to them."

"I'm glad you said he *had*. Because he doesn't *have* anything now, does he, *Père?* He's dead! Don't pick at the bones of the dead."

"That was an accident!"

"It was not!"

"The boy was in medical school, and he was tired. His parents told me about his long hours. It was an accident! He didn't deliberately take those pills! He was a good boy."

"Conveniently done, the day after my wedding. Then why is it that his parents still keep in touch with me after all these years? They cannot leave me alone. If it were an accident, why want his parents let go?"

"I cannot answer that. I'm sure they have their reasons."

"Could it be, guilt!" Bree raised a brow and looked at her father.

"Could it be simply that they are just fond of you?"

"Get real, *Père.* I'm not the same Bree that I was even four months ago."

"His parents said it was an accident! And that's good enough for me. Besides, you were my lookout and he was theirs. Now, you're married to a good, *Creole* man—which is the way it should be! I had to save you. I was not going to tolerate such madness. I was right then, and I'm right now!"

"Right... now! For your information, I didn't love Reuven. And I had no intentions of marrying someone out of my own race! You insult me, *Père*. Why would I do such an unthinkable thing? If Reuven told his parents, or you, that we loved each other and had plans to run away to California to get married, then he was very much mistaken too. I merely considered us to be two people with a common interest—medicine." In shock, her father's mouth dropped.

You mean, you... didn't love... Reuven!" His voice was hoarse with disbelief.

"No. And all these years, you thought that..." Bree looked at her father's shocked expression and fell into a fit of laughter.

Wiping away tears of laughter, Bree's voice turned serious. "You see, *Père*. All the hell you put everyone through was for nothing. All you had to do was ask—something you have never done! Every decision that was ever made in my life, you made it." Ugly memories rushed to her mind. "I did everything you wanted me to do. I finished high school at fifteen. I finished college at nineteen, because you said I should. I had the grades to get into any university I wanted, but you wouldn't hear of it. You told me not to waste my time applying to other colleges. I was going to Grambling University, and it was not open for discussion. You wouldn't even let me go to Xavier University where you and mother attended. You wanted me stuck out in the country. You even chose my profession, *Père*. I wanted to be a gynecologist, but you said *your* school needed a biology teacher. So, I'm a biologist! Did you know that Harriette and I wanted to practice medicine in Africa? We wanted to help African women. But you made sure that that didn't happen, *Père*. I was needed at *your* school. And the *real* reason you sent me to New York that summer was because of Harriette's death—for no other reason! You have never wanted me to leave the State of Louisiana!" Though Mr. Boutte tried to conceal it, he reacted knowingly. "Oh, my God. You knew! You knew what my plans were. Damn you, *Père!* Only Dean Moreau knew about our plans. No wonder Dean Moreau... I guess your tactics work on everyone!" She made a vicious grunt. "It didn't take much for Dean Moreau to change my mind. I conformed. But a part of me never accepted it. Now you come barging in my home this morning using your same old tactics. Well, your tactics won't work on me this time! And don't you, from this day forward, ever mention Reuven's name to me again!"

"All right! I admit it." Mr. Bouttes anger had replaced his shock. "I may have been wrong *that* time, but I'm right *this* time!"

"Shit, leave me alone!" she screamed. "You badgering me won't change anything, anyway."

"What was that *gutter* word you just used?"

"Shit! I said, shit! Now, leave me alone." Triumph gleamed in her eyes. Her look disarmed her father.

"I'm not finished. I came to discuss something else." Bree folded her arms, leaned back against the kitchen counter, and gave her father a blank look.

"Lately, all you have been doing is staying inside this house feeling sorry for yourself. Okay, so you're hurt. But you've got to pack all of this under your feet and get on with life. Buck up! I need you to take over the funeral home here in St. Jamesville. You already know how to run the business from top to bottom, I saw to that. We have good staff, but your two brothers could use your help. They do have careers of their own to manage, too. It's high time that you take a more active role in the family businesses. We're all overworked. Your uncle Batiste has been a big help, but who knows when my dear brother will take to the winds..." Bree interrupted him.

"If everyone is so overworked, why did you open another funeral home here and in Shreveport? Weren't the funeral homes in New Orleans, Slidell, and Baton Rouge enough?"

"I opened the last two funeral homes for my brother. I pray that Batiste will stop his wanderings one day soon, and when he does, he'll have something of his own to come back to. If Batiste doesn't have anything, it will be an ugly blemish on the family."

"On your kingdom, your kingship," Bree murmured softly.

"What was that?"

"Let it lie, *Père.*"

"Let it lie, huh. My dear, little 'precious pearl,' you are very fortunate. Very fortunate, indeed! So you better take heed to all the silly choices you have been making in your life. I think you're trying to dismantle this family."

"I am not! You..."

"Shut up! Just shut up! I don't see you exactly bubbling over with enthusiasm. We need your help! I can handle the Insurance company, myself. I have good agents. They have been with the Company for years. But your two brothers need your help—mainly, Manuel. He's the one having to drive to St. Jamesville and Baton Rouge everyday. Durant lives in LaPlace, so he's closer to the funeral home in New Orleans and Slidell. He could do with your help one or two days a week, too. But you're mainly needed here in St. Jamesville."

"I'll think about it," Bree said.

Her father lowered his voice to a deadly whisper and said, "Bree, I have never struck you. But so help me God!" He pushed his hands deep into his pockets and started pacing the kitchen floor. "When it comes to this family, I'm not above doing anything!"

"I don't recommend you striking me, *Père*. You wouldn't like the end results."

"I run this family!" he shouted. He had lost control. "And I'll continue to run it! And if I don't see my family working with a passion to keep this family stable, I'll run this family from my grave if I have to!" He gave Bree a long, intense stare.

"I love my family, *Père*. If you need my help, of course, I'll help. Is it reasonable to ask for two months to let my family *situation* settle down?"

"Do I have a choice?"

"*Non*."

"Then, I'll wait. I'm going to speak with your husband about it, anyway. Tousant, your husband! Not that pitiful, Farras Jourdan who has the gall to call himself a man!"

"You do that, *Père*."

"One other question." She threw up her hands and leaned back against the counter. "Why don't you get yourself a housekeeper? Give one of our people a job. If you're that concerned about social levels, there's pride in earning a honest dollar. If the housekeeper is treated with dignity and respect, I cannot see a problem. Anyway, most Negroes take pride in whatever job they have. Being a domestic is nothing to be ashamed of. Many college tuition's have been paid by domestic work. I cannot understand your continual refusal to have a housekeeper."

"I do not have to discuss anything about my life with you anymore, *Père*." She stood silently before her father and gave him a direct look without any softness.

M'sieu Boutte stared back at his daughter and thought: *It's going to be a bother. But one day soon, I'm going to sit down and try to analyze Bree. What type of mind does it take to come up with something unheard of, unthought of, and then act on it!* "God's wrath awaits those who are involved in *unholy alliances*," he said. He gave Bree a determined look, made a slight bow to her, and walked toward the front door. *Madame* Muscadine III walked along beside him. Her short legs pounded the carpeted floor with an angry fierceness. She wore her owner's personality. Bree's whole body shook with rage.

A month later, Delphine stopped at Bree's house. "I can pay you five dollars a week 'till I pay the money back," she said, handing Bree a five dollar bill.

"If you cannot pay some weeks, pay me the next week, or whenever you can, Delphine. I'm in no hurry."

"Thank you for understandin', but I think I can manage five dollars a week. I'm doin' as much overtime as I can at the café."

"Won't you come in for a cup of tea?"

"I think I will." Delphine stepped inside the house.

"Lordy mercy! This is a palace, Bree," she said, looking around in awe. "I see why people are gossipin'." Delphine rested her hands on her hips. "Chile, this house is somethin' else. It's just plain old jealousy."

Bree wondered why other women envied her. Did they see something she did not see? Did they appreciate something she did not appreciate? "It don't make no difference how many husbands a woman haves. Whether it's *one, two,* or a *thousand* husbands," Delphine continued, "we all just trying to do one thing, live! And try our darndest to squeeze a little peace out of life."

"I wish everyone understood that. I got a letter from my ladies' club today. Suddenly, I don't fit in anymore. I guess I have added a black mark. My great-grandmother helped organize the club. I was a 'fourth generation' member. It's a closed club, open only to the offsprings of the 'original' members." Bree had never liked the blatant snobbishness of the members, herself, but the club raised a great deal of money for Black universities in Louisiana, so she had remained a member. "But like Farras always says, 'Their loss.'"

Though Bree sounded unaffected by the wide berth her friends had given her, she was lonely, and she missed them. She had often wondered how could she ever win in life if she kept losing people who were important to her? What was the point? " That's a shame," Delphine said, shaking her head. Bree's mind had gone adrift, but Delphine's words jarred her thoughts, and brought her attention back to her. Delphine looked at Bree. She knew that look of sorrow. It had shown itself in her house many times.

The next day, Bree walked out of the A&P holding a bag in each arm. She set one bag down on the hood of her car, and she struggled to open her car door with the other. She tried to set the second bag on the hood, but the bag wouldn't sit level. She looked around, and saw two boys walking slowly, licking two chocolate ice cream cones. "I'll give you two boys a dollar apiece if you'll give me a hand." The boys looked at each other. The oldest of the two yelled, "*Non,* 'cause *nos mère* said not to talk to you! You're living in sin!" They both started running; holding their ice cream cones like two fragile, crystal glasses. Bree knew that the grown-ups were maligning her, but to poison their children's minds was appalling. Even Father Andreau had given her a painful smile. When she approached him in the aisle at the A&P, he hurriedly walked past her, muttering something unintelligible.

She sensed that it was something insulting.

Everywhere Bree was greeted with hostility. A middle-age couple approached her. Bree spoke. They did not. They walked silently past her. The woman carried a fishing pole, and her husband carried some crabbing nets. A dead turtle hung heavily in the man's other hand. She knew the couple. She had once saved them from losing their land because of delinquent taxes. She stood and watched them as they walked down the road. The couple had bruised her soul, and all they thought about was cooking turtle soup! She pressed her lips together.

Tousant had had an experience the week before at the barbershop. A man had walked up to him, and asked him if he had a brain. The man had said that if he did, then he must be a *punk*, or he was *voodood*. Paupon had overheard several of his teachers talking about their *unconventional lifestyle*, but they had stopped talking as he walked past them. And Farras was still having problems with his parents. *Jesus!* she thought.

It was Monday. Bree had just taken fresh linen to the upstairs bedroom when the front doorbell rang. She opened the front door to find Deacon Hebert, Deacon Broadenaux, and *Madame* Blanque at the door. Deacon Hebert was holding his hat in his hand, looking down at the floor, almost shamefaced. He kept his head down and mumbled to himself. "This ain't my doing, Bree. I got elected to come here." He gave her an apologetic glance. When Bree looked at Deacon Hebert, she thought of Friday night boxing and 'Gillette' commercials. As a teenager, she remembered him coming to their house to see boxing on television with her father. Deacon Broadenaux, the chairman of the Deacon board, stood looking at her with bold contempt. She had guessed that he was to be the spokesman for the group.

As she held the door open for the group, a cold chill crept up her spine. *Their errand must be terribly important,* she thought, because Deacon Broadenaux believed any absence from his job was a *carnal* sin. She could not move from where she stood. Deacon Broadenaux spoke, "I know this is a surprise Bree. But we're the Committee that was elected and sent here by our church to talk to you," he said, sounding official. "Can we come in, please?" The calmness of his voice dissipated her fear.

"Yes, please, come in." She stepped back out of the doorway. "Can I offer you coffee, tea, something cool to drink?"

"*Non!*" Deacon Broadenaux said, a bit too loudly, stopping her next words. "This is not a social visit, Bree," he said, in a stern voice.

"Please, have a seat," Bree offered.

The small, Church committee sat down. But Deacon Hebert remained standing. "Bree, I'm gonna speak frank and straightforward. We were sent here by the Church to inform you that a meetin' has been called so that our church can vote on whether you can remain a member of Mt. Olive Baptist Church." Bree sat speechless, too astound to comment.

He reached into the inside pocket of his coat and brought out a long, white envelope, tore it open, and began reading:

"Date: March tenth, nineteen hundred and sixty-six.
Place: Mt. Olive Baptist Church, 2640 Claiborne Avenue,
St. Jamesville, Louisiana. Time: 8:00 P.M. "

Bree stared at Deacon Broadenaux in disbelief. *Surely, this is a nightmare,* she told herself. *This cannot be happening. This cannot be real.* She wondered if she closed her eyes and opened them again, would everything be different? The Deacon's words made no sense. If she had not been so stunned, she would have interrupted him:

"Charges:
1.Adultery.
2.Contamination of our church's youth.
3.Disrepecting the holiness and
   sacredness of God's house.
4.Destroying the outstanding reputation
   of Mt. Olive Baptist Church. "

Deacon Broadenaux handed her a copy of the Charges. She looked over at Deacon Hebert. He had his head down. He was still standing in the same spot. *Madame* Blanque sat with a smug look on her face with the corners of her mouth turned downward. Not one of them showed even the slightest glimpse of compassion for the pain they must have surely known they were causing. When Bree found her voice, she spoke directly to Deacon Broadenaux.

"Does this mean my son and husband, too?" she asked, in a soft voice, feeling herself the victim of a conspiracy.

Madame Blanque spoke for the first time. "Which one of yo' *husbands?*" *Madame* Blanque piped up. "You have *two* husbands, you know."

"Since my *second* husband is not a member of Mt. Olive Baptist Church, I'm obviously speaking about my *first* husband, Tousant!" Bree said, her eyes blazing.

"*Madame* Blanque spoke out, clutching her Bible in her lap. "You couldn't prove that by any of us. The way the three of you have been 'sassaying' down our church's aisle every Sunday! It's just downright sinful and unholy. Its *degoutant!* You are a festering sore on the body of *my* church! We prides ourselves on adhering strictly to biblical teachings." Her dark eyes were cold and hard, and they opened wide as she spoke. *Madame* Blanque was a women of average height with wide, rounded hips and bowed legs. She wore black dresses in every season with three silver bracelets on each arm. She was brown-skinned with thick, healthy, white hair that she wore in two thick braids across the top of her head. She had spoken her words very forcefully.

"How many men have you slept with in secret, *Madame* Blanque?" Bree inquired. Filled with rage and humiliation, Bree tried to keep the anger out of her voice.

"You are satanic! Over-proud. And you got too many evil airs, Bree Jumppierre. God's gon' send this little castle you manage to build for yo'self tumbling down in ruins. A castle you built with the income of *two* mens, I might add. God's gon' take all this finery away from you," *Madame* Blanque said, angrily getting up from the divan. "Deacon Broadenaux, Deacon Hebert, let's flee from this *domicile* of the devil."

"My life is not your business," Bree said. "I'll make my defense to the Church, not to the likes of you three."

"Bree, this meetin' is being held for the sole purpose of dismissin' you, not your husband. I want you to understand this," Deacon Broadenaux explained, standing up. "I'm speakin' about your 'legal' husband now. Because you ain't *M'sieu* Farras Jourdan's wife. You his *concubine!"* he sneered. His eyes held a malicious gleam. "You the guilty party here, not yo' po' husband, Tousant. You should start makin' yo' defense to God befo' you come to the meetin'," he said, in a hateful voice as he walked out the door.

"I already have. Have you, Deacon Broadenaux?" Bree asked, "I bet you don't even know how to pray!" He waved her off, not wanting to hear anymore. She had to steady herself to fight back tears. *Why not, Tousant?* she thought. *Why was she 'immoral' and Tousant was not?*

"I pray and I believe in God, young woman," Deacon Broadenaux said, his eyes wide with anger.

"Yes, but do you *know* God?" Bree shouted after him.

"Young woman, you got a lot of trouble ahead of you. I was born 'wid a *veil* over my face. I have a *gift*. I know 'bout these things," Deacon Broadenaux said.

Madame Blanque stood at the edge of the gallery opening her parasol. She turned and spoke to Bree again, "You wretch! I'm going to give you *tracas à n'en plus finir."* She shook her fist in Bree's direction. "I don't know what it is 'bout these *high- class* folks, but the higher they go up the ladder, the mo' they show their rumps. *Madame* Bree, you will find that I am an unconquerable, Christian army all by myself," she boasted.

Damn, Madame Blanque! Bree thought. *She needed to comprendre. For once! Just once! Why couldn't she be left alone?*

When the Church committee left, Bree re-read the Church's charges they had given her. She struggled upstairs to her and Farras' bedroom like an old woman. She was dead tired. She took out her little *music box* and fell heavily across their bed. It wasn't supposed to be this way! Was the Church mistaking her openness, her honesty, for arrogance? There were so many people clouding her vision that she did not know anymore. "Please, God, temper me with humility," she prayed. "Let me be honest but never arrogant," she whispered reverently. *How can all this be?* she thought. *Wasn't it just a moment ago that she was a wife and mother and had peace? Wasn't it just a moment ago that she had complete support from her family, church, and community? Wasn't it just a moment ago that....* It was as though she had never lived before, had never had a past life.

She knew that she had to exercise some common sense, but whether anyone liked it or not, her decision to keep Farras as a *second* husband, stood. She had to trust her luck. She could not rely on anyone to teach her how to handle her *unconventional lifestyle.* She either had to learn quickly herself, or she would lose. If she threw up her hands now, it would not be just a defeat, it would be a humiliating defeat.

After a long while, she rolled over and lay on her back. She reached over to her night stand, took two kleenex from the box, and wiped her eyes. Her *music box* played its gentle song while she lay silently, gazing, eyes vacant. She had withdrawn. She would have absolute balance for a period, but then someone would give her a look, or would say or do something, and she would again retreat inside herself. It was then that she wondered whether she was in over her head.

Her problems with the Church brought back memories of her childhood. She thought about Harriette. She had not let herself remember Harriette for a long time. Harriette had always given her comfort and support. She yearned for Harriette's friendship and her sisterhood. Her mother used to say that they were too close, that they were *deux t^tes dans un seul corps.* Harriette had been the *blackest* and the *prettiest* girl she had ever known. But Harriette had no "mental editor" to help her filter out bad things. Harriette had always searched for trouble, and when she couldn't find trouble, she created it. Harriette died a horrid death their freshman year in college. She got pregnant, and bled to death trying to cover up her sin. Weeks of her talking to Harriette had not stopped her from getting a back-alley abortion in New Orleans. Harriette had told her in confidence that she was pregnant, but she never mentioned anything about getting an abortion. For years, she wondered if she had broken her word to

Harriette, could she have saved her life. But looking back, it would have taken *God* to stop Harriette from getting that abortion. Until Harriette got pregnant, she had assumed that they led the same sheltered life. Harriette had looked directly into her eyes and said, "It's the way of the world, Bree. The piper must be paid. Anyway it goes, I cannot win." Still, she and Harriette always had the ability to *decode* each other's meaning on things. Did she deliberately not *decode* things then?

The day she found Harriette dead, the sky was a deep gray, but a sun-bright halo appeared to wrap itself around one low-hanging cloud. Harriette had crawled into a large hole that they, as children, had dug together alongside the levee. She had pulled and tugged at Harriette's body until she got her out of the dark hole. *Personne n' avait le coeur pour toucher les morts.* But this is Harriette! she remembered thinking. She's not just a dead body!

Once out in the daylight, she could see that Harriette's eyes were open. She tried not to look at her eyes. Even when Harriette was alive, there was a wild and desperate look in her eyes. The skin on Harriette's face had ashened, and pulled backwards, marking her previous agony. Her mouth was turned sideways and was fixed into a permanent grimace. This made her appear to her to still be in severe pain. Dazed and angry, she had slapped Harriette's dead face—slapped it, and screamed out her anger at her corpse. Then she heard herself laughing hysterically, her hysterical laughter turning to heart-breaking sobs. She had sat a long time beside Harriette's dead body, whimpering. Sometime later, there was a strange silence, and many things started to happen. Odd, inconsequential things; vague things that were—part real and part unreal—took her mind away from Harriette. Even now, she could not explain them. They were just "things and events" moving around her. She had watched the slow movements of bumblebees as they darted from clover to clover. Unfamiliar faces floated out from the bayous past her, crying. *Feu follet* sailed slowly in the air from the direction of the graveyard. The taste of sugar cane and hot, spicey *gumbo and curt bouillon and boudin* exploded simultaneously inside her mouth. *Zydeco* music caressed her ears. Seconds later, she saw herself dancing the *Second-*

line to the music of *Professor Long Hair.* Seconds later, she saw herself at *Mardi Gras* yelling, "Throw me something, Mister!" to the man on the *Zulu* float. All that had happened while she sat beside Harriette's body. Later, she found herself mourning all the "things and events," as if they had come to their end too.

After Harriette's funeral, she went to the levee and erected a *cairn.* It had taken years for her to sort out Harriette's death and finally accept it. She wondered whether Harriette would support her now? What would her reaction be to her *unconventional lifestyle?*

Bree got up, walked to the bathroom, and splashed cold water on her face. Her face felt hot, feverish. Her mother had said the day after Harriette's funeral. "Bree that goes to show you, you cannot go against the grain, not if you expect things to go right in your life." After her mother said that, she started going to *Mass* twice on Sundays, and read her Bible daily. She wanted to purge herself of any urges to "go against the grain."

She picked up her Bible from the dresser and sat down heavily on the divan. She laid the Bible across her lap, and wrung the damp towel in her hands. "That's what I have ended up doing Harriette. I've gone against the grain." Her voice broke a little on her last words, as she folded her hands, and rested them on her Bible. Her life seemed to reek with unrealisms. She wondered, crazily, if she weren't asleep and everything that was happening to her wasn't just a hellish nightmare. She looked around the bedroom and Harriette's words: *'The piper must be paid'* seemed to hang in the air and pulsate and cause the walls to vibrate. Her words seemed to penetrate her skull, ricocheting crazily inside her head. Her scalp tingled. She picked up her Bible again, and held it to her breasts. "An unholy alliance," she whispered. "God, you made me what I am. I am asking you to fix my *situation.* Am I just some insignificant *something* in your sight? That's... all that I have... to say," she cried, her tears almost choking off her words.

She walked over to the dresser, and laid her Bible back in its place. "No, Harriette. The quickest way to lose yourself is to give the world what it wants. Because a double-minded person is unstable in all their ways. I'm standing firm, Harriette. I just have to ride this one out."

She walked out of the bedroom closing the door quietly behind her. The faint sound of the song from her *music box* faded as she descended the stairs.

After Paupon had gone to bed, Bree showed Tousant and Farras the letter that the Church committee had given her. Through clenched teeth, she tried to explain what had happened. "Do we all agree that we still want to attend Mt. Olive Baptist Church?" Farras asked.

"Yes, I do," Bree answered, quickly, with a determined look on her face.

"Then, dammit, we gon' fight!" Farras stood hitting his fist in the palm of his hand.

The next day it rained and rained. It seemed that it was always raining in Louisiana. The constant rain made everything dreary and sad, and it depressed Bree. She got up during the night, and stared out her bedroom window at the black rain for hours. The levee had already reached the point of overflowing, and another hurricane warning was out. It made Bree anxious. But no one else seemed bothered by the hurricane warning. Everyone still went about their daily business, holding parasols over their heads, and giving each other cheery greetings.

All during the day, Bree paced the floor. Every so often, she paused, and glanced outside her living-room window. She saw people going out or coming in from the rain. Their loud, happy voices, and their jovial greetings meant nothing to her. She couldn't help wondering whether her grave *situation* gave them their cheeriness and foolhardiness.

The next morning, Bree looked outside her bedroom window and gave a sigh of relief. The sun was out. Before she could take a bath and get dressed, the telephone rang. It continued to ring all morning.

She got calls from people who had not spoken to her since she had taken Farras as her *second* husband. They all said that they would be at the Church meeting. Some of the members that called hadn't attended church for years. But she wasn't disillusioned by their calls. She knew that her *situation* meant something different to each of them. Their reactions were grounded by their own personal fears. But the majority of the callers were active church members who attended church on a regular basis. They were afraid that if she were brought before the Church for her private life, maybe the Church wouldn't stop at her. A few of them had made remarks that nobody's life was spotless or sin free. But none of her old friends called. They hadn't visited her since Farras moved in. She had expected it from some, but she was disappointed in others. She had written Malik X a letter. She did not want any members from her organization at her church. It was her own personal battle. A battle that only she could *win* or *lose*.

A second after Bree hung up the telephone, the telephone rang again. As soon as she lifted the receiver, before she could even say hello, an unfamiliar, woman's voice spoke. The woman's voice was cold and unyielding, and she spoke quickly and hateful. "You have fallen from God's good graces, Bree Jumppierre. This town will never forgive you. You will feel the heat of the fire! You are a weak, selfish bitch!" The woman started sobbing before she hung up. Bree stood with the telephone receiver hanging loosely in her hand, stunned. Had the entire town gone *mad!*

CHAPTER
TEN

*I*t was early afternoon. There was a strong breeze, and the clouds hung high and sparse. The doorbell rang. As soon as Bree opened her door, Delphine swept in the door past her. Delphine was the one person outside of the family who still visited her. "Lordy, mercy. I know without askin' that you're gonna fight this church thing," Delphine said, holding her open parasol over her shoulder. "You just got to, Bree."

"*Oui,* I am. I cannot give in on something that's right for me."

"Lord, chile, ain't that the truth," Delphine said. "No wonder before all this happened so many people looked up to you, including me. And it ain't got nothing to do with you helping me when I was down, either. I admired and respected you because of yo' love for our people. Lordy, mercy, I don't know if I got the guts to git beat up on and shot at. Ya'll crazy!" Delphine threw her head back and laughed. "But I'm a member of yo' organization." Bree gave her a look of pleasant surprise.

"I'm sorry, Delphine. I didn't know."

"Don't be sorry. The Organization is too large for you to know every member. I have to tell you the truth, Bree. I used to pray that the Organization wouldn't ever call on me to go with ya'll. Especially to Mississippi! Now, I'll go anywhere the Organization asks me to go. But Lord, I'll sho' be prayin' all the way." Bree chuckled. "Freddie just worships the ground you walk on, Bree."

"I'm flattered." Knowing that Delphine was a member of the Organization made Bree look at her with new recognition.

"Honey, ain't no need in being flattered. I'm tellin' the truth. God knows, you earned the respect of all these peoples, Bree. You are a damn good person. That's how come I don't understand these peoples. How can they treat you like this?" Bree gave Delphine a noncommittal look. It was against her nature to malign anyone. "*Si Dieu veut.* I'm gon' be at church with bells on. It's *my* church too, and I have a right to my say," Delphine said indignantly.

"I don't want you to put yourself in a position to be ridiculed too, Delphine. Because of what this town has put me through, I just couldn't stand to see anyone else suffer like that." Bree had discovered a strength in Delphine, and she felt drawn to her because of that strength.

"You just let anybody try to stop me," Delphine said, throwing her shoulders back proudly. "It ain't just you. I can't stand to see anybody suffer either, Bree. I've had my pains and my downs too. If I was gon' be—whatever that 'word' is you just used—it woulda started by now. Not to mention that I don't care! Honey, these people ain't gon' fool with me. I been tellin' 'em off 'bout the way they been treatin' you. They know I don't care what they say 'bout me. Well, I gotta be going, Bree," she said, walking towards the door. "I just drop by to tell ya' that I'm with you all the way, and I always will be. Remember that ancient African law?" Delphine asked, with a mischievous smile.

"*Oui*, fabulous law, that." Bree laughed. "I think I have found myself a sister." Pride gleamed in Bree's eyes.

"I s'peck it was meant to be," Delphine said.

When Bree opened the door for Delphine, Miss Rosette was standing there. Her presence startled Bree. Miss Rosette had made three attempts at ringing Bree's doorbell, but she had walked away several times before deciding. When Bree opened the door, she caught her standing with her hand hovering over the doorbell. When Bree and Delphine stepped outside the door, Miss Rosette walked to the edge of the gallery and picked up a tin pail with a rusty handle. The handle hung lopsided, as if it had been pulled and tugged into its present shape from repeatedly being overloaded. Bree's eyes fell on the pail, then traveled across the gallery and rested briefly on Miss Rosette's mud caked brogans. Miss Rosette and her father lived together in a little, four-room house deep into the bayous. The unpainted, weather-beaten house blended in with the gray Spanish moss that hung from the trees and appeared to be part of the bayous. A person would have to know that the little house was there to find it. There were no pathways leading up to the little house. Once, when she was a girl, she and Harriette had hacked their way through the bayous to the little house.

"Hey, Miss Rosette," Delphine said, breaking the silence, "It's been a long time since I seen you around." Miss Rosette stood holding the pail with her eyes fixed on Bree's face.

"I brung these blackberries to you." She spoke to Bree without acknowledging Delphine. Delphine walked over and peered down into her bucket.

"Lordy, mercy! Them sho' is some nice blackberries, Miss Rosette. A person sho' could make some nice blackberry pies outa them." Delphine kept gazing down in the pail at the blackberries, as if tasting the blackberries with her eyes. Bree stood staring at the pail and the woman. She had seen Miss Rosette on her walks out of the swamps. Except to speak in passing, Miss Rosette had never shown more than a spark of interest in her. She was a strange woman. Bree looked at Delphine. Delphine gave her a puzzled look, and shrugged her shoulders.

"Well, I better git going. I can't put a meal on a table standin' here eyein' them juicy blackberries," Delphine said, walking towards the steps of the gallery.

"I'll send some blackberries over by Paupon," Bree said, finding her voice.

"That's fine, but I ain't hintin'," Delphine said laughing.

"No kidding," Bree chuckled.

"No, I ain't hintin'. I slam that one right at you." Delphine laughed, as she walked away.

Miss Rosette stood, her body bobbing up and down, with her eyes still on Bree. She had rickets. Her father had the disease, too. Bree stood trying not to stare at her. She had never been that close to Miss Rosette. She doubted that anyone else had either. "Thank you for the blackberries. It's very kind of you to bring them to me," Bree said.

She wanted to make an offer to pay Miss Rosette for the blackberries, but something in the woman's eyes prevented her from asking. "Please, won't you come in?" Bree asked, moving to one side to make room for her to walk through the door.

"*Non, merci.* I just brung these blackberries to you. Papa's got to eat soon." She had never seen Miss Rosette in a dress before. She always wore overalls and a cap. She obviously viewed her visit to her house as something 'special' and had dressed for the occasion. The gesture was deeply moving to Bree.

"You must be tired from such a long walk, Miss Rosette," Bree said. "It must have taken you hours to pick those blackberries. It's so hot. Won't you rest a minute and have some ice tea?"

"*Non*, but I thank you. I heard 'bout yo' troubles... and.... Listen, Bree. These old, feeble-minded asses don't know nothin'! Anythin' that looks different scares they asses. They don't care 'bout yo' heart." Bree stood nodding in agreement trying to avoid looking into the pair of fast moving eyes. Miss Rosette's eyes seemed to flash from side to side rather than blink. Bree wondered how she could speak so passionately and still keep such an expressionless face. She had a long *Pall Mall* cigarette dangling from her loose lips. Bree had never, even as a child, seen her without a long, unlit, *Pall Mall* cigarette dangling from her lips. She seemed never to be smoking the cigarette. Her satisfaction seemed to come from its dangling. Bree wondered whether it was the same *Pall Mall* cigarette she had seen as a child. But when she saw Miss Rosette's tobacco-stained fingers, she dismissed the thought. Miss Rosette had folded her arms across braless breasts, and continued talking with her unlit cigarette dangling. As she spoke, Bree could see that some of her teeth were missing. "Now, take me. I'm breathin', ain't I?" She removed the *Pall Mall* cigarette from her mouth, wet her lips, and replaced the cigarette back into its previous position at the corner of her mouth. She had unfolded her arms, and was pointing her hand in the direction of Bree's chest, "so that means that I'm livin'. Ain't that right, Bree?" Bree nodded her head, but her eyes were on the fingerless hand being pointed at her. She wondered about the amputation. "Now, take you, Bree. You're breathin' too, ain't you? That tells me that you alive! Breathin' is life, ain't it? Well, these peoples here in St. Jamesville is scareda life. They rather back they asses into this life than to face up to it head on. I know what I'm talkin' 'bout." Bree couldn't believe that Miss Rosette was such a passionate and excitable woman. She stood listening quietly to the woman, looking at the *Pall Mall* dangling from her lips. "Look at the hateful name these asses calls me: Miss Rickety Rosette, Miss Bobbin' Robin, Miss Shake Rattle and Roll." Bree looked off. Because as a child growing up that was all she had ever heard Miss Rosette called. "Take me, I ain't never had a man. If Papa wasn't a man, I wouldn't know what a man looked like. But I don't go 'round punchin' holes in people's hearts 'cause I don't! Well," she said, walking over to the edge of the gallery, "I best be goin'. Papa'll be wonderin'." She turned around and looked at Bree. Bree saw kindness in her eyes; their sufferings had created some sort of strange bond between them. "It's strange," she said, "no matter what happens to us in this life, we still have to eat, doodoo, and clean our behinds up. It's somethin' terrible 'bout that!" A painful expression crossed her face. "I'll be keepin' my eye on you, Bree. I had to come, 'cause cruelty just gits me all unhinged." And without another word, she walked off abruptly.

Bree watched her as she walked. Though her body bobbed up and down, she held her head high and proud as she walked. Bree's heart warmed toward the proud woman. She wore a shapeless, carmine-colored dress, and as she walked her dress hung proud and stubborn. It seemed to refuse to be blown by the wind. "Wash them blackberries fo' you put 'em in yo' belly," Miss Rosette yelled out without looking back. She walked hurriedly along. Bree stood with her arms folded, and watched her departure until the tall weeds on the levee shut off her view.

"*Quelle femme!*" Bree spoke softly to herself. "I'm willing to bet my right arm that you washed those blackberries a dozen times before you brought them to me." She was grateful to have another woman as an ally, but she couldn't resist evaluating Miss Rosette as a possible enemy someday, too. She had discovered that a friend is not forever a friend, and an enemy is not forever an enemy.

Bree rose early the next morning full of confidence. It was the day of the Church meeting. Her confidence had held up all day long, and was still holding up, as they drove into the church's parking lot. She saw her family and Delphine waiting near the steps at the front entrance of the church. Seeing her father standing there with them surprised her. Her father was holding *Madame* Muscadine III gingerly in his arms. When she walked up and greeted them, they embraced her. "Lotta people here, ain't it?" Delphine said, looking around.

"Yes, it was announced in church every Sunday, three weeks in a row," Bree answered. Her eyes remained on her father's face.

"What! For three Sundays! Drawing things out to get as much of the Bouttes' blood as possible. I would have guessed that," her father said. Calming his voice down, he said, "I cannot believe that they announced this meeting with Paupon sitting right there in church!" Hurt showed in his eyes.

"Yes, they did," Bree said.

"That's what I say about the Baptist. They don't know how to handle things quietly in a Christian manner. They're just too 'messy' for me. They like to keep up a ruckus all the time. You should have stayed with the Catholic church like the rest of the family. Louisiana is a Catholic state, anyway. The few Baptist here no one takes seriously. Where's my grandson?" he asked, looking around. He did not want to open up a dialogue with Bree on the comments he had just made about the Baptist church.

"He wanted to come, but we didn't want him here, *Père*. He has a lot of homework to do, anyway. It's just as well. I don't want Paupon here wasting his time with these fools," Tousant explained.

"Tousant!" Bree warned. She looked around to see if Tousant had been overheard.

"Well, they are fools! This is just plain crazy!" Tousant retorted angrily.

"It's been a hard road and a forced change," her father interjected.

162

"But I have learned to respect the decisions you make for your life, Bree. That goes for all my children now. For the first time in my life, I respect my children as people. I respect your *two* husbands as people, too. You three are the finest people I know, and you've got guts, too!" he boasted, looking proudly at them. "Bree, I love you too much to just throw you away. My own ambitions are one thing, but my children's lives are another." His voice choked, and he turned his face away from her, but not before Bree saw that his eyes had moistened. She had never mentioned her father's visit to Tousant or to Farras. She never told them how *naked* her father had made her feel, how she felt *raped* of protection. After he left, all that day, she felt as if she didn't have any clothes on. "I suppose this is the closest I'll come to an apology, Bree." Bree knew it would be nothing less than miraculous for her father to make such a rapid change. She didn't trust her father and doubted if she ever would. "I love you, Bree. Let's try again," he whispered.

"We'll see what time brings, *Père.*" Her father's weak apology was not enough to convince her of any permanent changes he had made.

One of the deacons came to the door and beckoned for them to come in. It was time. Bree was ready.

"Well, I guess it's time," Tousant said, squeezing Bree's hand.

"I guess so, Tousant."

"Nervous?" Tousant asked.

"*Un peu.*"

"*Je t'aime,*" Farras said. He straightened his back, and pride gleamed in his eyes.

As they walked towards the door of the church, a few faces nodded to her, but Bree's brown eyes returned no greetings. An angry woman's voice said, "We gon' put a hurtin' on Mrs. Bree's butt."

Then she heard a familiar voice saying, confidently, "I knew last month the Church was gon' git her. Knew it! I'm one of 'dem peoples born with a *veil* over my face. I know 'bout these thangs." Bree shuddered, and wondered in an uninterested way, why the familiar voice never knew about anything but pending doom.

As she entered the church, another woman's voice growled behind her, "Some people can sho' change up on people."

The three of them walked inside church together. Bree heard whispers and talk around her. All eyes were upon them. She felt their cold stares as she walked past them. She stared straight ahead, undaunted. An usher seated them in the empty seats on the left front pew. Bree guessed that they knew that her family would be with her. The usher seated Bree between her *two* husbands. Murmurs and grunts could be heard from members. The night was hot. The church was packed with bodies. The ceiling fans were useless.

Bree glanced around the church. It seemed to her that an unceasing effort was being made to destroy her. She had become a criminal, or the *Scarlet* woman that Satan himself had created.

"Look at the little blind mice!" All heads in the church looked back towards the vestibule. Miss Rosette was standing in the vestibule of the church with her arms folded across her bosom. She held her long *Pall Mall* cigarette defiantly in the corner of her mouth. "They blind asses can't see," she smirked. "They can't even hear!" She let out short, mocking laughter. Then she turned and stomped out. Her black, mud-caked brogans thumped rhythmically against the tiled floor.

After Miss Rosette left, silence filled the church until Deacon Broadenaux cleared his throat and called the meeting to order. Reverend Littlejohn stepped up to the pulpit. His voice boomed through the microphone. "Let us bow our heads in prayer. Let us pray, and ask God to direct the decision that'll be made on this young woman this evening." He prayed a sad and solemn and lengthy prayer. When he finished, he sat down on a gold-colored, cushioned bench facing Bree. The bench was far out enough for the minister to see the whole of the church. He sat wiping his sad face with a white handkerchief. He motioned to the pew on the right of the church where all the deacons were seated.

Deacon Broadenaux walked over to the church organ and picked up an iron folding chair lying against it. Bree's eyes followed him. She watched Deacon Broadenaux pick up the chair and unfold it. She knew that the chair had been clearly put there for her. She was finding out that society required a high price for *individuality* and *freedom of choice*. Deacon Broadenaux set the chair on the floor directly in front of the pulpit in full view of the members and stood next to it. "Will the accused... *excuser moi*," he stammered embarrassed, and corrected himself. "Will Bree Jumppierre..." He paused and cleared his throat. "I don't know if Bree's using the last name of that *second* man or not," he stated, in a loud voice looking at the members. The members roared in laughter. Farras made a motion to get up, but Bree squeezed his arm keeping him still. She looked at Farras. Farras gave her a weak smile and remained seated. When the laughter subsided, Deacon Broadenaux spoke again. "Will, Bree, please step forward and take the chair in front of the pulpit." Holding her head high, Bree got up and walked over to the chair. She sat down in the folding chair holding her body erect. She folded her hands on her lap and looked out at the members with wide, unashamed eyes. All voices came to a hush. For they had come to hurt, to wound, to draw blood. Bree looked into their faces and discovered that people loved pain— especially pain that belonged to someone else. She had always believed that her people hated pain. But within seconds, she saw that there was an excitement, an ecstasy, a joy among her people, as they witnessed her pain and degradation. *When they finished seeing my pain, what will they do with it?* she thought. *How will my pain help them?* "This is an outrage!" a voice exclaimed. Bree's head snapped in the direction of the voice. Her father had risen from his seat. *Madame* Muscadine III had risen, too. Her gray, wooly hair bristled, and she growled hatefully. Her father patted the dog's head, and she lay back down. The members grew silent. "This is an outrage!" her father repeated. *"Sainte mère de pitié!* In all my years on this earth, I have never seen anything like this! This isn't a church meeting. A church meeting is when Christians come together in prayer and pray for a fellow Christian that they believe is faltering in their life, not to persecute them! This church is set up as if it's a courtroom, with the minister the judge, the deacons the jury, and my daughter the accused. This is being handled in very poor taste. It's a three-ring circus! A free spectacle!" he said, looking around at the members. "I will not stand for it!" He shouted up at the pulpit to the minister. After her father voiced his strong disapproval, Bree stood up.

"*Père*, please sit down. I have something I want to say. Let the meeting continue, please, *Père.*" Bree sat back down. Her father made the sign of the cross and sat down. One of the deacons handed Deacon Broadenaux a long white envelope. Deacon Broadenaux read off the charges again, turned, and looked at Bree.

"I've read the charges. I believe you have something to say before the members starts the voting procedure."

Bree hesitated before she spoke. She looked at the assemblage. Her eyes stopped on almost every face. "First of all," she began, turning to face Deacon Broadenaux. "I think I have a right to know what–person or persons—brought these charges against me." Deacon Broadenaux stood looking grim; his mouth moved without sound.

"I did," *Madame* Blanque replied, standing up. "Everybody done got so quiet. Because yo' father done scared 'em, or they scareda me, but I fears no man! Ain't but one that I fears, God!" she said, pointing up at the ceiling. In a high pitched tone, almost preaching. "Yes, Mrs. Bree, I'm sayin' that you're sinnin'! I'm sayin' that you're openly committin' adultery, and I'm sayin' that you openly livin' and sleepin' with *two* mens at the same time!" She left her seat, walked down the aisle, and stood facing Bree. There was a hint of some sort sick delight teasing the corners of *Madame* Blanque's mouth. Bree looked in awe at her as she stood, cold and erect, with her bony fingers curled around the Bible she had clutched in her hand. Bree walked over to the pew where she had been sitting, and picked up her Bible. *Madame* Blanque stood watching. "Ain't no need in you gittin' yo' Bible, honey. Yo' Bible reads just like mines do. They all say the same things, and I know it from cover to cover. Ain't nothin' you can read, say, or do to change the Bible. The Bible tells you plain as day that the life you are livin' is wrong in eyes of God and man." Bree walked up to *Madame* Blanque, reached out her hand, palm up, and laid her Bible there.

"*Madame* Blanque, how long were you married to *M'seiu* Blanque before he died?"

"Forty-six years," *Madame* Blanque spoke up, proudly. Her voice was loud enough to be heard by the entire church.

"I asked you this same question in my home, when you and the Deacons came to bring your glad tidings. I asked *Madame* Blanque if during her forty-six years of marriage, had she ever committed adultery?" Bree stated calmly, looking around the church. "You didn't answer me then, *Madame* Blanque. Now, I'll ask you the same question again. Have you ever—at any time in those forty-six years of marriage—slept with another man? Please place your hand on my Bible before you answer me. The Bible you just said reads the same as yours. Put your hand on my Bible and swear, not before me, or to the members, but before God!" Bree held her Bible out to *Madame* Blanque and looked deep into her eyes. With anxious looks, the members sat waiting on the edges of their seats. Bree could feel the tension. *Madame* Blanque looked around at the members, then looked back at Bree, and gave her a long, scornful look. Bree could see the hate in *Madame* Blanque's eyes. At that precise moment, she thought that *Madame* Blanque would have loved to kill her. She felt that there was something intrinsically evil about *Madame* Blanque.

"That's playin' with God!" *Madame* Blanque huffed. "And I don't play with God. Only an evil, satanic person like you would come up with such foolishness," she cried. At that moment, Bree felt some strange and irrational pity for *Madame* Blanque. To her own surprise, she backed off from her, and let her walk, shoulders back, to her seat. *Madame* Blanque rushed down the aisle and took her seat. She crossed her heavy, bow legs; folded her arms across her heavy breasts, and stared hatefully at Bree.

Bree directed her attention to the congregation. "All of you are nothing but liars and hypocrites! And you're a long ways from being Christians. I'll place my hand on my Bible and say that I have been married for sixteen-years to my *first* husband, and that I have slept with but *two* men in my lifetime and both men are my *husbands.* Yes, that's right. *Husbands!* Anyone else here want to put their hands on my Bible and make the same claim?" Bree asked. She walked down the aisle arbitrarily picking out members; pushing her Bible at them. She had lost her patience with them. "Come, make the claim that you have never, nor are you now, sleeping with someone other than your own spouses!" She couldn't tell from their silence whether they were angry or guilty. "You single women, divorced women, put your hands on my Bible and swear that you have slept with but *two* men. You married women, come, swear," she repeated, still holding out her Bible. "I won't say, men, because: married, single, divorced, or widower, society sanctions your behavior. You men don't think about sin when you're up to your shenanigans—and you sure don't care what people think, either!" A few men looked awkwardly down to the floor. Others looked, uninterestedly, at nothing. "Some of you don't even care what your wives think, do you? What's the matter? Do I pose a threat to your small-minded, boring lives. Maybe you're afraid that my *unconventional lifestyle* just might change some others."

"Call it the way you see it, *chèri*. Make 'em listen to the drums of the *Congo*," Uncle Batiste yelled out, jumping up. "Reverend Littlejohn's sittin' up there on his throne wipin' his face like a damn fool. Jesus, I hate fools!" Bree looked quickly in her uncle's direction. He smiled sheepishly and sat back down. Bree turned and looked boldly into Deacon Broadenaux's eyes.

"So, you're one of the leaders of this...whatever this is. Put your hands on my Bible and swear." Deacon Broadenaux stared at her hand, as if he were not sure that he had heard her right.

"I don't care what you just said, Bree. It's wrong to be 'pleasurin' *two* mens at the same time!" Deacon Broadenaux growled. His eyes blinked, angrily.

"Do you know for a certainty that I'm—to use your word— 'pleasuring' two men at the same time?" Bree asked, holding her Bible in front of him. "That is a complete and utter lie!" Bree stated forcefully. "Why are you doing this, Deacon Broadenaux? I have been kind to you and your family. Now, all I get from you is *un paquet de sotises*."

"You being good to me ain't got nothin' to do 'wid you sinnin', Bree. Don't you go tryin' to make out like it is. And don't you go tryin' to make out like I'm wrong or crazy, either. You the one 'wid *two* different horses pullin' the same wagon. I don't mean at the same time. I mean, one after or before the other—whichever way you wanta put it," he added, with narrow eyes. He gave her a cold stare, with such fierce intensity that, Bree knew she would never forget that look.

"Do you know for a certainty that I'm sleeping with *two* men at the same time, Deacon Broadenaux?" Bree asked.

"No, I don't know for sho'. But any fool would..." his voice wavered.

"Ah, ah, Deacon Broadenaux. You're assuming now. The trouble with you people are you're joining forces on the wrong thing. As we speak, there are forces at work trying to stop you from seeing the sun rise tomorrow. You are ignoring the things that matters. You people literally thrive on gossip. But we all know the old saying: *Those who shout the most, talk the most, have the most to hide.* Some of the members looked directly at her, some looked at the walls or down at the floor, some withdrew into themselves, and closed their faces off; some sat looking at whatever they had been looking at before without making a sound. Bree looked at them, and a deep humility came over her. They were good people. People that had been beaten down and trodden. Was her family their hope, their ray of sunshine? She had heard her words to them, and knew that the words she heard herself saying were insensitive and cruel. Her words were harsher than she meant them to be. Why didn't she just tell them that they had hurt her and be done with it. She just could not believe that they really knew how much they had hurt her. For them, her *situation* was a new game to be played in an otherwise dull and hopeless life. She looked at the bowed heads, and saw that they were sorry they had hurt her and were ashamed. She saw indecision in the eyes of some of the deacons. "I'm one of you. You are my people! You hold my heart in the palms of your hands. We've respected each other all of our lives. *Vois-tu pas?* I'm sorry that you've done this to me. I do one thing different, one thing that you people do not understand, and you crucify me! Can you be just a little more tolerant? Can you people see that I must be free to choose my own path in life? Everything cannot be clean and tidy all the time. Don't you know that I am being as good as I know how to be—thank God nobody can be God but God." Silence. Bree wept. Her eyes were fastened onto the faces of the ones who still looked at her with embarrassment. She was glad that she saw no pity. Because where there was pity there was no respect.

"I don't want no parts of this no mo'!" a male voice, in a half sob, broke into the stillness. "We done gone plumb crazy. Doin' this terrible thang to po' Bree." The Deacon picked up his hat and walked softly out the front door. Without another word, other members got up and filed out of the front door.

After the church had cleared, Bree stood staring at her *two* husbands. A tear traced a path down her cheek. "I'm proud of you, sugar," her father said.

They all walked joyously out the front door of the church. When they got outside, Deacon Broadenaux stood waiting for them. "What do you want, now? You ain't done enough harm for one lifetime, Deacon Broadenaux?" Farras asked, his arms hanging loosely at his sides. Bree could see he had balled his hands into fists.

"No, wait brother," Deacon Broadenaux said, holding his hands up.

"So now it's, brother!" Farras raised his voice and tried to nudge Tousant's out of his way.

"Wait, man," Tousant said. "Let the Deacon talk. Let him say what he has to say." Farras moved slowly back out of the Deacon's face.

"Can we all go into Reverend Littlejohn's study? He wants to talk to ya'll," Deacon Broadenaux said.

"You're the errand boy now, Deacon Broadenaux?" Manuel asked.

"It won't hurt us to hear what Reverend Littlejohn have to say," Durant said.

They followed Deacon Broadenaux, with Farras protesting, to Reverend Littlejohn's office. When they entered the office, Reverend Littlejohn was on the telephone. From the sound of his voice, and the course of his conversation, he sounded as if he were talking to his wife. He motioned for them to sit, but there were only two straight back chairs lined up against the wall. Bree and her mother sat leaving the men standing. Farras was still upset. He stood in front of the door with his hands still balled into fists, breathing hard. Tousant stood next to Bree with his back up against the wall. His face was creased into a deep frown. Her father stood next to Tousant near Reverend Littlejohn's desk. He shifted his weight, impatiently, from foot to foot. Her Uncle Batiste stood watching the minister, absentmindedly, pulling at his gray beard. Delphine had squeezed herself inside the door and stood next to her uncle. Delphine had whispered into Bree's ear, "I'm sticking all the way." She had walked out the church door behind them.

Deacon Broadenaux stood a few feet behind Reverend Littlejohn. He wore a black suit with silver cross on a silver chain around his neck. His black shoes were polished until they shone like glass. He was small in stature with small, darting eyes and a bumpy complexion. His eyes were red and set into the brown, leathery skin of a face that appeared dried-out, lifeless. They were the only thing that stood out on his wide, featureless face. Bree sat staring boldly at him. He appeared to be making an effort to hide himself away from her. Each time Bree glanced at him, he moved a few feet farther behind Reverend Littlejohn's desk, and pulled nervously at the silver cross around his neck. She wondered about Deacon Broadenaux and his *veil*, his self-proclaimed *gift* to see into the future, and wondered seriously whether he wasn't insane. She wanted something unnatural to occur, something to shake the very foundation that Deacon Broadenaux based his life on. *Maybe the moon should cough up blood. Or the devil, painted-up like a whore, should seduce him,* she thought. She felt cheated. She wanted to taste the deliciousness of vengeance. Her mind screamed for it. Deacon Broadenaux and *Madame* Blanque had tried to crush her.

Reverend Littlejohn looked up from the telephone. His eyes pleaded for patience. He made a frown at the person on the other end of the telephone and continued talking. To keep her eyes from wandering to Deacon Broadenaux again, Bree concentrated on every detail of Reverend Littlejohn's small office. A vase of assorted plastic flowers sat on his desk. There were no pictures on the walls—except a painting of a "blasphemous image" of Christ with his arms held out from his sides. The hands were held palm sides up showing bright, red bloodstains. There was a picture of Reverend Littlejohn's wife, looking sad and withdrawn, with sick, unhealthy eyes. Each time she saw Mrs. Littlejohn, she was walking hurriedly; with her arms wrapped around her small, delicate frame, as if she were trying to hide herself from the world. Her smooth face looked puffy, as if her face had been swollen by the water of too many tears in her life. She saw no traces of her ever being youthful and pretty.

Reverend Littlejohn hung up the telephone and turned to Bree. "I wanted to see you, Bree. I wanted to personally say that I'm truly sorry. I'm speaking not just to you, Bree, but to your whole family. Tonight's meeting wasn't held to hurt or to embarrass you. I was convinced by some that it was right." Reverend Littlejohn spoke in a quiet voice so low that Bree had trouble hearing him. She sat doubtful that she was hearing exactly what was being said. "It's regrettable, but I want you to know that I prayed over having this meeting. Bree, I watched you grow up into a fine, young woman." he said, with sad eyes. His eyes looked old and as ancient as the world. At that moment, Bree looked again at Deacon Broadenaux and found all traces of vindictiveness gone. She could never hold anger long, and she found hate, vulgar. She was free. "I wouldn't, deliberately, hurt any of you. I went to school with your father and your Uncle Batiste," Reverend Littlejohn said, looking at her father and uncle. "Maybe I'm just getting old and narrow-minded. I know what you said in the meeting tonight was right, Bree. You shouldn't be judged by anyone but God."

"I know that my *unconventional lifestyle* goes against our religion, Reverend Littlejohn," Bree said, "but some people don't even believe in God. I believe in God, but I don't go around shoving it down other people's throats."

"Bree, I haven't the remotest idea of what's going on these days. But what went on here at church tonight just feels wrong. I'm proud of the way you conducted yourself tonight. You stuck to the issue and won your argument." He stood up and shook her hand.

As they started out the door, Lawrence Woodward opened it. "Am I too late?" he asked, looking at them.

"Man, you're always too late," Tousant said laughing.

"Man, I swear. I tried to get here on time. But *M'sieu* Boutte left too much work to be done by tomorrow morning."

"I know, man," Tousant said, patting him on the back. "My father-in-law knows how to work an insurance agent for his money. Let's go to my house and celebrate."

"Celebrate," Lawrence said. "Man, it's too late to celebrate. It's way pass my bedtime."

"Not for us, it's not. Now, let's all go by my house," Tousant said.

When they arrived home, Bree looked in on Paupon. He was asleep. She stood in his doorway and reflected on the conversation she had with him over breakfast. Because of the recent development with the Church, she had to find out if Paupon was still coping. He had told her that after his father came home from the hospital, he was too sad to be her husband. That's why it was okay for Papa J. to be her other husband. Paupon's words sounded like something her uncle Batiste had told him. When Paupon finished talking, she had excused herself, and stayed in her room until she dressed for the Church meeting. She couldn't help wondering whether Paupon wasn't being forced to grow old beyond his years. This raised more questions: Was she conning herself? Was Paupon conning her? Was he saying everything that she wanted him to say? How would she ever know? When he became an adult, would he despise her? What was Paupon's thoughts when he was alone in his room or in other private places? Why did she expect a ten-year old child to understand and accept the things that she could not fully understand? Was it too late for her to turn back? Questions, questions. But where were the answers?

Bree shook off the chill that had started to creep up her back. She quietly closed her son's bedroom door and went into the kitchen to make sandwiches. A few minutes later, her father yelled into the kitchen, "We're hungry, Bree!"

"The sandwiches are almost ready," she yelled out. Her thoughts soon returned to Paupon, and her heart leaped. Paupon was an exact replica of Tousant in appearance, but he had her eyes and four dimples above his upper lip. His dimples weren't noticeable until he smiled.

"Bree, what are you thinking about?" Tousant asked. "I have been standing here for five minutes, and all you have been doing is frowning."

"Just thinking about a face that looks like yours. Will you bring the other tray of sandwiches, please?" she asked, walking quickly out of the kitchen.

Bree's family was preparing to leave. They all stood on the front gallery. "I better go ya'll," Delphine said. "Cause I got to git my beauty sleep," she laughed. The porch light caught her gold tooth at the right angle and made it sparkle. "I got a hard day's work tomorrow. Tomorrow is *Vendredi*, you know? Fish day. Lordy, mercy! The cafè will be packed. *Adieu*," Delphine said, as she slipped into the darkness.

When everyone left, Bree announceu, "I'll leave the cleaning up until tomorrow. It's late. I'm too tired to clean up." She yawned.

"I'm tired, too. I'm going to bed," Tousant said, stretching and yawning.

"Havin' fish for supper tomorrow night would be nice, Bree." Farras said.

"You haven't had any fish since we have been married, have you, Farras? I know that you are Catholic, and you probably miss having fish every Friday."

"I'm not Catholic, anymore. And it don't bother me. I didn't go to 'Mass' all that much, anyway. I've gone to church more since we've been married," Farras said.

"But old habits are hard to break, huh?"

"No, it's not my habit of eatin' fish every Friday—even though *Mère* is a devout Catholic. I just heard Delphine talkin' 'bout fish, and I got a taste for some, that's all."

"I'll go to the fish market tomorrow, and buy some fish for the whole family. It'll be a nice change," Bree said.

"Don't buy catfish, buy perch, okay."

"A fish supper sounds great. I'm sorry I have to miss it," Tousant said.

"Oh, Tousant, why?" Bree asked.

"Business, my dear. I won't be going back to Houston for a few weeks."

"Another trip. You just got back a couple of weeks ago."

"I know. What can I say? All I *can* say is that I'm going to Germany." His eyes telling her he couldn't say more.

"I understand. What time are you leaving tomorrow?"

"Six o'clock in the morning."

"How long will you be gone?" she asked.

"I'll call you tomorrow night and let you know."

"Well, I better get some shut-eye if I'm going to function tomorrow," Tousant said, stretching again.

Bree reached for his hand and looked at Farras. She never knew what went on with Tousant's job, or how he would be when she saw him again. "Don't forget to set your clock, Farras." Bree said, looking into his eyes.

"All right, good night you two," Farras said. Tousant and Bree stood with their arms around each other.

CHAPTER
ELEVEN

*B*ree had just stepped out of the shower when she heard a loud banging at the back door. *That must be Oncle* Batiste, she thought. She was glad that he had come. She needed to talk. Her conversations with her uncle were always satisfying and reassuring. She hurriedly dried off, and reached for her white robe that hung on a hook behind the bathroom door. When she opened the door, her uncle stood scraping his shoes on the back steps. He held a handful of pecans. "The pecans needs pickin'." He chewed as he spoke. She looked past her uncle at the pecan tree. The nuts had fallen, and they were piled up around the tree.

"I'll get Paupon to gather the nuts up this evening." Her uncle walked past her through the door. "What! No rose today, *Oncle* Batiste?" she said, half-jokingly.

"Bree, please. I'm not in the mood." She gave him a puzzled look and followed him into her kitchen. She walked over to the stove and started a fresh pot of coffee. "I've had a grave thing to happen to me, Bree." She looked at her uncle with sympathetic eyes. "I'm scared to go away and leave you with yo' troubles." Bree looked stunned. "Okay, damn it! So I'm yo' *placeé*. I guess I always will be."

"I thought you said you were going to let me fight my own battles. You said that you wanted this town to kick my behind righteously, remember?"

"I know what I said! You don't have to remind me." He shook his head. "I'm in a mess. My heart have always been in yo' hands, but I ain't gon' meddle." He dropped his voice, and his eyes moistened. "I just wanta stick around to make sho' damn snake it's a fair fight!"

His voiced choked. Bree smiled.

"Why are you, smiling? It's horrible!" he shouted. "I'm lettin' a woman control me for the first time in my life. I ain't stayin', permanent. Just 'til your 'troubles' blows over," he added.

"What's so horrible about you staying for a while? I love you, and I think *c'est merveilleux.*" She tugged at his beard. "There are two things one can never defeat, *Oncle* Batiste—love and death." He gently slapped her hand away from his beard. "I thought you were as tough as nails as far as women were concerned. Now, I find out that you're just an old cream puff." She couldn't resist teasing him.

"Just pour up my coffee," he growled. Bree knew that her uncle was embarrassed at expressing his feelings. He held his head down, and sat fidgeting in his chair. He did not want to look at her. He pulled sharply at his ear and cleared his throat and stirred his coffee. Bree had a serious look on her face.

"It'll sure make the family happy if you stayed with us for a while. We worry about you, Uncle Batiste."

"Why worry about an old geezer like me?"

"We love you. Now, how do you like that, Mr. tough as nails?" He grunted.

But when he looked up at her, he smiled a toothy smile.

"Between the two of us, we gon' set this pitiful, little, sad-sack town ablazin' with change. Have them where they won't know their behinds from a hole in the ground."

"This town may have *us* not knowing our behinds from a hole in the ground," Bree retorted. *God, help me. Where will it all end?* she thought.

"Well, we just gon' be happy and not dwell on a damn thing," her uncle stated. He got up and danced a jig. "You sho' damn snake better believe it. You know somethin, *chèri?*" he said, sitting back down at the table. "I've read lots of books in my day. I've even read up on quite a few religious beliefs, too. But I ain't never read any books or Bibles that says a woman can have *two* husbands and live with both *husbands* under the same roof! Damn, if the three of you ain't somethin' else. I swear, you was meant to be my daughter. You sho' damn snake was meant to be."

She gave her uncle a slow smile. He smiled back at her. A few seconds later, his smile broadened, and he fell into a fit of hearty laughter. Bree looked surprised. Then she opened her mouth wide, and joined her uncle in his laughter. He pulled her up from the table, and they danced happily around in the kitchen. When their laughter subsided, they sat down at the table, held hands and looked at nothing.

After a brief silence, Bree started another topic of conversation. "When you retire, *Oncle* Batiste, will you come back to Louisiana to live?"

Her uncle let out a soft sigh, and another-world look came to his eyes. He spoke softly. "Louisiana is a place where: honey is wrapped around each spoken word, where jazz and gospel music rides together on thick, humid air and wraps itself around you like a passionate embrace, where attending Mass, *Mardi Gras,* funerals, and makin' love are the very same thing, where people can be corrupt one moment and saintly the next, where *voodoo* is a religion and the cause of everythin', where people love harder and hate harder than anywhere else on earth, where walkin' down any street can whip loneliness into a fine powder, and where just eatin' a bowl of *gumbo* can be a sexual experience—and you ask me will I come back to live in Louisiana!" When he finished talking he was winded. He had spoken rapidly and with great intensity. Bree sat with a warm smile on her face.

"Remind me never to ask that question again."

"Well, you asked this time, and I answered you this time, niece."

"I don't want to rush you, *Oncle* Batiste, but I have to get to the fish market before all the perch are sold out. Thanks to Delphine, Farras wants fish for supper tonight."

Bree had to hurry and get out into the sunshine. She felt fluid, as if she were slipping away from herself again. Her conversations no longer made any sense. Her mind felt as though it had been squeezed dry. Her uncle gave her a long look. "*Qu'est-ce que vous avez?* You look..."

"Nothing is the matter with me. I'm sorry that I have to rush you."

"Nothin' to be sorry about. You best be going. I'll see you tomorrow, niece."

"*Au revoir, Oncle* Batiste," she called after him as he walked out the door.

⚬⚬⚬

Bree walked into the fish market and was grateful that no one else was there. St. Jamesville was a Catholic town, and on Friday mornings, buying *Bourbon* street would be easier than buying fish. On Fridays, every fish in town was bought out. Being detained by her uncle had caused her to come later than she had planned. "*Bonjour, Madame* Jumppierre. Um... um...." *M'sieu* Mouton stammered in surprise. He was the owner of the fish market. He was surprised to see Bree. She had never been in his fish market before.

"Jourdan, is my second husband's name," Bree said, finishing her name for him. "*Bonjour, M'sieu* Mouton. *Comment allez-vous?*" She greeted him cheerfully.

"*Je vais bien, merci.*"

"*M'sieu* Mouton, do you have any perch?" she asked, hopefully.

"You in luck. The man just brought them in a few minutes ago. I ain't had time to put 'em out yet. I won't be open for another half hour. I have to git around to eatin' my dinner, sometimes," he chuckled, "I musta forgot to lock the front door." *M'sieu* Mouton saw disappointment on Bree's face. "But I'll go on and serve you. I'll take you in the back, and you can take yo' pick of fish. Most people like catfish, you know," he said, leading her to the back room. He gave her a quick, unreadable look.

The small room was dark and wet and smelled of mold and fish. The odor made her slightly nauseous. A small, cobwebby closed window, near the ceiling, let in streaks of dirty, diffused sunlight. *M'sieu* Mouton walked over, Bree guessed from memory, and pulled a string hanging from a naked light bulb. The brightness of the light, momentarily, blinded her. The light was too large for such a small

179

room. She stood scanning the small room without turning her head, or moving from her position in the doorway. A large, double, cement sink hung heavily from the wall. One side of the sink held catfish and the other side held perch. She stood in the archway of the door. She thought about walking out without buying the fish, but her mind fell on Farras. *M'sieu* Mouton motioned to her. She walked over and looked inside the sink. The fish lay inside the sink with a thick layer of ice covering them. "Don't smell too good in here, do it?" *M'sieu* Mouton said, seeing the frown on Bree's face. "Have to keep it damp and cool for the fish. Keep it dry; the fish'll spoil. I don't stay back here too long myself. I just haul the fish out to the front and put 'em on ice. I gits myself in a hurry too," he said smiling, showing jagged teeth. From a nail on the wall, he unhooked a white, granite pan. He rinsed the pan out and poured the water from the pan into a floor drain. He rolled up the sleeves of his plaid shirt and stood holding his pan waiting her choice of perch.

As Bree pointed out the perch she wanted, *M'sieu* Mouton reached in, picked the fish up out of the sink, and dropped the fish into his pan. She bent down, and rolled up her pants legs to prevent the bottoms from touching the floor. She noticed *M'sieu* Mouton's eyes following the movements of her body. He stood holding a perch in mid-air looking at her round behind. Perspiration ran profusely down his face, and wet circles had formed under the arms of his shirt. His facial muscles jumped spasmodically. She stood up, and started picking out her choices of perch again, but *M'sieu* Mouton did not move. He stood staring at her; resting the pan against his side, holding it in place with one arm.

Puzzled by *M'sieu* Mouton's silence, she waited. She thought that *M'sieu* Mouton was listening for the bell in front signaling him that a customer had walked in.

He walked over and stood close to her. "*Madame* Bree, listen," he whispered, his face twisted with passion. Bree moved a few paces back from him. Her heart pounded in her chest. "I ain't gon' hurt you. Just listen ta me, *Madame* Bree," he begged, his voice growing a little louder. "I'm a good man," he said, with a pleading look in his eyes. "I work hard, and I gots my own business. I know it ain't much, but I do pretty good," he said, setting the pan of fish down on the floor. *M'sieu* Mouton's face was thin, and he looked ill. But there was nothing sickly about his eyes or in his expression. He stood blocking the doorway letting his eyes roam greedily over her body. His mouth fell open as he gazed. He murmured something else under his breath that she couldn't catch. A sick fear rose in her. "I could spend a lifetime just 'maginin' what it's like for a woman ta have *two* husbands. You ought not ta go 'round tantalizin' us po' bachelors."

"*M'sieu* Mouton, keep away from me!" Bree yelled. Panicking, she continued to back away from him. She backed up against the far wall looking wildly around for another exit. But there wasn't another exit. The only way out of the room was the door that led into the market. She stood in helpless terror. She was too confused to observe anything with any accuracy.

"I wouldn't hurt you fo' nothin' in the world, *Madame* Bree. I been secretly in love 'wid you fo' a long time. I was just too scared ta say anythin'. I thought you wouldn't have me. I wanta be one of yo' *husbands*, too."

M'sieu Mouton walked, menacingly, closer to her. Bree was trapped. She looked around the small room for something to fight him off, but she saw nothing, except the sink that contained the fish. It was a terrible feeling not knowing what to say, what to do. She saw a table with a wooden top that was used as a carving block. *A carving block!* her mind screamed. *If there was a carving block, there had to be knives! But where were they?* she thought, glancing quickly around the table.

"You already gots *two* husbands. What difference would havin' *three* husbands make? I heard you at the Church meetin'. You said it was all right. I'll be good ta you, *Madame* Bree. I'll take good care of you just like yo' other *two* husbands do. I'm a easy man to git 'long with. Anybody in St. Jamesville can vouch fo' that. I can git 'long 'wid anybody. I'll git 'long with yo' other husbands. I promise," he pleaded. "I'll be good." He stood next to her with tears rolling down his cheeks. "I'm a lonely man. Please, let me be one of yo' husbands, *Madame* Bree," he kept pleading. "Oh, God, somebody needs ta tell me somethin'." *M'sieu* Mouton wrung his hands. His face was distorted by crying,. But only one tear trickled down his cheek. *His mind's snapped. He's insane,* she thought wildly. *My God, what have I done? What... have... I caused? "M'sieu* Mouton, it doesn't work that way," she explained in a patronizing tone. She didn't know which frightened her more, *M'sieu* Mouton's apparent loss of reality, or wondering whether his reaction was brought about by her having *two* husbands. She didn't know what to do because she seemed to be thinking too many thoughts at once.

"Why, it don't work that way?" he inquired. He reached out and ripped the front of her blouse open and roughly grabbed one of her breasts. His face hardened. He squeezed her breast so hard, Bree felt her chest going numb.

"Please, *M'sieu* Mouton. You're hurting me, please," she begged.

"No, you think you too good fo' *ol'* Mouton, don't you, *Miss High-Class Lady?* You and that 'high and mighty' family of yours. What's the matter? I smell too bad? You usta that fancy after-shave stuff on them *two* husbands of yours, huh? Well, I can buy myself some of that stuff too. Oh, I got it. I ain't *educated* 'nuff fo' ya'. Is that it, *Miss High-Class lady?"* he sneered.

Bree started screaming and tearing at *M'sieu* Mouton's face. He tried to put his hand over her mouth, but she bit his hand. "Oh, you little tiger you. That bitin' and kickin' and screamin' don't cut no mustard with *ol'* Mouton. He grabbed her wrist, and held it so tightly that, her whole hand throbbed and burned. "I ain't gon' rape you. All I wants fo' now is a little *tittie* feelin'." Bree stopped struggling and stood still. *M'sieu* Mouton was grinning insanely as he dug his nails deep into one of her breasts. "Now, that's mo' like it. See, *Miss High-Class Lady,* I ain't hurtin' nothin'!" His voice trembled with passion. He relaxed his grip on her wrist taking her stillness as submission. He kissed the side of her neck with chapped, full lips. She could smell the foulness of his breath as he panted.

Bree turned swiftly, reacting in a way that surprised even herself, and kicked *M'sieu* Mouton in his groin. He doubled over, and fell to his knees, howling in pain. Bree ran quickly out the door through the market to her car. "I'll git you. It ain't over. You hear, *Miss High-Class Lady.* It ain't over by a long shot!" He yelled out painfully as

Bree exited the door.

Bree sat in her car crying. She tried starting her car, but her body shook, violently. *M'sieu* Mouton's words were still echoing in her mind.

"Bree, what's the matter?" The voice spoke into the car window. Startled, she jerked her head up and looked into Deacon Hebert's face. When she saw Deacon Hebert, a fresh wave of tears wracked her body. Deacon Hebert stood looking at her not knowing what to do. He never knew what to do with other people's discomforts. For some absurd reason, other people's discomforts embarrassed him. He knew that it was not rational. He had always helped people, but always from a distance that he chose himself. He had often regretted being that way. It had stopped him from embracing his children—sometimes when his children needed it the most. But that was the way he was. He looked around for assistance, but he saw no one to relieve him.

Deacon Hebert was a tall, gangling man. Though his posture was erect, he appeared to be melted and poured into his clothes. He wore a large straw hat that made him look absent of a body. Sweating profusely, he kept casting worried looks at Bree. Finally, he reached out a shaking hand, and patted her timidly on her shoulder. "Drive me home, please," Bree begged between sobs. She tried to cover up her breasts with her hands.

Deacon Hebert felt faint. His facial muscles went spastic. He feared that he might soon pass out. With a shaking hand, he took in a deep breath, and opened her car door.

"Move over, Bree." He felt as if he were being choked by his own words. He got inside her car, but he did not start the engine. "Bree, what's the matter? What happened?" he asked, "What's wrong wid yo' clothes all tore up like that?" His voice quivered. "You sick?" She shook her head. "Well, if you ain't sick, then somethin' or somebody musta hurt you," he said. His body had finally stopped shaking. Joyous relief flooded over him. He took off his shirt, and reached in the back pocket of his pants, pulled out a handkerchief, and handed them both to her. "Maybe I should go git the police."

"*Non!*" Bree yelled. "Please, drive me home."

"Not 'til you tell me what's wrong, Bree. Maybe I can help," he added kindly.

"You cannot help me." She moaned and started crying again.

"Tell me, and let me be the judge of that," he said.

She gave Deacon Hebert a sick, defeated look. Between sobs, she told him what happened. When she looked up into his face, she saw anger. His anger surprised her. Deacon Hebert had always seemed so low-keyed to her. "I'll take care of this. You just stay here in the car," he said, reaching for the handle of the door.

"No, please. I just want to go home," Bree pleaded, holding onto Deacon Hebert's arm.

"Somethin' got to be done 'bout this, Bree. Let me get the police," he said, in a sympathetic tone.

"Non, he didn't. He held my wrist and tried to make me listen to him. He bruised my wrist," she said, holding up her hand. She was too embarrassed to tell Deacon Hebert about *M'sieu* Mouton's digging his dirty nails into her breasts, bruising her. When Deacon Hebert saw the bruises on Bree's wrist, he grabbed the handle of the door again.

"This is shameful. I watched you grow up, Bree. You just like a chile of mine. I know yo' father would do somethin' if this woulda happened to one of my daughters. He wouldn't be sittin' here mincin' words. He woulda been in there by now," he said angrily.

"No, please. My family will handle it. I want to go home now, Deacon Hebert."

"All right, but you be sho' to tell yo' *père* that I tried to help you," he said.

"I will, Deacon Hebert. Thank you."

When Deacon Hebert started backing out of the driveway of the fish market, he saw *M'sieu* Mouton peeking through the front window of his fish market. "There he is," Deacon Hebert said, pointing at the window. Bree turned her head away. "You in a lotta trouble this time, man. You just don't know how much trouble you in. You have stretched yo' good luck beyond the line now, buddy. You done mess with the wrong woman this time," Deacon Hebert said. When Bree turned and looked at *M'sieu* Mouton again, her heart raced.

"What did you say, Deacon Hebert?" she asked, with growing

excitement in her voice.

"I said *M'sieu* Mouton was in a lotta trouble," he explained, looking at her.

"No, I mean, after that. Please, try to remember. It's important. I was only half-listening to you."

"Let me see," he pondered. "Oh, I said Mouton done *messed* with the wrong woman this time. 'Cause if yo' *husbands* don't do him in, yo' *père* sho' will."

"You mean, he's done this to other women?" Bree asked, feeling a great sense of relief.

"Sho' he has. Lots of times," he answered. "He got a reputation 'round town for meddlin' with womens. That's a commonly known fact. With some he tried to do more than meddle. That Mouton's a strange, funny-actin' man. He's full plumb to the brim with *manies.*"

"Why do they let him get away with it?" Bree cried.

"Well, most of the people knows him and figure him harmless. They figure he's lonely since his wife died some years back."

"Yes, I remember when his wife died," Bree said slowly.

"Most times, the lady husband or her man friend, just talks to Mouton. I guess that stops him from foolin' with that woman, but I guess he just turns right 'round and picks on somebody else's wife or girlfriend."

"Yes, but the man is ill. He needs professional help. He's not harmless! Look what he did to me," Bree said, holding up her bruised wrist again. "It could have been worse, much worse. He could have hurt me badly. He might have even killed me! Something has to be done. He has to be reported. If *M'sieu* Mouton had been reported before, this wouldn't have happened to me!"

"Most womens knows 'bout him and keep away. They don't go in his market by theyself. They always take somebody with 'em. That's why Mouton's market always seems crowded. All of them womens don't be buyin' fish. They be watchin' out for each other."

"*M'sieu* Mouton could get overly excited and kill someone. That man's dangerous. If it does happen, the women he's attacked before would be to blame," Bree said, getting upset.

"No, they won't be the blame. They don't get the police for the same reason you want. They let their man take care of it. Besides, everybody thinks Mouton's harmless. Fortunately, it ain't happened where he done hurt nobody."

"I have to be the one to change it then," Bree replied. "Why do they continue to trade with him?"

"Cause you know he got the only fish market in town that sells fresh catfish, perch, or buffalo," he answered.

"They should go to the A&P and buy fish, or catch their own fish. That'll close *M'sieu* Mouton down."

"Well, you been in St. Jamesville all yo' life, Bree. You know these peoples. Since you married yo' *second* husband, you probably know 'em better than anybody," he said, giving her an embarrassed look. "You know, I didn't want to come to yo' house that day," he interjected. "I let 'em talk me into it. I guess I'm just weak-minded. I felt real bad after we got there. I knowed we was wrong, and I'm real sorry," he said, his voice trembled.

"The minute you entered my front door, I could tell by the way you acted that you felt bad about coming. I accepted your apology that day, and I have forgotten about your part in it. You weren't the only one talked into trying to vote me out of the Church."

"Shows you how weak-minded some people is," he said.

"I wouldn't say that. I think most members thought what they were doing was right. He has to be closed down and given help."

"Who?"

"M'sieu Mouton."

"Yes, that's true. What you gon' do 'bout it?" he asked.

"I haven't decided, but something will be done. This is a small town. I cannot understand why I didn't know about *M'sieu* Mouton," she continued.

"Yes, that's true. Because people 'round here is like Southern ice boxes. They can't keep nothin'," he chuckled. "Course the biggest portion of his customers are Catholics. Maybe they just keep they mouths closed and confess to the priest. What's that priest name that's here now?" he asked, in deep thought, trying to recall the priest's name.

"Father Andreau," Bree answered.

"Yes, that's him. Them Catholics confess everythin' to the priest. They trained that way. You were raised Catholic, Bree. You know what I'm talkin' 'bout. Maybe that explains it."

"Maybe," she said. "I'm glad to know that *M'sieu* Mouton has done this before. I don't mean glad. You... know... what I mean."

"Yes, I know exactly what you mean, Bree."

"I mean now something can be done about him," she said sharply.

"You mean that, too. But you also thought that Mouton done this to you 'cause you got *two* husbands, didn't you?" he asked.

"Yes, I did think that."

"And you thought that if he did it 'cause you got *two* husbands, maybe some other mens will do the same thang. Well, now, you can rest yo' mind. 'Cause Mouton's done it to womens with only one husband and some with no husband. Most peoples here have always respected you and yo' family. Since the meetin', they gained a lot more respect for you. I know what I'm talkin' 'bout, Bree. 'Cause you been the talk of the town all mornin'. I don't think you gon' be gittin' no mo' passes from mens that you didn't git befo'. No more than any other pretty womens gits. Whether you got one husband, *two* husbands, or none at all, don't matter."

"Thank you. I needed to hear that, Deacon Hebert."

Deacon Hebert stopped the car in Bree's driveway. "Now, you just stay put, Bree. I'll help you out of the car. I'll git you into the house safe and sound."

After they got inside the house, Bree turned to Deacon Hebert and said. "Let me give you taxi fare to go back uptown to pick up your truck."

"I won't hear of it. I'm just glad that I could help. You just go lie down and rest. I'll git somebody to take me to pick up my truck. You want me to call yo' family?" he asked.

"No, I think I'll just lie down and rest. I'll call my family later."

"You sho'. I hate leavin' you all by yo'self shook up as you is. That was a bad thang to have happen to you."

"I know it was, but I'll be all right. I'll take a couple aspirin and rest."

"You want me to stay with you a little while? I don't mind it a bit.

You just like one of my daughters. I'm so sorry that I ever had to hurt you, Bree. I guess I'm going overboard now, but I'm tryin' to make amends."

"You don't have to do that. I told you that I have forgotten about that 'church business.' One cannot move forward looking backwards," she said.

"Well, now, you know that's right," he said, walking toward the door.

She walked towards the kitchen to go upstairs to her *music box*. All she wanted was rest, aspirin, and her *music box*. "Thank you, Deacon Hebert. Thank you for everything," she said, as she climbed the stairs.

"Bree, if you need me just holler," he said, as he walked out the front door.

Bree hesitated on the stairs for a moment until she heard the door close. When she entered the bedroom, she went straight to the night stand and took out her *music box*. She sat down on the side of the bed and closed her eyes and held her *music box* to her breasts. After a few minutes, she undressed and lay naked across the bed. She lay deeply engrossed in thought. When the doorbell rang, it startled her. She lay letting the person repeatedly ring the doorbell. Annoyed, she walked into the bathroom for her robe. "All right, I'm coming!" she yelled, as she descended the stairs. The doorbell continued to ring. The constant ringing pierced her already aching head. Was peace too much to hope for?

When Bree opened her door, her father bolted past her. "I asked Deacon Hebert not to tell anyone for now. I told him that I wanted to rest," she murmured, rubbing her temples.

"Never mind all of that," her father shouted, pacing back and forth in the living-room. "Did that bastard hurt you, Bree? I'll kill him! I swear! I'll kill him! Besides your wrist, did Mouton hurt you anywhere else?" As he inquired, he lowered his voice. He looked at Bree with pain and anger and hate in his eyes. Her father's angry eyes reminded her of the eyes of the soldiers who had fought and killed in Vietnam. Her organization was still committed to go to the V.A. Hospital every weekend to serve refreshments, read, write letters, and

188

talk to the injured soldiers. They all had a desperate look, filled with hatred, in their eyes. Until she got use to it, their looks had frightened her. Now, her father had that same look in his eyes.

"No, father. He didn't hurt me any place else. He frightened me. *Père*, I was just so frightened. *M'sieu* Mouton was squeezing my wrist so tightly that he stopped the blood from circulating. But he did not *rape* me." She answered the question that her father's eyes were asking.

"Thank, God." He let out a sigh of relief. "Let me see your wrist." She reached her arm out to her father. "My God, look how bruised and swollen your wrist is," he said, turning her wrist over to look at the inside of it. "Look at all the little gashes. Mouton must have dug his fingernails into your skin." He looked closer running his finger over the broken skin. "These gashes look deep." When Bree looked at the inside of her wrist, she saw the small breaks in her skin. "Get dressed, Bree. I'm taking you to the doctor to get a *tetanus* shot. Fingernails are poisonous. Especially when they're filthy like Mouton's handling dead fish all day. There's no telling what Mouton has underneath his finger nails."

"I had a *tetanus* shot two years ago, *Père*. They're supposed to be good for five years." He pulled her gently to him and held her.

"Everything's going to be all right my little 'precious pearl.' Don't you worry. Everything will be taken care of," he assured her in a soothing voice.

"I'll call your mother. She'll come sit you. You go back and lie down and rest. I have something to do," he said, anger rose in his voice again.

"Father, please don't harm *M'sieu* Mouton. The man's sick. He needs professional help," Bree pleaded.

"He's going to need more than that when I get through with him." He pushed her back from him and walked towards the door.

"*Père!*" she begged. "Please. Let Farras or Tousant handle *M'sieu* Mouton. You're too upset. I don't want you to get into trouble.

He's not worth it," she said, her face wet with tears.

"Me! Durant Boutte! Get into trouble! Not in this town, I won't! I'm not waiting for your husbands, brothers, nobody! You're Durant

Boutte's daughter. And Durant Boutte takes care of his own!"

"Stay with me, please, father. I'm too nervous to be left alone. I took some pills to rest. *"Père, je ne me sens pas bien.* I'm afraid to be alone. I was going to call to see if I could get someone to stay with me until Farras got home, but since you're here, couldn't you just stay until Farras comes home from work. Don't call mother. You know how upset she gets. She could wreck her car." He eyed her suspiciously.

"What kind of pills did you take, Bree?" he asked.

"Three sleeping pills." She lied.

"What! Are you crazy? That'll knock you out like a light!" he said, walking back to her.

"I know," she agreed, feeling relieved.

"Why did you take three? That many could be dangerous." He placed both of his hands on her shoulders and looked deep into her eyes.

"I guess I was nervous and didn't think. Help me to the bedroom upstairs," Bree prompted, appearing weak.

"I'll stay only until Paupon comes home from school. Then I'm going to attend to that Mouton," he said, helping her up the stairs.

"Paupon, won't be coming straight home from school. He's going by a friend's house to use his microscope. Something is wrong with his microscope. Farras always gets home before Paupon does. He changed his work hours after we got married. He'll be home by three o'clock."

"Oh, yes, Farras works those funny hours."

When they walked into the bedroom, he pulled back the covers and helped her into bed. "My *music box,*" she said, looking on top of the covers. He found it near the foot of the bed and handed it to her. "Deacon Hebert told me *M'sieu* Mouton has a habit of bothering women. Did you know that, father?"

"I heard rumors of it. But you know how rumors are—lies mostly," he said, sitting at the foot of her bed. "This will be taken care of. You just close your eyes and rest. I'll be here. I won't leave this room." She was glad to hear her father say that. Because that's what she had counted on.

190

"Wonder whether he's hurt any of the other women? "

"Shhh." Her father put his finger to her lips.

As soon as Farras walked through the door, he yelled out Bree's name as he usually did. Bree got up out of bed and stood at the top of the stairs. "I'm up here, Farras," she said. She turned around and looked at her father who had sat up on the divan. He was putting his shoes back on. He had lay on the divan across from the bed. "Let me talk to him, *Père*, please," Bree begged.

"This is men's business, Bree," he replied, pushing his shirt neatly into his pants without loosening his belt. She knew she wouldn't win against them both. So she sat quietly back down on the bed.

When Farras walked into the bedroom, he was surprised to see *M'sieu* Boutte standing there. *M'sieu* Boutte immediately started telling Farras what had happened. Farras looked at her wrist. She saw the same look in Farras' eyes that she had seen in her father's eyes.

Farras ran across the room and opened the closet door. She knew that he was getting his gun. "Farras!" she screamed, "No, Farras, it's not worth it," she cried, "He's sick!"

"That bastard ain't sick!" he cursed. "You're my wife, Bree. It's worth it to me!" he yelled.

"Farras, you're acting like a wild man. Sit down for minute and let's talk," she begged.

"I tol' you once before that there was a time for talkin' and there was a time for doin'. Now, is the time for doin'!" he yelled, loading his gun.

"Father, don't let Farras leave this house with that gun," she cried.

"Farras, listen. I felt the same way you're feeling at first, but there's other ways we can deal with Mouton. I can put him out of business and have Mouton locked away for good. Take time to think the way Bree made me do."

"No!" Farras yelled, "Now git out of my way, Bree. I know why Mouton did this to you. I've been expectin' somethin' like this to happen."

"It's not what you think, Farras. I thought the same thing," Bree explained. She rushed to Farras and held him tightly around the waist.

"No, Bree. Move, now!" Farras retorted, angrily. He pulled at her arms, trying to break her grip.

"Mouton only did this because he felt that if you already had *two* husbands, then why couldn't he be number *three*, right!" he yelled.

"No, Farras. Son, you have it all wrong," *M'sieu* Boutte protested. "He's done this to lots of women before."

"Deacon Hebert told me the same thing, Farras," Bree added. "He said that *M'sieu* Mouton had a habit of doing this sort of thing to women. That's why the women won't go into his fish market alone. I didn't know about *M'sieu* Mouton, Farras." Farras sat down on the divan.

"Then why wasn't anythin' ever done 'bout him?" he asked, looking at her father.

"I thought it was just rumors, hearsay."

"Okay, let's go talk to Mouton, now! We can figure on how to stop him permanently later," Farras said, unloading the gun and putting it back into the closet.

"Let's go," Farras said. "You stay here, Bree." he ordered. When Farras and her father left, Bree nervously paced the floor.

Farras walked up to the doors of the fish market and kicked the door open. *M'sieu* Mouton was behind the counter waiting on customers. The market was crowded. When *M'sieu* Mouton looked up and saw Farras and *M'sieu* Boutte, he looked at them as though he had expected them. Farras jumped over the counter in one motion. He grabbed the front of *M'sieu* Mouton's shirt, and twisted it close up to his throat. The customers stood watching in silence. "If you ever touch my wife again, I'll kill you!" Farras threatened. He twisted *M'sieu* Mouton's shirt even tighter. He held *M'sieu* Mouton's shirt so tight that he could hear the material of the shirt tearing. He let go of *M'sieu* Mouton's shirt, grabbed him around his neck, and started choking him. *M'sieu* Mouton tried to pull away from him. The two men stumbled against the wall behind them. Farras continued to choke *M'sieu* Mouton. He started bumping *M'sieu* Mouton's head against the wall. "Don't ever touch my wife again, Mouton," Farras kept repeating. He bumped *M'sieu* Mouton's head against the wall with each word. *M'sieu* Mouton screamed.

"I ain't hurt yo' wife, man." *M'sieu* Mouton screamed, trying to get away from Farras.

"My wife don't lie to me, Mouton. You just called my wife a liar!" Farras hissed through clenched teeth. He banged *M'sieu* Mouton repeatedly in his face and stomach with his fist. Finally, Farras hit him such a hard blow that, *M'sieu* Mouton staggered crazily around before sliding to the floor. Farras kicked him and spat in his bloody face. When Farras walked from behind the counter, *M'sieu* Mouton lay tattered and bloody, moaning. Farras turned around, but *M'sieu* Boutte held him back. "Come on, son. I think he's got the message. He'll never sell another fish in this town. He may as well hang up his 'out-of-business sign'."

As Farras and *M'sieu* Boutte walked out the front door, they overheard a customer say 'I've always held the utmost regards for *Madame* Bree, myself.'

When Farras returned home, he walked through the kitchen where Bree was nervously trying to prepare supper. He glanced at her and walked upstairs to their bedroom. Bree slid the lid back on the pot and followed him. When she entered their bedroom, Farras lay full length on the bed. She stood beside the bed looking down at him. "Supper will be ready, soon. Are you hungry?" she asked.

"No," he said, turning his back to her. She had noticed blood on the front of his shirt.

"Are you hurt?"

"No, I knocked a little skin off my hand that's all," he answered. His voice was muffled by his face being pushed into the pillow. "I don't want Tousant to hear 'bout this, Bree. I take care of the 'physical' part of you, remember. Promise me. I have to know before I..." he stopped, not finishing his statement. "Before you what?" she asked.

"Nothin'."

"Let me see your hand. I better see after it. You wouldn't want it to get infected. Which hand is it, Farras? The right one?" she asked, reaching for his right hand.

"Leave me alone, Bree! he said angrily. "I tol' you my hand's all right," he yelled. He lay breathing heavily.

"Let me be the judge of that, Mister," she replied, going toward the bathroom.

"I said, my hand's all right, dammit!" he yelled at her again.

Farras raised himself in a sitting position, and leaned his back against the headboard. *"Je suis navre,"* Farras. *Qu'est-ce qu'il y a?"* I was only trying to help," she said softly.

"Yes, yes. I know you, Bree. You always the one who wants to talk. Now, I want to talk. Sit down," he said, patting the bed. He moved over. She came around the bed and sat down. She tried to read the look on Farras' face, the look in his eyes, but she couldn't. She had never seen this side of Farras before. "We've always stressed being honest with each other, right!" he began.

"That's the only way it can be, Farras."

"I'm leavin' you, Bree," he said abruptly.

"You, what!" she exclaimed.

"I said, I'm leavin' you," he repeated.

"Are you serious, Farras? *Vous vousmoquez de moi.*"

"You know I wouldn't joke 'bout anythin' this important."

"Why? Is it because of what happened today?" Even though Bree's voice sounded calm, she felt faint.

"Partly, but I've been thinkin' 'bout leavin' you for over a week."

"I never saw any indication that..." She moved back from him as though she had been struck.

"That's because I wasn't sho'. I didn't want to tell you 'til I was sho'. It woulda only confused me, us," he said.

"And all this time I thought you were at peace," she remarked.

"I've had more peace with you than I ever had in my life, Bree." He reached out and touched her face.

"You can still be at peace, Farras," she whispered softly. "You can still remain part of this family. It was something you said you have always wanted. Do you still love me? Have you fallen out of love with me?" she asked. Tears formed in her eyes.

"Lord, lord, no," he whispered. "I love you more than anythin'. More than my own life."

"Then what is it? *Qu'est-ce que tu as,* Farras?"

"This set-up is causin' too much pain, too much sufferin', and too many embarrassments." Farras spoke quickly.

"This is your family too, Farras. You have suffered, too."

"Not as much as the three of you."

"We knew from the start there would be pain," Bree reminded him.

"Gossip, yes. But, my God, not all of this!" he moaned.

"I never thought you were a quitter, Farras."

"I ain't no quitter, Bree!" he protested. "It's just hard for a man to see people he loves suffer so. I want to protect you from pain, not cause it."

"That's what a family is all about, Farras. Family is about sharing everything: the pain, the joy, and the love."

"I want to give you up befo' any more pain is brought down on this family."

"Then Tousant should have left me, too."

"Tousant stayed, but look at what he had to give up, Bree. Don't you know deep inside of Tousant he's sufferin'. He's endurin' it because of his love for you. Every night that we walk up them stairs together, Tousant suffers. Can't you see that's what I'm doin' too? I'm willin' to give you up. Even though it feels like the pain is gon' kill me. Maybe then this family will be at peace."

"I cannot be at peace without you, Farras. I love you. Just as I cannot be happy without Tousant because I love him. Our love for each other will see us through all of this. Do you know how pearls are made? They're made when irritants get into the shell of the oyster. The oyster secretes a fluid to wash the irritant away. And after a while, a pearl is formed. Something of beauty results from the oyster's pain. We have to be patient, Farras. I believe our love is as solid as the earth and as enduring," Bree persisted.

"'Dems just words, Bree!" She sat transfixed staring at him. Her temples were pulsating rapidly as though drums were being played inside her head. "My decision to leave, stands, Bree."

"*D'accord*," she whispered.

"*D'accord.* Is that all you have to say?" Farras asked, obviously shocked by her reaction.

"What else is there for me to say, Farras? I don't want you to stay if you've decided to leave."

An Unholy Alliance

"So, I guess that's that," Farras said slowly.

"I don't own you, Farras. But I am hurting. My heart is busting loose. We have tried, and we have failed." Farras gave her a long, hard look.

"I better start packin'."

"*D'accord.*" She turned and walked unsteadily out of the bedroom. "I won't hide. I'll be sitting in the living-room."

As Farras packed, he tried hard to avoid thinking of what his life would be like without Bree, Tousant, and Paupon. He pushed the confusing thought from his mind and started packing faster.

When Farras walked into the living-room, Bree was sitting on the divan, her *music box* lay in her lap. "I'm gonna load my car. I really don't have that much," Farras said solemnly.

"Do you need help?"

"No, I'll manage."

After Farras finished loading his belongings into his car, he stood in the living-room holding his black saxophone case. "Had to take this last. I wanta place it in the car real careful." He tried to chuckle but it came out as a grunt. I..."

"Don't, Farras, please!" Bree sobbed. "Just leave." They stared at each other in silence. The space between them was electrified with pain.

Farras walked out the front door without looking back. Moments later, Bree could hear his car pulling out of the driveway. "Now, what?" she asked herself. Her voice choked. She stood up, then immediately sank back down on the divan and then immediately got up again. Farras was gone. She had come to rely on Farras. She loved him. She ran wildly out of the house and wandered aimlessly about the backyard. She turned swiftly and ran weeping towards the levee. Once more, Bree felt the heavy weight of her decision. Had everyone been right all along, and had she been wrong? She fell down amongst the tall weeds, and wondered how she could stop the disaster, the disgrace, the humiliation. As she wept, the melody from her *music box* played softly. *"An unholy alliance,"* she sobbed. Her words were carried away by the wind. She lay sobbing on the hard, unyielding ground.

CHAPTER
TWELVE

*F*arras sped away with no thoughts of where he was going. All he could think of was the mess that he had made of his life. It occurred to him then that he may not have intended for his marriage to work with Bree. He didn't know what his intentions were. At that moment, he couldn't even understand what his feelings were. Everything was just too confusing. Suddenly, he felt a tightness in his chest that threatened to shut off his breathing.

Thirty minutes later, Farras slammed on his brakes, scattering rocks and dirt. When the dust cleared, he realized that he was at the *Blue Door, a* rowdy nightclub frequented almost exclusively by men who cut and haul pulpwood; men who had seen hard times and relished them. Farras sat staring blankly at the closed door of the nightclub. The front and side windows were open, and he could hear a woman laugh loud and boisterous. From the juke box, a well-known blues singer was asking a sad and hurtful question:

> *"Do ya' feeel like dyyyin'?*
> *Oooh, can't stop yo' heart*
> *from crrryin'...*
> *'cause the shoes of bluuues is walkin'*
> *all over you..."*

Farras exhaled and grunted. The first blues song ended. Then the Blues singer's sad and hurtful voice cried out again:

"Oooh, I done ya' wrooong, baby.
And I swear ta God, I don't know whhhy....
Yeees, I done ya' wrong, I done ya' wrooong..."

He had left Bree. So why did he feel waves of him being deserted washing over him again and again; breaking up whole things inside of him? Later, shoutings of a friendly-sounding argument drifted in through his open car window and pushed the feeling away.

A truck pulled noisily up behind Farras' car. Metal scraped against metal, as the old, one fender, rusty truck screeched to a stop behind Farras' car, blocking his car in the graveled parking lot. Annoyed, Farras jerked his head quickly around ready to protest the driver's inconsideration, but the appearance of the driver and his two companions stopped him. He vaguely recognized one of the men from his many years of playing music in every type of nightclub that could be imagined. He had seen their rough type many times. They were men who wouldn't go to work on Monday mornings without a swollen lip, black eye, or a bodily cut. They showed and bragged about how many stitches it took to patch them up. He gave a light bang to his steering wheel, and cursed at himself for ending up at a place like the *Blue Door,* euphemistically known as: *The Bucket of Blood.* He looked in his rear-view mirror at the three men. They had stopped and were shoving their dirty shirts neatly down inside their grimy, work pants. They stood publicly with unzipped pants and loose belts. The three men had hot, tired looks on their scarred faces. Faces that appeared to Farras to have never been washed. The three men stood silent, occasionally glancing around them. Farras cursed underneath his breath at himself again. "Out of all the nice, comfortable nightclubs between here and home, why did I choose this hell hole? I must have a secret desire for total destruction," he murmured. "Maybe I don't want to live anymore." He thought about how useless he already felt without Bree. "Maybe that's the reason I came here," he murmured. *Now, why would I say somethin' that stupid?* he thought. *That's the stupid shit comin' out of me from bein' around Bree too long and 'dem damn books of hers. She got me*

198

believin' that psychology bullshit she's always readin' and talkin' 'bout. "Analyzin things," *she calls it. Shit on that bullshit! I wanta live!* he almost screamed out. "I just need a few shots of whiskey to make me mellow like the old Farras."

Farras opened his car door quickly almost hitting one of the three men. He stopped, sitting half-frozen in his position with one foot on the ground, and the other foot still in his car.

"Hey, man, what the fuck you tryin' ta prove? You musta come here to git a grand, ol' ass whoopin', huh?" one of the men asked, glaring at him. The man grabbed the upper corner of Farras' car door. With yellowish, popped-eyes, he held the door with a firm, angry grip. Farras could see veins running like black snakes on the back of his sweaty hand. The man's neck muscles bulged, and saliva had formed at the corners of his mouth.

"Hey, man. No harm was done, no harm was intended," Farras said, staring fixedly into the man's eyes. He never was a man to cause trouble, but he had never run from trouble, either. He had no qualms about holding his own with one, maybe even two of them, but not three! The thought knotted his stomach, and made it quiver. One of the three men walked over to a large fire ant mound and gave it a swift, hard kick. Farras tried to keep the man in his line of vision, and at the same time, keep his eyes focused on the man who still held his car door. The man walked back, and stood next to his companion at his car door.

"Let that som' bitch outa his car," he said, with a deadly edge in his voice. He hawked up a mouthful of phlegm and spat it out near Farras' foot.

"Well, let's just go fo' broke, baby," Farras said. Still looking at the three men, he slid cautiously out of his car. Once both his feet were firmly on the ground, he took a few steps backwards hoping to get clear of his car, out in the open. When he was clear of his car, he stopped and said, "My papa always said if a man's gotta die, he at least ought to do it standin' up." Farras bit down so hard on his teeth that his jaw bones moved in and out. He stood there in a kind of stupefaction, waiting for the three men to make their move.

"Hey, man, wait," the third man said. "I think I know this *Cat.*"

He pointed a dirty, work-worn finger up and down at Farras' chest. He looked at Farras, curiously. "Man, I know yo' ass from somewheres." Farras stood, muscles flexed, ready for any action that called to be taken. He didn't know whether his past encounter with the man had been a good one or not, so he kept his fighting stance. A fighting stance he hoped would give him good balance, and a chance to at least hold his own until... *until what?* he told himself. *Until help came! But he knew no help would come, not at the Blue Door! A chance to prolong his dying would be more accurate. No ambulance would come, either. He knew that for sure, too. Maybe a hearse! But he even doubted that.* The man's two companions stood, legs apart, with their fist balled waiting for a verdict from their friend. "I got it. Damn it! I got it!" the man finally said, snapping his fingers in recognition. "You the *Cat* that blows *sax*, ain't you? Uh, the Kingpins, right?" His face broke into a wide grin. "Do ya' know yo' band's 'sponsible for me havin' the sweet woman I got now?" He laughed, slapping Farras on the shoulder. Farras relaxed, slightly. Still distrustful, he kept a steady gaze on the three men. He didn't know whether it was a game being played on him to catch him off guard. "I had been after that woman for months, man. Then one Friday night, I saw her here at the *Door*." he said, jerking his head toward the nightclub. "I tol' her that the Kingpins was playin' over in *La Place*, and I asked her if she wanted to go to *LaPlace* with me. Man, that woman's sho' crazy 'bout the Kingpins. She just loves ya'll music. Wished I knowed that befo'. Sho' woulda saved me a heapa time and money," he laughed, almost hugging Farras. The other two men stood, their arms folded, listening intently. "Man, that night ya'll *Cats* sho' bump som' rump. God knows ya'll did. Man, that woman got a few drinks in her, and we started groovin' offa that mellow sound ya'll was makin'. We danced and danced, man, cheek to cheek. Me sweet talkin' that woman the hol' time." He started dancing around, holding one hand on his stomach, and holding his other arm out and curved in front of him. He was a tall, raw-boned man, and when he swung himself around, his arms and legs appeared disjointed. "I still got that sweet woman too, man. Come on, let's let them bottles behind that bar do some clinkin'. Now, dat's a mellow sound too, ain't it?" He laughed uproariously. "Hey, ya'll come here and shake my man's hand." The two men reached out, and pumped Farras' hand as if nothing had occurred, as if they had just walked up and spotted a long lost friend. The four men walked towards the front door of the nightclub.

When they entered the nightclub, the three men walked directly to the bar and spoke to the bartender in a friendly, familiar manner. Still not trusting his new-found companions, Farras hesitated inside the door. He looked around the nightclub for a familiar face, but in the dim light, he couldn't recognize anyone. Putting up a relaxed front, Farras strolled lazily to the bar, and sat down next to the man who had recognized him. "Hey, man. What's yo' name?"

"Farras Jourdan."

"Damn, if it ain't. Now, I remember. Hey, Scamp. Give my man, Farras, his poison," he said, to the bartender. He pointed at the bartender in the same manner that he had pointed at Farras outside. Farras guessed it to be a nervous habit since the pointing fingers seemed to jerk nervously up and down. "My name's Fin. Just plain ol' *Fightin' Fin.*" He let out a howl of laughter, banging his fist on the bar. "Gimmie 'nother drink, bartender! Gotdamit!"

Farras became more relaxed, but he still wasn't comfortable. He didn't like the unhealthiness of the atmosphere the nightclub seemed to project. He had made up his mind to leave as soon as he felt right in leaving.

The three men started talking about trucks and trees. While their attention was focused on each other, Farras looked around the nightclub again. His eyes lingered on the strange faces.

The front door opened letting in the outside daylight. Two women walked in. One of the women said something to the other one and walked in the direction of the ladies' room. The other woman walked swiftly to the bar with a serious look on her face. She was an attractive woman, but harsh looking, life beaten. Farras thought her too plump, but he eyed her longer than he wanted to or had intended. The woman sat at the bar, and she spoke to the bartender with the same familiarity as the three men. "Hey Pudgy, you ain't speakin' this even'?" one of Fighting Fin's companions asked.

"If M'sieu Farras Jourdan can sit here without speakin', I guess I can too," she said, looking around at Farras. He turned around on the bar stool and faced her. "I just got off work, and I'm hot and tired. I need a drink just like ya'll," she said. She was looking at Farras, but she directed her words to the three men.

"You know me?" Farras asked.

"Hell, yes," she said smiling.

"From my music." It was a statement rather than a question.

"You got it, handsome." Farras couldn't help being flattered. He hadn't thought his band different or better than the other bands in the area. But it appeared that they were. "I heard the news already, you know," she said. "It's a small town. News travels fast. Besides, the clothes in yo' car tells it all anyway." Her voice had softened as she spoke. "Why don't we go over to a table and talk," she said, her eyes on a table in the farthest corner from the bar.

"If you like. I ain't never not been gracious to a lady," Farras said smiling, as he slid off the bar stool.

Pudgy walked slightly ahead, glancing back at him as she walked. She chose a table down from the bar in a corner. She didn't wait for Farras to seat her. She pulled out a chair that positioned her back to the bar. As soon as they sat down, the second woman came out of the ladies' room. She walked towards them looking puzzled. Pudgy gave her friend a quick sign. And her friend turned quickly, almost making an about-face, and walked towards the bar. She sat down on the last stool that was farthest from the front door, looking annoyed. "That's my best friend, Elsie. She thinks I'm too good for the mens around here," Pudgy said.

"Are you?"

"Well, I don't know. That depends," she said, looking dreamily into Farras' face. "I know you a gentleman and probably wanted to seat me, but I ain't in no mood to look at Elsie's ugly, screwed-up face," she chuckled. Farras nodded. He preferred to sit facing the bar, anyway. His band had played in nightclubs like the *Blue Door,* but he had been up on the bandstand away from the people, which offered him some measure of protection. The atmosphere in the nightclub made his spine tingle. He felt fear and excitement at the same time.

202

The feeling both electrified and depressed him. It was a feeling he had never experienced together before. He loved and hated the feeling. He wanted desperately to stay and he desperately wanted to leave. He remained seated. "You know what, Farras? I been waitin' for this 'shit' to happen. No, not waitin', hopin'. I had hopes of this 'shit' happenin'. I knew you'd come to yo' senses sooner or later. You too much of a man to have to deal with a hassle like that. A man like you needs a woman of his own." Pudgy said her words purringly rather than speaking them outright.

"What you talkin' 'bout?" Farras asked, getting angry. With Bree, he paid strict attention to how he spoke, but with Pudgy he felt no need.

"Hurt that bad, huh," Pudgy said. A pained expression crossed her face, as if she were reminiscing.

"Yes," Farras whispered.

"*Madame* Bree may be too much woman fo' one man, but she sho' ain't woman enough for *two* mens," Pudgy said hatefully. "Don't she know there's a shortage of Black mens? She probably don't care. She should feel guilty. But I just bet she don't!" Pudgy spat. "Madame Bree's just a greedy woman. She wants it all. Well, she can't have it all!" Pudgy's face was contorted by rage.

"Shut up, bitch!" Farras growled. "Cause you don't know what the hell you're talkin' 'bout." Farras' eyes blazed.

"Hoa, let me make myself clear, Farras. I ain't bad-mouthin' *Miss High-Class* lady. I was just tryin' to ease the hurt. Take some of yo' pain away," she explained.

"Well, it damn sho' didn't sound like that," Farras said. Some of the tension drained from his face. "How come they call you Pudgy, anyway?" Farras asked, trying to steer their conversation away from Bree.

"Well, now, honey, where's yo' eyes?" she laughed. "Can't you see why?"

"Yes, I guess I can. You are... well... pleasingly plump, as they say." They both laughed.

"I can help you forget *Madame* Bree, Farras. "I'm good to my mens," Pudgy broke in, cutting off her laugh.

"What makes you think I wanta forget?" Farras asked.

"Cause you hurt. And nobody likes to hurt, not even you, Farras."

"You can't make me forget Bree, Pudgy," Farras stated blankly, ignoring her remarks. "No power on this earth can do that," he said, a distant look in his eyes.

"I think you scared to let me try, Farras. You scared I might succeed. That *high-class lady* got you less inclined to try new things?"

"It's not a question of being scared or less inclined, Pudgy. You seem nice enough. It just wouldn't be fair to you, that's all. I don't wanta hurt you."

"You let Pudgy worry 'bout her own feelin's, sweet thang. I can handle it. I know what I'm gittin' myself into. I can take care of myself." Farras sensed the deep need in her, a need that probably ran as deep as the pits of *hell*.

"I can see why yo' friend Elsie worries 'bout you, Pudgy."

"What do you mean?" she asked, rapidly blinking her eyelids.

"I mean, you don't know me. Yet yo' needs are forcin' you to take me in. What you actually sayin' is, that you'll deal 'wid me anyway you can git me. I bet befo' now, you never even thought 'bout, Farras Jourdan. You may have seen or heard me blow *sax*. But that's 'bout it."

"Now, that's where you wrong, Farras. I've wanted you in the worst way every since I first saw you up on that bandstand," she nodded her head towards the empty bandstand. "Every since the very first time I heard the mellow sounds you can make blowin' that *sax* of yours."

"So you a musician, lovin' freak? There's lots of womens who loves nothin' but musicians. Seein' musicians up there on that bandstand must give 'em some kinda sick thrill. Maybe womens like you looks upon a musician's hard instrument like it's a extension of they dicks! But *bèbè*, the instruments are also very *cold!* Maybe you in love with the 'junk and jive' most musicians prides theyself in talkin'."

"But you're not just a musician, Farras. You go to work on the docks everyday. And workin' on the docks ain't easy. I must admit that you being a musician do help thangs, too. I love nightclubs. I can follow you 'round on weekends. We both can have a good time, Farras. From what I understand, you never got... I mean... you never got *Madame* Bree to go 'wid you. She's above it, I guess." Farras gave her a cold look, but he made no comment on her remarks. "That whole family lives in a different world than we do, Farras. It's a world where peoples like you and me don't fit. You had *faire monts et merveilles.* She was makin' you into somethin' you ain't, Farras.

"That's a lie! And you shut the fuck up! 'Cause you don't know what the hell you're talkin' 'bout. I done tol' you that! Why you got to 'dog' another woman to git yo'self a man, huh?" Farras' heart felt like it had literally been broken, and he didn't want to, nor did he need to, think about the source of his pain.

"Farras, don't git mad with me. All I meant was.... Well... look... you need somebody right now, and I need somebody right now. That's all I meant, *bèbè.* I know it'll be right fo' us. 'Cause we cut from the same cloth."

"How do you know what kinda cloth I'm cut from, Pudgy? Hell, you don't even know me! You don't know what the 'shit' I'm cut from."

"Look, Farras. Just spend the night with me. If thangs ain't right by mornin', you move on. Fair enough." The need in Pudgy's eyes, and the desperation in her voice, made Farras both despise and pity her. He hated weak, desperate women. They clung dangerously close to their men, choking them, shutting off their air and space. But he wanted to be, needed to be, soothed and stroked. He accepted Pudgy's offer. His acceptance of her offer was not done with words. He answered her with his eyes and by his facial expression. Joy flew into Pudgy's eyes. Her eyes grew wild and strange like a half-starved animal. Farras' pity surfaced.

"Long as you know what you're doin', Pudgy. I ain't got nothin' to lose, *bèbè. "* Farras said.

"I know what I'm doin'."

"Okay," Farras said slowly, "let's go."

They got up to leave. Farras quickly gulped down his drink. When they passed by the bar, Elsie rolled her eyes at Pudgy, and she gave

Farras a look of pure hate. "You sho' yo' friend, Elsie, is all right? I mean she do like men, don't she?"

"Oh, Elsie's all right in that department. If she wasn't, we wouldn't be friends. She's been hurt a lot by mens, too. We just kinda took to lookin' out for each other."

"Oh, 'cause, man! The look that woman gave me, whew!"

As they approached the three men, all three turned sideways on their stools. They paused, holding their drinks in their hands and looked at them. Then they turned back to the bar, and proceeded with their mission of getting drunk, rowdy, and mean enough to bash in some person's skull. "See ya' my man," Farras said to *Fighting Fin*, as they reached the front door.

"Yeah, man. See ya' on the bandstand," *Fightin' Fin* said. "Don't break no flo' boards," he added. They all laughed.

"Hey, Elsie. Everythin's cool," Pudgy said, reassuringly as she passed by her friend.

"Cool," Elsie said, lifting up her glass.

When Pudgy and Farras stepped outside, it was just beginning to get dark. It surprised Farras. It didn't seem to him that he had been in the nightclub that long. "Hey, Pudgy. You gon' have to walk home. My car is jammed full of clothes, as you can see." Farras said, making a slight bow at his car.

"So, I see. No, problem. I can walk. I just live 'round the corner anyway. Just a two minute walk from here. I live above *M'sieu* Morant's grocery store. Well, actually behind the store, upstairs. Do you know where it is, Farras?"

"Yep, the band stops in there sometimes to buy some of that good baloney meat and crackers befo' a gig," he said laughing.

"You go on ahead then. There's a place to park yo' car by the stairs. Sit in yo' car and wait for me, all right."

"Whatever pleases the lady."

When Pudgy walked up, Farras had got out of his car, and was sitting on her bottom step. She smiled, as she searched through her pocketbook for her door key. "Sho' you don't want to back out on this deal?" Farras asked.

"I'm sho'," she replied, unlocking the door. "My place ain't much to look at, Farras. It's nothin' like that palace you just came from. But it's clean."

"You ever seen inside Bree's house, Pudgy?" Farras asked angrily.

"No, but I don't need to. I heard enough talk 'bout it. Seein' the outside of the house is enough, anyway."

When they stepped inside the door, Pudgy walked straight to her bed, and threw her pocketbook down on it. She sat on the side of the bed, and pulled off her shoes.

Farras stood inside Pudgy's door. He wasn't surprised by what he saw. Pudgy's house looked exactly as he had expected. He had been inside enough women's houses to know exactly what he would see— clean rooms, sparsely furnished.

"Come and lie down, Farras. Rest yo' self. See it ain't so bad, is it?" Her voice sounded desperate to Farras. But this time, her voice had the reverse effect on him. It made him despise her. A strong urge washed over him to hit her. He saw a distasteful 'something' in Pudgy, and he wanted to destroy it, kill it! He stood in his spot trying to void his hatred for her. But a few seconds later, he wanted to cleanse her, to make her whole and healthy. "You hungry, Farras, *bèbè?* I cooked some good ol' greens and corn bread, yesterday. It'll only take me a few minutes to warm it up. I don't know why I cooks so much food when it's just me. I guess it's because I came from a large family—eleven of us. It's habit. I did all the cooking for the family when I was growing up."

While Pudgy idly chattered, Farras stood looking at her bed. He still stood in the same spot at the door. Finally, he walked over to Pudgy's bed and sat down. The springs squeaked noisily under his weight. He didn't know what had drawn him to her bed. Weariness, or just wanting to fuck away his pain. He sat watching her. Her movements weren't graceful like Bree's. Her movements were awkward, like the movements of a young girl trying to impress her first boyfriend, but didn't know how to go about it.

"Farras, I bet you ain't had no good 'soul food' since you left yo' mama's house." Her words jolted his thoughts. Farras was irritated by Pudgy's insinuation, but he said nothing.

Pudgy prepared a good meal, and Farras ate heartily. He rose from the table and said, "I'd like to take a bath, Pudgy, if you don't mind," he added.

"Mind! I'm hopin' that this will become yo' home, remember." Loathing crept into his mind. He shook his head slightly, as if to physically shake the feeling away.

"I'll just go git some things out of my car."

"You need help?" she asked, rising from the table.

"No," he said, rushing out the door, not allowing her to pursue her intent.

Farras lay in the bed listening to the sounds coming from the bathroom. Pudgy had finished cleaning up the kitchen, and was taking her bath. He wished that she would hurry. He lay holding one hand over his erected penis. It wasn't that he desired Pudgy, he just wanted to have an *orgasm* to release some of his pent-up pain.

Pudgy walked out of the bathroom naked. Her eyes passed longingly over the full length of Farras' body. He looked at her body, and fought the urge to compare her body with Bree's, but couldn't. Bree's body was soft, the ultimate of femininity. Life had not touched her harshly, but had touched her lovingly and protectively. This enabled Bree to love a man beyond any love most women could even comprehend. Because life tarnished Bree's type of love early in most women. Bree's love was total. She had given him the type of love that a woman like Pudgy could never hope to match.

When Pudgy got into bed, she started kneading and kissing Farras' genitals. He lay fighting down the image of Bree, trying to grasp the pleasures Pudgy's hands and lips offered him. *God, let me feel sweet pleasure,* he thought. He rolled over to his side and drew up one leg.

"*Bèbè,* if you don't want to work, Pudgy will take care of you. You'll see. You won't have nothin' to worry 'bout." Farras froze. For a minute, he lay fighting a feeling of nausea. Finally, he sat up, and pushed Pudgy roughly away from him.

"So you wanta kill my ass with a big dose of nice, 'balls-killin' poison, huh. You want to make me a 'pussy slave' instead of a man!" Once Farras' emotions got wound up, his words were stinging, and ran swiftly like water rushing over a broken dam. "You wanta choke me, not let me breathe. What you want to do is strip me of my manhood and my pride and ruin me!"

"No, baby, wait! What I meant was..."

"What you meant is what I just said! You're not a woman. I don't know what you are. You uses yo' body to entice men to their death. You must be a goddamn black widow spider! And you surprised at not keepin' a man." He got up and started getting dressed. Pudgy lay whimpering.

"No, no, Farras."

"Yes, yes, Pudgy! Now, I know why I'd rather live in h*ell* with Bree than to die in *heaven* with a woman like you. Bree knows that I'm a man!" he yelled. "She respects me as a man. She wouldn't tolerate anythin' less. That's somethin' that a woman like you can't begin to understand. What I feel, what I think, matters to Bree. But you don't understand that, do you, Pudgy? Women like you always come down hard on women like Bree. My advice to you is, you better try like hell to git like her!"

"Farras, please," Pudgy begged.

"Please, what! That's another thing Bree would never do—beg a man or anybody else. And me with my dumb ass 'bout to give her 'sweet thang' away to somebody who don't even know what they gittin'. I'm goin' home!"

"Teach me, Farras. I'll learn what it takes to satisfy you, I swear."

"Jesus teaches fools, Pudgy."

He walked out of Pudgy's door leaving her heaving in violent sobs. He sat behind the steering wheel of his car, drained. He leaned his face against the cool glass of his car window. Now, he understood what his mother had been saying all these years. 'Son, sometimes a person have to be mean in order to be kind.' He had not wanted to hurt Pudgy. She seemed to have a heart of gold. But he had to show her that nobody had to accept less than they deserved. And as long as they kept their self-respect in tact, they didn't need to grasp at straws! "Self-respect was something a person oughta be buried with," Farras stated emotionless. Somewhere down the line, Pudgy had lost her self-respect. And he had wanted to knock her brains loose, so she would look for it. "Maybe I went 'bout it all wrong." His words fell dead in the dark stillness of his car. He exhaled deeply. A person have to have somethin' to hang onto. He looked up at the stairs and imagined seeing Pudgy naked; suspended in mid-air with nothing for her to hang onto, and finally floating off into oblivion. Hell, she had Elsie! But the thought made him sad. "Shit! I ain't no goddamn psychiatrist!" he bellowed, as he drove out of the dark, narrow alley, his car tires shrieking in the night.

Bree walked in the dark towards her house. As she drew nearer, she saw a small, red flicker of light. At first glance, she mistook the light for a firefly. But as she drew nearer, she saw the dark outline of a human figure and recognized the red flicker as a lighted cigarette. "Where you been, Bree? I been worried sick."

"Farras," she whispered. She could not tell him that she had lay for hours amongst the weeds, motionless, wishing for death.

"It sho' ain't no ghost," he said laughing.

"Oh, Farras. I thought that..."

"Oh, shut up," he teased, "I tol' you you talk too much." He pulled her into his arms. "Damn that old car. I got to put my car back in the shop. I didn't git three mile before it quit on me."

"Stop lying, Farras," Bree laughed.

"Okay, I'm lyin'," he laughed.

"Oh, good Lord. What time is it? I have got to get supper ready," Bree said, pulling away from him. "Paupon, where..."

"Slow down, Bree. I sent Paupon to yo' mother's for the night. And as for supper, we won't have time for that. Come to me, Mrs. Jumppierre-Jourdan," Farras said, with love and passion in his voice. They walked into their bedroom and closed the door.

CHAPTER
THIRTEEN

Ella Guidry-Harrison

Occasionally, lightening lit up the house. A loud clap of thunder had awakened Bree. She had always found it difficult to sleep in stormy weather. She gave a quick look at Farras sleeping peacefully and walked softly downstairs to the kitchen. She tried to turn on the kitchen light, but the severity of the electrical storm had knocked off the power. She reached up into the kitchen cabinet for two candles and lit them. She walked through the dining room into the living room and placed the two lighted candles on the mantle above the fireplace. She knew going back to bed was futile.

The steady, ticking sound of the grandfather clock seemed magnified a hundred times in the quiet room. The yellow light of the candles blended the furnishings in the living-room into one flickering, oblong shadow. The shadow steadied itself on the wall behind her. Somewhere near, a lightening bolt struck something, and the whole house shivered, as if cringing in fear. When she was a child, her Uncle Batiste had told her that lightening was God's flash bulb. He said that, periodically, God took pictures of mankind's wickedness. And each picture that God took, sickened Him. When God got sick and tired of man's wickedness, He would vomit on the earth and end man's existence. As she sat listening to the strong winds and the pouring rain, she felt sick to her stomach at how close she came to losing Farras. She imagined God having that same "sick to the stomach" feeling.

211

All during the next morning it rained heavily. By evening, the rain had stopped, and a foggy, gray wetness hung in the air. Tousant arrived home that Friday evening, exhausted. He had gone to bed earlier than usual. His body twitched and jerked in his sleep; he was in the grips of a terrible nightmare. Miniature, steel-colored men ran around his ankles taking painful bites out of his flesh on each pass, and their momentum was gradually increasing. And as their momentum increased, bright, red, translucent bubbles expanded larger and larger from their ears; threatening to enclose their heads. A voice; then pellets... no, stones... reached deep into the recesses of Tousant's nightmare, waking him up. He shot straight up in the bed. His heart pounded, and he was breathing hard with fright and fatigue. "Come *ouuut!*" Beads of sweat ran down his face, and his pajamas stuck to his skin. With shaky hands, he turned on the bedside light and looked at the clock. The hands on the lighted clock showed twelve o'clock. "Come out! Come out of there, *Miss High-Class lady.* When you step out the door, step out with not one, but both yo' titties showin'," the voice shouted.

Dressed in an ill-fitting, black suit, that he had years ago wedded his wife in; *M'sieu* Mouton had stationed himself underneath the master bedroom window. He stood weaving and looking up at the lighted window. "I can't hear *yooou,*" he shouted. He bent over sideways, and cupped his hand over his ear. After getting no response, he started throwing pecans upon the veranda. Some pecans landed on the veranda floor, and others fell back down on the ground near his feet, barely missing the top of his head. "You didn't think that a ass-whoopin' from Farras and pressures from *votre père* was gon' stop me, did ya'? Well, I got news fo' ya'; my two-tittied lady 'wid the *twooo* husbands, it won't! Now come on outa there. Come on out showin' yo' *twooo* titties. Keep 'em pointed out like two beacons of light so's I don't miss 'em, ya' hear." *M'sieu* Mouton's voice seemed to run across the damp night air and hang there summoning its listener.

He held a large bag of pecans in his hand.

When Tousant entered the dining room, he met Bree coming down the stairs. "What is it, Tousant?" she asked, with sleep still in her voice. "I thought I heard..." *M'sieu* Mouton's voice grew louder, but his voice could not be readily identified.

"That's what I'm about to find out," Tousant broke in. He headed for the front door. When Tousant stepped off the front gallery, he saw a dark form weaving and throwing something up at the veranda. The darkness prevented Tousant from focusing accurately on the weaving figure. Seeing *M'sieu* Mouton was made difficult by the black suit he wore. "Who are you? Are you crazy? What the hell are you doing? What do you want!" Tousant asked angrily.

M'sieu Mouton turned and faced the direction of Tousant's voice. "Who is me? What do I want? It sho' ain't you I want. You go back in there, and sen' out the two-tittied lady with the *twooo* husbands. I brought a 'peace-offerin',' he said, and held up his bag of pecans in the dark.

Tousant walked up to the dark form and discovered that it was *M'sieu* Mouton. A sound of drunken laughter tore into the damp night air. *M'sieu* Mouton fell to the ground and rolled around. "*M'sieu* Mouton, is that you?"

"Tousant," Bree called from the dark. She was standing on the edge of the gallery. "Tousant, come in and call the police," she said frightened.

"It's *M'sieu* Mouton, Bree. We don't need the police. I can handle him. You go back inside the house." Bree's heart sank. She didn't move.

After several attempts, *M'sieu* Mouton pulled himself up and leaned against the oak tree. "You wanta know what just struck me?" he said snickering. "I always wondered why womens had *twooo* titties. When all they needs is, one. Now, I know. Fo' *twooo* husbands," he said, holding up two fingers in the dark. "Cause don't no lil' itiddy biddy *bèbè* needs *twooo* titties."

"*M'sieu* Mouton, get the hell off my property before I call the police," Tousant warned.

"*Nooo*, not 'til I sees the *twooo* titties. *Twooo* titties pointed straight at me," he whined, as he walked up to the gallery; spilling pecans on the ground as he walked. "A 'peace-offerin'' fo' my lovely. I'm yo' slave, *Madame* Bree Jumppierre-Jourdan."

"Tousant, be careful. *Ne vous frottez pas a' lui.* He might have a gun. The man has gone completely crazy! I'm going inside to call the police," Bree said, turning to go inside.

"No, let me handle this, Bree," Tousant said, stopping her.

"You know, I just thought 'bout somethin'. *Twooo* titties and three *husbands* just ain't gon' git it! One of us *husbands* gots ta go. Since you is her *first* husband, Tousant, you can stay," he said, blowing foul breath into Tousant's face. "The way I got it figured, it's my turn now. That means that other som'bitch in there gots ta go. He just gots ta *gooo.* 'Cause he ain't gon' tow the line, even if we lets him stay."

It broke Bree's heart to hear *M'sieu* Mouton's insane pleas for something he could never have. It was an unbearable thing to witness. Something inside of her broke away, and she knew that whatever it was was lost to her forever. *"Qu'est-ce qui arrive?* Farras asked, standing in the doorway in his pants. He wore no shirt or shoes.

"Nothing, except the world wants my blood for upsetting it," Bree answered.

"What are you talkin' 'bout, Bree? For Christ sake, make some kinda sense! I sensed in my sleep that you wasn't there, and I woke up. I came..." Farras stopped talking and walked to the edge of the gallery.

"He gots ta *gooo!* You and me, we gots ta kill that mo' fucker," *M'sieu* Mouton said, slurring his words.

"Who's out there? What the hell?..." Farras jumped barefoot off the gallery without using the steps. Bree heard the wet, splashy sound of the grass as his bare feet trod over it.

"It's me, Farras," Tousant said.

"And, who else?" Farras asked, walking up to the two dark figures.

"M'sieu Mouton."

"M'sieu Mouton!" Farras could feel his stomach muscles begin to jump.

"Take Bree inside. I'll handle him, Farras."

"Like hell you will," Farras said.

"You gots ta *gooo,*" *M'sieu* Mouton said, staggering up to Farras.

"Git the hell outa my face, man! You right when you say somebody gots to go. I hope you know who that somebody is. When I finish with yo' ass this time, the undertaker gon' be hard pressed to take you."

"You don't understand nothin' do you, man?" *M'sieu* Mouton yelled in Farras' face. "Ya' see they ain't but *twooo* titties," he explained, whining, holding up two fingers again.

"What the hell are you talkin' 'bout, Mouton?" Farras demanded. He grabbed the front of *M'sieu* Mouton's jacket. "Don't nobody wanta hear this shit this time of night. This is the first Friday night I been off from my music in two years, and I sho' as hell don't plan on spendin' any of it with you!"

"Time of night! That's all left, you fool!" *M'sieu* Mouton shouted, weaving under Farras' grip. "I be damn if I'm gon' look behind me," he said, pointing behind him. "Cause that's what you wants me to do, ain't it! You wants me to do like Lot's wife, don't you you som' bitch! You wants me ta turn ta a goddamn pillar of salt! Well, I ain't! See. Look. I'm lookin' straight aheada me." He struggled awkwardly against Farras trying to hold his body erect. "*M'ap' aller fout' gris-gris sur, Farras,*" he shouted. "Don't you think fo' one goddamn minute I can't put a heavy *mojo* on yo' ass. I put a *mojo* on my wife's ass! She gotta live 'wid a belly full of snakes eatin' her ass from the inside out. And ain't no doctor in the world can help her ass either. She done been ta doctor after doctor, but it ain't done the po' chile no good!" Farras had loosened his grip on *M'sieu* Mouton's clothes, and he fell to his knees. "The night is so black!" he cried. "It ain't natural! Why ain't theys some light? Why do the sun keepa runnin' 'way from me. The moon's out even in the daytime. Anybody with sense loves the sun. The sun is warm and red like blood and full of life! Only fools loves the ice cold moon. Why ain't nobody in charge fo' me ta tell? It needs ta be somebody in charge!" he screamed. "Lord, I needs somebody ta go crabbin' and fishin' 'wid me." He wailed like a desperate child. "Lord, I needs somebody ta tell me somethin'."

Bree ran inside and called the police. She turned on the gallery light before she went back outside. She stood on the gallery leaning silently against a pillar. A hint of cape jasmine perfumed the damp night air teasing her nostrils. "He's drunk. We'll throw him off the property, and take care of everything in the morning when he's sober," Tousant suggested.

"This crazy fool ain't drunk! He's just a brazen bastard that's buckin' to die," Farras said.

M'sieu Mouton got up and started staggering about the yard, flapping his arms. "Ain't but *twooo* titties. What in the world is gonna happen ta *meee?* What in this som' bitchin' world gonna happen ta *meee? Twooo* titties is all she gots," he repeated to himself, holding up two fingers. He cocked his head to one side for a few seconds as if listening to someone; then fell heavily back down on his knees again. When he spoke again, his voice had changed to that of a young boy's. "I just pretend I'm readin' my comic books. 'Cause Mama's legs is startin' ta jump again."

"What the hell is this bastard talkin' 'bout, now!" Farras asked, in disgust.

"Let him talk," Tousant said. "It won't hurt anything. Maybe it'll settle him down some, and he'll leave. Anyway, his mother died a long time ago."

"Let's get him goin', now!" Farras said. "We don't need to stand here and listen to this fool ramble on. Let him talk somewhere else."

"Let him be!" Something inside Tousant made him hold Farras back.

"Mama won't look at her jumpin' legs." *M'sieu* Mouton's voice interrupted their discussion. Both men stopped talking and looked at him. "She just looks at me like she shame of herself. I used ta think that my evil looks made Mama's legs stop jumpin'. I was a fool! 'Cause nothin' can stop her jumpin' legs: evil looks, prayers, nothin'! I try to think what's it's like livin' in a wheelchair. In magazines, I see old, wrinkled womens in wheel chairs. But Mama is the onlyest young, pretty woman I see in a wheelchair. I didn't think that bad thangs happen ta young, pretty womens. I don't know what made me

think that shit! But Mama don't seem ta notice her wheelchair no
mo'. Sometimes when I thinks she ain't lookin', I looks at the picture
of her on top the radio. In that picture, Mama's wearin' her nurse
uniform with some other nurses, smilin'. I always forgits ta ask Mama
what 'R.N.' means." *M'sieu* Mouton's voice trembled. "Every night,
Papa puts Mama ta bed. She usta cuss Papa out, and beat him on his
head 'wid her fists. But Papa's stronger than she is, so he just
overpowers her. He holds her hands down hard on the bed 'til she
stops fightin.' He always laughs a stupid kinda laugh, and his eyes gits
real big like they gon' pop right outa his head. Like that cat's eyes got
that time I hung him from the fence. But Mama don't fight Papa no
mo'. She just lets him lay her down. Then she just lay quiet; folds her
arms across her chest, and stare up at the ceilin'. Since she can't do
nothin' 'bout 'em, I usta think that the water stains on the ceilin'
bothered her. But now, I don't believe it's the water stains. So I stop
standin' at her door ta tell her good night.
    A man came 'long. Mama said she thought the man could save her
from Papa tryin' ta drown her, but the man couldn't save her. She say
that's why she's in that wheelchair. I don't know how Mama gits
thangs all mixed up in her head 'bout how she got in that wheelchair.
That man didn't try ta save Mama from drownin'! My cousin Rovert
took Mama ta work that mornin'. I cried ta ride with 'em. When
Mama got outa the car that man come runnin' up ta her. When Mama
saw that man, she tried ta run away from him, but that man pointed his
gun at Mama's back and shot her—*pow, pow, pow!* Three times!" he
screamed. "Lord, Lord, Lord!" *M'sieu* Mouton started rocking and
hugging himself and crying. "Dem' shots was *sooo* loud. That man
left her layin' in a ditch! Cousin Rovert ran off and left me in the car
by myself. I was lookin' at Mama bleedin' in that ditch! Some
peoples come from the hospital and got her. When Mama came home,
she was in that wheelchair! I just can't understand how Mama gits
thangs all mixed up in her head like that...?" His words faded out.
    Farras gave *M'sieu* Mouton an impatient sigh and started to speak,
but before he could speak, *M'sieu* Mouton's voice penetrated the
night air again. "Papa is so big. Bigger than Alvin's papa. But him
being big don't mean nothin'! 'Cause don't seem like he's here, not

even when he puts Mama ta bed. He just ain't here.

Papa took me ta the doctor fo' bein' too bad. All the doctor did was sit up there with his chest stuck out listenin' ta Papa tell him 'bout all the bad stuff I do. When Papa tol' him 'bout the cat I hung on the fence, he tol' Papa ain't nothin' wrong 'wid me 'cept badness. He tol' Papa ta beat me ta straighten me out. Papa couldn't wait ta git me home. Papa didn't tell the doctor that he had give me water 'wid sand in it, and it give me the 'Gravels.' When we got home, Papa beat me bad. I begged Papa. Please, don't hit me on my back!" *M'sieu* Mouton hugged himself again and started crying out aloud. "But that seem ta be the onlyest place Papa wanted ta hit me. When he stopped beatin' me, my back looked like 'dem slave mens in Alvin's papa big book." Bree wondered off-hand, what the 'Gravels' were. But she continued to listen and was silent.

M'sieu Mouton's words had a fleeting sound like blowing wind running in all directions. Bree had sat down on the gallery, and was rocking herself back and forth. Every minute or two, she stopped rocking; held her face in her hands and wept softly. "The teacher don't want me in school no mo'." *M'sieu* Mouton's voice droned on. "He say he can't *contend*! He tries ta make me look at the blackboard. He tries ta make me act like the other children do. He tries ta make me read books, too. I wanta explain ta him that I gots ta watch my back. I gots ta. It don't matter if he's there. He can't protect my back fo' me. I gots ta do that fo' myself. It don't matter if I'm in school. While my mind is on what the teacher sayin', somebody can come snatch the door open and hurt me. Anybody can git a gun or a knife or even a stick! Then where will I be? Every time I gits ready ta tell the teacher this, I can't talk. I just feels like I gots ta *pee*. I sets in class and sweats a lot, and try ta keep myself from runnin' away. I go on and suffer and sits where he tells me ta sit. I tries hard ta listen, and say what I thinks the teacher wants me ta say. At recess, the children always picks fights with me. I guess I could run fo' the fightin' starts, but that would mean turnin' my back ta 'em. I have ta face 'em ta protect my back. But facin' somebody always means a fight. Lord, if they gits me... Some day somebody gonna git *meee*. I just wish it don't be in my back! When the children fights me, I have ta win! I have ta! They all wanta punch me in my back. I'm tired by dinner time 'cause I spends the mornin' protectin' my back. When the teacher walks us ta the lunch room, I gits my plate, and finds me a spot against the wall away from peoples. It's the other children that causes all the ruckus! But I'm always the one the teacher say he can't *contend* 'wid."

Tousant gave a quick, nervous, dry cough, and turned his back to *M'sieu* Mouton. His wet eyes were hidden by the darkness. *It's a shame*, he thought. *It's just a damn shame. He knew M'sieu Mouton when he "was" M'sieu Mouton. It was just a freaking shame. Just before his wife died, was the last time M'sieu Mouton talked with any sense and looked like anything.* He turned around and looked at *M'sieu* Mouton. He shook his head sadly; folded his arms, and looked up at the nighttime sky.

M'sieu Mouton was of average build and weight, but his body appeared to shrink smaller, as he lost himself in the throes of his childhood pain. "When Mama first come home in that wheelchair, Papa made me go ta Shreveport ta live 'wid Grandmama," *M'sieu* Mouton whispered, holding his hands up to his face. "I went ta school there, too. But the teacher up in Shreveport said the same thang—she can't *contend*! Even Grandmama said she couldn't *contend*! When she knows I had ta fight my cousins ta protect my back. Grandmama said she felt sorry fo' me, but she still sent me back home. Then Papa took me ta live with my aunt Rosa. Same thang. Aunt Rosa couldn't *contend*, either!" *M'sieu* Mouton started to whimper. After a few minutes, he stopped; dug his hand deep into his pocket and brought out an object. "Now, I have a knife." Farras reached down, and roughly took the knife away from him, but *M'sieu* Mouton continued to talk without noticing that his knife had been taken away. "I stole my knife from ol' peg leg *M'sieu* Julis. I didn't wanta steal the knife from him, but I have ta protect myself. *M'sieu* Julis don't need his knife anyway. What's gon' happen ta him done already happen ta him. He don't need ta protect hisself no mo', but I do! So I stole his knife. It's mines now. It don't b'long ta nobody else but me. My knife loves me. I talks ta my knife when ain't nobody listenin'. I keeps it real sharp, too!" With his last sentence, he struck himself in his chest with each word he spoke. "Mama sees me holdin' my knife, but she don't say nothin'. I keeps my knife in my pocket all the time." *M'sieu* Mouton's mind shifted again. "I wish I could be by myself, but I can't. Peoples is everywheres." He waved his hands around in a wide arch. "Yestiddy, my teacher came ta my house, and I heard him tellin' Mama that there's a place 'specially 'quipped' fo' bad boys like me. I guess Mama musta finally tol' somebody she can't *contend*! Mama tol' my teacher that she don't know what was the matter 'wid me. They don't understand that sooner or later somebody's gon' git me! It just ain't no need ta send me ta a place 'specially 'equipped' fo' bad boys like me. But I can't control what other peoples think. The only thang I got ta do is protect my back fo' as long as I can. Mama tol' the teacher she was helpless. She tells me that, too. She said she was drownin' and grabbin' at anythin' ta save herself, but Papa wouldn't try ta help her. I know Mama ain't lyin' 'bout Papa not helpin' her—just seems like Papa ain't never here."

M'sieu Mouton had his back to them. He started hitting his head on the ground. When *M'sieu* Mouton spoke again, his voice had changed. This time his voice was polished, smooth, and controlled. He recited his words, and the pitch of his voice rose and dropped like a newscaster's voice. "Did you ever want to just drive your car right off a bridge?" He lifted his hands and held them out from him. "Did you ever just throw up a nickel and say: "Heads the *Manchac bridge*, *t*ails the *Huey P. Long bridge?*" Did you ever just say that to yourself?"

Bree heard the sirens in a distance and relaxed her body. Farras spoke. "That pitiful bastard's gone nuts," Farras said.

"This mornin', a man on the television was puttin' on a fresh, clean shirt that was washed in some kinda washin' powder that s'pose ta make yo' clothes smell fresh and clean." *M'sieu* Mouton's own voice returned as his mind shifted to another thought. "I had ta make sho' that the man's smile wasn't a fake! 'Cause I always frown when I puts my shirts on. And I never thinks 'bout what kinda washin' powder was used, either!" he shrieked. "And I don't think 'bout if my clothes is fresh and clean," he stated, in a calmer voice. "I just frown and wait fo' the pain ta leave my head and slide down ta my back. Every day, I pray fo' it not ta happen, but it always do. So I taught myself a trick way ta hol' my body so the pain won't be so bad. Puttin' on shirts ain't as easy as it looks!" He let out a shrill cry. "Anythin' can happen. If yo' back itches, you can't scratch it. The skin might come off like the skin come off 'dem slave mens backs in Alvin's papa big book. That book show pictures of mens 'wid bad thangs done ta they backs: Holes! Bleedin' welts! Hangin', raw skin! Even when you sleepin' you got ta make sho' yo' back is protected–even the dark can hurt you sometimes." *M'sieu* Mouton stopped talking, and started twisting the front of his jacket in both hands. Dry sobs wracked his frame, as he cried for the sins of his parents.

Sick of the sound of *M'sieu* Mouton's voice, Farras said, "Allow me the pleasure." He walked up behind *him*. *M'sieu* Mouton was whining, holding up two fingers, and writhing on the ground.

"I tol' my wife last night."

"Yo' wife's dead, fool! And yo' mama's dead, too!" Farras said, fighting down the urge to choke him, to squeeze his neck until he died. He lifted *M'sieu* Mouton roughly off the ground and held him. *M'sieu* Mouton's arms fell limply to his sides.

On *All Saints' Day*, Bree had often seen *M'sieu* Mouton at the graveyard walking like a zombie, with a bouquet of flowers in each hand. But he always stopped at the first grave he came to. Blinded by tears, his flowers would drop from his hands, and always end up on the wrong graves as he stumbled away.

"It was my wife's ghost. I talked ta her. She's the one tol' me 'bout the twooo titties." *M'sieu* Mouton stopped squirming; cocked his head on the side, and broke out in song. He sang an old spiritual that Bree had heard troubled people muttering to themselves ever since her childhood:

> *"Beyond the smiling and weeping,*
> *Beyond the waking and the sleeping,*
> *Beyond the sowing and the weeping,*
> *I shall be soon. Beyond the blooming*
> *and the fading, beyond the shining*
> *and the shading, beyond the hoping*

and the dreading, I shall be soon."

As Bree listened to *M'sieu* Mouton's song, pools of water gathered in her eyes. While still in song, *M'sieu* Mouton started fumbling awkwardly with the zipper of his pants.

"Unzip yo' fly, and I swear I'll break yo' hand," Farras said, between clenched teeth. "If you wanta piss, wait 'til you git to jail. That's if I let you live that long. Best thing fo' you to do is cross yo' legs."

"Miss High-Class Lady," *M'sieu* Mouton's voice dropped to a deep whisper, as he pointed a trembling finger at Bree, "you ain't never gon' have no peace 'til you pass *waaay out there beyond the smiling."*

Bree cringed from *M'sieu* Mouton's pointing finger and thought, *Something needs to be said here.* But the pointing of a finger was a horrifying thing to a *Creole*, and she sat verbally paralyzed. She turned her face away from *M'sieu* Mouton. He continued to struggle; trying to free himself from Farras' vice-like grip. He stopped struggling; leaned his body heavily against Farras, and resumed singing:

> *"Beyond the parting and the*
> *meeting, beyond the farewell*
> *and the greeting, beyond the*
> *pulse's fever beating. I*
> *shall be soon."*

M'sieu Mouton's voice stopped. The silence was the loudest Bree had ever heard. Time had stopped. The crickets ceased their nightly serenade. Fireflies darted about, selfishly lighting up minute spaces in the dark for themselves. A fast moving cloud slipped silently by. Bree stiffened. In that great quietness, they heard voices coming from the direction of the levee. Some men walked along the levee with hunting lights on heads, going "bull frogging." They were having a loud disagreement. Bree held her breath. But the men walked briskly past, their voices fading into the night air. Again silence.

Finally, Bree willed her body to step off the gallery and walk over to Farras. "His heart's stopped hurting," Bree said. Her words seemed to break the stillness like bursting atoms. "Let him down, Farras," she said.

"He do feel heavier."

"Who, Mouton?"

"Who else?" Farras asked, annoyed by Tousant's question.

"Probably passed out. His brain's saturated with liquor," Tousant said.

Farras removed the arm he held around *M'sieu* Mouton's neck, and let him slide slowly to the ground.

"What are you saying, Bree? That *M'sieu* Mouton's dead?" Tousant asked.

"Yes."

"How do you know fo' sho', Bree? You ain't listened to his heart or felt fo' his pulse?" Farras' voice went hoarse with fear.

"I know, that's all. I just know."

"If that's true, they'll think I killed him. A lotta people seen me beat Mouton's ass. How we suppose to explain this?" Farras asked. "Now, we'll be involved in a lot of unnecessary trouble."

"The man obviously had a heart attack, Farras. Any coroner can verify that!" Tousant sounded annoyed.

"Yes, but why did he pick here to have his heart attack? Tousant, I tol' you that we shouldn't let that fool ramble on like he did. Long befo' he went outa his mind. No, you wanted him to wear hisself out talkin'! Well, he wore hisself out all right—for good. That crazy fool done *talked* hisself to death!" Farras said, in a deep whisper.

Bree could still hear *M'sieu* Mouton's screaming voice inside her head. She barely managed to choke an angry scream from escaping from her own mouth. She looked down at his body and said, "He sure did behaved badly. Now he's behaving himself so well and so quietly, not screaming, not talking, not swearing, not singing, just dead!" Her words were cruel. They housed all of her pain and suffering. But some unusual kind of calm replaced her anger, and in her heart came an indescribable sadness. Her next words reflected that sadness. "He lost sight of his life a long time ago, perhaps deliberately. Our *situation* must have triggered something inside him. He wanted a chance to live again. And, now, he's dead. We cannot be angry with *M'sieu* Mouton, can we?"

"No, I guess not," Tousant answered, looking down at the body, sadly.

"Sometimes, a woman gives meaning to a man's life, but in her absence, he ages. Sometimes, he dies.

When the police drove up, Farras walked up to the car and immediately started explaining. The two policemen looked at him. Then they looked down at *M'sieu* Mouton's body. "Get everything down," the policeman said to the one talking to Farras, "I'll call in," he said, as he walked to the patrol car.

A short while later, an ambulance drove up and two men got out. One of the attendants took *M'sieu* Mouton's pulse, and listened to his chest with a stethoscope. He stood up and announced, "Yep, he's dead, all right." He nodded his head towards the body, and the two men lifted *M'sieu* Mouton's body onto the stretcher and drove off without a word. "Officer... will... I mean... do you think there will be any problems?" Tousant asked nervously. "My wife...we have..."

"I don't think that there will be any problems, *M'sieu* Jumppierre. Because I see no evidence of foul play. If ya' story checks out, and I believe that it will, the coroner will make his report and that'll be it."

"Thank you. I would like to take my wife inside now if that's all right?"

"Sure, go right ahead."

As they walked away from the policeman, Deacon Hebert and his wife rushed up. They were gasping for breath from their quick run. "What's going on over here?" Deacon Hebert inquired, breathless. They did not answer Deacon Hebert. They walked inside the house, and closed the door behind them.

"Are you, okay?" Tousant asked, looking at Bree.

"Yes, I'm fine."

"What's next?" Farras asked, searching both their faces.

"Reporters will be makin' a nuisance of theyself again."

"I don't know what's next, Farras. I hope nothing. And the hell with pesky reporters," Tousant added. "Bree is my concern, now. I don't want her carrying around a burden of guilt."

"I don't feel guilty, Tousant. Someone had to be there. But what *M'sieu* Mouton needed, we could not give him. He was searching for some meaning to his life," Bree said. "Though it saddens me that he had to go insane looking for love, looking for some kind of meaning in his life. I can understand why *M'sieu* Mouton thought that I must have had an over-abundance of love to give." Bree let out a weary sigh. "There are so many people in the world. Why do some people have to die unloved? I wish *M'sieu* Mouton would have bled when he died."

"That's a strange thing to say, Bree." Tousant said, looking perplexed.

"Is it?" Bree asked, looking directly into Tousant's eyes. Tousant heaved a tired sigh and left the room.

CHAPTER
FOURTEEN

*I*t was hot and humid for May. Bree lay on a chaise with eyes closed. She just lay there, thinking about nothing, reclining lazily underneath the live oak tree. She had convinced herself that she had nowhere at all to go and nothing whatsoever to do. She wished she could make time stop forever.

She was barefoot, and she wore white shorts with a red halter top that exposed her midriff. Her *music box* lay against her outer thigh on the chaise. She laid her book down and stood up. She pulled a small piece of low-hanging Spanish moss from the branches of the live oak tree and stood running the moss through her fingers. She stepped back from the live oak tree and looked up at the sun. The sun seemed as if it were boiling with rage, as if it were upset with the earth for reasons unknown to her.

Bree liked the sight of growing things. She walked over to the rose trellis planted underneath the veranda. Sometimes the slightest breeze would bring the sweet fragrance of roses to her nostrils. She reached down to kiss a small rose bud, and she caught the sight of a hummingbird from the corner of her eye. She watched the hummingbird go from flower to flower sticking in its long beak. She walked slowly around the hummingbird observing the bird in awe. Her face was aglow in wonderment. Seeing the hummingbird heightened all her senses, and made her acutely aware of all the tiny life about her. Small, living things, that were trying hard to survive, trying desperately to continue their life cycle. The hummingbird fluttered near her for a few seconds, then flew off and landed on another flower a few feet away.

She walked back and stood underneath the live oak tree again. She looked up high into the branches of the oak tree. *Old Minnie,* do you know how at peace I am? How contented. I read somewhere that one cannot hope for happiness. So I only hope to obtain peace."

A car was coming down the private road that led up to Bree's driveway. Bree recognized the car. It was her two sister-in-laws, Belinda and Sabbath. As the car came nearer, she saw that their children were with them. This dampened her spirits. She resented their intrusion. Both her brother's children were spoiled, and their visits always tired her out. She loved Belinda as if she were a blood sister, and seeing her always brought joy to her heart. Belinda bubbled over with love spreading it to everyone who came in contact with her. She had never met anyone who disliked Belinda. She had *le gout bien fin,* and was always stunningly dressed. She was tall and attractive with naturally red hair. During her college years at Xavier University, she modeled for *the Sears and Roebuck* catalog. She was soft spoken and sensitive and an avid reader. Belinda was either smiling or on the verge of tears. There was no middle ground for her emotions. She had stood with Bree in her crisis. She had called her daily. Sometimes she even drove the twenty-five miles from La Place to visit.

Bree disliked her sister-in-law, Sabbath. Even when they were children growing up together, she disliked her. She had once asked Sabbath why her parents gave her a name like, Sabbath. 'Because I was born on *sur Dimanch*e, stupid!' Sabbath had said.

"There are a lot of girls born *sur Samadi,* but their parents aren't stupid enough to name them Saturday!" she had retorted, and slapped Sabbath's face. The incident had left a trace of bitterness. In the beginning, her dislike for Sabbath was subtle, but over the years, her dislike for her grew more acute. Sabbath had always been self-centered with brown, 'icy' eyes, and her 'icy' eyes always expressed arrogance which destroyed her good looks. She'd always thought that her two brothers had married the wrong women, but both seemed to have solid marriages. Both Belinda and Sabbath were overprotective mothers. Their children were always at the doctor's. Sabbath and Manuel's children were worse. She thought their children extremely neurotic.

She watched them as they got out of the car. Her nieces and nephews pushed past their mothers. They shoved and tore at each other. Belinda yelled at them, but the children paid no heed to her. They broke out running towards the levee. Bree closed her eyes and shuddered. She wondered why the children weren't in school. "*Bonjour*, Bree. We herded the tribe off to the dentist today," Belinda said, as she walked up to Bree. "It's such a nice day. We hated to go right back home. So here we are. It was such a pleasant drive up here." When she reached Bree, the two women embraced.

"Yes, it is a lovely day, Belinda. I just finished studying nature."

"Studying nature." Belinda looked baffled.

"It's not important. *Faites comme chez vous.* This is an unexpected pleasure." Belinda walked over and sat down on one of the benches at the end of the table. Sabbath was still standing at the car brushing and smoothing out her dress. She held her parasol with an unsteady hand. Sabbath represented a Louisiana that belonged more to Ante-bellum times. Her dresses were always long with lace on them some place. She was rarely seen without a hat and gloves. She had never seen Sabbath wear her hair in a modern style. On the rare occasion that she was without a hat, she wore her hair pulled back with a long braid hanging down her back. She was an accomplished pianist and still performed on certain occasions. She was a pretty woman who looked fragile but wasn't. She had an ample bosom, and her skin was pale with yellow undertones, that made her look like a faded, antique doll. And she always carried a cold, aloof look on her face.

When Sabbath walked up, she did not embrace Bree. She spoke and complained about the heat. Bree wanted to tell her that if the world was perfect, she'd still find something to complain about, but she offered them lemonade instead. "Lemonade sounds great," Belinda said.

"I'll have some too, *merci*," Sabbath whined. Her formal airs always grated on Bree's nerves.

"Us, too, Auntie Bree," the children chimed in.

Bree got up to go inside the house. "Need any help Bree? We

didn't come to put you out. I thought maybe the pool would be ready and the kids could swim. We didn't bring their swimming suits. They could always swim in their underwear," Belinda said, laughing. Sabbath sat quietly with a smug look on her face. She was fanning herself with a small, white, lace handkerchief. Bree looked at her because Sabbath's mood could quickly turn ugly.

"No, to both of your questions," Bree replied. "I don't need any help getting the lemonade. I can put it all on a tray. Thank you for your offer." Though Bree's words were directed to Belinda, her eyes were on Sabbath. "As for the pool, it's not ready yet. As a rule, we never bother with the pool until school closes for the summer."

Bree sat the tray down on the table. She and Belinda served everyone. Afterwards, the children ran back off towards the levee. "How has it been going, Bree?" Belinda asked. "We haven't talked in almost a week."

"Great! Just great, Belinda." Bree answered. "I have no complaints."

"I talked to Nina a few days ago, and she seemed really hurt. She said she's been trying to call you for weeks. She said she wrote you a brief note offering you her support. She also said that you were asked to rejoin the ladies' club, but she hasn't got a response from you yet. Bree, you have been accused of avoiding your friends."

"I'm not avoiding my friends, Belinda. Not the people whom I found to be my friends or family," Bree added, looking again at Sabbath.

"Why, are you looking at me like that, Bree?" Sabbath asked, blotting imaginary perspiration from her forehead.

"Well, if you don't know. I'll be wasting precious energy trying to explain, Sabbath."

"I would have come to the Church meeting, but I had menstrual cramps. You know what a problem I have with that. I guess I could have called, but dealing with four boys hardly leaves me time to think. Besides, it's quite a drive from La Place to St. Jamesville. I'm usually exhausted at the end of the day. I do have my household duties, you know," Sabbath said, fanning again, sipping lemonade.

"And, of course, you do have your bridge club over every

Thursday. It is on Thursdays, isn't it, darling? It's amazing how much energy you can muster up on Thursdays, Sabbath."

"Oh, come on you two. Let's have a nice visit," Belinda encouraged, acting overly cheerful.

"Everything you just said is all weak excuses," Bree continued, not heeding Belinda's plea. "Belinda stuck by me, and she has the same responsibilities you have, Sabbath. She drove the distance, twice, to visit with me and talk. It has been my experience in life that people act on situations based upon how they truly feel."

"I had planned on being with you at that church meeting until little Durant came down with an ear infection."

"Liar! Stop patronizing me, Sabbath. Remember, this is Bree you're talking to. I know all of your damn tricks!" Bree said, in a tone full of contempt. She hated talking to Sabbath that way, but Sabbath always seemed to bring out the worst in her. After her arguments with Sabbath, she always ended up disliking that part of herself that said such nasty things. And their arguments never brought about a better understanding between the two of them. Her dislike for Sabbath always seemed to increase after each disagreement. She had resigned herself to the fact that she would never be fond of her brother's wife, and she had accepted the fact that Sabbath would never be fond of her.

"I don't have to take your insults, Bree," Sabbath huffed.

"Then stop with your lies!" Bree exclaimed.

"Hey, you two. You have got everything out now. Let's forget it and have a nice visit," Belinda pleaded, looking at each of them. "Now, Bree, tell me are you happy? I know that you are. I'm so glad everything's over and done with and things are back to normal," Belinda said. "You are happy, aren't you?" Belinda asked, again.

"No, but I'm at peace," Bree answered.

"*Bon*, I'm glad." Bree knew that Belinda meant it.

"It was rough going there for a while. At times, I almost gave up, but I am glad that I stuck it out. I have learned a valuable lesson from all of this."

"Have you?" Belinda asked, giving Bree her full attention.

"Yes, I have. I have learned to live my life as an individual and by my own principles. I no longer depend upon others to carry me through my life. I don't have to do what others expect of me, either. I can do what I want to do with my life. It's mine. It belongs to me to do with whatever I choose. Before I was in the right clubs, had all of the 'so-called' right friends, and did everything that my family and the community expected of the Bouttes. My *situation* has given me a freedom I cannot describe. If I had it to do again, I would do it exactly the same way. I'm not afraid of life anymore. That puts me way ahead of most people. A person has to grow or perish. And if that growth is undesirable to society...so be it," Bree said, shrugging her shoulders. "I have defined my *responsibilities* to my family, society, and to myself."

"That's wonderful," Belinda said. She walked around the table and kissed Bree's cheek.

"Yes, that is wonderful," Sabbath said. For once there was no insincerity in her remark. Bree looked at Sabbath, and for the first time, she saw respect in her eyes. She had never seen respect in Sabbath's eyes for anyone in all the years that she had known her.

"Looks as if more company is coming," Belinda said, looking down the road. Bree looked, but she didn't recognize the car. When the white sedan pulled in the driveway, Bree could see that it wasn't an ordinary car. It appeared to be some type of official car.

A woman got out of the car and walked towards them carrying a brown briefcase. She was middle-aged, with graying, red hair and very white skin. She wore a pale, green cotton dress with brown oxfords. "I'm looking for, Mrs. Bree Jumppierre. When she spoke, she seemed nervous. Her voice came out in a high-pitched, squeak.

"I'm Mrs. Jumppierre," Bree said, getting up from the table.

"I'm Miss Bartley from St. Tammy Parish Children's Services," she said, with a cool professional aloofness. *"M...i...s...s."* She spelled *Miss* slowly and deliberately, looking at the three women, as if she were waiting for an unfavorable response.

"Yes," Bree said, waiting for her the woman to state her business.

"I was sent here to investigate a report given to us that a minor child is living in an 'immoral' environment," she said, with the same professional coolness.

"What!" Bree exclaimed. "Are you sure you have the right person?" The woman laid her briefcase down on the edge of the table and thumbed through some papers.

"Are you, Mrs. Tousant Jumppierre?" she inquired, looking at the paper she held in her hand.

"Yes, I'm Mrs. Tousant Jumppierre," Bree said again.

"We have a report brought to our office by a," she hesitated, bringing the papers up close to her eyes, "by a *Madame* Blanque," she said, looking unfeelingly at Bree.

"*Madame* Blanque," Bree whispered. She sat back down at the table, stunned. "Why won't she leave us alone?" Bree asked, in a low voice. Her question was not directed to anyone. "What is that woman's problem?" She had half-expected something more from *Madame* Blanque. Yet, when she actually did something, it came as a shock.

"I'm sorry, Mrs. Jumppierre. Please try to understand, we have to follow through on all complaints," she said, in a nonapologetic tone.

"The best home possible is being provided for my son. All his basic needs are being met and much more," Bree added. "He attends the best private school in the area. He gets all the attention he needs and an over-abundance of love. You see our home. Look at our home," Bree cried. "My child is at peace. He has lots of friends. This is unbelievable! What is the matter with *Madame* Blanque, anyway?" Bree asked again. "This whole town will vouch for my family. My family helped to build this town. This is part of my family here," Bree said, waving her hand in the direction of Belinda and Sabbath.

"Mrs. Jumppierre, I'm well aware of your family standing in this community. I know who you are. I have known your father quite a number of years, myself. Still, all reported cases must be investigated."

"Is everything based on your report?" Bree asked, looking at her squarely in the eyes.

"Basically, it is, Mrs. Jumppierre,"

"I cannot give you anymore information than I already have," Bree said.

"Not quite, Mrs. Jumppierre. It was reported that you're living in

the house with *two* men claiming them both to be your husbands."
"That's correct," Bree said, with a stern face. Miss Bartley's look concentrated on Bree's face, as if she could not quite believe her words. Bree wanted to explain but decided it was pointless. She really didn't see what difference any explanation would make. She could tell Miss Bartley had already branded her 'guilty as charged.' Miss Bartley appeared to Bree as being a woman who overtly glorified the straight and narrow while secretly doing the most wicked things.

"You mean you're living with *two* men under the same roof claiming them both as your *husbands!* You mean you have a minor child living in this environment?" Miss Bartley stated in one breath. "I cannot believe it! You mean, it's true!?" she almost shouted, turning red in the face. "Well, I never! I'm... afraid..." she stammered, "that I cannot give a favorable report on this case, Mrs. Jumppierre. You have placed yourself at risk of losing your son. We need to sit down and draw up a forty-five day 'service agreement.' The 'service agreement' will state that your current lifestyle with *multiple* husbands will stop! And that your current lifestyle is not in the best interest of your minor son. Also, some other things will be expected of you if you want to retain custody of your son." she added.

"You have no right!" Bree shouted. "I won't have a stranger, or anyone else, dictating my lifestyle. Don't you dare write out a 'service agreement' or any other kind of 'agreement,' because I won't follow it! I don't trust words like 'service agreement.' Get away from me! Get off my property!"

"Oh, but the State of Louisiana do have the right! There are laws to protect minor children, Mrs. Jumppierre," she said, closing her briefcase, preparing to leave.

"My son needs no protection from the State of Louisiana or *from Madame* Blanque. He's being raised in a perfectly healthy environment." Bree's voice had turned ice cold.

"Oh, I don't know about environment, Mrs. Jumppierre. The Juvenile Judge will decide that question at the *hearing.* I have done my assessment of this case, and there does not appear to be any immediate danger to the child. So your son will remain in your custody until the *hearing.* You will be notified."

"And if we decide we won't go along with this madness!" Bree asked.

"I wouldn't advise that, Mrs. Jumppierre. But if you insist, then I suggest you call your attorney. But be prepared to attend a *hearing* in juvenile court. Judge Micads, based upon the evidence, will decide whether you will retain custody of your son. The judge might turn the child's custody over to a responsible relative. I will be petitioning Juvenile Court for a *hearing* in this matter. Good day, Mrs. Jumppierre," she said, walking to her car. The social worker kept shaking her head, as if she could not believe what she had just heard.

"The least you could have done was talk to me in the privacy of my home, or don't you even consider me a human being?" Bree shouted. "Miss Bartley was being so judgmental. I didn't think social workers were supposed to do that."

"Why don't you make a request to talk to that Miss Bartley's supervisor? She has to report to someone." Bree looked at Belinda.

"The hell with it! Let her make her damn report. Why is *Madame* Blanque maligning me?" *Somewhere, some place, there was a rightness about her situation,* she thought. How would her life be if she had made the decision to remain celibate? What great harm would *Madame* Blanque want to do to her then? What would the town say or do then? "This town's attitude has rubbed me raw, Belinda. When will this awful time pass?"

Belinda came around the table and sat beside Bree. "Honey, listen, we're all behind you. They cannot get away with this. You'll see. I know that you cannot help being upset, but try not to worry. *Madame* Blanque is old, lonely, and miserable. She feels unloved. She's just a jealous, nasty woman. The way she sees it, you're getting love from *two* husbands and a fine son, and she's not getting any love at all. I'm glad that you dressed that old heifer down good-fashioned at the Church meeting, Bree. All she has is her Bible. That's been the real problem with her. It has nothing to do with morals. She could care less." When Belinda finished talking she was crying. "You want me to stay with you until Farras come home?" she sobbed. "Sabbath can take the children home. Durant can come pick me up later." Tears ran down Belinda's face as she stroked Bree's face.

"*Non, merci*, Belinda. I'd much rather be alone. I wish people weren't so fond of illusions. If they weren't, they might be able to understand themselves and others better. It might even help them understand me and my *two* husbands. That damn *Madame* Blanque really sets my teeth on edge. What a terrible tongue that woman has."

"You're sure you don't want me to stay?" Belinda sobbed. "I don't mind staying, Bree."

"I know you don't." Bree had started to cry. "But I really want to be alone, Belinda." She picked up her *music box* from the chaise and started walking toward her front door.

Bree wondered whether *Madame* Blanque was human. Her wrath toward her was unaccountable. It was hard to interpret her motives. It went beyond any rational, religious objections that she might have to her lifestyle. It went beyond her ability to comprehend. People like *Madame* Blanque were the kind of person her uncle had said sickened God and made Him vomit.

"*Je regrette*," Sabbath called after Bree. Bree didn't answer. She kept walking. She had retreated into her pain. *Effing 'service agreement.' Does she think that I am stupid?* she thought. *Reporters will be snooping again.* "*Cette femme! L' armée ennemi!*"

That Saturday morning, Bree, Tousant, and Farras sat at the dining room table with their attorney, Mr. Moires. He sat looking at Bree with piercing, blue eyes. Bree told him what had happened. When she finished, he sat in deep thought. "I don't think we'll have too much of a problem here. I'll speak with Miss Bartley's supervisor."

"I don't want Miss Bartley's report changed or dismissed. If that happens, there will be no resolution. Someone else will come up with something. I think this *hearing* will resolve everything," Bree stated. "I want a full scale public hearing, open to all."

"Might cause you some embarrassment," Mr. Moires said looking at Bree. "Perhaps you should consider having this *hearing* in the privacy of the judge's chambers?"

"*Ce ne fait rien.* No, thank you. I think that this is the best way. I can handle the embarrassment," she replied.

"Mrs. Jumppierre, I want you to understand completely that the *hearing* will not, specifically, be to decide whether you can keep your son. The *hearing* will be, specifically, about your way of life. You're taking a chance. I could put a stop to this right now," he stated.

"That's just it, Mr. Moires. It won't stop! This way, I believe it will. I just have to take a chance. I'm terrified, but it's the only way!"

"But there is one advantage. Judges do not like taking children from their parents. Especially a healthy specimen such as your son. You just may have a point. This will probably stop the townspeople cold. Now, what about your families? Will they be behind you in this? It will impress the judge. What about your family?" he asked, looking at Tousant.

"I'm originally from, *Thibodaux.* My parents were killed in an automobile accident four years ago," Tousant said. "My grandparents are both too old now and cannot be bothered."

"Oh," Mr. Moires said. "And you, Mr. Jourdan," he said, looking at Farras.

"I don't know, Mr. Moires. So far my parents ain't come 'round, but we really ain't been married that long, either. I'll work on 'em," Farras said.

"When you two married, you didn't get a marriage license, did you?" Mr. Moires asked, a concerned look on his face.

"No," Bree said.

"I'm glad you didn't because that would be illegal," he said, looking relieved. "Well, everything looks good. I'll take care of everything. You'll be notified as to the date of the *hearing,*" he said, getting up to leave.

"Mr. Moires," Tousant said suddenly. "I have something to tell you that I feel you need to know. How our family got to be the way that it is."

"No!" Bree shouted.

236

"Mr. Jumppierre, you don't have to explain anything to me. You people have a right to pursue your own life without interference from the State of Louisiana or anyone else. As long as you're not breaking any laws. So far, no law has been broken. I think we have a good case already, Mr. Jumppierre."

"Yes, but I would feel better if you knew *our situation* and what brought about our *unconventional lifestyle,* Tousant said. Mr. Moires sat back down with a look of mild curiosity.

"Tousant, please. No!" Bree pleaded again.

"My *sexual dysfunction* doesn't make or break me as a man, Bree. I have grown way past that. I am just as much man as any man."

After Tousant told Mr. Moires about the accident, he sat, stupefied. "My God, man. I don't think I have ever had the pleasure of meeting a man of your caliber. I read your story in the papers. But who in their right mind believes what they read in the papers, but hearing the story first hand.... It's remarkable!" He looked at Farras. "I have never met a man like you, either, Mr. Jourdan. What I see here is a man who loves his family and is trying to do everything necessary to keep his family together. The *hearing* shouldn't last long. But there is one other thing. Would Mr. Jourdan mind being questioned by the judge?"

"No, I don't mind doing that at all." Farras spoke up.

"And your son, Paupon. What about him?" he asked, looking at Tousant.

"No problem. Paupon's quite a man for his ten-years," Tousant said proudly.

"Then I don't foresee any problems," Mr. Moires said, walking towards the door. "You'll be hearing from me soon."

Bree shook at the thought of being in a courtroom and being questioned by a judge. She had read about trials and hearings in the newspaper. Somehow, in court, the truth always came out sounding like lies. When she thought about the possibility of losing Paupon, her shaking grew worse.

Word had got around the state again about her latest problem. There were more write-ups in newspapers. Bree had seen a few of the headlines: *"THE CONTINUING SAGA of ST. JAMESVILLE'S*

WOMAN'S FIGHT AGAINST the SYSTEM." But the possibility of her losing her son was never mentioned. At the time, she told herself, *perhaps losing one's children doesn't sell newspapers.* A few reporters from New Orleans and Baton Rouge came to her door trying to get her side of the story. At that precise moment, she felt like giving up, but something gave charge to her body and rang out loud and clear to her—fight! Fight for control over your own life, over your own destiny.

Bree had always wondered at the inconsistencies of Louisiana. The southern region of the state was dominated by French influences in architecture, food, and language. The attitudes were supposed to be freer, more progressive than the northern, agricultural region of the state. But the hostilities towards her came from both regions of the state.

The telephone rang, but Bree did not answer it. She had stopped answering the telephone. Her family had stopped calling and started coming by her house. She was afraid that this new crisis in their lives would affect Paupon. She had kept him home from school a few days. Both Tousant and Farras talked to him. Farras asked Paupon was he still at peace with him in the family. Paupon had said "yes" without hesitation.

A few minutes later, the telephone rang again. Out of habit, Bree's hand hovered over it. The telephone blared out three more rings. Bree lifted up the receiver and held it to her ear. She heard a familiar voice yelling through the receiver. She recognized Sabbath's voice. "*Allo*, Sabbath."

"I have been calling and calling," Sabbath said, sounding distraught.

"Belinda, should have told you that I am not answering the

telephone," Bree said impatiently.

"What if something happens to Paupon at school? Or to Tousant or Farras for that matter," she asked, "How could anybody contact you?"

"We have already made arrangements at Paupon's school in the event of an emergency, Sabbath. If something urgent happens, they will contact my father's office at the high school. In the event of an emergency about Tousant... actually that's the only reason I even lifted up the receiver." She held the receiver and waited for Sabbath's next words.

"Oh, come to think of it. Belinda did tell me that you weren't answering the telephone," Sabbath said. *It's just like you to disrespect other's wishes,* Bree thought.

"But I called, anyway." Sabbath purred. "You need to get out of that house, Bree," she whined. "It's not good to stay in for too long." *Since when have you ever been concerned about my welfare,* Bree thought. "Now, listen, Bree. I'm having a few ladies over this afternoon, and I thought you would like to come. It will be a nice outing for you. Besides, it is a lovely drive."

"I'm not up to it, Sabbath. Not today."

"I won't take no for an answer."

"Sabbath, I'm not up to it today," Bree said, more firmly with a trace of anger in her voice.

"I thought that we had settled our disagreements, Bree," she said, putting sincerity in her voice.

"That's not it, Sabbath. I'm just not up to talking with a bunch of women I don't know."

"It'll do you good to get out and meet new people. Come on, please. Don't say, no." Sabbath pleaded.

"Oh, all right, Sabbath. If that will shut you up, I'll come." Bree said. She hated letting Sabbath get to her like that. "I'll come, but only for an hour or so."

"Great! Then I'll expect you around eleven o'clock." *Maybe it won't be so bad after all,* Bree thought. *Sabbath's voice sounded cheerful enough.*

"All right," Bree said, and hung up the telephone without saying good-bye.

Sabbath's invitation made her feel a little uneasy. As soon as she hung up the telephone, the doorbell rang. When she opened the front door, Mr. LaPorte, the postman, was standing at the door holding a large, brown paper bag.

"Good morning." The postman greeted her, taking off his postman's hat.

"Good morning, Mr. LaPorte," she said, looking at him curiously. He had already made his mail delivery to her house. "Did you forget to deliver something?

"Oh, no mam. I didn't, Mrs. Jumppierre. Um...um...," he stammered. "I don't know your other *husband's* name," he said, looking at her.

"Jourdan, Mrs. Bree Jumppierre Jourdan," she said.

"I don't mean no harm. I just wanted to give your other *husband* all due respect," he explained. "I'm sorry for what's happening to you. I feel real bad about what's happening to Black people, period," he said. "Bombing little children in churches, cattle prods! I was just wondering whether I could help in some way?"

"Don't speak!" Bree interrupted the postman. Her face was frozen with rage. "Do not tell me how badly you feel about what's happening to my people. It's been happening for centuries. You keep delivering mail and watching your television and watch us die." She looked him up and down and thought: *So he's sympathetic to Blacks suffering such inhumane persecutions. The postman has found that Black people are human beings! she thought. That is not good for any oppressor to find out. Some White person should explain the perils of that to him.*

"I just wanted to apologize," he said remorsefully. She saw the sorrow on his face.

"Apologize! For what? There's nothing important going on. Just the destruction of millions of human beings." Her eyes held him. His mouth moved but no sound came. His eyes pleaded with hers for release, but Bree's eyes held steadfast. He started slowly backing off the gallery while her eyes continued to hold his. He stepped off the gallery with a confused look in his eyes. As the postman trotted to his mail truck, Bree looked at him and wondered whether, during *Hitler's* regime, did a German postman say the same things to the 'suffering Jews' as he delivered mail with the stench of human flesh in his nostrils? She looked down at the bag of 'preserves' that the postman had left sitting on the gallery, and tears of fury ran down her face. What 'peace-offering' did the German postman bring to the suffering Jews?

When Bree arrived at Sabbath's house, Sabbath met her in the driveway. "I have a 'special' surprise for you, Bree," Sabbath said, with excitement in her voice. Before she could say anything, Sabbath had caught her hand and led her into her house. "Ladies," she announced in a formal voice, "this is my sister-in-law, Mrs. Bree Jumppierre-Jourdan." The women spoke and looked at Bree in awe. "Bree," Sabbath said, catching Bree by her hand again. She led her across the room, "this is Ms. Raleigh, the President of our very own local 'women's lib' movement."

"Pleased to meet you," Bree said, and sat down in the chair next to Ms. Raleigh. She hoped that Sabbath hadn't dragged her to her house to join Ms. Raleigh's "women's lib" group.

"We have a 'special' award for you today, Mrs. Jumppierre Jourdan. That's why it was so important to get you here," Ms. Raleigh said.

"Oh, what type of award? And what on earth for?" Bree inquired.

"For being a 'trail blazer' for women's rights, of course," Ms. Raleigh, quipped. "You're to be commended," Ms. Raleigh, continued. The other women sat nodding their heads in agreements. They sat distant and aloof like painted, *plastic dolls.*

"Yes, Ms. Raleigh. I read one of your newspaper articles. You expressed your outrage about what's happening to me very eloquently," Bree said. Ms. Raleigh smiled a stiff smile, and nodded her head.

"And we'll be at that *court hearing* to support you too, Mrs. Jumppierre-Jourdan."

"With all your banners, signs, and flags too, I bet?"

"We have spent a week coordinating our project," Ms. Raleigh stated, with a hint of pride in her voice. "We refuse to stand by and watch a woman of your stature be treated in this manner."

"Oh," Bree said, surprised. "I'm sure that you are aware that I have had conflicts with the 'System' many times before. But I am only one of millions. I'm puzzled, Ms. Raleigh. Three months ago, half of my organization was either in jail or in the hospital. Where were you and your 'women's lib' group then? That made the papers as well. I guess... I'm wondering how did I manage to *miss* your support then?" The room grew quiet. The women gave Bree a cold stare.

"Mrs. Jumppierre-Jourdan, we thought that you'd be grateful for our support. This is a woman's issue. At the risk of sounding vain, we do know quite a bit about what's needed for the 'liberation' of women. We felt it our duty to support you, and give you the benefit of our experience. We have a few pointers to give to you that we have found to be quite effective. History shows...."

"You want to give *me* some pointers on how to get myself *free!*" Bree interrupted her and stood up. *"History!* You're looking at a woman who walked around with the *Nile River* in a rusty bucket until *God* told me where to put it. I'm the woman who gave birth to the 'human race' millions of years before *Hippocrates'* help. And you want to give me some pointers on how to get myself *free!* Please! *Au revoir, dames,*" Bree paused. "I don't know what you women know, Ms Raleigh, but I know what you don't know!" One of the women stood up poised to speak. "Don't speak. Please, do not speak!" Bree stood trembling in rage.

"Je regrette, Bree," Sabbath apologized, walking down the hallway behind her. "I thought since..."

"I just want to be left alone, Sabbath. I want *paix. Au revoir,* Sabbath." Sabbath stood holding the door.

"Give my nephews my love. Look, Sabbath," Bree said, her voice softening, "I'm sorry that I had to insult guests in your home."

Bree walked angrily to her car. She was upset with herself for losing control, and for dishonoring the house of her brother.

CHAPTER
FIFTEEN

At sunrise, Bree got up, and went into her vegetable garden to gather vegetables. It was a bright morning. She wore a large, brown straw hat that shielded her eyes from the sun's brightness. The fresh morning dew wet her sandals and soothed her feet. She stood holding a basket of vegetables, and she thought about how past generations of her family had loved and tilled the soil.

She sat the vegetable basket down at her feet, and stood pushing stray strands of her hair back underneath her straw hat. She watched a green "garden snake" sit unafraid on top of a tomato plant. His tongue darted out smelling the air. She ignored the harmless snake.

The garden brought thoughts of her past back to her. Before she had Farras, the early morning hours only brought loneliness. In Tousant's long absences away from home, she would touch his side of the bed while silent tears wet her pillow. It was during Tousant's absence, to fill the lonely days, that she had started a vegetable garden. But that *life* seemed like a lifetime ago. Now, having a yearly garden had become an important part of her life. Since her marriage to Farras, he and Paupon had taken over the vegetable garden, and that year's vegetable garden was much better than all of the years' before. Farras had taught Paupon things about gardening that she had not known herself. Even though she had read every book that she could on the subject. Though Tousant had a great love for the land, his job never allowed him the time to work a garden.

She reached down, picked up the basket of vegetables, and started walking towards the house. As she approached the back screen door, she heard the faint, muffled voices of Tousant and Farras. When she entered the kitchen, Farras and Tousant were sitting at the table. They both held strange looks as they looked up at her. She sensed that something was wrong. Instead of using the large, iron sink in the garage, she dumped the vegetables into the kitchen sink. The past three weeks had been hard. Prolonged tension had taken its toll on her. It was as if a cloud of doom hovered over her house, as if *something* nameless was poised, ready to demolish her. She knew the *force* she would be fighting this time was much more powerful, more equipped to virtually destroy them. As she stood at the kitchen sink washing vegetables, she was tempted to just give in to her feelings. She was tired of fighting seemingly endless battles. But whenever she felt down in spirit, she would remember that her family was still together, and..."Bree." Tousant's voice jumped into her thoughts. He called her name in a more serious tone than he usually did. She turned her attention to him. "This is very important, Bree." He motioned for her to sit down at the kitchen table. Bree stood frozen at the sink with her back to them. "Would you just stop a minute and come sit at the table with us?" Tousant asked, in an annoyed tone.

"Where is Paupon?" Bree asked.

"You were in the garden. You didn't see your father pick him up?"

"*Non*, where did they go?"

"They went to the restaurant. They'll be gone all day."

"Oh, Lord," Bree cried.

"What's wrong, Bree? Paupon has gone with his grandfather to his restaurant before. I happen to agree with your father. Paupon needs to learn the business. There's nothing wrong with him spending some Saturdays there. He was excited."

Bree turned and gave Tousant a doubtful look. "I guess, our Saturday morning tennis games are over."

With her eyes on both Tousant and Farras, she tore off two paper towels to dry her hands. Trying hard not to let her face show her anxiety, she walked over to the table, and tiredly pulled out a chair and sat down.

"Mr. Moires, called me at work yesterday," Tousant said.

"Why, would he call you at work?"

"Because, I asked him to," Tousant replied.

"Why did you do that?"

"We decided that any calls pertaining to the *hearing* would come to my office."

"We, who?" Bree frowned.

"Me and Tousant," Farras spoke up. "I know how our protectin' you freaks you out, but we can see what this *hearin'* is doin' to you. We ain't kept nothin' else from you. So, I don't care if knowin' this upsets you. We is men. Any man will protect his family. Excuse us for tryin' to make yo' sufferin' a little less. If you think that we wrong..." Farras said, leaving off his last words.

"I guess, you both were right. This time, anyway," Bree added. "What is it we have to talk about?" she asked.

"The *hearing* is set for next week," Tousant said.

"Why, so soon? I thought these things took time," she said.

"I thought so, too. But it's a small town. Which means that the court docket isn't backlogged. I mentioned the same thing to Mr. Moires and this is what he told me," Tousant said.

"Oh," Bree said, suddenly more dispirited.

"We want you and Paupon to go away for the week and come back home maybe the day before the *hearing,*" Farras said.

"No way!" Bree yelled. "You two have really been planning and talking, haven't you? We're staying here together until this *court hearing* is over."

"Just listen to yourself, Bree. Look how you're shouting. You have been having these flare-ups often. We have always discussed things in a calm manner."

"Yes, I know," she sighed. "It's my nerves."

"I know your nerves are shot. You need some rest. A week away from all this would work wonders for your nerves. I know that you want to show the world that we stand together, but that's not necessary. We are a family–maybe not by 'copy book standards–but a family, nonetheless. We don't have to prove it to anyone," Tousant said. "We don't have to be in each other's physical presence every day to stay strong, either. Each of us is a very strong individual. If we weren't, we would have been beaten as soon as we started out."

"If you worried 'bout Paupon, don't be." Farras interjected. "Sometimes I think he mo' together than we is." Farras had a proud look on his face. Bree sat looking at them.

"Where did you two plan for us to go?"

"We ain't planned nothin'," Farras said.

"We thought we'd leave choosing the place up to you," Tousant said.

"Oh, I see. You two planned everything else, but where we're to go is up to me, huh?" she said.

"Well, we figured we would let you do a little something," Tousant said smiling. "But the place you choose cannot be too far away."

"Why not? There's airplanes now, Tousant. Modern transportation is here. Gone are the horse and buggy days," Bree said irritably. "Since it's my choice. I think I would like to go to *New Iberia* and visit my mother's sister, *mon Tante Marie.*"

"I think that would be fine, Bree. That's not too far away, either. I have always liked *votre Tante Marie et Oncle Thos.* They are good people. They just feed you too much when you visit them," Tousant said smiling.

"How far is *New Iberia?* I heard of it, but I don't know where *New Iberia* is," Farras asked.

"*New Iberia*, is about one hundred and twenty-five miles from here," Tousant said. "It's a little over a three hour drive."

"That sounds good," Farras said.

"Can I say something here?" Bree asked.

"*Oui, la dame*," they both said.

"I was wondering if they knew about the *hearing.* I wonder if the *les journaux* in *New Iberia* carried the story. If it did, how did *Tante Marie et Oncle Thos* take the news?" Bree asked, sounding apprehensive. "I cannot believe that our 'lifestyle' has sparked such an outrage in this state. It surpasses anything I have ever seen."

"I cannot believe it either," Tousant said. "But you can bet if one newspaper carried our story, they all carried the story. Not much excitement happens in small towns, and when it does, they break their necks writing about it. But don't worry about it, Bree. We know

246

better than anyone you cannot stop talk. If you're concerned about how your aunt and uncle are taking all of this, call them. I'm sure that your aunt and *votre mère* have already talked about our *unconventional lifestyle*. *Votre mère* probably already called her. They are sisters, you know. Even though they only visits each other a few times a year, they still talk to each other on the telephone. *Votre mère* probably called her sister when we first decided that you would take Farras as a *second* husband. Your mother was really upset about us. It's only natural that she would call and discuss our *unconventional lifestyle* with her sister."

"I'm not so much concerned about my aunt knowing. But I would hate to visit her, and have someone find out who I am. It could trigger almost anything. I don't want their life disturbed. They still have to live in *New Iberia* after I'm gone."

"I know, so call your aunt," Tousant said. "If she and your uncle don't think that a visit will be wise, I'm sure she will tell you, and you can choose some place else. It's simple. But knowing *Tante Marie et Oncle Thos,* they'd be glad to have you two. *Tante Marie* is tough and so is *Oncle Thos.* They would love the company. *Oncle Thos* is just wild about Paupon. He will have a fishing buddy. I know Paupon would love it, too. And you can rest, read, and let your aunt stuff both of you with food."

"You're right, Tousant. My thinking has been bad these last months. I'll call them tonight. And, anyway, *Tante Marie et Oncle Thos* have such good hearts. It wouldn't matter to them how I have chosen to live. Still, I wonder why *Tante Marie* hasn't called me."

"Maybe, she wanted to. But she thought it wasn't her business to get involved. Maybe she felt that if you wanted her to know anything about your life, you would have called her. It could very possibly be that she was waiting for you to call her. They wouldn't have invited themselves into our affairs, Bree," Tousant said.

"I should know better," she said. "This will give me the opportunity to do some shopping in *Lafayette.* I have always loved shopping in *Lafayette.*"

"Then everythin's fine," Farras said. "I think I'm gon' git myself a beer."

"Not, quite," Tousant said. Farras hesitated.

"What do you mean, not quite," Farras asked.

"I think you should go with them, Farras. You need to get away from all this, too. You just told me this morning you could take time off for the *hearing*. You said that you have built up a lot of sick leave," Tousant said.

"No way, *bèbè*. I'm stayin' right here," Farras said angrily.

"It makes sense, Farras. I would go myself if I could take time off work. I cannot take time off right now."

"No way, *bèbè*," Farras said, again, "We both the mens in this house. You don't tell me, and I don't tell you. We discuss, remember!"

Bree sat watching the *two* men. She wondered why men placed so much importance on being men and not on just being human beings. She braced herself for Tousant's inevitable reaction. She knew that one day a confrontation would occur between Tousant and Farras. She knew, too, that one day they would have to get each of their roles as her husbands straightened out between the two of them. If there hadn't been external troubles, or if Tousant were home all the time, it would have already occurred. But their "troubles" had caused Tousant and Farras to stand together. They had been kept busy by a common purpose. But they had not shown the other the 'weakness and strength' of their own personalities. Now the time had come for them to deal with each other, and the outcome would be based on the way each of them had been socialized to be men. Farras and Tousant were dissimilar in temperament—an unmatched pair. There was a strong possibility for them to become rivals. If that happened, it would completely destroy the relationship between the three of them.

Farras and Tousant glared at each other for an eternity it seemed to her. "Farras, is it necessary to prove to Bree which of us is the better man?" Tousant asked. "I mean, she's our wife. We don't have to do combat to see who wins her or to see who rules the roost. If we have to do that, then all is lost anyway. There has never been a question in my mind as to who was the better man. I'm my own man, and you're your own man, Farras. I thought that was understood," Tousant said.

"It was never understood by me. I never thought you put yo'

manhood on the same level with mines, Tousant. You never tol' me or led me to believe you did. I always felt since you a educated man, you looks down on me. This suppose to be my house too. But I don't own a damn thing here but my clothes," Farras continued.

"I didn't know you felt that way, Farras. But so much has been going on that we haven't had a chance to talk, earnestly. Farras, I do not place your manhood any lower than I place my own."

"Oh, so now you want me to believe that you respect my manhood like you do any other man, huh?" Farras glared at Tousant.

"If I didn't respect you as a man, Farras. You would not be in my home. I would not have a man around my son, or my wife, that I do not respect," Tousant said.

"Did you respect me at first. Or did you want a 'stud' for yo' wife? If I was a educated man like you, would you let me be in yo' house?" Farras asked.

"The answer to your first question is, no! I didn't respect you at first..," Tousant said.

"You see, I knew it!" Farras interrupted.

"Let me finish Farras," Tousant said. "Did you respect me as a man at first? Now, be honest, Farras." Farras sat back down at the table.

"Well, I don't know if I respected you as a man, but I..."

"But you admired me. You admired a man that did what I agreed to do. Something that you thought was impossible for any man to do, right? You thought that you could never do what I'd done under any circumstances, right?" Tousant asked. "You see, Farras, that's your problem. You put doubts in your own mind, not I. You thought, this man has a beautiful wife, and not only does he agree to let me live with them, but he's got guts enough to marry us too! Hey, man. I know that was a 'head trip,' and probably a little freaky to you, too. But I have learned to admire you as a man, Farras. Loving another man's wife, and having the guts to agree to live an *unconventional lifestyle* took courage. Most men would have said, 'The hell with this!' And tried to take Bree away from me and have her all for himself. You see Farras, we admired each other for doing what we both thought was the *impossible!* But you didn't respect me and I didn't respect you.

Respect is earned. And I think we have earned each other's respect. I know you earned my respect, Farras."

"You got my respect a long time ago, man," Farras said.

"And to answer your question about being a stud, Bree wanted a husband, not a stud. Farras, you could have left a long time ago, especially when trouble started, but you stayed. As far as your manhood goes that said everything to me. It said a lot about your love for Bree."

"I did leave. Well.., fo' a few hours, anyway." Farras said.

"I would have figured as much. That was only being human, Farras. Good, Lord! You're a man, not a saint. This is new to all of us. To answer your question as to whether I would have let an *educated* man be a *second* husband to Bree, the answer is, no!"

"Was you *testin'* my knowledge, too?" Farras asked.

"In a sense, weren't you testing mine, Farras?" Tousant asked.

"Sometimes," Farras admitted.

"But you were testing me for a different reason than why I was testing you," Tousant said.

"How, so?" Farras asked.

"Now I can finish answering your last question, as to whether I would have agreed to you being Bree's *second* husband if you were college educated. I repeat–no! I'm human, too. If Bree would have met a man that satisfied her both 'physically and intellectually,' I would have lost her. Why would she need me? Quite honestly, Farras, that's why 'our situation' works. It's simple. You don't pose a threat to me. As far as the 'physical' love that you so jealously hoard, I don't pose a threat to you. I have no desire to reclaim anything 'sexual' from my wife. We each have what we want. Some would say that we have our cake and are eating it too. It's the way of the world, Farras. Deep down inside of every man, there's hatred for another man getting more than his fair share. That's why poor people hate rich people. If that same poor person became rich, he wouldn't hate rich people anymore, and all the reasons he had for hating the rich would fly right out of the window."

"How do you know that I don't pose a threat to you, Tousant? I could be 'intellectually' stimulation enough for Bree," Farras said.

250

Bree's heart leaped. She sat trying to keep her feelings channeled into neutrality.

"I have tested your knowledge, Farras, remember. I have tested your knowledge in areas that I know Bree has to be intellectually stimulated in," Tousant said. "The arts, politics, science, currents affairs, philosophy, etc." Tousant gave Farras a look of arrogance.

"So, Tousant, you sayin' if you died tomorrow, I'd lose Bree."

"Bingo! That's exactly what I'm saying, Farras. "I am also saying that no matter how much you hate reading, or any formal learning, you would have to get your behind in gear and enroll in some night classes, or become the most well-read man in the State of Louisiana. Farras, you know, I know, and Bree knows too, that what I'm saying is the truth. There's no denying it. You satisfy her *physical* needs. Let's don't forget that. Bree loves what you do to her in bed. But I satisfy her 'intellectual and spiritual' needs." Bree knew that there was a thin line between cruelty and candidness, and Tousant was skirting dangerously close to pedantry. "And as for either of us being head of this household, neither of us is. We are all adults here. I didn't mean to imply that I was. You are right. We do discuss things, and try to come up with answers that would make us all happy."

"I understand that, Tousant. I don't know why I flew off the handle like that. I guess this *hearin'* business is gittin' to me too."

"I disagree, Farras. I do agree that this *hearing* business does have us all under stress, but this confrontation had to come sooner or later. I'm glad it came and it's over. It wasn't as bad as I thought it would be," Tousant said, looking at Bree. Bree hadn't moved. She had almost ceased breathing while the 'verbal sparring' took place. She sighed with relief. "Farras, this was not our first hurdle in this relationship, and I'm glad that this one's over." Tousant exhaled deeply.

"Yes, I'm glad it's over too, Tousant. Now, we both know where we stand. I still ain't goin' on no trip with Bree. I'm stayin' right here. Bree will have Paupon and her *Tante et Oncle*. I'm stayin' and that's final."

"Okay."

"I would like to leave Monday morning if I can get a train out,"

Bree said.

"The train!" Farras said. "Can't you fly? A plane will git there in no time. It takes too long by train, and you already tired."

"It'll be a treat for Paupon. Which one of you is going to take us to the train station?"

"I can," Tousant hurriedly injected. "I'll go back to Houston Tuesday," Tousant explained. "You have to leave to go to work so early, Farras. Unless you were planning on taking the day off too," Tousant added.

"No, I'm just gonna take a few days off fo' the *hearin'*," Farras said."

"Then *c'est entendu,*" Tousant said.

"What about Paupon's last week of school? The school year won't end for another week," Bree said.

"Who does she think she's married to *two* dummies?" Tousant said, looking at Farras. "It's been taken care of, Bree. Paupon passed to the sixth grade with flying colors. The teacher will mail us his report card. Satisfied?"

"Yes, now all I have to do is call *Tante Marie et Oncle Thos.* I'll have to let them know when my train will be arriving."

"Farras," Tousant said, "there's just one more thing that I'd like to say. Then we're going to leave this kitchen before Bree throws us out. After the *hearing* is over, I'll speak to Mr. Moires about arranging for you to buy an acre of land here to build yourself a house."

"Whatever is fair, Tousant," Farras said. "I have one last question to ask you too, Tousant. How did you meet Bree?"

"Well, I finally got my master's degree, and had come back to the States for a visit. I stayed here in St. Jamesville with a fraternity brother for a few days. He was teaching, naturally. There was nothing else that an educated Negro could do in those days. Anyway, he gave a party in my honor, and I met Bree at the party."

"You were overseas somewhere?" Farras interrupted.

"*Oui*, France."

"France! Sweet Jesus!" Farras gave a low whistle in awe.

"I have an uncle who lives in France. He never came back to Louisiana to live after WWII. I had graduated from Southern

University, but I still had a burning desire to be an *astro physicist*. My parents contacted my uncle in France. Since I spoke the language, they didn't think that school in France would be too difficult for me. I don't even want to think about the financial hardships my schooling put on my parents, but my uncle took his share of the financial burden, too. A thousand letters later, and another visit to the States, Bree finally consented to marry me. One year later, we got married. Two months after our marriage, I went back to France and stayed until I completed my doctorate. When I came back home, I got a teaching position at Southern University. But I was not happy! And I remained unhappy until I finally got the job in my field at the 'Manned Space Flight Center' in Houston. And now, here we all are." A quick, hostile look passed over Tousant's face.

It had dawned on Tousant during the course of their conversation that Farras was a *fool!* And he hated *fools!* They always did things the wrong way. And they sure as hell did not wrestle, *morally*, with the wrongness of it either. They were "natural born hell raisers," and they never allowed too much thinking to dominate their lives. That made him hate men like Farras more. And men like Farras didn't have bodies that trapped them inside, and have them running on the inside like a *pet* hamster on wheel in a cage, either. They did not get "sick-to-the-soul" pain. They were minute-by-minute men. Their senses did not get stunned by "tomorrows." They did not have to weather any storms in their lives. *Impotency* could never happen to a man like Farras, *he told himself.* Somehow, men like Farras just seem to skate by the "shit heaps" of life. Unstoppable, with balled-up fists, they: bullied, flirted, fucked, teased, and walked arrogantly around *Fate*. And for reasons unknown to men like himself, *Fate* never viewed men like Farras as good candidates for mental cruelty. And the big payoff for *Fate* was to mess with the minds of brilliant men, and to let men like Farras walk around with stiff, dagger-like dicks, dripping blood.

"That figures," Farras said. The sound of Farras' voice disrupted Tousant's angry thoughts.

Tousant looked at Bree with troubled eyes. He could not stop himself from longing for their old life together. He hesitated at the doorway. "One small detail that I neglected to mention to you, Farras.

You do not earn enough money to maintain Bree. She hates poverty with a purple passion. Of course, being rich wouldn't rest too well with her *social* conscience, but poverty doesn't rest too well with her *personal* comfort. And besides, you don't look the best either, Farras." Tousant raised his brow. "Am I being cruel?" he asked, as he exited the door. Tears, not flowing... just two, lay in each of Tousant's eyes.

Feeling a terrible anxiety, Bree looked full-faced at Farras but made no comment. She tried to shake the image of Tousant's eyes from her mind. *What was it with Tousant?* she thought. *He said "yes," but somehow he really meant, "no."* She shook her head in confusion.

It was Sunday evening. Bree and Paupon had spent a week in New Iberia. On the train ride home, the word *hearing* played through her mind. But she was glad that Tousant and Farras had talked her into taking the trip. Her visit with her aunt and uncle had been enjoyable, and she felt completely rested. She could face the ordeal of the *hearing*, which was at nine o'clock the following morning.

She turned the key in the front door and she and Paupon walked into the living-room. Paupon gave a loud holler bringing Tousant and Farras rushing into the living-room. "Surprise!" Bree yelled.

"Surprise!" Paupon yelled.

They all embraced. Paupon immediately started talking. *"Pe're,* every day, *Oncle Thos* bought me a *peaux boy,"* Paupon said, excitedly. "He laughed at how fast I could eat them. He would say, "Oh, Paupon, eating is the *joie de vivre.*" Then he would pop his fingers and say, *"Laissez les bons temps rouler, Paupon."* I had a good time. We rode the *Teche Queen.*"

"Paupon, please, slow down. At least slow down enough to breathe," Tousant said laughing.

"*Père*, every night *Oncle Thos* played his *Zydeco* music, and the four of us danced and danced. I'm going back to the *Zydeco* Festival next year. *Oncle Thos* wants me to come back to celebrate *Mardi Gras* in *Lafayette*. *Then* we're going to the *Mardi Gras in St. Martinsville*, too. We're going to both *Mardi Gras*. *Oncle Thos* plays a mean game of chess, too. He said I'll always be his best buddy." Tousant and Farras were in deep laughter as Paupon spoke. "Talk about *boudin* and *gumbo*." Paupon licked at his lips. *"New Iberia and Lafayette* have more than their fair share of it. I'm definitely going back. Man, I had a good time. I sure am glad we went." When Paupon finished talking, he stood with a dreamy look in his eyes.

"Glad we could oblige you, *fils*," Tousant said smiling. "How come you didn't call us to pick you two up at the train station? We knew you would arrive tonight, so we waited for your call," Tousant said, happily to Bree.

"We decided to surprise you two," Bree said.

"And you sho' did," Farras said. "Paupon looks like you growed a inch in a week." Paupon did not answer. He stood with his hands in his pockets, smiling. "Where's the suitcases?" Farras asked.

"We carried the luggage from the taxi and left them sitting on the front gallery," she answered.

Farras took Bree's luggage upstairs to their bedroom. When he came back downstairs, they were all sitting in the living-room. "Hand over yo' little *music box*, Bree." Farras said. He held his hand out in front of Bree.

"What for, Farras? Don't spoil things tonight, please," Tousant said. His eyes gleamed in anger.

"Will you please hand me your *music box*, Bree. I got a surprise fo' you. Don't git nervous." Bree looked at Tousant and back again at Farras. Cautiously, she handed her *music box* to Farras. He kissed her little *music box*, and gave it back to her. She looked at him.

"Merci," she said, her voice choking up.

"I want you to have it. I've grown... I mean... I'm not...," he stammered.

"Shhh," Bree said. She reached up and pressed her fingers to his lips.

"I understand, perfectly," she said softly. When Farras looked around at Tousant and Paupon, they pretended that they hadn't noticed.

"I missed you two. I don't know 'bout, Tousant. But I was a lost man," Farras said. "We done fixed food fit fo' a queen and king. And the only fuss we had since you been gone was 'bout supper tonight," Farras said, looking at her. "I like *shrimp and mirliton* and Tousant likes steaks. So we flipped coins. I lost," he said laughing.

"So we fixed steak."

"I'm so hungry, anything will taste great," she said.

After supper, Tousant and Bree sat out on the veranda. Exhausted, Paupon had gone directly to bed after supper. A slight breeze was blowing cool air from the levee. "Cannot stay out here too long, the mosquitoes are giving me fits," Tousant complained.

"Let's just stay a little while longer, Tousant," she said. "At least until Farras can join us. You *two* have a pretty good system. You do the cooking, and Farras does the dishes."

"Was the trip enjoyable?"

"The trip was great! But I'm glad to be back home."

"I'm finished," Farras said, walking out on the veranda, "It was a ton of dishes to be done. Next time, I'll cook. At least, I don't dirty every pot, pan, and dish in the kitchen." Tousant did not comment on Farras' remarks.

"I been thinking," Tousant said, looking up into the nighttime sky.

"You have," Farras joked.

"Yes, I have," Tousant said. "Maybe after the *hearing* we should sell out and start fresh some place else."

"I don't think that's a good idea. As a matter of fact, I know it's a rotten idea," Bree said. "For one thing, if we go some place else, all of this *mess* could start all over again. People are the same everywhere, Tousant. You know that. Our families are here. These are our roots. It's all we know. No, Tousant. I wouldn't be at peace living some place else. We have a good life here, and I'm not running. I want to live and die on the soil of my ancestors."

"And whata 'bout me?" Farras asked. "I ain't like you, Tousant. I

256

can't git a job just anywheres. I think Bree is right. This our home. I'm stayin' right here in Louisiana."

"All right. Just because I'm educated doesn't mean that I'm smart all the time," Tousant said. "It was a dumb idea. I'll admit it. Let's go to bed. I'm bushed. I know Bree is bushed, too." He directed his last words to Farras. "These mosquitoes are giving me fits," he said, slapping at his neck, "We won't be leaving Louisiana. *C'est entendu.*" Tousant said, a slight edge to his voice.

"Why you always say that?" Farras asked.

"Say, what?" Tousant asked annoyed.

"*C'est entendu.* Why you always sayin' that? Nothin' in life is ever settled, Tousant. Life changes constantly from day to day. There's other words to say instead of, *c'est entendu.*" Tousant stood mildly shocked by Farras' words. Suddenly a rush of hatred, out of nowhere, clutched his chest.

"Don't git nervous, Tousant. I didn't suddenly get smart. Bree read somethin' like that to me one day—and I learn fast," he said smiling. He saw the tenseness leave Tousant's face.

"Well, it's been a long day," Tousant said. It surprised him how weary he felt in Farras' presence for any length of time. And Farras' excessive politeness towards him angered him, dangerously. Killing someone had always seemed far-fetched to him, the mark of a mind out of control. Yet, there were those peculiar moments when... He was glad that most of Farras' weekends were taken up by his music. When he was home on weekends, he was glad that he had only brief encounters with him. Anything more would have been *too* much. There were nights when he thought he heard sounds of their love-making. Of course, he did not. The sheer distance of the two bedrooms made that an impossibility. So he could not have heard. Still... there were times when he thought that he did, and it wounded him. He knew that *Time* could never heal such wounds. How could his heart ever heal marred by such deep wounds? Why was it that people usually survived large, gaping wounds, but they usually died from inconspicuous wounds? Before, he had never believed in the *foreverness* of anything, but... now... His suffering had taken him over. Lord, knows, he had tired to overcome his suffering. At work, he tried to hide his suffering, and tried to carry on just as he had before, but he found that he had to constantly watch what he said or did. Where before there was certainty, now was uncertainty—he constantly check every decision.

The worst part of his *impotence* was knowing that sex was being had by lesser men. Men who stayed sexually fulfilled; yet, they kept grabbing and reaching for more sex. His *impotence* kept him with a feeling of sitting at a table that held a *feast*, but he wasn't allowed to eat. "I'm going in with Tousant a while," Bree said. "I'll be upstairs later, Farras." The sound of Bree's voice interrupted Tousant's angry thoughts. He turned and gave Bree and Farras a hostile look.

Bree sensed that something had happened between her *husbands* in her absence, something she could not yet define. She had sensed that something was wrong during supper, now she sensed something again. She said nothing.

"If I'm asleep, wake me up, Bree," Farras said, winking at her as he exited the veranda. "Oh, I forgot to tell you *votre me're* called, Bree." He walked back and stood in the doorway. "She said to tell you that they will see us at the *hearing* tomorrow. She said fo' you not to worry that thangs gon' work out fine. And fo' me to be sho' to tell you that she will fix a 'victory dinner' at her house. We should come to her house after we leave the courthouse," Farras said.

"That sounds fine. At least we're not alone in this," Bree said.

"I forgot to tell you. We got a dozen or so telephone calls from well-wisher's," Tousant said.

"Did you talk to your parents, Farras?" Bree asked.

"*Oui*," he said.

"*Et?*"

"And—I don't know. We won't worry 'bout it," Farras said, "I'll see you upstairs."

After Farras left the room, Tousant turned to Bree and said, "Bree, I figure I'd let you have all the bad news at once. I got fired today." He kept a light-hearted voice as he continued. "The record states: *Fired with cause.* It seems there is a 'moral clause' in my contract. They know the end results of my accident, but they don't agree with our *unconventional lifestyle.* I think a discreet affair would have been more to their liking. Because of the sensitive nature of my work, the Lab. really frown on an employee's name being in the papers. Especially the negative articles being written about us. They cannot tolerate the publicity. Bree stared at Tousant full in the face. A false smile had frozen on his lips. Tousant's chest protruded a bit too far. She could tell that he was putting up a brave front. She knew, too, that if Tousant did not get another position soon, he would crumble. His whole identity was wrapped around his profession. He had become his profession. It defined who he was and gave his life order.

"Jesus! They're crushing us, Tousant!" Bree said. Her voice had a heavy weariness in it. "You'd think that what we do was our own business. Perhaps *Père* was right when he said that this is *an unholy alliance.* Perhaps there is some 'universal moral code of conduct' that must be adhered to. Perhaps when we leave that pathway, the universe trembles and gets thrown off balance."

"We have always known that there was a price." Tousant stated, matter-of-factly. "And we were willing to pay it. And..."

"But its such a high price, Tousant!" she wailed, interrupting him, "Such... a... high..." She became too emotional and couldn't finish her sentence. Her eyes held pools of water.

"Being fired with 'cause' will probably prevent me from ever getting a 'security clearance' again." Tousant ran his his hands over his head. "I'll have to find a position completely out of 'Research and Development.' He gave her a stern look. "We're not whipped, yet. I'll teach again if I have to," Tousant added.

"You hate teaching, Tousant. You know you do. This..."

Tousant broke in. "We're be all right, Bree," he said reassuringly. "Please, try not to worry. First things first. Let's just concentrate on tomorrow." Her face went blank. "Bree, find the strength. We have yet another battle. We have got to fight to keep our *fils,*" Tousant stated, passionately gripping her by the shoulders.

CHAPTER
SIXTEEN

*I*t was a windy and cloudy morning. The windswept sky held twirling, dark clouds. The wind had pushed puffy, gray clouds, with faint, indistinct lines, back to one side, and shaped them into peaked, skyward waves. Behind the clouds, the sun reflected red with silvery lights that snaked its way along thin, horizontal openings. On their way downtown to the courthouse, they passed by *M'sieu* Mouton's fish market. It was boarded up. Bree sat quietly in the back seat with Paupon. The song from her *music box* played in her mind. She leaned her head against the back seat and glanced up at the unusual looking sky. *I'm going mad and no one's noticed it,* she thought. "Hey, why are you so quiet back there, Bree?" Tousant asked, glancing back over his shoulder at her. "Don't tell me you don't have anything to say." He reached back with one hand and squeezed her knee.

"I have nothing to say," she murmured. "Nothing." Bree was more frightened than she had ever been in her life. Restless and nervous, she feared the worst. Fear knotted her stomach. The thought that she might, indeed, lose her son almost cut off her breath. Before she left the house, without anyone knowing, she went into every room that had a clock and stopped them.

When they drove into the parking lot of the courthouse, there was a large crowd. The crowd milled around as though they were waiting for *Mardi Gras* floats to pass by. Bree got out of the car and stood briefly looking at the crowd. "Nervous?" Tousant asked, as he glanced quickly at the crowd. He gave Bree no chance to answer before he spoke again. "This is pitiful! These people! It's just a *hearing* for Christ sake!" Tousant exclaimed. "There must be some out-of-towner's here too, Bree." He guided her along. They walked across the street towards the courthouse. Bree looked to her left, and she saw Malik X and some members from the Organization. She held up her fist in salute to them; then threaded her way through the crowd. Someone in the crowd pointed and yelled, "There they are. That's them." They ignored the voice, and continued walking towards Mr. Moires, who was standing outside the courthouse door waiting for them.

As they stepped up on the sidewalk leading to the front door, someone else in the crowd said. "There they are." This time, a hush fell over the crowd. Some strained their necks trying to get a quick glance. The crowd stood in the liquid heat their clothes stuck to their sweaty bodies. Camera bulbs started flashing. Reporters seemed to be everywhere. Bree saw that there was even a television camera pointing at her face. It made her feel as if she were a specimen underneath a microscope. Reporters were yelling questions at her. She held her head high and kept walking.

When they walked inside the front door of the courthouse, there were more reporters, more questions, more flashing bulbs. Tousant saw Mr. Moires waving his hand near the door that led into the courtroom. Tousant gently nudged Bree, Paupon, and Farras ahead of him. They shoved their way through the crowd. Next to Mr. Moires, Bree's family stood against the wall near the door. She looked at them, and she gave them a weak smile. Farras looked around, and saw his parents leaning against the opposite wall. He tapped Bree and Tousant on the shoulder. "My parents are here. I'm going over and speak to them." Bree looked in the direction where Farras had just pointed, and saw his mother clutching her purse. Farras father stood next to her. Bree looked over the crowd. To her left, she saw Ms. Raleigh and her "women's lib" group. They nodded to her. She nodded back. But her eyes were hard. Standing directly behind Ms. Raleigh's "women's lib" group, was the postman and his wife. They looked at Bree, and Bree gave them a warm smile as she threaded her way through the crowd towards them. She shook the couple's hand.

"Thank you both for the preserves and for your moral support,"

Bree said smiling. "You must forgive my manners. I'm afraid I have not been myself lately." With sad eyes, they both nodded their heads in understanding. "After this blows over, if you still want to help my people in some way, of course, it would be welcomed."

The postman whispered in Bree's ear, "All White people are not bloodthirsty, you know."

"Of course not. I'm sorry if I implied otherwise. I should get back to my family now." She smiled back at the couple as she threaded her way up front. She glanced again at Ms. Raleigh and her 'women's lib' group. She wondered whether all the women of the world would ever learn to genuinely bond to each other. She seriously doubted it. *What a tragedy,* she thought. She gave a quick look again over at Farras and his parents, and saw Farras making exaggerated hand gestures, as if he were hotly pursuing a useless argument. She saw Farras drop his hands at his sides, and shake his head. He walked away from his parents looking sick and defeated. He threaded his way through the crowd. As soon as he reached Bree, he said:

"I tried." He exhaled deeply.

Bree gave him a tender look and said, "I'm sorry, Farras."

"It'll be a cold day in h*ell* befo' I beg again. I got my pride too," Farras said. "Besides, we got more important thangs to worry 'bout right now, anyway." Bree looked over at *Madame* Blanque. She was leaning against the wall on the opposite side of the room. She stood, arms folded, looking triumphant. Their eyes held for a moment. Her hatred for *Madame* Blanque, vanished, and was replaced by a deep and stirring sadness.

Bree's throat felt hot, parched. To her left, she saw Miss Rosette sandwiched in by the crowd. She appeared to be shaking more acutely. Her body seemed to be in one continuous, jerking motion. She smiled, and prayed silently that Miss Rosette would not scream out her hostilities. Delphine fought her way through the crowd. When she reached Bree, she spoke quickly, "If you lose, I lose. It's an ancient, African law." She held up her thumb and smiled.

"Mr. Jumppierre, let's get your family inside the courtroom," Mr. Moires said, "I had no idea that there would be this many people—and reporters, too! I thought there would be a few curiosity seekers, and maybe one reporter, but nothing like this!" Mr. Moires exclaimed, throwing up his hands. "Had I known, I would have made some other arrangements. Maybe had you people enter from the rear," he continued. Bree looked into Mr. Moires' blue eyes, and she did not believe him. She sensed that Mr. Moires had, in some underhanded way, planned it all.

By nine o'clock, it was already unbearably hot. The courtroom was packed with people. Some stood mopping their faces with soggy handkerchiefs. The ceiling fans offered no relief. People choked the front entrance and covered the front steps. Hot air filtered in through the large, double doors. No policemen asked them to leave. Perhaps they feared a riot if they had. The crowd's eyes were fixed on the door that led to the judge's chambers. They had come to see Bree's blood spill and would not settle for anything less.

Tousant sat next to Mr. Moires. Bree sat between Tousant and Paupon. Mr. Moires leaned over and started talking to Tousant. "I have talked to the judge already. This won't last long. I've explained to him about this case. The judge will begin with Mrs. Jumppierre. Then, your son. You'll be last," he told Tousant.

"And what about, Mr. Jourdan?" Tousant asked.

"I don't think so. I have run a small check into his background. Though, he has never been in trouble with the law, his reputation with the ladies... I don't want the judge to get a crack at him. This whole case is based around 'morals' as we understand them to be, Mr. Jumppierre. I don't want to take any unnecessary risks."

"If you think Farras will hurt the case, then by all means, he should not get on the stand," Tousant said.

Bree didn't trust small town justice. She thought the 'justice system' in small towns was never handled properly. Too many things were handled in their own unique way. How can the supposedly, brilliant minds that run the State of Louisiana, be so stupid as to hire people such as Miss Bartley?

Bree sat with her hands in the pockets of her jacket craving the pretty sounds of her *music box. Everything is wooden,* she thought. *Maybe the shine of the wood represented the shining light of, so-called, justice, and the wood itself represented how hard and cruel justice can be.* At that moment, she had a sense of unreality. Her eyes fell on her son's stern face. Paupon sat poised and silent.

When Judge Micads walked quickly into the courtroom, they all rose. He was about her father's age, but, unlike, her father, his hair was completely white. He looked kind to her, but she had built up a distrust for anyone connected with the possibility of her losing Paupon. Bree sat trying to imagine what would happen, but she could only dimly imagine what would happen to them.

Bree was grateful that it was only a *hearing.* She couldn't have held herself together if she had to sit in a courtroom with hostile jurors.

As soon as Bree was sworn in and sat down, Mr. Moires asked, "Are you, Mrs. Bree Jumppierre-Jourdan?" Mr. Moires asked, talking louder than she had ever heard an attorney speak before. She had guessed that he did it to be heard clearly by Judge Micads. "Do you go around advocating *bigamy?"* he asked, in that same loud, professional voice. Mr. Moires was putting on a crazy showiness for the reporters. He held his hands behind him and reared back on his heels. *He was se pavoiser comme un paon,* she told herself.

Bree repeated to Judge Micads what she had said at the Church meeting. She concluded by stating. "I'm not an *unfit* mother, your honor. And my husbands' fitness as fathers is not in question here. Why that is so, I do not know. I'm a woman who, for my own private reasons, has *two* husbands. If it were my *first* husband living with *two* wives, we wouldn't be here at all. No one would be here trying to prove him an *unfit* father. Maybe a few people might gossip and wonder, but that would be all," she said. "My life doesn't exist for anyone else to understand it, Judge Micads. I have not broken any laws," she stated, very quietly with the coldness of steel in her voice. "But I'm being branded a *Jezebel.* Mr. Moires looked at Judge Micads, then he looked at Bree. His eyes stopped briefly on Paupon.

"I know your whole family, Mrs. Jumppierre. They're decent people." As the judge spoke, Bree's fears took flight. Judge Micads' eyes softened, and he looked at her with kindness. "I'll speak to your son, now."

As soon as Paupon sat down, Judge Micads asked, "Paupon, where do you attend school?"

"Larper's Academy, sir," Paupon replied.

"That's a fine, private school." Judge Micads noisily ruffled some papers in front of him. "You have been attending a private school ever since you started school, Paupon?" Judge Micads continued.

"Yes, sir," Paupon answered.

"What do you think about living in the same house with *two* fathers? I mean, one real father and a stepfather at the same time. I want you to take your time and answer in your own words."

"I feel lucky to have Papa J. That's what I call my step-father. I have *two* fathers who love me. That's a lot better than most children. Some children don't have fathers at all," Paupon said.

"How old are you, Paupon?" the judge asked.

"Ten-years old, sir." As her son spoke, Bree felt her hands loosening from being held in tight fists in her lap. "I have never had a case like this, not in twenty-two years on the bench," He smiled wearily and continued. "Let's not waste this court's time. This young woman has not broken any laws. This family should not be here. This is a waste of the state's time, my time, and this family's time. Someone will give an account for this. I promise you," he said. "The State of Louisiana is not in the business of dictating 'morals' to its citizenry." Judge Micads dismissed the case. Bree squeezed Tousant's hand tightly as tears streamed down her face.

So that they could avoid the crowd, Mr. Moires suggested that Farras park their car at the back door, but a reporter had anticipated this and was standing at the back door as they exited. He walked up to Bree asking questions. Bree stopped his stream of questions when she said, "I am ready to make a statement. Everyone else has talked about my life. Now it's time for me to say something about it."

"Yes, ma'am," the reporter said excitedly, "start talking." He held his microphone to Bree's mouth. A few seconds later, other reporters came. Both Tousant and Farras squeezed Bree's hands, simultaneously.

"No, Bree," Tousant said, gently pulling her toward the car. "They'll not print the truth. They'll twist around everything you say, and you'll hate yourself in the morning," Tousant contended. His eyes pleaded with her to let it be over, but Bree saw the need in the reporter's eyes for answers. They, too, were products of 'Western Civilization.' She ignored Tousant. She felt that this would be the last time she would have to defend herself. She put her hands into the pockets of her jacket and hesitated before she spoke.

"When my church tried to dismiss me, most of the members wanted me to *win,* because they were afraid that the Church wouldn't stop at me. At the *hearing* today, most people wanted me to *lose.* Because they were afraid that my victory might set yet another precedent. I read in this morning's papers that if I *won* my case it would change the 'lifestyle' of others. Some articles even suggested that my *win* today might even change the whole institution of marriage. Some newspapers even went as far to say that my *unconventional lifestyle* may change the family structure of *Western* Civilization! I don't think that you have to stay up nights worrying about that happening. Though I am not a sociologist, I do know that societies undergo crisis and do change. A prime example is the spiraling divorce rate in this country. An answer must be found. I'm not saying that my *unconventional lifestyle* is the *Answer* or even that it is *an answer.* I'm not advocating my *unconventional lifestyle* for anyone."

"So you don't have any feelings of guilt?" one reporter asked. "You don't feel that you're wrong?"

"No, I do not. My decision was based on my own personal circumstances. If I thought that it was wrong, I wouldn't have *two* husbands! I don't think what I'm doing is alien to human nature at all."

"Why did you choose another husband rather than a lover? It would have been more acceptable in our *Western society?*" another reporter asked.

"That's true. If I had chosen to take a lover, it would have been more acceptable, but it wouldn't have been more acceptable to me," she explained.

"What makes you so different from the rest of us?" the same reporter asked, with malice in his voice. He leaned towards Bree and said something else to her under his breath. She could not make out his words. But she could tell by the coldness in his eyes that it was something humiliating, something punishing, something unkind.

"Am I really that different from other people? I think not. But I do know what makes me different from you—I am a human being!" she snapped at the reporter, and turned her back to him.

"Is it possible to have one's pleasures without paying for it?" another reporter asked, with a deliberate, mocking logic.

"Pleasures! Every human being alive must find some way to live. I didn't make this world. The world was like this when I got here. This is a meaningless exchange of words. End of interview." She walked away with Tousant and Farras to their car.

When they got into their car, her father stuck his head out of his car window and said, "I don't think you should have given that interview." He looked at her for the first time with genuine respect. "But... I kept Paupon in the car with me."

"*Merci*," she said. "Paupon can come with us now."

"Don't forget our 'victory dinner.' Follow me," her father said happily.

When they got a few blocks away from the courthouse, Farras started singing; Paupon joined him in song. Tousant had enclosed himself in silence. Bree sat in the back seat of the car looking quietly out the window.

Definitions to Creole words, phrases, and sentences used in this book.

A la debandade. To rack and ruin.
A vous de meme. The same to you.
Adieu. Goodbye.
Ainsi soit-il. So be it.
Algarade. A ruckus.
Allo. Hello.
Alors que. When.
Avez-vous de cafè. Do you want coffee?
Bèbè. Baby.
Beignets. Fritter, sprinkled with confectioner's sugar.
Berceuse à bras. Rocking chair.
Betise. Foolishness, nonsense.
Bonjour. Good morning.
Bonne Annèe. Happy New Year's.
Bonsoir. Good night.
Boudin. Spicey sausage
C' est entendu. That's settled.
Ce n'est pas ma faute. It is not my fault.
Ce ne fait rien. Never mind.
Cela est egal. It's all the same to me.
C'est de la communaute. A common person. A person who lacks education and polish.
C'est merveilleux. That's marvelous.
Cette femme. That woman.
Chacun son gout. Everyone to his liking. To each its own.
Chantez ia. Sing that.
Chère. (mas.) Dearness.
Chèri. (fem.) Beloved, cherished.
Chevrefeuilles. Honeysuckles.
Comment allez vous. How are you?
Curt bouillion. Fish stew.
D' accord. Okay, agree.

Dashiki. A brightly colored, loose-fitting African garment.

Dègoutant. Disgusting.

Demain. Tomorrow.

Des gens du commun. Common people.

Dèsolee. Crushed, heartbroken.

Deux te^tes sur un seul corps. Two heads on one body.

Dieu. God.

Doux. Sweet, mild, soft.

Enfant unique. Only child.

Est comme ca. That's the way it is.

Et. And.

Excuser Moi. Excuse me

Fait tres froid ce matin. It's cold this morning.

Faites comme chez vous. Do it like you do at home.

Feu follet. Playful little fires.

Fille. Daughter.

Fils. Son.

Folle. Crazy.

Foutu. To deal blows.

Gumbo z'herbes. A dish of nine greens eaten on New Years Day to insure having something to eat the whole year.

Je croit que non. No, I do not want any.

Je `devenir folle. I'm going/becoming crazy.

Je ne sais pas. I do not know.

Je regretta. I'm sorry.

Je suis narve. I'm terribly sorry.

Je t'aime. I love you.

Joie de vivre. Joy of life.

L'armée ennemi! The enemy.

Laissez les bons temps rouler. Let the "good times" roll.

Le gout bien fin. A keen eye for fashion.

Le poisson. A fish.

Les bonnes manieres. Good manners.

Les gens raffine. Well-bred. People of refinements.

Les journaux. Newspapers.

Livre de priere. Prayer book.

Lui donner ma facon de penser. To give him my thinking style.

Madame. Married woman.

Mais qu'est-ce que vous. What are you saying?. Pain, trouble, hardship, badly.

Manies. Peculiar ways or habits.

M'ap' allor fout' gris-gris sur. I'm going to slap a voodoo spell on.

Mari. Husband.

Marraine et parrain. Godmother and Godfather.

Merci beaucoup. Many thanks; thanks a lot.

Merci encore. Thanks again.

Me're et Pe're. Mother and father.

Me're la dame. Mother lady.

Me're. Mother.

Miriliton. Pear-shaped fruit.

Mo p'tit `zange. My little angel.

Mon amour. My love.

Mon Dieu. My God.

Mon me're et mon deux freres. My mother and my two brothers.

M'sieu. Mr.

Ne vous frottez pas a' lui. Do not provoke him.

N'est-ce pas. Isn't that so. Isn't it?

Non, j'ai a vous dire quelque chose. No, I have something to tell you.

Non. No.

Nos me're. Our mother.

Oncle. Uncle.

Ou est-ce qui vous prend. Is this what's bothering you?

Oui, je sais. Yes, I know.

Oui, J'en ai. Yes, I have some.

Oui. Yes.

Pain-patate. Sweet potatoe pudding.

Paix. Peace.

Pas un soupcon de sentiment. Not a trace of feeling.

Pe're. Father.

Pére, je-ne me sens pas bien. Father I don't feel well.

Perle de perfection. Pearl of perfection.

Personne n' avait le coeur pour toucher les morts. Nobody has the heart for touching the dead.

Petit amie. Little friend.

Peut-etre. Perhaps.

Placee'. A protective friend or relative.

Pour le grand monde. For high society.

Pourquoi. Why; what for; for what reason.

Presque. Almost.

Professeur. Professor, teacher.

P'tit diable. Little devil.

Quel dommage. What a pity.

Quelle femme. What a woman.

Quelle heure est-il. What time/hour is it?

Qu'est-ce que tu as. What is it that you want?

Qu'est-ce qui arrive. What's happening?

Qu'est-ce qui erreur. What's wrong.

Qu'est-ce qu'il y a? What is the matter?

Qu ést-ce que vous avez. What's wrong with you? What's the matter with you?

Quoi. What, which.

Sainte me're de pitie'. Holy Mother of mercy.

San tambours ni trompettes. Without drums or trumpets.

Se pavoiser comme un paon. Display himself like a peacock.

Second-line. A traditional dance done by African-Americans in southern Louisiana.

Si Dieu veut. If God allows.

Sur Dimanche. On Sunday.

Tante. Aunt.

Tisane de sassafras. Sassafras tea.

Toutes les larmes de son corps. Shedding all the tears in her body.

Traiteur. A healer.

Un coup d'apoplexie. Have a stroke.

Un paquet de sotises. A package of insults.

Un peu. A little.

Un signe de croix. Sign of the cross.

Une amie. A friend.

Vendredi. Friday.

Vite. Fast, swift, quick.

Vois-tu pas. Don't you see

Votre me're et pe're. Your mother and father.

Votre me're. Your mother.

Zut alors. Vous avez fort. Damn it! You're wrong.

Zydeco music. Afro-Creole music of southern Louisiana.

BIBLIOGRAPHY

Ella Guidry-Harrison, was born in New Orleans, Louisiana. A graduate from California State University in San Jose. She also studied "Creative Writing" and was a campus reporter at San Jose City College. She studied "Creative Writing" under Donald Barthelme at the University of California at Berkeley. Some of her work appeared in San Jose City College Literary Magazine and Baltimore's Fairfax Magazine.

In her field of Social Work, her work as a fund-raiser and coordinator for "Save the Children" during the Ethiopian famine, resulted in being awarded "Woman of the Year" in Harrogate, England where she lived for three years. She was awarded a "Proclamation" by the Mayor of her hometown–which proclaimed September 28, "Ella Guidry-Harrison Day."

Ella Guidry-Harrison have lived and traveled across America and throughout the world. She presently resides with her husband in Maryland.